ALAN POPE WASN'T READY
FOR ALL THE JOYS MONEY COULD BUY.

There was no light in the plane cabin. Nadia had told the radioman not to disturb them.

"Do you always live this way?" Alan asked.

"Yes, always."

"Aren't you ever scared?"

"Of what?" she asked.

He couldn't tell her. He had never met such a beautiful woman. Nor such a wild one. He was overflowing with tenderness, with warmth, and he wanted to take her in his arms. She stopped him short and asked in a panting voice, "Do you want me?"

"Oh, yes, so much, Nadia, so very much..."

"Well, what are you waiting for?"

RIVIERA

RIVIERA

Pierre Rey

Translated by Harold J. Salemson

BANTAM BOOKS
TORONTO · NEW YORK · LONDON · SYDNEY

RIVIERA
A Bantam Book / September 1983
Published in France under the title of Palm Beach.

ISBN 0-553-20900-0

Published simultaneously in the United States and Canada

Bantam Books are published by Bantam Books, Inc. Its trademark, consisting of the words ''Bantam Books'' and the por-
trayal of a rooster, is Registered in U.S. Patent and Trademark
Office and in other countries. Marca Registrada. Bantam
Books, Inc., 666 Fifth Avenue, New York, New York 10103.

PRINTED IN THE UNITED STATES OF AMERICA

O   0 9 8 7 6 5 4 3 2 1

NOTICE

The locale and setting of this novel are true and famous the world over. On the other hand, its story and the characters in it are purely imaginary.

> "Woe unto those who are content with little."
>
> Henry Michaux (*Ecuador*)

BOOK I

1

At nine that evening, the police blocked off the two ends of the Croisette, closing it to all traffic.

It had just gotten dark. The night was soft, fragrant, and sweet. The crowd, assembled along the balustrades overlooking the beach cabanas which covered virtually every square inch of sand, was shoving forward by the thousands. A happy, urgent rumble of shouts of joy, laughter, and music, combined with the muted swell of the Mediterranean endlessly licking against the shore as it had done throughout the centuries.

It was July 21, the barest shank of the season, the start of the vacation reprieve that would last until the fall. Now was the time for fun. Between the unbroken line of luxury hotels and the sea, the crowd continued to grow denser, coming out of the little side streets that led to the Croisette, invading the terraces of cafés and overrunning them in an unconcerned and good-natured assault.

Down at the end of the bay, maître d's and captains at the Palm Beach Casino were ushering the first guests, dressed in evening gowns and white tuxedos, to their open-air tables, each of which was graced with lighted candles, to watch the gala. People fortunate enough to have gotten accommodations at the Majestic, the Carlton, the Martinez, or the Grand Hôtel, looked out of their own windows to watch the goings-on. Out at the end of the pier in the Old Port at the foot of the lighthouse, the fireworks handlers checked their installations one last time. Their boss looked at his watch.

"Touch 'em off in five minutes," he called. "Stations."

Then, suddenly, all the lights in Cannes went out. A dull clamor arose from the strand, soon drowned out by the music from dozens of loudspeakers placed over a length of several miles on the trunks of palm trees, in the branches of plane trees, on the cornices of buildings, among the tiles of roofs. Applause and bravos rose from the multitude, rolling like some huge wave, and swelling in the almost-complete darkness which was dotted only by the brief glows of burning cigarettes.

At the same moment offshore, an outboard started up, and at full speed, headed for the floating pontoon on which the rockets of the fireworks were set up. It cut sharply through the waters, leaving behind a powerful phosphorescent wake that was not visible from the shore.

Over the roar of the motor, the four men in the outboard could distinctly hear the ritual phrase which opened the World Festival of Fireworks:

"Spain presents..."

The boat hooked around the pontoon and pulled up against it. Two of the men jumped up onto the slippery boards. The idling motor gave off a dull, hoarse snarl covered by the first notes of the Aranjuez "Concerto," coming from the pitch-dark Croisette.

"Four minutes," said the man who had remained at the tiller. Dressed in dark slacks and a black polo shirt, he bent over and effortlessly lifted the trussed, gagged body of a man over his shoulder.

"Need any help?"

"Just hold the boat still," he answered.

The last of the four men was already at work on the deck of the pontoon, a veritable forest of wheels to which firecrackers of all sizes were attached. The trussed man looked at them helplessly, with desperate, begging eyes. He was dropped between two rows of Bengal lights, and a very powerful bomb was attached to his belly. The man who had carried him up connected its detonator to the bunch of cylinders that would explode into the final bouquet climaxing the pyrotechnics. The victim fought back with the energy of a wild animal, but was unable to loosen his ties even the slightest bit. His face was bathed in sweat. His temple veins bulged frighteningly against his livid face.

"Look at the fuckin' dope!" Marco said. "We give him the best seat in the house, and he's complaining!"

The other two laughed.

"Ever get this close to a fireworks display before, Marco?" his sidekick asked.

"Never!" he replied. "And it was always my dream when I was a kid."

"Just two minutes more," the man in the boat muttered impatiently.

They clipped some wires with a pair of pliers.

"Go!"

They jumped back into the boat, and sped off. The outboard skipped up out of the water, made a big swing, and disappeared into the night.

The man they left behind was named Erwin Broker. He was twenty-eight years old, and he didn't want to die. He was trying every which way to dislodge that bomb from his solar plexus. The bomb moved slightly. He made an even greater effort to try to break the electric wires that bound his wrists to one of the boards. His muscles were taut as ropes; he was gritting his teeth to keep the pressure up despite the fact that he was tearing his skin off. He had to fight to keep from passing out.

But the others had timed their movements perfectly. The touch-off would take place any second now. He knew that he was about to die, that nothing in the world could save him any longer. He stopped struggling, let his head fall back against the moist, sticky boards, and looked up at the sky. From shore, he could make out the confused murmur of the crowd and the sharp, airy notes of the concerto. Never before had he had time to contemplate the stars. They pierced through the warm night with their cold brilliance, and he found them beautiful.

Then, a thousand suns burst before his face, he screamed through his gag into the horrifying noise of the rockets.

They caught fire one after the other, lighting the sky with violent arabesques, the lightninglike traces of which slowed almost to a halt at the end of their trajectory, only to explode once more into an infinity of shattering suns that fell toward the sea in whimpering curves. He felt his clothes start to burn, and he fiercely bit his lips as the first lick of the flames reached his flesh. He was terrified by the bomb pressing against his gut, for he knew it would explode as soon as the great wheel began to spin.

His eyes bugging with horror, he saw it start to move, at first slowly, then suddenly speeding up until it hit a giddy pace. The first flames sprang from the pinwheel, and they were the last images that the retinas of Erwin Broker's eyes recorded in his lifetime. The explosion shook all of the improvised wharf and the whole thing went up in a phenomenal bouquet of pyrotechnical wonder.

BOOK II

2

At 1:00 P.M., the lunch-break buzzer sounded through the eight floors occupied by the offices of Hackett Chemical Investment Corporation. Almost as one man, the 622 executives, receptionists, department heads, bookkeepers, file clerks, secretaries, typists, and legal eagles now rushed toward the elevators that would drop them twenty-five to thirty-two floors below and discharge them in impatient bunches into the suffocating humidity of Forty-second Street.

The only person in the whole Rilford Building who didn't rush out was Alan Pope, in 3021. He sat glued to his chair, staring into space, as if he hadn't heard a sound. Sam Bannister, his best friend, already had his hand on the doorknob and was staring quizzically at him.

"You trying to get in some overtime?" he asked.

"Who'd pay me for it?" Alan replied dismally.

Bannister looked at him more closely. "I'm lunching at Romano's," he called. "Want to come along?"

"Not hungry, thanks," Alan said.

This being quite unlike Alan, Sam shuffled from one

foot to the other and asked, "What's the matter? Murray?"

"Yeah, Murray."

Anxious as he was to get out, Sam let go of the knob. He took a couple of steps toward the double desk across which he and Alan Pope had faced each other for the last four years.

"Want to talk about it over a beer?" Sam said.

Alan shook his head and slumped further down into his chair. "Go without me, Sam. I've got to think."

Bannister hesitated a moment, started to say something, then thought better of it, and asked, "What time you seeing him?"

"At three," Alan conceded.

"Think he's going to give you a raise?"

"Very funny," Alan smirked.

"Look, you're worrying over nothing. I'm sure he'll have something good to tell you." Sam stopped on his way out the door, shrugged, and in as carefree a tone as he could muster, added, "In case you change your mind, remember Romano's."

Alan stayed by himself. His gut knotted with apprehension, he sighed, got up, stuck his nose against the window and peered out, but he wasn't seeing anything.

Ten minutes went by without his moving. Then he hurried over to the phone and called home. He had to see Marina. With luck, she'd still be lying in his bed, naked and warm.

The line was busy! He suddenly felt a mad urge to talk to her, touch her, make love to her. He didn't have much time. He hung up, flung his jacket over his shoulder, and went out into the empty hall.

"What woman, Penny? Did you get her name?" Abel Hartman asked in exasperation. He was an insignificant little neighborhood lawyer who occasionally got a divorce case, but most of the time he dealt with arguments over adjoining walls, flooded apartments, or fender benders. His clients were poison to him.

"Mabel Pope," his secretary calmly told him, "you know, the ex-Mrs. Alan Pope."

Hartman groaned. "What does that pest want from me now?"

"The usual. Alimony overdue."

"She should have married a guy with money. Tell her I'm in Turkey."

"She saw you outside when you went to pick up the Leyland file. You'd better see her, or she'll start chewing the scenery."

"Does she owe us anything?"

"Not a cent."

"How I hate those female bloodsuckers," he said. "God pity the poor guys that fall for them. They bleed 'em to death!"

He noticed that Penny was sneering at him, and suddenly remembered that she was a divorcée herself. He cleared his throat and said, "Okay, show her in. I'll swear out a complaint for nonpayment against Alan Pope for her."

The taxi taking him home seemed to be slowed down by the heat.

"Can't you go any faster?" Alan asked.

"You want she should blow up on me?" the hackie retorted.

Alan drummed nervously on the armrest of the ancient Pontiac. It was steaming like an old nag. Marina must have gotten up by now; Alan visualized her in the shower. What had struck him the minute he met her was how much she looked like Marilyn Monroe. He had wandered into a bar on Sixth Street to use the cigarette machine. She was sitting there on a high stool, alone, sipping something that had cherries and mint in it. Forgetting about the smokes, he sat down two stools away and ordered a Scotch. While he tried sneaking looks at her, she calmly turned and spoke to him.

"Tell me why you're ogling me like that and I'll buy you a drink," she said. "No, don't cheat, now! You're getting ready to lie. Just answer right off."

"Well," he stammered, "I think you . . . that is, you . . ."

"And I remind you of . . ."

"Exactly!" he concurred.

"I've heard that one before, believe me. Everybody says it."

She dipped her lips into her glass and her pointed tongue licked at the crushed ice around its edge. Five or six drinks later, his heart thumping and the palms of his hands all wet, he shyly asked whether she'd have dinner with him. She stared him down, realizing how uncomfortable that made him and delighting in it. Then, she burst out laughing.

"Aren't you the one, though?" She took a toothbrush out of her purse and tickled his upper lip with the end of it.

Her skin was soft, milky, warm, and firm.

Among other qualities, she had a total lack of modesty, and was as free with her body as a newborn babe. She walked around his place stark naked, striking poses that would have made a hardened soldier blush. She would lie on the rug with her legs in the air, one foot stuck in each corner of a stool, a cigarette dangling from her lips while one of her hands mindlessly caressed her breasts and the other was raised high, the fingers spread and waving at the end of a stiff arm, so the scarlet polish would dry on her inordinately long nails.

Alan had given her a key to his two-room flat. She might or might not be there, as she often disappeared for several days at a time, never deigning to offer the slightest explanation. She'd come back with armfuls of exotic flowers that cost a mint, ask whether there was any butter left, say she had to go out and get some, and return with grapefruit, a bright-colored parasol, a transistor radio, a stray kitten, or stalks of celery to put into the coffeepot on the windowsill like a bouquet of posies.

Overwhelmed by Marina's footloose and fancy-free nature, and physically more than satisfied by her, Alan rewarded her with presents he could ill afford and which didn't impress her. She would regularly leave her rings, gold chains, or earrings in the ladies' rooms of the bars they occasionally went to. One evening he made the mistake of questioning her.

"Listen, Alan," she answered, "I'm here with you because I like you. Ask questions and I won't like you. If I don't like you, I go away. Clear?"

"Marina...," he begged.

"You're free, I'm free," she said. "The only way I know how to live is with all the doors open. Take your choice."

Since then, he knew better than to ask anything. All he wanted was not to lose her!

"Hey, stop, this is the place!" he called out.

The driver, who'd been dozing at the wheel, jammed his brakes on. Alan was almost thrown off the taxi seat as he reached into his pocket for change. There was a crash of crushed metal.

Fuming with rage, the driver of the refrigerator truck that had just rammed them jumped out on the sidewalk. "You crazy or what?" he yelled.

The taxi driver called back, "Some noive! You run inna me an' you bawlin' me out!" By this time he was out on the sidewalk, too, and he could see that the rear end of his taxi had crumpled like a paper cup.

"Hey, you see wot dat guy done to me?" he said to Alan, whom he wanted as a witness. But Alan slipped him a five and shrugged fatalistically.

"It's not your fault, fella," he said. "It's mine. Today's my unlucky day."

When the taxi driver got around to asking for his name and address, Alan was already up on the eighteenth floor, nervously trying to unlock his door.

Even though the place was air-conditioned, the smoke in Romano's was thick enough to cut with a knife. The upstairs room was jammed with upper-bracket clerks and very junior executives grabbing a quick drink with their sandwiches. The waiters and bartenders had to elbow their way through the tide of humanity standing five or six deep in front of the bar.

Sam Bannister was in luck. He only had to share his barstool with one other guy, but he had to yell to make himself heard over the cacophony of crisscrossed conversations.

"Wrap it up nice, will you, Tom?" he was calling. "It's a present!"

Tom smiled and did as he was told. He liked Sam, who sometimes gave him a tip on the market. He tied a string bow around the package and handed it to him.

"Thanks, Tom, you're a pal. Put it on my tab," Sam said.

He slipped off his half of the barstool, which was immediately assailed by a mob of would-be sitters. Head down, his arms to his sides, he made a broken-field dash toward the door, winking to several guys he knew.

Outside, it was 104 in the shade. This was July 22, after

all. Alan must be eating worms in the office, Sam said to himself. The dope's scared so shitless of Murray, he even forgot today's his birthday!

Alan kicked the door open. Marina was in—and wearing nothing except long, black kid gloves and a flowered straw hat—what she referred to as her "house dress." She was doing one of her favorite exercises, reverse push-ups. She was on her back, propped up on her forearms, with her head thrown back and her body arched so as to make the most of the smooth, round line of her belly. Alan felt the hots for her. His eyes glued to her, he slipped out of his jacket, kicked off his shoes, and started to unbutton his shirt, which was sticking to his skin.

"Hi," she said, without interrupting her push-ups. "Alan, you know Harry, don't you?"

"Hi," said Harry. He was sitting on the floor in a neutral corner with his feet up on a chair.

Alan noticed that Harry was wearing old sneakers. It made him sore that here he was quickly getting back into his shirt when Harry, the intruder, was the one who ought to have been feeling ashamed. But Harry was not at all ashamed. As if Alan weren't even there, Harry was helping himself to another shot of his best whiskey.

"Pleased to meetcha," Alan muttered.

"Twenty-five," Marina called, as she collapsed back on the rug.

"Twenty," Harry corrected her.

"Twenty-five," she insisted.

"Listen—" Alan tried in vain to cut in.

"Be a nice guy and get me a glass of milk, will you, Alan?" Marina asked.

Bemused, he headed for the fridge, saying, "You two old friends?" Then, not knowing just how to take all this, he turned to Harry and asked, "You want some, too?"

"No, thanks. I prefer Scotch. I've got it already."

Alan went back to Marina. "What's this all about?" he asked.

"What's what all about?" she innocently replied.

She was still lying on the floor, but had put the ridiculous straw hat over her face. Alan felt like he was talking to the hat.

"What's he doing here?" he demanded.

"He's an old friend," Marina said, as if that made it the most natural thing in the world.

"You mean me?" Harry asked in a huff.

"You shut your trap!" Alan yelled. "I'm asking Marina!"

"What the hell! Do I live here or don't I?" she countered.

"Yes," Alan shouted.

She sent her hat flying. "Then, why should I have to explain? I can invite anyone I want to my house."

"Dressed like that?" Alan wanted to know.

"I like that!" Harry protested. "I've never been treated this way in my life!"

"Excuse him, Harry. He's always edgy when he gets home from work," she put in.

"Well, I'm leaving," Harry said. He got to his feet with amazing agility, finished off his drink, and nodded good-bye to Marina.

"And what if I smashed you in the face?" Alan asked matter-of-factly.

Feeling the situation was getting out of hand, Alan, purple with rage had set himself up barring the door, fists clenched. Marina got up, slipped on a pair of Alan's slacks and one of his blue dungaree shirts.

"Where are you going?" Alan demanded of her.

She fluffed her hair and said, "With him."

"That's if I want you," Harry put in.

"Oh, come on, Harry, don't be a shit," she pleaded.

"All right, then hurry up," he answered. "I don't like the looks of that guy."

"Marina!" Alan shouted.

"You're a goddamned bore," she told him.

The door closed behind them. Speechless, Alan mechanically poured himself a drink. He kicked over a chair that went waltzing into the wall.

"Goddamnit to hell!" he swore.

And then the bell rang.

Back in the comforting intimacy of his own office, Oscar Vlinsky rubbed his hands. Three weeks alone with his wife in Florida had disgusted him with the whole idea of vacations. With Annie, he was a nothing; here at the Burger Bank, he was God. As comptroller, he had the power to interfere in the lives of people he didn't even know, and determine their fates according to his personal whims.

All he had to do was touch a key of his computer in order to see the whole list of defaulting or overdrawn customers pass before his eyes. Abel Fischmayer had warmly congratulated him on the tough way he had of handling fudgers.

"Good work, Vlinsky," he had said. "Here at Burger we could use a lot more men like you!"

But Oscar knew he was a loner. He greedily pressed down a red key on the computer board, and was appalled to see how many names appeared before his eyes.

Vlinsky hardly knew where to begin, but he decided he'd knock off the name that was at the top of the screen after he counted ten. He started counting. At ten, he stopped and looked at the top name: Alan Pope, overdraft, $327.00.

Alan figured Marina had just been playing a joke on him. She'd now changed her mind, dumped that idiot, and was coming back. He delightedly rushed to answer the doorbell, slipped, almost fell, and then stopped in front of the door. He had to remember not to let her realize the hold she had on him; he'd have to show her how sore she had made him. He wiped the happiness off his face, put on a frown, and went into the kitchen to hide the remains of the chair he had smashed before going back to open the door.

"Hi, Alan. Won't you ask me in?"

It was Mabel standing there, smiling at him. He eyed her in amazement.

"You dyed your hair green!" he exclaimed.

"So what?" she replied, coming in. She gave the place a quick once-over and commented, "Nothing's changed, I see." She picked up a book and tossed it down again. "Except, of course, there are no more pictures of me on the walls. But then, why should there be?"

She sat down in an armchair, and as she did so, her Indian skirt rode up and exposed a healthy hunk of thigh.

"I was on my way out," Alan said. "I'm due back at the office."

"You still have one?" she asked nonchalantly.

"How else do you think I can pay your alimony?"

She laughed that rippling little condescending laugh he knew so well.

"Oh, Alan, dear Alan. It's July twenty-second already, and I still haven't gotten the check due last June thirtieth. That's no way to run a railroad."

She crossed her legs high so that he could see the hem of her flesh-colored panties.

"You'll get it!"

"When?"

"I'm a little short," he told her. "I couldn't even pay my rent on time, and I'm overdrawn at the bank."

She looked flirtatiously at him.

"You're always overdrawn," she said. "What's her name?"

"Who?"

"The gal you're overdrawn for. You were always a sucker for women."

"You're a fine one to say that!"

She sighed deeply, looked at him indulgently, and uncrossed her legs—but without pulling her skirt down.

"It's all too stupid," she said. "Maybe we shouldn't have been so hasty. Sometimes I wonder. It wasn't so bad, you know."

"What wasn't?"

"Us," she said modestly, lowering her eyes like a schoolgirl.

"What are you trying to get at?"

"It's silly, living separated like this, not sharing anything."

"We share my income," he answered tartly.

"Well, don't think I enjoy taking it from you. It really bothers me. But I'm all by myself, and what else can I do?"

Trying to seem as natural as possible, she opened her blouse slightly and carelessly rubbed her chest with the back of her hand. He could fleetingly see a bit of a nipple.

"It's hot in here," she said. Then, lying back in the armchair, her legs spread, she added, "How about starting over from scratch?"

Alan pretended not to get her meaning.

"You know," she said. "It wouldn't be the first time a pair of divorced people got hitched all over again."

In spite of the heat, he shivered. They had been married only for a short season. Had he ever really wanted to marry her in the first place? Somehow, there they had been, in front of the justice of the peace. And everything that had seemed so adorable in her before, became unbearable the minute the marriage was consummated.

To live up to the women's magazines' version of what the ideal woman ought to be, Mabel played exotic Indian music until five in the morning, stuffed herself on fried oysters, covered her face with mudpacks, wore a reducing girdle, and several times a day doused herself with an allegedly aphrodisiac perfume that stunk up the place wherever she went. Considering herself to be the very epitome of culture, she tried to give Alan lessons in posture, yoga, and good manners.

However, once she had landed Alan, she was saved from worry about herself. On the rare occasions when she deigned to open a can of organic macrobiotic soup, she was hard put to find a pot to heat it in or a decent dish to serve it in. And as he devoured this unusual treat of "home cooking," she looked scornfully at him, appalled by the vulgarity with which he went at it, saying, "You're supposed to eat it, not lap it up."

Nor were the nights any more satisfactory. If, during a break in her endless symphony of sitar music, his hand would wander over to her thigh, she would jump away from him as if she had been electrocuted and tell him off. He would curl up fetuslike at the far edge of the bed, trying to get some sleep. At break of day, he would feel his way into the kitchen and make himself a bitter cup of coffee. After eleven weeks of abstinence and assorted other frustrations, he begged her for a divorce—and to his surprise, she agreed without too much of a fight. There were just two conditions: He was to take all the blame for the failure of their marriage, and he was to share all of his earnings with her on a straight fifty-fifty basis—for life, if she did not remarry. In desperation, he also agreed to pay her legal fees, just to have her out of his hair that much faster.

"What do you say?" she was now asking.

He gazed at her greenish mane, her phoney smile, her gaping shirt, and answered, "I'm late, Mabel. I've got to go."

"Well, yes or no?" she demanded.

"No, it was all a mistake," he answered. "We never were meant for each other."

She shoved her skirt back down, hopped up, and eyed him with unconcealed hatred.

"I just saw Hartman," she hissed. "He's going to swear out a complaint against you. You'll see what it'll cost!"

But words were no longer strong enough to express how she felt. She spat at him.

Except for her black kid gloves and the flowered straw hat pulled down to her eyes, Marina was stark naked as usual.

Hands to the floor, she was doing push-ups.

"Fifty," she counted, as her breath gave out.

She let herself roll over on the rug, legs spread, arms crossed.

"Not even thirty," Harry corrected her. "What you lying for?"

"I can't help it," she answered candidly. "How about giving me a glass of milk?"

Harry let some red paint drip out of a hole in a tin can onto the ocher ground of a canvas lying flat on the floor. "Go get it yourself," he told her.

"Harry . . . please . . . ," she begged.

He sat down on the floor, and with his bare toe started to spread the paint he had just dripped onto the canvas. "You think I'm your next sucker?" he asked.

Without getting up, Marina dug her teeth into a red apple that was at hand and looked up thoughtfully at the ceiling.

"He's very nice, though," she said.

"You miss him already?" Harry twitted her.

"He makes love real nice."

Harry burst out laughing. "A bookkeeper! A lousy, stinking colorless little bookkeeper! You mean to tell me a square lunk like that really knows how to screw? C'mon over here."

Obediently, she moved over to lie down alongside the wet paint.

"Roll over," he commanded. "Some more. . . ."

"I'll get my gloves dirty," she protested. Still eating the apple, she rubbed her bare buttocks in the bright red oils.

"Just wait till I sell this masterpiece," he said. "I'll buy the whole store for you."

"You never sold a painting in your whole life," she told him.

"People are too damned stupid to understand. So how can you expect 'em to buy? Go on, rub your ass in it harder. I'm gonna call it 'Ass Print.' How you like that? Hey, where you going?"

With the paint running down the backs of her legs, and her hat askew, Marina nonchalantly went to the refrigerator and began to drink out of a carton of homogenized milk.

"You crazy or something?" he asked. "That paint's gonna dry! What you thinking of?"

She threw herself down on the low couch which began to take on the color of his masterpiece, but before Harry could complain, she answered him.

"I'm thinking of Alan."

3

When Alan came in, a broad smile spread over Sam Bannister's horsy face.

"Quarter of three! I was beginning to be worried!" he said. "What the hell were you doing?"

"Oh, not much. Just stopped off at my place."

Sam didn't like Alan's worried look. "Something wrong?" he asked.

"Not really—just that in less than two hours I was in a car accident, Marina walked out on me 'cause I caught her entertaining another guy, and Mabel came to let me know she's suing for back alimony. Situation normal, as you can see!"

Sam couldn't keep from laughing nervously.

Alan sat on his desk and looked bleakly out the window. With shy awkwardness, Sam held the package out to him, saying, "This'll all blow over. Here—for you."

"For me?"

"Yes, take it."

Alan held his hand out distrustfully. "What is it? A bomb?" he asked, and Sam nervously laughed again.

"Open it and see," he replied. "Today's July twenty-second. Doesn't that mean anything to you?"

Alan shook his head blankly, and Sam gave him a hearty clap on the back.

"It's your birthday, you dumb ox!" he said.

"Jesus! I forgot all about it," Alan mumbled.

"But I didn't, pal."

"Listen, Sam, you're nuts. You shouldn't have."

"Oh, what are friends for, anyway?" Bannister said.

Alan tore the wrapping paper off and revealed the embossed carton with the coat of arms. He took out the bottle, and Sam looked delighted.

"Real French cognac," he said. "Old as the hills!"

He took two paper cups out of his desk drawer and tossed one to Alan. "You'll feel better after you have a shot of this," he said. "Remember, this is the first day of the best year of your life! How old are you? A hundred? A hundred and ten?"

"Like your brandy. Old as the hills," Alan replied.

"Seriously?"

"Thirty."

"You trying to rub it in? Here I am forty-six with no past to speak of and too old to have a future. So, let's drink to yours!"

"And yours!" Alan answered, raising his cup.

They both bottomed up.

"It was real nice of you," Alan said.

Sam winked back as he smacked his lips. "It may not be the best drink for a hot day like this, but it sure beats New York water!" he said.

Alan poured a second round. They downed it, and Sam set up a third. "Happy birthday, shortass!" he toasted.

"Thanks and here's to you, fart!"

"Old fart!" Sam sententiously corrected him, as they gulped the brandy down.

"Sam," Alan said.

"Yes?"

"You ever hear anything as lousy as what Marina did? And I'm not even sure she'll come back."

"They all come back," Sam replied philosophically. "I've

tried everything I could think of on Crystal, and she's always come back."

"I think I'm in love with her."

"Let me have your glass. I'm pouring."

"You weren't listening, Sam. I said I love her."

"You're too soft on your dames. Drink up!"

"You're probably right. Down the hatch!"

The intercom buzzed. Bannister grabbed it and answered, "Nobody's in!" But suddenly his expression changed, and in a colorless voice he answered servilely, "Yes...okay ...sure...right away." He hung up.

"Did I tell you that Mabel spat in my face?" Alan asked, repressing a burp.

"That was Murray," Sam said noncommittally.

"What about Murray?" Alan asked.

"You had a three o'clock with him. He expects you."

Alan poured himself another hefty shot, gulped it down too fast, coughed, grabbed a tissue to wipe his mouth, and disdainfully declared, "Murray is a brown-nosing son of a bitch!"

He solemnly put both his hands on Bannister's shoulders, looked him square in the eye, and said, "Let me tell you a secret, Sam." He paused to give more weight to his pronouncement. "I got no use whatever for Oliver Murray."

Sam's good-natured face lit up. "Me either," he said.

"I'm gonna tell you somethin' else," Alan went on. "If Murray thinks he can push me around on my thirtieth birthday, he's got another think comin'."

Bannister nodded his approval vigorously, while anxiously looking at his wristwatch.

"'Cause Oliver Murray's just a brown-nose son of a bitch!" Alan concluded.

"Right," Sam said, "right. But now go on to his office."

"And how!" Alan shot back, as he crushed the paper cup in his hand and slammed the door behind him.

Oliver Murray was nasty by nature. He boasted he could recognize any person's weak points after just fifteen seconds. And with the infallible instinct that most mean people seem to develop when they have a little power in their hands, Murray knew how to hit where it hurt the most. As head of personnel, he relished being the terror of all eight floors of the Hackett offices. He was always on the lookout for one more chink in the armor of any of those under his thumb. He was often known to go into people's offices after hours and search through their desks or even empty their wastebaskets to piece together the scraps of personal letters—which then became part of the dossiers on everybody's private lives that he kept as up-to-date as possible.

He himself didn't drink, was never known to laugh, was always the first one to arrive in the morning, and the last to leave at night. His life seemed to consist of nothing but his concern for the well-being of Hackett's. And his office reflected that fact: It was bare, austere, without the slightest personal touch about it. It was furnished with a large, clean glass-topped desk behind which he operated like a monarch on his throne, a large safe that contained his personnel records (duplicates of which were in a bank vault), and a digital clock that clicked audibly every second, reminding his visitors that time was money. On the desk nothing was to be seen, not a scrap of paper, not even a pencil. On the wall there was a picture of Arnold Hackett, founder and presiding officer of the company. Across the desk from Murray, three stiff, straight-backed metal chairs were available for his victims whom he treated with sadistic courtesy: Somebody, after all, had to pay for his strict virtuousness.

After being announced, Alan Pope came in. Murray eyed him stonily a long moment. For an endless number of seconds, there was a visual duel between Alan, standing up, and Murray, seated; the loser would be the first one to break the silence.

"Well, here I am," Alan said.

Still staring at him, Murray clearly enunciated, "Mister Pope, do I need to remind you that drinking during office hours is strictly forbidden?"

Alan rolled with the punch, and answered, "Was that all you wanted to tell me?"

Murray's cold face almost smiled. "Sit down, please," he said.

"No, thanks," said Alan.

"As you wish. But before I get around to the main subject of this interview, I'd like to check on a few points. You've been with us now—just how long?"

"Four years," Alan said.

"Four years, two months, and one week to be exact," Murray corrected. "Would you please tell me what you are presently earning?"

"You know better than I do," Alan replied.

"That is correct, Mister Pope. After deductions, your take-home pay is one thousand six hundred and seventy-two dollars a month." He shook his head at the figure, and commented, "Not bad."

"Do you have any idea what my rent, my clothing, my alimony, and food bill come to?"

Murray ignored that challenge and went on, "Your private life is no concern of mine, young man."

"Well, then, why should you decide whether my salary is good or bad? Or did you call me in to offer me a raise?"

"Not quite, Mister Pope," Murray gloated. "Raise is not quite the word. As I am sure you know, what with international market conditions, things are not as bright as they might be in the pharmaceutical field right now. There's a bit of a crisis, which Hackett will pull through all right, of course, because this is a dynamic company, ever on the move..."

Alan found it harder and harder to keep from weaving as he stood there, so he said, "Can't we get to the point, Murray?"

"Oh, I'm getting there, Mister Pope, don't you worry! In order to get over this temporary hump, Hackett is going to have to effect some retrenchment of personnel."

Alan felt his legs giving way under him, but in order not to give Murray the satisfaction of knowing it, he kept a blank expression on his face.

"Since you have been with us for four years and we have a very enlightened personnel policy, your accumulated benefits, including severance pay, will come to eleven thousand seven hundred and four dollars."

The repeating flavor of the cognac in Alan's mouth turned sour. He was being fired! But he was going to make the bastard come right out with it. "Just what are you trying to tell me, Murray?" he asked.

Undaunted, and with just the slightest trace of contempt in his voice, the maker and breaker of careers at Hackett stated, "Very well, Mister Pope. There is no need for you to return to your office. You are off our payroll as of this moment."

* * *

Sam Bannister could hardly concentrate on the papers in front of him. He feared the worst. Whenever Murray called someone in, it could be assumed that that person was being fired. And for the last few days, the Hackett men's rooms had been full of rumors of wholesale dismissals. Alan was a prime target. Only four years' seniority, always friendly and helpful, never buttering up any of the bosses' wives, never trying to cut anyone else's throat so as to get promoted, he was the ideal pigeon. To get ahead at Hackett's, one had to be ruthless, brown-nosing, and capable of any betrayal or about-face. Every office neighbor was automatically looked upon as a potential enemy. Every superior was a power to fawn on until the time came when he could be brought down. No one survived in Hackett's atmosphere without a minimum of hypocrisy, and to Sam Bannister's despair, Alan Pope just didn't possess it. Although his work left nothing to be desired, it was just too obvious that for Alan, working at Hackett was only a job, not a religion.

Sam was furious to think that a fellow as gifted as Alan did not have a drop of the killer instinct that was so indispensable to success within the closed shell of Hackett Chemical. Alan was attractive to women, but then fell in love with them and was too ingenuous not to let them know it. His women, of course, had a genius for making the most of that. Mabel was bleeding him white, and Marina was two-timing him with a carefreeness that even Sam, redheaded, nearsighted, and ungainly as he was, would never have stood for.

Sam suddenly jumped up. Alan had walked right by, not even seeing him, like a robot.

"Alan!" he cried.

"Any booze left?"

"Come on, what'd he have to say to you?"

"Lemme have a drink, Sam," Alan replied.

Bannister opened the drawer with the bottle in it. He nipped from it first, and then poured a cup for Alan.

"Was it good news? Or bad? Huh?" Sam demanded.

Without pausing for breath, Alan downed his cognac. He looked at Sam as if he were seeing him for the first time in his life, then tried opening his mouth several times, but no sound came out. Hurriedly, Sam poured him another. Alan grabbed it, and turned his back on him.

In a broken voice, he said, "I've been kicked out, Sam. Flushed away like a turd!"

The super stopped Alan before he got to the elevator. "There's some trouble in your apartment, Mr. Pope," he told him. "Had to turn the water off. The plumber's taken a look at it, but he says he can't do nothing till he rips up the bathroom floor to see where the trouble is."

"No water at all?" Alan asked.

"Nope."

"No shower? No toilet?"

"Nothing."

"Oh, shit!" Alan said, and walked away. Then, turning back toward the super, he smiled apologetically.

"Oh, Mr. Pope," the super called. "Remember, you still haven't paid your July rent."

"I'll take care of it very shortly," Alan replied.

Everything came at once. In the elevator, he was sure the cables would break, and then he was amazed to be able to find his key. Inside, he took off his soaked shirt, balled it up and tossed it on the bed, went into the bathroom and turned on the tap, but all he got was an out-of-order gurgle.

He took off his shoes and socks and pants, and headed for the bookshelf where he kept his whiskey bottle. It was empty! He repressed his fury at the sneakered pig who had finished it on him, went back into the bathroom, and gave himself a rub with a big terry cloth towel. He reached for his bottle of lotion. It slipped through his fingers and smashed on the tile floor.

For a moment he just stood there, his arms dangling at his sides. From the smallest detail to the most vital, everything was going wrong today. Out of sheer discouragement, he sat down on the closed toilet seat, took his face in his hands, and closed his eyes.

He suddenly felt that he had to have a cigarette. He feverishly searched the pockets of all his suits, moved some books around, opened some drawers—but there wasn't a smoke to be had. Going out for a pack was just too much trouble. The way he felt, he didn't dare face the people on the street, let alone go in anywhere and buy a pack of cigarettes.

In the kitchen, he finally lucked out. In a canister marked Flour he found a Camel that had been put out with barely a puff taken on it. One end was thick with lipstick. He smelled it, trying to see whether he could detect the aroma of Marina through the flat odor of the stale tobacco.

He lay down on the couch, lit a match, and took a deep drag. His mind was a blank as he stared at a crack in the ceiling.

He needed an ashtray, reached out and turned to see whether there was one at hand.

That was when he saw the letter.

It had been left halfway under the door. How come he hadn't noticed it before? he wondered. Maybe Marina had just put it there?

His hope-filled heart skipped a beat, and he hopped up, walked along the carpet, and grabbed the envelope. But he no sooner looked at it than his heart sank. It was from the bank.

Yes, he knew he was $327 overdrawn at the Burger Bank. So, what were they writing him about now? Were they canceling his account? He tore the envelope open, unfolded the printed form inside, and glanced quickly at it. At first, it didn't make sense. He read it again, more slowly.

The blood began beating at his temples. His throat constricted, and he rubbed his eyes, and then read it once again. It had two lines of text that were just too crazy to believe.

This is to inform you that we have this day credited to your account the sum of $1,170,400.00.

4

"I'm in a hurry, Miss," Bannister urged.

He held the forms out to be signed across the counter.

But the brunette didn't seem to hear or even see him. By the shaking of her shoulders, he could tell she was engaged in something mysterious that he couldn't quite make out. He knocked.

"I have to catch a plane," he called. "All I need is for you to stamp these forms. It's very important!"

The brunette looked at him, her eyes distorted by the thick lenses of her heavy tortoiseshell glasses. Without missing a beat of her shoulders, she murmured, "I'm busy."

"Doing what?" Bannister wanted to know, now worried that he'd miss his flight.

"Can't you see I'm masturbating?" she said. "Here, stick your head through the window. See for yourself."

Sam leaned over the counter, his head going through the opening of the glass and practically reaching her shoulder. She was sitting on top of three telephone directories with her legs spread and her right hand rubbing her clitoris. Inky pubic hair curled over her thighs and climbed toward her belly button, half hidden by the garter belt holding up her flesh-colored hose.

"How do you like it?" she asked, without breaking her rhythm.

Sam stared at her, eyes popping out of his head, his face flushed.

"Here, feel it," she said. "It's all real. Wanna put your hand on it?"

"May I?" he asked. "Really?"

"Of course, dumbbell," she said. "Look, try it with your fingers."

Sam dug his stiff fingers in where the brunette was showing him. . . .

"You sex maniac!" Crystal roared.

Not knowing where he was, Sam was suddenly awake. He found himself on top of his wife's overblown body, his fingers digging into her crotch, in the unexciting, familiar decor of their conjugal bedroom. They had been married for twenty-six years, and had three grown kids, the youngest of whom, Henry, was away at college.

Sam could hardly remember the last time they had had sex together. That last time must have been four or five years before, and even though Crystal had seemed perfectly willing, she had broken off right in the middle of the act, saying that she thought it was obscene and ridiculous for people of their age to engage in the phoney pretense of fornication. Once her children were grown, she had devoted all of her deeper urges to her work in the local Presbyterian church, of which she was one of the most devoted parishioners. Sam understood that that had meant the end as far as intercourse was concerned. But you couldn't stop a man from dreaming. . . .

"I must have been having a nightmare," he apologized, blushing to the roots of his hair.

"Disgusting! Utterly disgusting!" she commented.

She hopped out of bed, looking furious. An old flannelette nightgown clung to her elephantine shape. Sam turned away so as not to have to watch her go. He closed his eyes resignedly, hoping to get back into his vanished dream. But there was no brunette now. She remained in the dream world, playing with herself behind the counter instead of stamping the ticket that would have sent him off on a trip to who knows where. . . .

The phone rang twice. Crystal stood in the doorway, hideous to behold with her bleached hair in a ridiculous bun. Her head seemed to be screwed onto her overly heavy body with practically no neck between her chin and the curve of her shoulders.

"It's Alan Pope," she announced, and turned on her heels like an outraged queen.

Sam jumped out of bed, and in his bare feet hurried down the hall, aware of the aroma of toast and freshly ground coffee. In the vestibule he picked up the phone, and said, "Alan?"

"I've gotta see you, Sam."

"Now?"

"Right away."

"No can do," Sam groaned. "I'm late as it is."

"Then when?"

"Want to have lunch at Romano's?"

"No, that's too crowded. Meet me at the grill room of the Pierre. Okay?"

"Say, that's kind of fancy. Can you tell me why—" he was asking, but Alan had already hung up.

"What's he want from you now?" Crystal called from the kitchen.

"I don't know."

"If he calls you at home, he must want something."

Sam sat down at the table. "Just wants to see me."

Crystal shoved two more slices of bread into the toaster and grumbled, "He's no company for you, Sam. That Pope's a woman chaser, he's divorced, and lazy."

"And my best friend," Sam went on thoughtfully as he buttered his toast. "He happens to be in a bind. He just got fired."

Alan had walked by the bank three times without daring to go in. From the minute the double glass doors were unlocked, there had been a degree of activity he never would have suspected so early in the morning. Within ten minutes, twenty or more customers had gone in and come out. And others were now on their way in. He fell in with them and went up the two steps leading to the entrance.

The Burger Bank was a commercial bank that specialized in the financing of big multinational firms. General Motors had an account there, as well as General Foods, ITT, National Shipbuilding, National Steel of Detroit, Hackett Chemical, Lloyd's of London, and many other American and European conglomerates. The one thing all these companies had in common was that each employed at least fifty thousand people and did an annual gross business that ran into the kind of figures represented by a government's budget.

However, in order to appear democratic, the demagogic Burger Bank maintained a small department for individual accounts, mainly restricted to its major clients' personnel, so Alan Pope was one of those who had been permitted to bank there. It was most convenient, since that way each payday his paycheck could just be credited to his account by transfer from Hackett Chemical's account.

He knew the exact amount of his overdraft—$327—and with a trembling hand, he made out a check to Cash for $500. The teller looked at him with cordial indifference, and asked, "In hundreds, Mr. Pope?"

Alan nodded; he was too tense to get a word out. He quickly shoved the five C notes into his pocket and walked quietly out.

Once outside, he had to repress an impulse to run. He turned at the corner, leaned against the building, and let out a deep breath. Crossing the street, he went into a bar, and let himself collapse on a stool.

The bartender reluctantly put aside his *Racing Form*. "The way they write it, you ought to hit a winner every time. So how come I leave all my paycheck at OTB? What'll it be?"

"A double scotch," Alan said.

"On the rocks?"

"No, straight up. And make it a triple, not a double."

The bartender looked disapprovingly at his watch: It was 9:12 in the morning. Even his regular lushes didn't start hitting it that hard until about noon.

"Oliver Murray's been trying to get you for the last ten minutes," Patsy informed him; and Sam Bannister's blood turned cold.

"What's he want?"

How should I know? was what Patsy's face said. But she answered, "I've got enough to keep me busy all morning with those fluorite papers. And it's nine-twenty already. Maybe you'd better go and see him."

Mentally, Sam computed his earnings on his way to Murray's office, while running down the list of contacts who might be able to offer him a job. In the corridor, he wiped his forehead, tightened the knot of his tie, walked as inconspicuously as possible, and took the stairs up to the executive floor.

Outside Murray's office, he almost did an about-face, thought better of it, knocked twice, and opened the door. Murray was looking at the 9:22:12 on his wall clock.

"Sorry to hold you up," Sam said, "but I was on the phone. How are you?"

But he got no answer. Murray just stared him down, and played with his pencil.

"I was talking to Tokyo," Sam went on. Murray froze him with his eyes. "It was Mashibutu, about the fluorite," Sam persisted. "They were calling from the home office."

Murray's face gave a dangerous twitch.

"It's eleven twenty-three at night in Tokyo right now," he commented.

"Really?" Sam mumbled. "Are you sure?"

"I'm disappointed in you, Bannister," Murray replied. "What are you making?"

"Twenty-two hundred odd..."

"That's not bad."

"I've been here twenty-one years."

"That's a pretty long time."

Sam stood stock still; he knew he had just heard his death sentence. "Look, there's no reason to say that," he told Murray. "I haven't done anything wrong. You can't fire me the way you did Alan Pope. I'll appeal it. What have you got against me, huh?"

"You may leave," Murray dismissed him. "I'll have to note your hostile attitude in your file."

Sam suddenly wanted to kiss him. If he still had a file, he wasn't being fired.

"Listen, Mr. Murray—"

"You may go."

"It's just my wife, she kind of upset me this morning..."

Sam couldn't resist reaching over and shaking the hand of the man who terrorized him. Murray didn't like that one bit, and pulled back. Bannister let go of his hand, smiled a conciliatory smile at him, and tiptoed out of the office. Once outside, he did a couple of jumps for joy. He hadn't been fired!

He couldn't summon up the guts to make the next test. But in order to be sure, Alan had to go into another Burger branch—there were a dozen or more around midtown—with a check to Cash for a thousand dollars and walk out as if he did it all the time. The problem was, his legs weren't willing. So he stood there on Eighth Avenue looking at the branch door. The first time it had worked. This time he knew they would see their mistake, arrest him, throw him in jail. He murmured a little prayer, and forced himself to go in. Once inside the bank, he felt twice as panicky.

Clenching his teeth and sweating bullets, he made his way up to a paying teller. He took three tries to sign the check properly, and he noted that the teller hadn't let him out of his sight. He thought he would faint when he handed over the check.

The teller quickly glanced at a list of names, while Alan's heart skipped a beat.

"How would you like that, Mr. Pope?" the teller asked.

"In hundreds," Alan croaked.

"Eight, nine, ten, one thousand," the teller counted, and handed him the crisp new bills.

Alan held his hand as steadily as he could, and started to turn away when he heard, "Mr. Pope."

Pinned to the spot, Alan summoned all his nerve in order to turn his head back slowly and nonchalantly, but his pallor could not have gone unnoticed.

"Yes?" he inquired.

"I thought you might be interested in this," the teller said.

And he handed Alan a folder.

"It's all explained inside," he went on. "The bonds pay six and a quarter percent, tax free. They're a very good investment. Let me know if you're interested." He gave Alan his card.

Alan nodded his thanks, and thought, dying must be exactly like what I just went through.

The noonday sun flooded the studio and woke Marina. She opened her eyes, closed them again, and pulled the sheet up over her head.

"Harry?" she called.

"Yes."

"You here?"

"No."

"Whatcha doin'?"

"Working."

"What time is it?"

"Late."

"Is there any milk left?"

"Dunno."

"Wanna go see?"

"Nope."

Marina rolled over on her belly, and realized she had slept with her black kid gloves on. They were sticking to her skin. She took them off.

"Harry," she called again.

"Yes?"

"You're not very helpful."

"Nope."

"You gonna get me the milk?"

"Nope."

Marina yawned, stretched, threw the sheet off, sat up in bed, and rubbed her eyes. Harry was crouching at the other end of the room, stirring a mixture of colors in a dish with a piece of wood. She got up, and went toward the bathroom. Through the open window, she could see waves of heat coming up from the sidewalk. She turned the shower on full force, placed her hands on the floor of the stall and did a handstand against the wall under the icy spray. She stayed in that position for several seconds, letting the water run down from her toes to her face, her mouth open, her hair hanging, and her eyes half-closed. Then she nimbly righted herself and began to lather. When she was done, she carefully brushed her teeth but, instead of putting the brush back in the glass, she shook it out and put it in her bag. She dried herself, walked silently across the studio, got into her jeans, T-shirt, and sandals, and rolled her gloves and black dress inside her flowered straw hat.

The hat followed the toothbrush into her bag.

Harry glanced at her out of the corner of his eye. "Going somewhere?" he asked.

"Yes," she said. She grabbed half an apple that lay idle on a table, and bit into it. "I'm going back to Alan's."

"Hah!" said the artist, but he didn't turn to watch her go.

A maître d' courteously but firmly told Bannister he'd have to wait for a table. "But I'm meeting a friend. Ah, there he is over there!" he replied.

At the table farthest away in the right-hand corner, Alan was waving to him. The Pierre's grill room was jammed. Sam squeezed between the tables, inadvertently knocked over a glass of water, and apologized without stopping.

He was out of breath by the time he sat down opposite Alan. "Well, for a member of the newly unemployed, you seem to be free with your dough!" Sam quipped. He looked around the room. "It's a wonder that so many people can afford to come here. Tell me. What's this all about?"

Then he noticed the bottle of wine lying in its wicker basket.

"Whatzat?" he gulped.

"Pomerol. '61," said Alan, pouring him a glass.

Sam sipped the wine, and asked respectfully, "What do they charge for it?"

"Forty-five bucks."

Bannister nearly choked. "You in your right mind?" he gulped.

"Sam," Alan asked, "can I tell you something in absolute confidence?"

"Certainly not! Now, listen to me. There's an air of crisis up at Hackett. So I can only spare twenty minutes. Tell me what's on your mind."

"Yes or no: Can you keep a deep dark secret?"

"You know I never could!"

Alan took an envelope from his inside pocket and said, "Read this."

Bannister immediately saw it was a bank notice, and said, "If you brought me all the way over here just on account of your lousy overdraft, I'll kick your teeth in."

"Read it," Alan replied.

Sam unfolded it and read the two lines aloud. " *'This is to inform you that we have this day credited to your account the sum of one million, one hundred seventy thousand, four hundred dollars.'* "

He dropped the letter on the table with affected calm, and asked, "Can I order a hamburger here or will they look down their nose at me?"

He helped himself to a radish from the dish of raw vegetables on the table, buttered half a slice of black bread, began to eat it, but he was bothered by Alan's silence. He stopped.

"What's the matter?" Sam asked.

Alan looked daggers at him. "Hackett's just paid me over a million dollars. What do you mean, what's the matter?"

Bannister shrugged. "Fine," he said. "Did I tell you I had dinner at the White House last night? Come on, man. These things happen all the time. Nobody pays attention to them. Last month I got a phone bill for eight hundred thousand dollars. Do you think I paid it? How far do you think you can get with that one million plus?"

"Just a minute," Alan replied darkly. "That money's really in my account."

Sam burst out laughing.

"Okay, okay. Lemme get the guys with the butterfly nets."

"No, they've actually paid it to me," Alan repeated.

For the first time, Bannister noticed how pale Alan was, how tense he looked. "Alan," he started to say.

"For over a week," his friend cut him off, "I've been wondering how I'd pay Mabel's alimony. I was three hundred and twenty-seven bucks overdrawn at the bank. But I went to two Burger branches this morning. I cashed checks for five hundred dollars at one and a thousand dollars at the other. And they thanked me for coming in. How do you like that?"

"I don't," Sam replied, "because it just didn't happen that way."

Alan showed him a roll of bills, and challenged, "What do you call this? Spinach? I'm telling you I didn't have a dime, couldn't even pay my rent!"

"I don't believe it," Sam insisted. "It just can't be."

"Maybe not, but the dough's in my account!"

"Says you!"

"Says the bank. And it's there. They let me draw on it!"

"Come on," Sam retorted, "you're an old customer. They didn't check your account for those two withdrawals. Five hundred, then a thousand bucks—that's peanuts to them."

Alan waved the credit notice under Sam's nose. "Is this peanuts, too?" he demanded.

"But they never credited that money to you, Alan," Sam said stubbornly. "I just don't believe it."

"I could kill you!" Alan muttered.

Bannister smiled his best phoney smile. "Okay," he said, "maybe you're right after all. Why not go over and cash a check for twenty grand. If they honor it, I'll believe in miracles. You see what time it is?"

Sam got up, nearly knocked his chair over, started to turn away, and then stopped. He leaned on the table with both his hands and looked Alan straight in the eye.

"Look," he said, "this whole story is nothing but some wild computer error. You know it as well as I do. So why the hell are you carrying on like this?"

Alan made a face like a child caught with his hand in the cookie jar. He bit his lips. "Frankly, Sam, I'm damned if I know," he said. But then, looking up at his friend and acting childishly stubborn, he added, "I have no idea at all. But just the same, I'm gonna do what you suggested."

5

Marina kicked her sandals off with her toes. She had walked from Harry's studio to Alan's apartment, and was very warm. She brushed her sweaty hair off her forehead. Crossing the room, she dropped her keys in an ashtray, threw her bag on a chair, took off her T-shirt, opened her jeans, but had to stop to wriggle out of them because they were so tight. She was stark naked.

Her first stop was the kitchen. She opened the refrigerator door and smiled tenderly at seeing two cartons of milk. Alan hated milk, yet even though she had gone, he had been thoughtful enough to get some for her.

She opened one carton and drank from it, then went back into the living room and took the straw hat out of her bag. Her black dress and long kid gloves fell out, but it was too warm to put them on. She popped the hat on her head and opened the window. The outside air was even hotter. She went into the bathroom, thinking of the delicious feeling of cold water running down her body. But when she turned the faucet, nothing happened. At the kitchen sink, she had the same disappointment.

Marina took off her hat, picked up her dress and gloves, rolled them together and shoved them into her bag, wriggled back into her tight jeans, put on her T-shirt and sandals, and picked up her keys. She liked Alan a lot, but not enough to do without a shower when she felt like one.

She wondered where she ought to go next. She thought a few seconds, consulted her address book, and dialed a number.

* * *

Arnold Hackett was lounging in his mauve silk robe on the low sofa in Poppy's apartment. Arnold had been paying Poppy's rent for almost two years now. He was also footing the bill for her brother Peter's architectural schooling, not to mention her $2,000 monthly allowance. It amused him to think that despite all this, Poppy was always broke. Sometimes she scolded him for not coming to see her more often; that made him feel loved, even though his business didn't leave him much time.

Even if he had had more time, Arnold would not have come here any more often. Five years ago, he had had a slight cardiac warning. The specialists he saw had told him to take it easy. "What about sex?" he had asked.

"Fine—but only in moderation," the specialists had said.

Taking their advice to heart, Arnold indulged once or twice a month in one of the call girls whose numbers some of his peers passed around with lecherous leers. But Poppy was different—she loved him. She was a delicate child, barely twenty-two, almost exactly the same age as his daughter Gertrude. But unlike Gertrude, Poppy had her feet on the ground. Instead of turning up her nose at money and wasting her time with what was left of the flower children, Poppy was studying ballet with a very good Sixth Avenue teacher.

And in Arnold's eyes, Poppy had another great quality: She loved him precisely because of the fact that he was seventy-one. She hated young fellows. She found them dull, uninteresting, insignificant, and totally without personality.

"You can't imagine how bored I get with those young punks," she would say, and Arnold loved it, patting her affectionately on the head and reveling in the self-assurance that a successful man feels from his acquired wisdom. He knew he had never been handsome, but all his life women had admired "that little twinkle in your eyes"—all women, that is, except his wife Victoria.

Arnold's business took care of itself. People suffered from bronchitis, asthma, blisters, and bruises; whatever it was, his chemists found cures for it. Arnold raked in the profits, and all was right with the world. In forty years, he had made Hackett Chemical into one of America's most profitable enterprises with sixty thousand employees scattered through its many branches and subsidiaries, and doing an annual business of $459,000,000. Arnold Hackett's advantage over the competition was that his company was totally controlled by him. The only dark spot in his highly successful career was that he and Victoria had not had any male offspring to carry on his name and tradition; their daughter Gertrude was too busy being a hippie to take any interest in the family business. Sometimes, as he looked at Poppy's frail, lithe body, he would dream of a secret son who might take up where he left off. But it didn't make sense to become a father again at his age.

Arnold walked over to the closet's three-way, full-length mirror and decided to take a good, unbiased look at himself. He let his robe drop, but hesitated to take off his green-striped drawers, as he peered into the mirror to see whether his twinkle was still in his eyes. He squinted, wrinkled his brow, winked, and then he caught a glimpse of it—sparkling, ironic, laughing. Of course, the rest of him wasn't quite that attractive. Anyone not knowing who he was would have seen in the mirror only an image of a little, full-bellied, bald man, with spindly legs and too much hair on his body. (He had a team of researchers working on this one special problem: how to do away with body hair while replenishing the hair on the head.) He inspected his side views in the mirror, but found he was no more alluring in profile. All he saw was a pear-shaped figure, bulging at the waist, held up by two hairy matchsticks.

"You're handsome," Poppy said.

She was standing in the open bathroom door and looking at him. A towel was wrapped around her waist, and her little round breasts stood out at ninety-degree angles from her ramrod straight body.

"Only in your eyes, because you love me," Arnold protested, honest for once.

"I love your body," she assured him. "It's a man's body."

She came over, pressed her belly against his, and laid her head on his shoulder. Arnold put his arm around her, intoxicated by the wholesome aroma of her hair, the smell of her youth.

"Come on," she said, pulling him to the bed.

He wondered how he would get away from her wave of loving desire. Their party half an hour ago had fulfilled all of his own needs for the next two or three weeks. The temporary exhaustion he had experienced after his orgasm had worried him for a second, until Poppy crowned his effort with one of those comments she was so adept at. "Oh, what you do to me!" she had said. Her low voice had a hot and dreamy way about it, something that made her totally his.

"Please, Poppy, not now, dear. I have to be at a board meeting in an hour," he begged her.

She softly rubbed the top of his shiny head, and murmured, "You drive me crazy. Please don't go away tomorrow."

"I have to. I'm expected over there. Won't you come along?"

Poppy's eyes clouded over. "You know I can't leave Peter alone in New York."

He kissed the tips of her toes, then dialed a number.

"Hackett Chemical," a voice answered.

Hearing his own name announced by the switchboard operator gave him the same little thrill it always had for forty years. Poppy's nails skillfully teased his nape.

"Let me talk to Murray," he said.

"Yes?" said a secretary's voice, after the usual clicking sound of the telephones being connected.

"Murray!" he barked.

"Who shall I say?"

"Hackett!"

"I'll see whether Mr. Murray is free."

Arnold turned purple.

"I said this is Hackett, Arnold Hackett. What's wrong with you?"

"I'll put him right on, Mr. Hackett!" the trembling voice came back.

Poppy grabbed his free hand and bit lightly at the fingertips. Arnold was running his index finger in and out of her mouth.

"Murray?"

"Yes, Mr. Hackett?"

"How are things, Murray?"

He slipped his hand out of Poppy's lips, covered the mouthpiece with it, and whispered, "Stupid, mean, they hate his guts, and he's just the man I need in that job! Scares the hell out of 'em. He's head of personnel in our New York office."

Poppy gazed devotedly at him.

"Well, Murray," he asked, "are those heads rolling?"

"Absolutely, Mr. Hackett."

Arnold was feeling playful. "When do you think it'll be your turn, Murray?" he quipped.

No answer at the other end.

"Come on, you know I was only joking," he finally added. "How far have you gotten?"

"I've drawn up a first list of forty, Mr. Hackett."

"Not enough," he growled back. "I want action. Lots of new faces—people with ideas, people with enthusiasm. I want some young blood in there. How old are you, Murray?"

Arnold laughed to himself and whispered to Poppy, "Nothing gets results like keeping them off balance!"

Arnold resumed his commanding voice. "Well, Murray? I asked you a question."

"Fifty-two, Mr. Hackett."

Arnold indulged himself with a rather extended silence.

"Of course...Oh, well, that doesn't matter, Murray. Key people don't have any age! What's the atmosphere like?"

"A little hostile."

"And you put up with that? Fire the ringleaders! I'll back you up!"

"It's mostly the old-timers," Murray said. "You know, twenty years' seniority goes to their heads, and they think they can't be touched."

"What's his name, Murray?"

"There are several."

"Name me one!"

"Bannister," Murray said.

"What does he do?"

"He's head of Claims Settlement."

"Fire him!"

"Anything you say, Mr. Hackett!"

"Come on, I don't want any lame ducks around. Knock off fifty of 'em, understand? Don't go soft on me!"

He hung up abruptly, burst out laughing, and looked paternally at Poppy.

"I know you must feel upset by things like that," he said to her, "but if I didn't fire a hundred or so from time to time, the others wouldn't feel there was anyone running the company."

Alan Pope rode up Sixth Avenue until the taxi stopped in front of the Burger Branch he had selected. After paying the driver, he walked authoritatively into the bank.

Sam Bannister's dare made him rise above the terror he had felt at his two previous tries. He stopped at the first available teller's window, took out his checkbook, and made out a $20,000 check to himself. He looked insolently at the teller, signed his name, and handed him the check.

As if by some curious feat of astral detachment, he seemed to stand outside himself, watching himself doing all this, fascinated by his irrevocable action. What he was doing was so unlike his usual self that he forgot he was not only the dreamer but also the dream, and the principal actor in it, too.

"Do you want this in cash, sir?" the teller asked.

"Of course."

The teller looked worried. "Would you mind waiting a moment?" he asked. "I'll have to go to the safe."

The teller got up from his stool. Of course, he was going to give an alarm: Alan would head out of here and go straight to jail. He lit a cigarette calmly. What point in running away? The die was cast. He saw that the teller had returned with a man in a gray suit; at the same time, he saw two policemen, one on either side of himself.

The man in the gray suit spoke to him in a low, but firm voice. "My name is Abel Scott. I'm the assistant branch manager. Would you be kind enough to go along with these gentlemen?"

Alan started to hold his wrists out for the handcuffs. "You're carrying quite a large sum, Mr. Pope," Scott went on. "They'll see you to your car."

"We had a holdup here last week," the taller cop put in. "Better safe than sorry."

Alan noticed with embarrassment that he was still holding his wrists out. He quickly rubbed his hands together, brought them back down to his sides, and then cleared his throat. "That's very nice, but it won't be necessary," he said.

Scott looked at him with disapproval, but accepted his decision. The teller placed a thick manila envelope on the counter.

"I'll count it once more, Mr. Pope," he said.

"Go ahead," Alan heard himself say.

Under the cops' fascinated eyes, the teller's short, thick fingers flipped through the packs of bills like lightning.

"Good-bye now, Mr. Pope," Abel Scott said. "If you have occasion to call on us again, please let me take care of you personally."

Alan mumbled his acquiescence, picked up the bulging envelope, shoved it into his pocket, and nonchalantly walked out. The heat of the street hit him like a wave again. He had to walk almost a whole block before he found a bar he could duck into. Once inside, he rushed to the men's room and threw up.

"Look, Alan, how can I do it? What can I tell Crystal?" Bannister said as he tried to see whether Patsy was listening. She turned away and pretended not to know what was going on. Actually, she was taking it all in. Sam cupped his hand around the phone, and went on, "Where? What's the name of the place? Lemme write it down...okay, now repeat that number...I'll be there."

Alan hadn't given him any further details, but insisted that they had to meet for dinner. He had been speaking in a strange, colorless voice. And this date didn't suit Sam at all. The few times he had spent an evening out, he had prepared Crystal for it two weeks in advance, and she had still carried on a regular private-eye investigation to find out whether his business for the evening was really on the level. How would he ever get her to hold still for this?

"Excuse me," Patsy said to him, "but I'd like to ask you a question which is really none of my business. That is, it's my business a little. What I mean is, it doesn't affect me directly."

"I have to go and see Murray," Bannister replied.

"Yes, I know," she went on, "but the thing is—people are talking. There are rumors."

"What kind of rumors?"

"About a wholesale housecleaning."

Bannister shrugged. "You can't believe everything you

hear," he assured her. "You've been around here long enough to know how little these things mean."

"That's true," she replied. "But where there's smoke, you know . . ."

"Well, this is summertime," he told her. "And during the vacation period, people always start to worry."

"They say that Alan Pope—"

"What about him, Patsy?" he cut in.

"That he's been fired."

"What an idea!" Sam exclaimed, not sure whether he should confirm a fact that everyone would find out shortly anyway. "How is the fluorite matter coming along?"

"It's got me stymied."

"Try to make some headway with it," he urged. "I'm on my way upstairs."

What followed was quick and to the point.

"Come in, Bannister," Murray told him. "I have good news for you."

Sam tensed up. To Murray, the only good news was that somebody else had died.

"This is July twenty-third, Bannister," Murray went on. "On December thirty-first, I'm happy to inform you that you will get a closing check for twenty-eight thousand, seven hundred and forty-two dollars." As Sam looked wide-eyed at him, Murray continued. "As of January first, you are retired by the company."

The young woman walked blithely through the bar to the door of the poolroom at the back. A fellow coming out bumped into her.

"Hi, Poppy!"

"Hi, John," she said. "Is he in there?"

"Getting skunked," he answered.

She smiled at him and went on in. Through the smoke, she could see a dozen or so men caught in the bright light shining down on the pool table. They were watching a husky young man in a T-shirt who was about to attempt an impossible shot. Poppy took a couple of steps forward and called, "Peter."

The husky lad turned and looked daggers at her.

"Well, you shooting or not?" Maxie asked him, then looked distastefuly toward Poppy. "This is a poolroom, not a tea shoppe!"

"I'm sorry, Peter," Poppy mumbled, as several of the men standing around snorted knowingly.

"Beat it!" Peter snarled.

Poppy nodded and said, "I'll wait for you outside."

Peter bent all the way over the table, adjusted the cue in his right hand, and stayed stock still for a few seconds. The silence was absolute. Then the cue ball rolled...

"You owe me eight hundred bucks," Maxie said.

Peter took him aside. "Gimme ten minutes," he said. "I've got to settle something, and then I'll pay you."

Maxie looked inquisitively at him, but reluctantly agreed, "Okay, ten minutes."

Peter walked out and saw Poppy sitting on a barstool.

"You made me lose," he told her.

"A lot?"

"Fifteen C's. John, lemme have a double."

Poppy timidly put her hand on his forearm. His eyes stared at the various liquor bottles on the shelf, as if he wasn't aware of her existence.

"You angry at me?" she asked.

"Not at all. I'm delighted with you," he snapped, still without looking at her.

The minute she was with him she felt ten years old. Peter was so handsome that she melted at the sight of him.

"Peter—"

"Shut up!"

She looked at his long sinuous hands, the fine shape of his nose, his broad muscular shoulders bulging inside the white T-shirt, and felt helpless.

"I'm sorry I was late, Peter," she said. "Arnold barged in."

"Old lady Hackett?" he snorted.

"Maybe I can help you out, Peter." Once again, she put her hand on his forearm. His biceps tightened up, but he didn't push her away.

"You get anything out of that old skinflint?"

"Some."

"How much?"

"A couple of thousand."

"Gimme," he said.

She slipped him the roll of bills which he shoved into his pants pocket with a mean laugh.

"I'll never understand how such a stupid jerk can be

that rich," he said. "Maybe it makes sense that he thinks I'm studying architecture—but how the hell can he believe you're my sister? My sister, of all things! Why the hell would he think I was fucking my own sister?"

Victoria was tall, soft, blonde, and defeated, with skin as white as paper and eyebrows and lashes to match. She was perfectly colorless. Pasteurized. She was already transparent when Arnold Hackett first met her, and now, after thirty-seven years of marriage, she had become virtually invisible. The only child of a well-to-do pharmacist, she now wandered through her huge Park Avenue apartment, a ghostlike apparition stuffed to the gills with tranquilizers, surrounded by her servants and lapdogs.

"Are you happy to be going?" Arnold asked her.

She looked at him as if he had been speaking a foreign language, and said, "What?"

"I asked if you were happy to be going."

"Oh yes, Arnold, sure..."

"Did Richard let Gohelan know we were coming?"

"Yes, of course."

"Will we have our usual suite?"

"Yes, the big living room with the balcony and the two corner bedrooms on the third floor," she told him.

"Did Richard have Gohelan change the color of the wallpaper?"

"I don't know."

"Is the weather good there?"

"Very."

"Fine," he said.

"Gohelan told Richard that Korsky was there already," she informed him. "He's waiting to see you."

"Who?" he asked.

"Korsky. That man you play backgammon with."

"Oh, him! That crook's not gonna get a cent from me this year. I'm going in for tennis instead."

Victoria looked at him with worry in her eyes. He answered her unspoken question.

"My heart is a hundred percent. How's the water?"

"Seventy-seven degrees."

"Do we have our tickets?"

"I put them in your wallet this afternoon before you went out."

Arnold Hackett mechanically felt his pockets; they were
empty. He looked at his wife, but she was no longer
watching him. In her own world again, she was petting
Tristan, her favorite Pekingese. Arnold suddenly realized
the only place his wallet could be was at Poppy's. A wave
of heat swept over him at the recollection of his recent
sexual prowess.

"I must have left my wallet at the office," he announced.

"Send Richard for it," she said, coming back down to
earth.

"No, no, I'll go get it myself," he replied. "Richard
wouldn't know where to look for it."

He picked up the intercom and told the chauffeur to
bring the limousine around. With luck, Poppy would not
have gone over to her brother's yet. He might get a
chance to give her one last hug.

Nothing had been moved, but something in the air told
Alan he had had a visitor. He stopped, sniffed, searched
the living room with his eyes, and went into the bedroom.
The bed was just as he had left it, unmade, the sheets
dragging down on the floor.

He went into the kitchen. He turned on a faucet, and
got nothing but a hollow gurgle. He shrugged and
mechanically opened the refrigerator door. A charge of
excitement ran through him; one of the cartons of milk
had been opened and was almost empty. Marina had been
there!

He went back into the foyer to make sure she hadn't
slipped a note under the door, moved a few knickknacks
about, looked on the telephone table, and checked some
old grocery bills. It would be just like her to leave a
message on one, he thought.

He laughed nervously. In his haste, he had tossed aside
the envelope with the $20,000 in it as if it were a piece of
junk mail.

Now he became aware again that that money represented
what most men dream about—freedom, time of one's
own, travel, luxury. Sam would never get over it when he
saw the bundle. Now Alan was sorry he had insisted that
they meet for dinner. Not because of Crystal, who would
never let Sam hear the end of it, but because Marina
might come back in the meantime. She was so unpredictable,

popping in and out like a cat, never getting any place when she was expected, but materializing when one least imagined she would.

He looked with little interest at the envelope on the floor with his stack of hundred-dollar bills in it. Right then, he would gladly have turned it over to anyone who could tell him where Marina was.

6

Arnold Hackett listened at the door. A pop tune came through: Poppy must be home.

Arnold loved surprises. He put a proprietary look on his face, then turned the key in the lock and quietly walked in.

What he saw boggled his comprehension. Behind the large studio couch—which had cost him no less than $3,800—two divine legs seemed to be floating in the air, undulating to some supple rhythmic movement. The feet at the end of the legs were wedged against an antique Italian console table that had also cost him a bundle. He tiptoed around the bed; a naked creature he had never seen before, leaning on her forearms in elbow-length black kid gloves, was doing exercises. Her head was covered by a strange straw hat decorated with flowers, and as she moved, she counted her push-ups, "Twelve, thirteen, fourteen, fifteen..."

Open-mouthed before her perfect body, Arnold couldn't decide whether to slip out discreetly so as not to intrude upon her, or to stay and feast his eyes some more. After all, it was his place.

"Twenty-one, twenty-two, twenty-three, twenty-four..."

He eagerly dwelt on the nipples of the slightly heavy breasts, which grazed the carpet at each downward motion. He fervently hoped her face, hidden by her hair, matched the rest of her.

"Thirty, thirty-one, thirty-two..."

Arnold was hoping she'd go on to a thousand. But at

thirty-five, she collapsed, rolled over on her back with her legs spread wide, and saw him.

"Strange!" she said. "When I'm in shape, I do fifty easy. How about you?"

He blushed all over his bare scalp and said, "I don't really know. I never count."

She got up without any embarrassment whatsoever, took the carton of milk that was at the foot of the bed, and asked, "Want some?"

Arnold hated milk, but answered, "Sure. Why not?"

She took a long swig from the spout and then passed the carton to him. "I don't know where Poppy keeps the glasses," she said. "This place sure is a mess."

But Arnold's eyes kept going from her dark-brown pubis to her face.

"It's amazing," he said, "how much you look like—"

"I know. Don't say it."

In order to appear composed, he gulped down some milk, but almost gagged on it.

"My name is Arnold," he said. "What's yours?"

"Marina."

"I don't think I ever heard Poppy mention you."

"If she's letting you ball her, that beats all. You're old enough to be her grandfather."

That hit him solidly, but he rolled with it, and said with a paternal smile, "I'm Arnold Hackett."

He watched to see what her reaction would be. There wasn't any.

"I left my wallet here," he said. "Do you mind?"

He went into the bathroom where Marina's clothes were thrown in a pile, surreptitiously picked up her T-shirt and smelled it, found his wallet under a large sponge, and returned to the living room.

Still stark naked, Marina was straddling a Louis XV chair, and eyeing him attentively. He blushed.

"It must be lousy to be old," she said.

Among the sixty thousand men and women who worked for Hackett Chemical, none had ever dared say anything so bold to him. Yet curiously, he was not upset by it. He tried to get a little twinkle into his eye.

"If I had my choice, I'd rather be your age," he opined.

He wasn't exactly young anymore it was true, but what time he had left was that much more precious to him. He couldn't afford to pass up his remaining chances any longer. He had to grab, grab everything he could. He knew that he'd give anything just to have the right to touch this girl's skin. As he started to talk, he was so fascinated by her spread crotch that he could not tear his eyes away.

"Listen, Marina," he said. "We hardly know each other, but I'd like to make you a proposition..."

Should he tell her he had been pink-slipped? How was he going to break the news that he wasn't dining at home?

"Crystal! Crystal!" Sam called.

She wasn't in the foyer or the kitchen. Sam started hoping against hope that he wouldn't find her in the living room either.

But he had no sooner called her name again than he saw her sitting there in the purple wool dress that showed off every fold of her overfleshed body. She was reproach incarnate.

"What's the idea of yelling like that?" she demanded. "You know what time it is? Go put your slippers on."

"I'm going back out," he said.

Eyes wide with disbelief, she looked at him as if he had said something utterly incongruous.

"I beg your pardon?"

"I'm having dinner with Alan Pope."

"Forget that bum and go wash your hands," she declared. "You're not going anywhere."

Like a revelation, Bannister suddenly felt released from the full weight of his fears, his twenty-five years of marital slavery, the permanent sense of insecurity at Hackett, his terror of Murray, his dread of finding himself out of a job at an unemployable fifty, and the humiliation of always being treated like a little boy by his wife.

"Whether you like it or not, I am going out," he challenged her.

"You gonna insult me so you can go running around with that whore chaser?"

For the first time in his life, he was ready to stare her down. "The whores he chases are just as good as a lot of others I know," he said, and turned to leave.

"Samuel, where are you going?" she demanded.

Filled with a wild joy he could not remember ever having felt before, he called back without even bothering to turn around, "I'm going to get drunk with the whores!"

Alan had arrived early at Man Ling, a small Chinese restaurant where he and Sam often had lunch. It was inexpensive and quiet, and served good food. From where he sat, he could see all the tables with their red-and-white checkered tablecloths, the green fire-breathing dragons in bas-relief against the walls that were softly lit by colored balls serving as lamps. Next to his plate, he had placed the bank envelope containing the $20,000. Since he had gotten it, he hadn't touched the money. In fact, all day long he had acted only by reflex action.

The more time went by, the less he understood what had possessed him to go and withdraw money which didn't belong to him, which he had no right to spend, and which under any circumstances he would have to return eventually.

He was wondering about his own motivation, when he saw Sam come in. Bannister, squinting as most nearsighted people do when they're bothered, spotted Alan, came to the table, and sat down stiffly without a word. Alan saw how sweaty and livid he was.

"What's wrong?" he asked.

Sam took the rosé wine Alan had ordered, poured himself a glass, and gulped it down.

"Hey, Sam, I asked you a question," Alan said.

Sam looked at him tragically, and said, "Me, too."

"You, too, what?"

"I got fired."

"You're kidding," Alan said.

"Murray put my head on the block."

"Come on, Sam, cut the jokes."

"Do I look like I'm joking?" he asked.

"That can't be!" Alan said. "When did you see him? What did he say to you?"

"Early retirement mandated as of January first next. That does it for me. At my age, do you think I'll ever be able to get another job?"

"He can't do that!" Alan protested.

"You go tell him!"

"Does Crystal know?"

"Not yet."

"Did he give you any reason?" Alan asked.

"None."

"Well, do something about it. Consult your lawyer," Alan advised him. "I don't know what—but you can't take this lying down. You getting your severance pay, at least?"

"Sure, but how long do you think that'll last?" Sam asked. "And then what do I do?"

"Look, you're well known in the industry. You have a lot of contacts. You ought to be able to get a spot almost anywhere—at Bayer, Squibb, Glaxo, Schering Plough."

"Nope. Overage."

"At forty-seven?"

"Stop fighting it. This is it for me!"

"Goddamn," Alan said. "Son of a good goddamn!"

"Are you ready to order?" the waiter wanted to know.

Alan didn't even look at the menu. "Fried shrimp, spareribs, chicken with almonds, and pepper steak," he reeled off.

The waiter left. Alan thought he could see tears behind Sam's glasses. It upset him. "Oh, Sammy," he said.

Bannister turned his head away. Out of embarrassment, he took off his glasses and carefully wiped them with a corner of the napkin. But he didn't look at Alan. Then, he rubbed his eyes with his two fists and just sat there, his head in his hands.

"Oh, Sammy," Alan repeated, with awkward affection. But he didn't know what to say after that. What had happened was too cruel; nothing he might say could make up for it. For two minutes that seemed as long as a whole life's failure, they sat there in silence.

Ill at ease, unable to do anything about it, Alan cast a worried look upon the petrified statue that was his friend. Then that stone was shaken by a deep shiver and Sam seemed to come out of his terrifying coma. He suddenly seemed to realize that Alan was there, looked him straight in the eye, and muttered in a muffled voice, "I'm gonna get even."

"Yes," Alan answered with relief, "of course you are."

"It was your turn yesterday," Sam told him, "and mine today. Tomorrow it'll happen to hundreds of other little guys like us, moved around like pawns, yelled at, threatened, and finally kicked out like dogs. They treat us like old horses sent to the glue factory. Not for me, Alan! I'm not putting up with that kind of shit anymore! For twenty-one years everybody's been pushing my nose down into the dirt. Well, now I'm gonna hit back!"

Alan nodded agreement. Sam grabbed him by the wrist and squeezed it, as if he were trying to crush it.

"I'm gonna get even," he repeated. "You know what that means?"

"Yes, of course," Alan said.

"I'm gonna shaft them the same way they shafted us. They fucked up our lives. Now, by God, I'm gonna fuck up theirs!"

Alan quietly withdrew his hand. "They're stronger than us, Sam," he said. "We're licked before we start."

"I'll get those bastards, never you mind!"

"The two of us alone can't knock over the whole system, Sam," Alan argued.

"I want to see every one of the bastards crawl and croak!"

"You mean Murray?"

"Hell, Murray's just a cog in the wheel," Sam decreed. "He's nothing but an errand boy. I want the head man—I want Hackett!"

He savored the name he had just spoken.

"That's who I'll go after," Sam repeated. "Hackett. Hackett himself. I'll ruin the bastard if it's the last thing I ever do!"

"Whoa, boy!" Alan tried to calm him. "Hacket Chemical rakes in almost half a billion bucks a year, and employs more than sixty thousand people all over the world. All the banks are behind it and so is the government. What the hell can we do to hurt Arnold Hackett?"

"I don't know, but we'll do it," Sam insisted. "Are you with me?"

Alan could hardly hold back his nervous giggle. "That's like Monaco declaring war on the Soviet Union!" he said. And they were both silent.

The waiter was bringing their meal, and Alan ordered another bottle of wine.

As he reached for his glass, his elbow caught the envelope and knocked it off the table. He bent down and picked it up. Sam looked quizzically at him.

"Money," Alan said simply.

Sam's eyes opened wide.

"Money I withdrew from the bank. Twenty grand..."

Alan helped himself to a shrimp while Sam gulped down his wine.

"You really got twenty grand in there?" Sam asked.

Alan nonchalantly slit the envelope open and said, "Look."

Sam took a long look at the packets of greenbacks. "Holy smoke!" he exclaimed. "Real, honest-to-God dough!"

He stretched his hand out, but didn't dare touch.

"Go ahead," Alan allowed.

"Crazy, absolutely crazy," Sam said dreamily, as he spread some of the bills on the table.

Sam's eyes rolled back; they seemed to be going around in circles in their sockets. He discreetly placed his napkin over the currency, and in a changed voice said, "But, then...that means...then Hackett really did credit your account with..."

"That's what I've been trying to tell you since this morning," Alan told him. "One million, one hundred seventy thousand, four hundred dollars. Not a penny more, not a penny less."

Bannister pounded the table as if he wanted to break it.

"We've got 'em!" he almost yelled.

"Huh?" Alan asked.

Sam triumphantly picked up the napkin with the envelope inside it. "This is the first link in our chain!" he said.

"Hold your horses, baby," Alan warned him. "I may have over a million in my bank account, but don't forget I'm flat broke."

Sam threw the envelope back down on the table, saying, "What's this? Toilet paper?"

"It doesn't belong to me. I wouldn't touch it with a ten-foot pole," Alan replied.

"Did Murray kick you in the ass with a ten-foot pole?" Sam wanted to know. "Did you swindle anybody? Did you steal this dough? Who can hold anything against you?"

"It's just not mine," Alan repeated stubbornly. "Don't try acting funny about it. If you were me, you'd do the same thing!"

"I'd be long gone, man!" Sam told him. "You've got the

money in your bank account through none of your own doing. Grab your chance while you've got it, you dope! What have you got to lose?"

"Just my freedom," Alan said. "I don't wanna go to jail."

"You know why we're a couple of poor slobs?" Sam countered. "Because we never had any seed money to start with. We never had the one buck we needed to make ten more. But that's over! Now you've got the capital. You know what having a million bucks in your pocket means? With that kind of a stake, any fool can turn it into three million in a week!"

Alan started to contradict him.

"No, you listen to me," Sam cut him off. "We've had enough of trying to make ends meet. I know exactly what we have to do now. And you're going to hear me out!"

"I'm not going to get into anything until I know exactly how I happened to get all that money by mistake," Alan averred.

Sam gave him a withering look. "You've got it all wrong," he said. "What the fuck does it matter where it came from? You've got it; now use it. All that matters is to keep it long enough to get even with those bastards and make a pile for ourselves."

Oscar Vlinsky wasn't feeling very chipper this morning. When Abel Fischmayer got sore, the whole Burger Bank shook to its foundations. And it was obvious that Abel Fischmayer was about to have a fit. The signs were unmistakable. His ruddy skin turned livid. His fleshy lips magically disappeared to become straight, hard, pitiless lines. Oscar had dared to voice an opinion instead of sticking to the "Yes, sir" or "No, sir" that was expected of him. He had said to Fischmayer, "I'm certainly surprised, sir. My computer never makes an error."

Fischmayer stood up to crush him from his six-foot-plus.

"Vlinsky," he scolded, "you're talking tomfooleries. Do you want me to get the tellers to bring up the customer's account in cash so you can count it before me?"

"That won't be necessary, sir."

"You take my word for it?"

"Certainly, sir."

"Thank you, Vlinsky," Fischmayer spat at him.

Fischmayer was one of the three managing directors of the Burger Bank, and when he pointed a threatening finger thick as a sausage at Oscar Vlinsky, it made Oscar flinch.

"Any more mistakes like that and you'll find yourself looking for a job," Fischmayer scolded.

Vlinsky ought to have known enough to tiptoe out and go and hide in his own office. But, by some unconscious association, he thought of the words Galileo had spoken when he was almost burned at the stake for being right when everyone else was wrong. In spite of himself, he mumbled, "Nevertheless, it was moving..."

"What was that?" Fischmayer thundered at him.

"You're absolutely right, sir," Vlinsky came back. "But just the same, on one point I can assure you—"

"And who are you to presume to assure me?"

"Just on this one point, sir," Vlinsky continued. "When I notified our collection department about the customer's overdraft, which was very small, of course..." It was too late for him to backtrack, despite the fury he could read in Fischmayer's eyes. Oscar took a great gulp and finished, "That overdraft was really there, sir."

"What kind of nonsense are you trying to tell me, Vlinsky?" Fischmayer thundered. "I have Mr. Pope's read-out in front of me. He has over a million dollars on deposit with us. Are you crazy? Are you trying to get him to transfer his account across the street? From now on, I want that man treated with kid gloves, do you understand, Vlinsky? With kid gloves! Now, out of here!"

Oscar was out in the hall, feeling completely at sea. He was sure his computer hadn't make a mistake. But on the other hand, Mr. Fischmayer was the boss, and the boss's computer couldn't be wrong. So who was he to believe?

At just about the same time Fischmayer was confronting Vlinsky, Sam Bannister looked at his watch. 9:00 A.M. He glanced over at Patsy who was doing her nails while pretending to be working on the fluorite file. Sam coughed violently, and she quickly hid her nail file under the stack of papers.

"Can I get you a glass of water, sir?" she asked.

His face congested, Sam was coughing harder than before.

"I'm not feeling too well, Patsy," he said. "I have a sore throat, and I think I'm running a fever. Go over to the drug store, won't you, and get me some cough drops?"

"What kind?" she asked, already on her way.

"Ask the druggist," he said. "Whatever he recommends."

As soon as she was out of the office, he picked up the phone and dialed the Hackett home number. He had wondered all night how he'd get hold of it, and then he had found that it was listed in the directory. When he heard the phone picked up, he straightened his spine in spite of himself.

"Mr. Hackett, please," he said.

"Who's calling?"

"Oliver Murray, head of personnel at Hackett Chemical," he lied.

"Mr. Hackett isn't here, sir."

"Do you know where I can reach him?"

"I don't believe he wishes to be disturbed, sir. Mr. and Mrs. Hackett have just gone abroad on vacation."

"Let me be the judge of that," Sam replied. "Mr. Hackett told me to be sure to contact him directly when I had this very important problem solved. He'll appreciate your telling me where I can reach him immediately."

"Very well, sir. It's the Majestic Hotel, Cannes, France."

"Thank you very much," Sam said politely. "I think it's pretty shitty of Arnold to be over there sunning his ass while I work mine off here in New York. Good-bye."

Agog with contained excitement, Sam dialed another number.

"Alan, I know where the enemy is," he yelled into the phone as soon as it was answered. "You're leaving tomorrow."

"For where?"

"France! The Majestic Hotel in Cannes."

He pressed the button down and then dialed the operator.

"Can I have International Information, please?" he asked. "I'd like the phone number of the Majestic Hotel in Cannes. Yes, in France, that's right. I'll hold on..."

7

Lying flat on his stomach on the floor, Alan reread the paper on which Sam had written the day's schedule. It was just past 9:00 A.M. Despite the oppressive heat, New York was alive with the hum of work from its thousands of slaves. The thing to do now was not think, not crack up, just act. He called the broker.

"Arthur Dealy? My name is Pope, Alan Pope. I'd like to buy some gold. What's it going for today?"

"A hundred and eighty dollars an ounce, Mr. Pope. How much did you consider buying?"

"Two hundred thousand dollars' worth."

"Very good, sir. Two hundred thousand dollars. How will your payment be made?"

"By personal check on my account at Burger Bank. I'll bring it in to you later this morning."

"Would you like me to send a messenger for it?"

"That won't be necessary, thanks. I'm just passing through."

"What hotel are you staying at, Mr. Pope?"

"I'm with friends. Would you like their number?"

"Yes, if you don't mind."

"399-0733."

"I've made a note of it. Can I call you back in five minutes? Someone's paging me. I'll get right back to you."

The man hung up. Alan shook his head. Of course, Dealy would check during those five minutes to see whether his account at Burger Bank was any good. In spite of every positive sign, Alan himself could still not believe it was.

He put on a clean shirt and slipped into some slacks. He felt ridiculous wearing a tie in such weather, but Sam had insisted on it. He was tying the knot when the phone rang.

"Sorry, Mr. Pope," Dealy told him, "but I was called up to our front office. I'll expect to see you in an hour, sir, so I

58

can place your order. Do you know where we are located?"

"Of course."

He got into a light jacket, finally convinced that he was a man of means. He glanced around his apartment, slipped Sam's schedule into his pocket, and went out. He was at an American Express travel office twenty minutes later.

The place was unbelievably busy. At each teller's window, there was a long line.

"Miss, I'm leaving for France tomorrow," he told the clerk who finally waited on him. "Can you have a car waiting for me on arrival?"

"That's kind of hard," she answered indifferently. "We've been mobbed with requests. What make?"

"A Rolls-Royce with chauffeur."

She now looked at him with interest. "Just a minute . . ."

She got busy on the phone as Alan lit a cigarette.

"What luck!" she came back to him. "We do have one of those available. It's two hundred and fifty dollars a day, plus insurance."

"What about the driver?" Alan asked, gulping.

"He's included. Of course, any gratuities are up to you, sir, Is that satisfactory?"

"Fine."

"Your name, please?"

"Alan Pope. Oh, and I'd like some traveler's checks at the same time."

"How many?" she asked.

"Two hundred thousand dollars' worth."

She looked at him with awe. He asked her for a pen and wrote out his check for $200,000 to American Express. He ran his finger between his neck and his shirt collar; it was soaked. She smiled as she took the check.

"Would you excuse me a minute?"

She came back shortly, smiling more than ever.

"Fine, Mr. Pope. Could you come back, say, in an hour? We'll have your checks and your car reservation ready for you."

"Yes, of course. Oh, I almost forgot. I'd like to rent a yacht, too."

"How large a crew?"

Alan had no idea. "Maybe eight or ten," he hazarded. "What do you think?"

She was petite, very well shaped, with long black hair

and big blue eyes. "That's up to you, Mr. Pope. Unfortunately, I won't be the one who'll be sailing on it." There was no mistaking her expression: Just tell me where and when!

She took out a file, glanced through several folders, and handed one of them to Alan. "How does this strike you?" she asked. "Ten sailors and two chefs, one Moroccan, his assistant French. Fifteen knots, six cabins, including the master bedroom which is furnished with period drapes and furniture and is a hundred and twenty-five square meters—that is, about thirty-five by forty feet."

His throat choked up, Alan nonchalantly glanced through the brochure. "Yes, that looks quite nice," he said.

"It's more than that, it's superb. And only four thousand dollars a day, not including supplies, of course. How long would you want it for?"

"I'm not quite sure," said Alan.

"Well, it won't be free until three days from now. But it will only be available for two weeks at the most. And this is another stroke of luck, because it's not often you find anything satisfactory unless you reserve it a year or two ahead. Look at this."

She showed him a rental schedule for the boat. It was full from May 15 through October 30. Except the period from July 26 to August 9 was marked Cancelled. Alan wondered what kind of people fought each other for the privilege of renting a $4,000-a-day yacht.

"We just got the cancellation this morning. It was rented by some people named Garcia; Spanish, I guess. The man's wife was in an accident. And that's why you're in luck. Besides, if you rent it on July twenty-sixth, that'll bring you luck, too. That's my birthday. My name is Ann."

She looked up at Alan and ogled him mercilessly.

"The name of the yacht is the *Victory II*, and it's berthed at Cannes at the Canto Port. You're sure lucky to be going over there. Is this your first trip?"

"No," he lied.

"I'll have it all ready for you when you come back. Is there anything else?"

She looked at him insistently.

"I'm afraid that's all," Alan said.

"At your service, sir."

"I'll be back in an hour or so."

"I'll be expecting you. Just ask for—"

"Ann, I know," he said. "And I won't forget."

He turned and walked out, aware that her eyes were following his every step. Outside, he hailed a taxi and went to Gucci's.

Sam had told him, "You'll be judged as much by your bags as by your looks."

He picked out a set of matched luggage, almost choked when he heard the price, thought of putting them on his credit card, but reconsidered and wrote out a check. This way, he thought, if they put it through fast enough, it will be honored. He left the luggage there to be picked up later.

At Saks Fifth Avenue, he picked out six summer suits in colors ranging from eggshell to anthracite black. They needed some minor alterations, and he was told they could be ready in the morning.

"No go," he told the salesman, with a tone of authority that surprised even him. "Today or forget it. I also need some underwear."

The buyer, who had been called over, assured him the alterations would be done in time, and Alan went to Men's Haberdashery.

"I'll be back for everything at four o'clock" he said, after giving them a check for $1,759, and then headed for the Burger Bank. He picked up another $20,000 in cash which he put into a new Gucci wallet. "You'll need some pocket money," Sam had told him.

When Alan got to the broker's, Dealy immediately received him in a tiny office. "Here's the check," Alan said.

Dealy took it, picked up the phone, and placed the order. The whole thing took less than half a minute, and he turned smilingly to Alan and said, "You're now the owner of one thousand, one hundred and eleven point eleven ounces of gold, Mr. Pope. I think it was a very wise investment. Practically everything else seems to be risky these days, but gold is almost sure to go up. Do you expect to hold on to it very long?"

"I don't really think so."

"You know best, sir. But if you're looking for some promising short-term investments, might I suggest trying drug stocks? There's been a real boom in the industry since the beginning of summer. All the pharmaceutical stocks are going up daily."

"You don't say!" Alan commented, reminded that he had been fired because of the poor market conditions.

"Take my word for it, Mr. Pope, you could reap a twenty-five percent appreciation in three months!"

"I'll think about it," Alan promised.

"Good. Now here's your receipt."

Alan put it in his pocket. It was almost noon. He went back to the American Express office, where quite obviously Ann was eagerly waiting for his return.

"Everything is ready, Mr. Pope," she told him. "When you get to Nice, the Rolls-Royce will be waiting for you. The driver's name is Norbert. And as for *Victory II*—"

"What happened to *Victory I*?" Alan interrupted, as he gazed insistently at Ann's bosom. "Did it sink?"

She smiled and continued. "*Victory II* will be ready for you on the twenty-sixth, as we agreed. Captain Le Guern will be awaiting your orders as to where you wish to go—Italy, Sardinia, Sicily, Greece, Corsica, you name it. They report magnificent weather. The sea is smooth as oil. Are you interested in renting a villa for your stay? We have some elegant estates available anywhere from two weeks to several years—servants included."

"I'll stay at a hotel," he said.

"Majestic, Carlton, Negresco?"

"The Majestic."

She nodded appreciatively. "Here are your traveler's checks."

As he leaned over the counter to start signing them, his fingers grazed against hers. Both of them were aware that the other had sensed the fleeting contact.

"What time do you get off work?" he asked as he wrote.

She looked at him in wide-eyed innocence. "At five-thirty. Why?"

Shy though he was, Alan took the plunge. "If you're not doing anything, I thought... that is, I don't have a dinner date, and maybe we could get together—"

Before he could finish his sentence, she assured him, "I'll have to go home first. Where can I reach you?"

"I'm staying at the Pierre," Alan lied.

"Could we meet there, then?"

"Sure."

"In that case, I'll be at the Pierre bar at seven. How's that for you?"

"Fine," Alan said. "They really mix a mean martini there."

"Mr. Pope?"

Alan was afraid she was going to change her mind.

"I didn't see you counting those checks while you were signing them."

"Don't worry your little head over that," he quipped.

As he left the place, he felt a bit uneasy. He hardly recognized himself anymore. Everything since this morning had been done by some stranger with his name, who didn't act at all like him and with whom he felt no kinship. In the space of a few hours, he had bought gold, acquired a complete new wardrobe and fancy luggage, drawn thousands of dollars from the bank, rented a chauffeured Rolls-Royce and a yacht, pretended to know the Riviera inside and lied about living at the Pierre! Only yesterday, such extravagances would have seemed unbelievable to him. Obviously, Sam had become paranoid and had dragged him into something inexcusable.

Had he gone out of his mind? Why was he throwing all this money around as if it really belonged to him? When he got into his taxi, he huddled into a corner as if hiding, and whispered to the driver to take him to the Pierre.

A short time later, as he sat down opposite Sam Bannister in the grill room, he frowned at the fancy bottle of wine in its wicker basket.

"Who ordered that?" he asked.

"Me," Sam said. "It's called a Haut-Brion '61. It goes for two hundred bucks."

Alan went white. "Who's gonna pay for it?"

"You are. And I ordered caviar as an appetizer. We'll have vodka with it. Okay with you?"

"You've flipped out completely!"

Sam shrugged. "You have to spend money in order to make money," he said. "Did you do everything I told you?"

"Yes," Alan muttered.

"Have any problems?"

"The only problem I've got is you! Gold, fancy clothes, Gucci bags, Rolls-Royces, yachts. And now this tab!"

"At this point, four hundred bucks more or less won't mean a thing," Sam commented.

"Suppose I were to leave and let you pick it up?" Alan challenged, but he had to lower his voice, because the wine steward was pouring some of the nectar, saying, "If you'd be good enough to taste it..."

Bannister put on a connoisseurlike air, inhaled the bouquet at length, sipped from the glass, and swished the wine around in his mouth before swallowing. Standing at attention, the sommelier awaited his verdict.

"Superb," Sam finally decreed.

"Oh, thank you, sir," the sommelier said. He filled both their glasses with the same careful attention and left.

Sam stretched sensuously. "This is what I call living," he said. "Too bad I had to start so late!"

"Are you kidding me?"

"First commandment: Never lose your self-control."

"Well, I'm the one who stands to be held responsible, not you!"

"Second commandment: Rise above it. Having no financial worries, the rich therefore have no moral concerns. Their bank accounts guarantee that they can come out unscathed from almost any bind they get into. The rich don't have to raise their voices; they are listened to. They don't have to hurry; people wait for them. If they're stupid, they're called deep. If they don't say anything, they're called mysterious. When they do talk, what they say is called witty. If they get a cold, somebody else coughs for them. And all they have to do is express a wish, any time, any place, and it will be fulfilled immediately."

"But I'm broke!" Alan fumed.

"Wrong! You're a millionaire, and you've been proving it yourself all morning."

"The dough's not mine!"

"What does that matter? As long as other people believe it is..."

"How long can that last, genius?"

"If you don't screw up, the rest of your life. Money comes to money. Even if you're only rich for two weeks, that's long enough for any person of average gifts to set himself up very comfortably."

"But what if I fall on my ass?"

"All my life I've dreamed of having your chance!"

The caviar was brought in a crystal dish surrounded by crushed ice. The wine steward served their vodka. Their glasses frosted up. Bannister raised his glass for a toast. "To good luck, Alan!" Then pointing to the caviar, he added, "It's the best kind, large eggs. A hundred bucks."

Alan could no longer keep from smiling. "You're really spaced out!"

"Rich man's food, Alan, a king's wine. You'll see how much better your brain'll work. People who are stuffed with spuds can't have anything but clodhopper dreams."

"Where did you ever pick that up?" Alan asked as he spread a spoonful of caviar on a thin slice of black bread.

"We are what we eat," Sam pronounced gravely.

Alan contemplated him. "You really amaze me, Sammy," he said. "I don't know what's happened to you, but since yesterday you're a changed man. I don't recognize you anymore."

"Did you buy the gold?" Sam asked.

"Yep, two hundred thou'."

"The market closes at four. No later than three-thirty, give Dealy your sell order. As soon as that's done, have him give you a payment order on Citibank. You can negotiate it in France without attracting the attention of the exchange commission. How about the traveler's checks?"

"Got 'em."

"The cash?"

"That, too."

"As soon as you get there, you go to the Palm Beach casino. This is the season for heavy gambling. You write yourself a check and set up a draw account of half a million dollars. They'll cable Burger Bank for confirmation of your bank account, then set up their own account for you without a question. The next three days, you'll draw chips in moderate amounts until they total the full figure of your credit. Lose a few of 'em. Not too many, but have yourself some fun. Then you can turn in all the other chips to the cashier and get his casino check for them. You can cash it at their bank. That way, you'll have exported close to a million dollars without the U.S. or French authorities having any record of it."

"A brilliant scheme," Alan said, looking unconvinced. "But what about Hackett?"

Bannister looked away and scratched his head.

Alan suddenly pointed a finger at him. "Don't think you're gonna sell me a pig in a poke, Sam, because I won't buy it! If you don't tell me what the hell I'm supposed to do about Hackett, you can count me out. I want it all spelled out—a precise plan, and one that holds water!"

"Shit, you're no baby, man! You can play it by ear! You and he are gonna be breathing the same air, swimming in the same water, eating the same things, mixing with the same people, and fucking the same broads. See what comes up! What kind of a chance would you ever have in New York of getting next to a big wheel like Hackett?"

"None, and I like it that way. I'm not going!"

Bannister glanced sideways at him, thought for a moment, and then tried a new tack.

"You have exactly two weeks to find the way to get to Hackett. I know how the mistake happened."

Alan jumped as if he had been bitten by a snake. Sam motioned to him to settle down.

"I turned it over in my mind all night long, and I think I got it figured. Anyway, it's the only answer I can find."

"What?" Alan barked.

"Computer error, that's what. Answer my question without getting sore. When Murray told you you were finished, what kind of severance pay did he say you'd get?"

Alan thought a minute, then said, "Eleven thousand, seven hundred and four dollars." He took out a pencil and wrote $11,704 on the tablecloth.

"Now," said Sam, "what was the figure that the Burger Bank credited you with?"

"One million, one hundred seventy thousand, four hundred dollars."

Sam smiled victoriously. "Now, do you get it?"

"No."

Sam wrote $1,170,400 under the first figure. "Don't you see that it's the same number with two more zeroes tacked on?"

"Goddamn!" Alan exclaimed. "Son of a bitch! They'll put me in jail for this for sure!"

"Who is 'they'? Who's gonna press charges? Hackett or the bank? Which one fucked up?"

"I don't know. All I got was a credit notice."

"Well, either our computer left out the decimal point or the bank's did. In either case, it makes no difference. We have two full weeks from tomorrow to make the most of it."

"How do you figure?"

"Well, if they notice the mistake—and there's nothing to say they will—it won't be before August eighth, because that's the date on which the monthly payroll is made up at Hackett. On the eighth, the computer also prints out an up-to-date financial statement for the company."

"What if the bank made the mistake?"

"Same difference. Hackett Chemical is Burger Bank's biggest customer. And Burger is the only bank that finances Hackett and covers its payroll. All the money involved goes through both joints in one direction or the other. Four hundred and fifty-nine million dollars every year. And you're worrying about that tip they gave you! Now, what do you say to that?"

Alan shook his head powerlessly. "Beats me," he said.

"I've taken care of everything," Sam told him. "You pick up your first-class ticket at Kennedy Airport. I got you one of the best suites at the Majestic Hotel. And you're in luck, man! It was chock full, but tonight I'll let you in on the secret of how I worked it out so you could stay there."

"Tonight?" Alan stammered. "No can do. I'm not free."

"You crazy? We got a million things to work out!"

"I told you I can't. I got a date."

"Screw your date. This is more important."

"You should see her! Name's Ann. And I hope to!"

Sam picked up the ball right away. "Blonde?"

"Brunette."

"Where'd you find her, you dog?"

"She took care of me at American Express. I told her I was staying here. She's meeting me in the bar at seven."

"You got a place to take her?"

"No, of course not."

"Lemme have a twenty. Psst, captain!"

Sam gave the captain the bill that Alan had just reluctantly slipped him under the table.

"Mr. Pope is on his way through New York," Sam told

him. "He forgot to make a reservation. Would you see what you can do about getting him a suite?"

"Of course, sir. I'll do whatever I can."

He slipped out among the tables, ignoring the customers signaling or calling to him.

"Did you see that guy go?" Sam asked. "I've always dreamed of giving big tips. Makes things so much easier!"

"Yeah, especially when it's my money. What do they get for a suite in this fleabag?"

"What a vulgar question! When are you going to stop talking about money?"

The captain returned, brimming with importance, and leaned over to whisper to Sam, "The hotel was full, but I was able to work something out. Mr. Pope is in Suite Seven two five."

The waiter brought their steaks.

"Are you really coming over to France with me, Sam?" Alan asked.

"Absolutely. Just give me three or four days to work it all out, I give you my word."

"You're not gonna back out, are you?"

"Do I look like it?"

"What about Crystal?"

"I'll take care of her."

"And Hackett's?"

"I'll take sick leave. There are too many things I wanna do before I cash in my chips."

After coffee and cognac, they agreed they'd talk on the phone the next morning.

"Happy hunting!" Sam wished him lasciviously, as he headed back to his office.

Alan got a taxi. Strangely, the knot in his stomach had now disappeared. He picked up his luggage at Gucci's, and then his suits at Saks. The boxes were piled on top of the bags. It was a quarter past three. For a second, Alan thought of going back to his own apartment, even though the idea of no water was repugnant to him. Then he remembered that he was registered in Suite 725 at the Pierre, and burst out laughing.

The Haut-Brion '61 had temporarily calmed his worries. He was a little bit giddy, and felt at peace with the world. Everything was so easy. The bellhops came rushing for his bags and parcels, which he sent ahead to his suite.

Then he went to the desk and asked for a safe-deposit box. They took him back to a vault the size of a small room, lined with safe-deposit boxes. One was opened, he put his traveler's checks and the wallet with the $20,000 in it. The attendant had discreetly stepped out while Alan did this. Then he returned, locked the safe-deposit box and gave Alan a key. Back in the lobby, Alan went into a phone booth.

"Arthur Dealy?" he said, when he got the broker on the line. "This is Alan Pope. Remember me?"

"Of course, Mr. Pope. What can I do for you?"

"Sell that gold immediately at the closing quotation and have the proceeds put into a sight draft on Citibank. I'll come by to pick it up in twenty minutes." He hung up without waiting for an answer.

When Alan got to the broker's office, Dealy looked strangely at him.

"Congratulations, Mr. Pope," he said. "How did you know?"

"Know what?"

"About Iran."

"Iran?" Alan said.

Arthur Dealy smiled and looked knowingly at Alan.

"I understand, Mr. Pope. Please excuse my curiosity. But if you get on to something else like this, don't forget me, will you? I'd like to piggyback."

Alan blew his nose so as not to look too stupid.

"When you bought this morning, gold was at one-eighty, and it closed just now at two-fifteen. You made a net profit of nearly thirty-nine thousand dollars. My hat's off to you, sir! Do you think it's reached its high?"

"Well, with gold . . ." Alan paused.

"Depends on the wells," Dealy concurred. "If they close the wells. . . . What times we're living in!"

"Do you have my payment order?"

"Here it is, sir, on Citibank as you instructed."

"Thank you, Mr. Dealy."

"At your service, Mr. Pope. I hope to see you again soon!"

Riding back to the hotel, Alan fell into deep reflection. Everything that was happening was beyond him. By merely believing he had $200,000 to invest, he had been able to make $38,888.65 in a few hours. Maybe Sam Bannister was right, after all.

When he entered his suite, he saw that all his packages had been lined up neatly in the foyer. The large living room had a magnificent view of Central Park. Alan could hardly believe that it was he who occupied this suite.

He threw himself on the bed, bounced on it, did a somersault. He felt crazy. He went into the bathroom and played with the shower faucets, aiming the water at various spots on the marble-tiled stall.

He took off his clothes, and went back to the living room for the gin and tonic he had ordered from room service. He drank it totally naked, sitting cross-legged on the Turkish rug. He put some music on, and did a few dance steps, holding his glass against his cheek as if it were a girl.

Through the window he could see the crush of people lining up in the heat to catch buses and taxis home from work. Their activity seemed ridiculous to him; where he was, it was quiet and cool. He returned to the bathroom, picked up the clothes he had shed, and threw them into the wastebasket. Then he took a long cold shower.

After drying himself, he took a swig of his half-finished drink and headed back to the foyer to start opening the boxes with his clothes in them. He laid the new things on the bed, looked them over, and selected the darkest jacket to put on over his naked body. He looked at himself in the long mirror. The jacket fitted perfectly. Then he tried on the other suits. With a sigh of satisfaction, he lay down on the bed and lit a cigarette, but soon got up and paced around. All that space for himself alone made him dizzy. In his apartment, he could get from one side of the room to the other in three strides.

He lay down again, settled his head on three pillows, and contemplated the ceiling. It was so high that a penthouse could have been built in the bedroom without crowding anything. He went to check whether the price of the suite was posted on the inside of the door. Except for fire exit instructions printed in discreet good taste, there was nothing there. He shrugged, and tried to silence the still little voice inside him that kept saying he was crazy, that all this was just too easy.

Five minutes before the time for his date, he put on a

new shirt and necktie, got into a dark suit, looked at himself one last time in the mirror, and went out.

In the bar, he took a nice corner table that was not too brightly lighted. He put down his key for all to see. Ann came in and motioned to him. She was wearing wide black slacks that hid the height of her heels, making her look four inches taller. He held out a chair for her.

"Am I dreaming, or have you grown since noon?" Alan asked.

"You're not dreaming. The American Express clerk is shorter than this gal."

"Does that change take place every day?"

"Not necessarily. Depends how I feel."

"How do you feel tonight?"

"Wonderful. How about you?"

"That depends on you." They both laughed.

Three martinis later, Alan said, "Look, Ann. This is my last night in New York. I'm expecting phone calls from France and Japan. May I suggest something?"

"Try me and see."

"My suite is on the seventh floor overlooking Central Park. I've had the same grueling day as you—people, people, and more people to see. My head's still swimming from it all. I'd really enjoy just having a quiet dinner alone with you somewhere. What do you say to having it in the living room?"

"Living room?" she queried.

"Of my suite."

She slowly turned the glass around in her fingers, and without looking up said, "Why not?"

"I'm dying of hunger," Alan replied.

When they entered the suite, Ann went straight to the window to see the view of Central Park at twilight. Alan joined her. She had her back to him. He hesitated a second, then put his hands on her shoulders. She let herself slip back against him.

"Beautiful view," she said.

He quietly hugged her. She replied by taking his hand. He buried his face in her hair.

Below, as night fell, the headlights of cars were tracing long arabesques. Looking into space, she whispered, "Night in Central Park. How lucky you are!"

He grazed her cheek with his lips, aroused by the

warmth of her skin coming through the thin fabric of her blouse.

She turned to face him, took his face between her hands, and molded her body against his.

"Everything must come so easy when you're rich," she said.

BOOK III

8

Hamilton Price-Lynch lit his eighth Muratti of the morning, put a serene look on his face, and walked toward the balustrade of the balcony, carefully averting his face from what he wanted to see. Even at this distance, he felt he was being watched. Yet, from the seventh floor of the Majestic Hotel where his four-room suite was situated, the swimming pool seemed no larger to him than a sparkling blue-green bean. He inhaled the air, oxygenating his lungs which were permeated with the poison from the millions of cigarettes he had already smoked during his life, then peeked below. He saw his wife Emily and her daughter Sarah having tea at one of the tables around the pool. Emily spotted him immediately. With trepidation, he waved to her, but got no response. Even if she were to come up right away, it would take four or five minutes for her to get here.

When he was alone, he usually took advantage of the fact, to open a perpetually locked, metal briefcase and take out a flock of pornographic magazines, perusing them page by page with a magnifying glass. His situation only allowed him to dream his erotic fantasies. He knew that if he indulged the slightest of them, he would be pitilessly thrown out. At fifty-five, that might mean he would be on the street without a cent after years of having lived the dolce vita of the wealthy. It would be hard to start all over again.

Today, however, he rushed back into his suite and feverishly grabbed the copy of *Nice-Matin*, of which he had dared read only the headline, paralyzed as he had been by Emily's presence. He was sure that if he had so much as glanced at the article in her presence, she would have smelled a rat. He was so scared of her that even when she was thousands of miles away, he could feel her mistrustful eyes upon him. The blood now rushed to his face as he read the newspaper account.

VICTIM IN BAY OF CANNES IDENTIFIED
Erwin Broker, American, 28 Years Old

Police Commissioner Agnelli and Inspectors Berdot and Coumoul today identified the body of the man killed during the Cannes fireworks display. His wallet, floating beneath the surface, was brought up in the nets of some fishermen off the Cap d'Antibes. In it were identification papers for one Erwin Broker, American citizen, of New York City. Mr. Broker had checked into the Carlton Hotel twelve days earlier. He seemed completely unknown here on the Côte d'Azur, where he was apparently visiting for the first time.

He thought he heard some noise at the door of the suite, and quickly put the paper on the bed. He opened the door hurriedly, but no one was there; the hallway was empty. He went back out on the balcony, glanced over the guardrail again, and in a fraction of a second Emily's eyes met his. It wasn't possible, he thought, that she constantly sat looking up at the seventh floor. So what intuition told her that he would be looking down at just that second? He went back into the room to finish reading the article.

Identification of the body was made possible by the picture in the passport of Erwin Broker. Described as a company executive, he was scheduled to stay on in Cannes for another ten days or so. As of press time, the police had no theory as to what might have led to his tragic death. Commissioner Agnelli is continuing the investigation locally, after having alerted Interpol.

He realized that his cigarette had burned down to where it was searing his fingers. He snuffed it out in the ashtray, lit another, and took a deep drag on it. He threw the newspaper into the bathroom wastebasket, then deciding against that, took it out, considered clipping the article, but immediately realized he had better not. With her instinct, Emily would be sure to notice what he had done. Nothing that ought to be kept from her ever escaped her notice. He wiped his hand over his face. How stupidly he was acting! Emily had never even heard Broker's name. The man had only been to see him at his office once, one among his endless daily callers. The other times they had met, it had been in a bar on Eighth Avenue where no one knew who he was.

Finally, he slipped out of the suite, leaving a door open, and shoved the newspaper through the mail slot of Room 751. Then he went back in, put on some sunglasses, and went out on the balcony where he flopped down on a steamer chair. The sun at its zenith burned his shoulders through the light silk of his shirt. Yet he was freezing. Waves of ice flowed from his solar plexus through his body, out to the tips of his limbs. He was reliving the gala party at the Palm Beach three days before.

At the climax of the fireworks display, the final explosion had been so violent that the guests had not been able to keep from glancing at one another with fleeting looks of worried surprise. Everyone had laughed a little too loud and clapped a bit too heartily.

That was when the woman had shrieked, the kind of shriek that makes one's blood run cold. Price-Lynch was only a few yards from the woman's table, and Emily had looked quizzically at him. Then, they were all gathered around trying to revive the woman. Several people, helped by the waiters and captains, were lifting her from her chair to get her off the terrace. It all took place in semidarkness, because the man handling the lights had had sense enough not to turn them on again right away. A number of the guests, their eyes still dazzled by the pyrotechnics, had not seen what went on. Many of them had not even heard the cry through the brouhaha of overlapping conversations.

But, at the end of the dinner, Price-Lynch had gotten the details from Louis, the captain whom he buttered up with wildly overgenerous tips behind Emily's back. Louis had the lowdown directly from the waiter who had been serving the woman's table. When she had brought her soup spoon up from the bowl of lobster bisque, on it was a human finger, sliced off at the last knuckle and wearing a gold signet ring.

The waiter had had the presence of mind to dispose of the finger immediately in a paper napkin which he shoved into his pocket, and then lividly present it to Jean-Paul, the restaurant manager. Repressing an urge to throw up, Jean-Paul had passed it to the police inspector on duty and the latter had immediately taken off in his car at breakneck speed.

Naturally, the press had made no mention of the gruesome discovery. Nothing must be allowed to mar the summer tourist season. The papers had merely said that the shattered remains of a body had been fished out of the water beyond the lighthouse shortly after the unexplained explosion on the floating platform where the fireworks had been set up.

So, Louis's bloodcurdling story was true. The severed finger belonged to Erwin Broker. And Broker's death meant not only the collapse of a plan that had been carefully nurtured over a period of years, but also Price-Lynch's own demise if he didn't immediately come up with an alternate solution. Unfortunately, he didn't know what that could be.

It was already July 25. The mechanism that had been set in motion months before would go off as planned on August 8.

Barring a miracle, he could never find himself another pigeon in the intervening thirteen days.

9

Marc Gohelan ran the Majestic and its empire from a small office at the back of the building on the ground floor. Its two windows, hidden by growths of blossoming camellias in winter, looked out on Rue St.-Honoré, a quiet provincial street on which there was a service entrance for the 250 employees. This was the hidden side of the glamorous facade on the Croisette.

The season here lasted virtually all year. At the height of the season, Gohelan sometimes put in eighteen-hour days. He was a man of medium build with the face of an attractive pirate. Women liked his dark eyes and blond hair.

A confirmed bachelor, he made a rule of never mixing business and romance. Any woman guest who made a play for him drew a blank. But he would turn her away with so much charm and elegance that none could ever resent being spurned.

In Cannes, heartaches were as flimsy and ephemeral as the sea spray on the beach. The Majestic attracted beauty and money like a magnet. And they got along together very well. For one tourist season, anything went. People lived with an intensity that precluded duration. All that counted was the pleasure of the moment. In this wild whirligig were industrial tycoons, princes, swindlers, society women, middle-class families, millionaires, international celebrities, and crackpots of every description, whose social existence in some cases would not outlast the summer.

With one glance, Gohelan could size up a person, unmistakably picking out the fakers, the bad actors, the athletes on the make for a matronly friend with moolah, pretty dolls seeking a well-fixed "good and great friend." But Gohelan treated all of his guests with the same respectful familiarity, whether they were dethroned kings, water-skiing champions, ruling prime ministers, or politicians temporarily out of office.

While the closed-circuit tv screen danced with panoramic pictures of the main lobby, Gohelan looked at Albert Gazzoli, his chief cashier, and asked, "How much is Goldman into us for?"

"He got here on July eighth. I've had his weekly bill rendered to him three times already."

"Has he paid it?"

"Not yet."

"How much?"

"A hundred thousand and some francs."

"Restaurant charges?"

"Pretty heavy. He's been doing his entertaining at the pool, lunches and dinners for twenty and thirty people at a crack."

"Did he sign the tabs?"

"No."

"Come on, Albert. What the hell?"

"Well, you know how he is. It's difficult..."

"Bar tabs?"

"A lot."

"Paid?"

"No."

"Well, if he asks for any more advances, say no. No more cash for that character."

Albert looked at the boss with regret. "You should have told me that yesterday," he said. "We gave him forty thousand francs this morning."

"Let me see his goddamned check."

"He didn't give us one. Told us to put it on his bill."

"Are you crazy? He still owes us a hundred thousand francs from last year!"

Albert Gazzoli seemed to shrink into himself. "There are flowers, too," he added.

"What flowers?" Gohelan barked back.

"Fifty bouquets of red roses for his guests' wives."

"Don't tell me you laid out the dough for that!"

"Twenty-five thousand francs," Gazzoli mumbled.

"Did you ever get taken!"

"Well, he's supposed to be getting ready to do a superproduction with Brando, Newman, Redford, De Niro, Peck, Faye Dunaway—"

"Yes, I know, from a script by Victor Hugo, with Leonid

Brezhnev and Jimmy Carter playing themselves! Did he mention anything more about that cockeyed prize?"

"The Leader Award?"

"Yes. Who's paying for that?"

"Goldman, so far as I know."

Marc Gohelan banged his fist violently on the desk.

"We've been had, Albert," he yelped. "Laid, relayed, and parlayed!"

The young man in the light suit came through the gate from the arrival area into the Nice airport. He looked pale, slightly peaked, carrying a light brown leather briefcase. He had just arrived from New York and this was the first time he had ever been on the Riviera. He winced at seeing two uniformed cops channeling the travelers. But they were telling one another stories, interrupted by huge outbursts of laughter, and paid him no attention whatsoever. Everyone seemed in good humor, happy to be alive. Vacation was in the air, along with salt water and sunshine. The young man was startled at feeling a hand grasp his. A hostess in a bright red uniform, her arms full of flowers, was smiling at him and handing him a yellow mimosa.

Alan Pope took the flower, timidly returned a smile to the beautiful, suntanned girl, and read *Bienvenue* on the paper around the stem. It seemed a good omen. Whatever else might happen, at least he would have been welcomed with this flower and this smile. Sighing, he headed for the phone booths to let his driver know he had arrived.

Smiling mysteriously, Duchess Armande de Saran was dreamily contemplating her black eye. That plumber had not beaten around the bush. He was a stocky fellow with a low forehead, thick hands, a bull neck, and his body gave off a strong animal odor. The duchess figured he couldn't have been more than twenty-five. This kind of delightful encounter made thrills of pleasure run over her flesh. She loved being suddenly face to face with a stranger whose arrival had been planned and awaited by her. She had reported a leak in the bathroom of her suite— Number 19, one of the prize suites in the hotel—and had asked Gohelan to send someone up right away. As soon as the brute came in, she knew he would be the one, right then. It hadn't taken him long to see through her icy, haughty facade, one of the most elegant aristocratic women in the world. In order to provoke him while he was checking under the sink to see what might be wrong, she had barked orders at him as if he were the lowliest of servants, while making sure that, naked under her robe, she brushed up against him several times. Her head was already light with the contrast between the perfumes on her dressing table and the sweaty odor of the young bull. He was on his knees, his metal toolbox open revealing pincers and wrenches, heavy steel instruments made to bite, to tear.

"Hurry up, young fellow, hurry up," she snarled at him, and he looked up challengingly at her.

"Look, you don't like it, you can—"

"I beg your pardon?" She cut him off. "What insolence! I'll report you for this. Do you know whom you're talking to?"

His eyes unabashedly boring in at the top of her long thighs, he mumbled without opening his teeth, "A bitch, that's who!"

She slapped him. With one leap he was upon her, hitting her, trying to kiss her mouth, kneading her flesh in his powerful hands.

"Harder! Harder! Hit me! Hit me!" she moaned delightedly.

He stood her up, shoved her against the wall, and took her right there with the violence of a wild animal. The black-and-blue marks on her body were one thing, but that black eye he had given her was quite another.

She looked longingly at the powerful black pincers she had swiped from his toolbox—the duchess was also a kleptomaniac—and put a cold compress on her eye which was beginning to swell. What a man! The only kind that turned her on were tramps, hoodlums. The more brutal and vulgar and dirty, the more her body reacted with depths of voluptuousness frowned upon by the aesthetes of her own caste.

The living room door opened. It was her husband Hubert, the Duke de Saran. He immediately sensed what had happened.

"Mandy?" he asked, coming toward her, excitement in his eye. "Who was it?"

She shrugged with a sign of satisfaction. "A guy."

"Tell me. Did he beat you? Did he hurt you? Tell me, Mandy, tell me."

"I have to finish getting dressed. Later."

"Fuck the party. Tell me," he begged. His voice broke and he sounded like a helpless little boy. "Please, Mandy, give me a blow job now."

She looked attentively at him. He was in his sixties, of below average height, but unusually distinguished and noble. He had known all about her adventures for ten years now. She would tell him every little detail until this heir to one of the greatest bloodlines of France swooned in uncontrolled orgasm.

"No," she said, "not now. I want to go downstairs. Maybe you can have it tonight."

She took a rose from the bouquet that Goldman had sent her and rubbed it softly against her swelling eye.

Norbert and the two porters took their time loading his bags into the trunk of the Rolls-Royce. The car was parked in the Absolutely No Parking area reserved for departing passengers. Not once did the two uniformed officers make a move toward it.

Since he didn't know whether he was supposed to get into the car or wait until Norbert had finished with the loading, Alan lit a cigarette and stood among the crowd of people with his jacket over his arm. Once again he had a feeling of unreality, as if he were not part of the activity which was centered on him.

"Monsieur," the chauffeur called.

"Yes?"

"Would you prefer to have the top of the car down?"

Alan could feel the eyes of all the passersby who had turned to admire the immaculate whiteness of the luxury car. They all seemed fascinated by the choice he was about to make.

"Yes," he said, not wanting to disappoint them.

Norbert slipped behind the wheel and pressed a button. The top rose up with a soft hum and then folded back. After taking off his cap, Norbert opened the door for Alan. The gaping crowd had by now grown larger.

"Monsieur," Norbert said, tentatively. Alan almost answered, "Who, me?" Then he awkwardly slipped a hundred-franc note to the porters and climbed into the Rolls-Royce, embarrassed by all those eyes staring at him. The two policemen gave him a mechanical salute as Norbert shifted into gear. The Rolls-Royce moved off in total silence. Alan scrunched down into the back seat, scarcely daring to breathe.

Louis Goldman owed so many people so much money that no one could touch him. The very enormousness of his debts protected him from his creditors. None of them dared try to have him locked up, for fear this would dry up the source from which some day they might still be repaid. For the fact was that, through his fantastic bluffs, his deals so involved that they made your hair stand on end, Louis Goldman, when he did hit the jackpot, made money hand over fist. For any seven of his movies, six were usually such duds that the investors never saw a cent and the stars rarely were ever heard from again. But the seventh movie would be such a worldwide smash that it would return over a hundred times the money invested in it.

Then Goldman would condescend to settle his most pressing debts, but not without making his creditors feel he was doing them a favor. He referred to himself as a full-fledged genius, expressed nothing but contempt for all his contemporaries, set forth his own ideas as if they were dogma, brooked no contradiction whatsoever, and was firmly convinced that the world owed him everything.

He felt that those who were privileged to be allowed into his company should be honored if he let them pick up the astronomical tabs he ran up from hotel to hotel in Paris and Munich, Rome and Tokyo, Helsinki and London, anywhere from Tierra del Fuego to the Carribbean.

Whatever he owned was in the name of his wife Julia. The advances he got from banks for his film productions were immediately split up and dispersed among a multitude of wholly owned companies and their endless subsidiaries. On paper, Louis Goldman didn't even own his own toothbrush. He never carried a cent on him, consistently forgot to take his checkbook along, and rarely signed the bills people were tactless enough to tender him. But he was so famous that nobody dared kick.

He was very proud of his oversized belly—a contrast to

his once undernourished frame—and his large, babyish head with the thick lips that looked as though they had gone directly from sucking his mother's breast to nursing on a bottle to the everpresent cigar with a band bearing his own name, the symbol of ultimate success. His usual expression was one of scorn for the world.

He had arrived at the Majestic two weeks earlier, and had taken over the most sumptuous of its suites. The bay windows of its living room opened onto a huge balcony with climbing plants and brightly colored flowers through which one could see the shimmer of the sea. In each of its four rooms, there were large bunches of the red roses that Julia so loved.

Goldman took the unlighted cigar—that erect phallus sticking out from his jowls—from his ever sucking lips just long enough to down a gulp of Dom Pérignon. The champagne was lukewarm and he spat it back into the bucket, then shoved the cigar back into his mouth and poured himself a glass of chilled wine. In fifteen minutes a hundred or so of his guests would be arriving, the hand-picked crème de la crème of this season's Riviera set.

For the past three years, Goldman had been living on credit. His last big hit, *Parano's Blues*, had allowed him to get a position in the electronics market. Not because he had any real interest in it, but because he wanted to settle a grudge he had against John-John Newton, a leading manufacturer of missile and satellite equipment.

The last time they played golf together in the Bahamas, John-John Newton had not only beaten Goldman all hollow, but he had gone on to say publicly what a lousy golfer the producer was. And Goldman had vowed to get even. He had invested twenty-one million dollars in a rival company, Van Velde, and been wiped out in less than a year. Ever since that disaster, he had been floundering, looking for another deal that would put him back in the saddle.

Now he had his angle: He was setting up a movie deal that reversed the process of other pictures he had made. Instead of starting with a good screenplay which would provide a vehicle for a star or two, he had decided to sign the top thirty box-office names in the business as the basis for what would become the most colossal movie ever made.

With that kind of a cast, he figured, who would care about the story?

Nevertheless, he had made a deal with ten best-selling novelists, each of whom was writing one segment of a science-fiction epic from an outline titled *The Night the Sun Died* which Goldman himself had concocted. All of them, naturally, were on deferred salary—to be paid only after the grosses started rolling in. He had given each writer such a magnificent participation in the profits that if he ever had to make good, he would owe 160 percent of whatever he netted. Up to now what he had seen of the script was disappointing, but the publicity for his project had been so widespread and covered in such detail that even the most doubting of professionals thought it was actually under way. The toughest part was still ahead—getting the $50,000,000 that would justify Goldman's great catchline, "The Most Expensive Film in Movie History."

Up to now, the customary banks had been playing hard to get, and the major American distributors, burned before, were holding off—even though they knew they might have to come up with better terms once they could be sure Goldman's brainchild was worth having. So, he had had to look around for virgin fields of film finance. That was why Louis Goldman had agreed to be party to the charade known as the Leader Award, which was to be bestowed on him this very day.

Awarded periodically by Cesare di Sogno, a onetime Italian gigolo, the Leader Award was supposed to honor the most dynamic personality or company of the year. No one had any illusions about its true value, but it made a great impression on the suckers—of which there were plenty at the Majestic. The hotel's guest list was a veritable who's who of high finance, heavy industry, banking, aristocracy, and landed gentry. What Louis Goldman had to do was get this choice game to rise to his bait. He knew how fascinating the movies could be to tycoons bored with handling their own fortunes. And all of them were right here at hand. Cesare di Sogno had sent them all an engraved invitation, gilded in gold leaf.

"Lou?"

It was Julia, standing in the bathroom doorway, in a red terry cloth robe, a dress balanced over her forearm.

"Do you like it?" she asked.

"Terrific," Louis answered, without even looking.

"Aren't you ready yet?"

"All I have to do is put on my shirt."

"Well, put it on, darling. We have to be downstairs in ten minutes."

Louis Goldman shook his head with distaste, forced himself to get up, relighted his cigar, then crushed it out in the ashtray, and walked into the bedroom.

Standing there bare-chested, he glanced over the list of innocents among whom he expected to find his new investors. At the head of the list was Hamilton Price-Lynch, known as Ham Burger ever since he had married Emily Burger, the widow and sole heiress of Frank Burger III, owner of Burger Bank.

In second place, not too far behind, was the titan of the pharmaceutical world, Arnold Hackett.

The car went alongside some parking lots under construction and up a ramp, onto the expressway, where it merged into heavy traffic to Cannes. It was just past six in the evening, and the sun was still high; the air smelled of mimosa, gasoline, sea, and suntan lotion. Alan peeked out toward the left, toward the beaches along the road. He was aware that the drivers who passed him were staring curiously. He put on dark glasses.

"Do you wish to take the expressway, sir, or the beach road?"

"Take the beach road," he answered.

"Very good, sir."

Alan suddenly realized that Norbert had been speaking to him in perfect, scarcely accented, English.

"You speak very good English," he commented. "Are you British?"

Norbert laughed slightly. "Certainly not, sir," he said. "I'm French, of Italian ancestry. My family name is Testore."

"Do you speak Italian too?"

"Yes, sir. But that came naturally."

"What else do you speak?"

"Oh, a few words of Russian, and now I've started studying some Chinese. Although around here, there's no great need for knowing that tongue." He paused, and added, "At least, for now."

Alan wondered what he meant. He turned to watch

two magnificent girls walking along the beach on the
other side of the road, their bare breasts attracting no
special attention. Then he saw Norbert watching him in
the rearview mirror, and felt as if he had been caught with
his hand in the cookie jar.

"What do you mean—for now?" he asked.

"Well, sir, the Chinese are certain to get here sooner or
later."

"Why, what would they come here for?"

"The same as the rest of us, sir, to enjoy the country. To
my way of thinking, this region is one of the most
beautiful places in the world."

Nadia Fischler lived for gambling and would die from
gambling. She had known this ever since the first time her
hands felt the cards she got from the baccarat dealer in
Monte Carlo. She was just nineteen at the time.

At thirteen, Nadia had been introduced to sex by a
butcher's helper who had rewarded her with a bag of ham
and sausages which she took home, telling her mother
she had earned them running errands for the butcher. The
cold cuts had been very tasty, but that first, awkward
amorous encounter had left her with only a vague and
unpleasant memory. She had made up for it since.

Now at forty, her amazing violet eyes still exerted the
same irresistible power over men. She was well aware of
it and used it cynically and pitilessly on the pigeons she
plucked with terrifying regularity in order to keep feeding
her pathological passion for the gaming tables. She had
no interest in money as such, didn't care whether she
won or lost, and lived only for her one real thrill, an end
in itself—to gamble amid the muted murmur of the casino.

Having caught the public eye through her beauty, for
several years Nadia had appeared in movies. Producers,
lusting for her charms, tailored roles to suit her. The
heavy fees she earned were immediately gambled away.
Now she was much more famous for her suicidal bets at
the tables than for her brief, sensational fling in the movie
firmament. Rich and powerful men were always ready to
support her, for a week, or two days, or three hours, or as
long as they could take it. But they all had to give up. At
the rate at which Nadia lost, no one could keep feeding
her for too long.

Years before, she had had a brief affair with Lou Goldman. They had remained friends. And she had promised him she would put in an appearance at his party before going off to the casinos. Many a time, Lou had helped her out of a tight spot. And Goldman had never hesitated to hit her up for help when the roles were reversed.

She slipped into the black gown that had become her signature, fluffed up her ash-blonde hair, and called to Alice, her Tahitian maid.

"Are you ready?" she demanded.

"Yes, madame."

"Let me see."

"I'm ashamed."

"Come on! Show me!"

Alice appeared, hiding her face in her hands. Nadia burst out laughing. Alice wanted to crawl into the ground.

"Stay where you are! Let me look at you!" Nadia said.

"I won't dare..."

"You're magnificent," Nadia told her. "You'll be the high point of the party." And she burst out laughing again.

"I'm very thirsty, Norbert," Alan said. "Do you think we could stop off for a drink?"

"With pleasure, sir," the chauffeur replied. "But may I point out to you that the compartment to your right, behind the front seat, has a bar in it. You'll find it has all the usual assortment of whiskies and several kinds of mixers. I think there may even be some Coca-Cola."

"Thanks, I'd rather stop."

They were coming into Cros-de-Cagnes. Norbert unconcernedly parked the car in a No Parking area, got out and opened the door for Alan, and indicated a café terrace with brightly colored sunshades.

"Would this do, sir?"

"Just fine. Will you join me?"

"With pleasure, sir."

Their arrival had attracted attention. Young girls in swimsuits, lounging in steamer chairs, ogled Alan with unmistakable meaning.

"Say, Norbert," he said, "would you mind taking off your cap?"

The chauffeur smilingly complied, as they sat down at a small table.

"What will you have, Norbert?" he asked.

"A pastis, if you don't mind, sir."

"Well, I guess I'll try one too. Is it good?"

Alan suddenly felt kind of ridiculous. His brown shoes and tie, against his white shirt and light-colored suit, clashed with the casual wear about them. Whether young or old, everyone was as near naked as possible, shorts and espadrilles being the main articles of clothing. Norbert's severe black uniform looked almost funereal against the varicolored assemblage around them.

From what Sam had told him, Alan had imagined the Riviera as a sophisticated place in which everyone dressed just so.

Obviously, this was one more place Bannister had never seen.

10

Betty Grone made sure that two of the hotel's gorillas were outside her door, nodded to them, closed the door again and bolted it. She drew the drapes in her room, turned on the night lamp and angled it to shine on the bed, and then cautiously opened her jewel chest. She closed her eyes, lifted the lid, and dug her fingers into the treasures—gold, sapphires, topazes, diamonds, and emeralds; rings, necklaces, earrings, brooches, and pendants. As she touched each piece, she named the man who had made her a gift of it.

Some men had ruined themselves to get her these jewels, others had embezzled or swindled, still others had thrown them into her face in fury. Contact with the gems gave her a greater thrill than she had ever gotten from any of her lovers. She wished she could sleep with her jewels wearing all of them all the time, feeling the gems against her skin, comtemplating them as she ate. But they were too expensive.

The slightest carelessness on her part would have endangered the insurance she carried to protect them from theft or loss. After Betty had sated herself by fondling the jewels, she would ring for the armed men who would take them back to the safe.

She opened her eyes wide again, and reminded herself that it was her ass, her ass alone, which had garnered this wealth for her. And her head, too. For hers was an art that no school taught, the art of trading on her favors, of milking a man's feelings for all they were worth. Little did she care that behind her back jealous women referred to her as a whore. At her rates, whoring was an aesthetics, a high art that soared far above mere semantic considerations.

With her eyes still closed and her hands deep in her collection of treasures, she recalled her triumph of the night before, at the Signorellis'. As she stepped onto the terrace, she had seen out of the corner of her eye her hated rival Nadia Fischler, deep in conversation with the man they were both after, Honor Larsen, the head of a big aircraft firm, Larsen Aeronautics. Honor was built as delicately as a huge sack of silver dollars with a pair of heavy horn-rims perched on top. He was famous for the extravagant presents he gave to the women who shared his life for a few days, or even just a few hours. True to form, Nadia had done her best to get her hooks into this walking gold mine, and had dazzled him at the casino.

Betty had been waiting for her own chance to go on the attack. She knew that Larsen was going to be at the Signorellis' party. Confident in the power of her beauty, her flaming mane, and her green eyes, she had spent several hours on a spiderlike arrangement of jewels on her emerald silk sheath. When she walked into the lighted ballroom, all conversation had abruptly ceased, all eyes had turned toward her, as she glistened like a shining sun, radiating an infinity of fleeting sparks at every slightest movement of her body.

Honor Larsen had reacted to her just as the others did, shamelessly devouring her with his eyes in spite of Nadia's presence beside him. Nadia, in the black dress that was her trademark, was dimmed to insignificance by Betty's brilliant appearance. It was an instant neither one of them would ever forget.

Later, Honor had phoned Betty to ask her to have dinner with him, and she had accepted. He was going to pick her up at Goldman's cocktail party in the hotel lobby.

With a little luck, Nadia Fischler would see them go off together.

She reopened her eyes, took a deep breath, regretfully closed the jewel case, unlatched the door, and called to the armed guards. One of them took charge of the jewels, while the other led the way, his right hand meaningfully deep inside the opening of his jacket. Betty kept watch on them as they disappeared down the corridor. At the most recent estimate, her fortune in precious stones came to some six million dollars. Or just about what Nadia Fischler had gambled away in the last three or four seasons. Betty smiled to herself, thinking of the poverty in which her rival would end her days.

She went back to her dressing table, and pinned onto her coral dress one single, sublime, blue-white diamond, which had been given her by a citizen of Kuwait. Downstairs, Honor Larsen was probably already waiting for her.

The waiter brought their pastises. Alan took out the roll of French bills he had exchanged some traveler's checks for at the airport. But Norbert had already settled for the drinks.

"With your permission," he said. "The usual thing is that I lay out whatever expenses there are. You can settle for all of them when you leave."

Alan put the money back in his pocket. They each took a sip of the pastis.

Norbert smiled. "Would you like something else?"

"No, I'll try to get used to this," Alan replied.

"For instance," Norbert went on, "perhaps it would have been better if you had not tipped the porters yourself. You gave them much too much."

"Yes, but—"

"Oh, I'm not worrying about you, sir, but about those who come later. If they only give the usual amount, they'll get hassled, I think you say."

"Well, I won't do it again," Alan said. "It's very educational having you around."

Norbert smiled broadly. "Thank you, sir."

In the same spot as Arnold Hackett's suite, but two floors below, was the suite occupied by Cesare di Sogno.

The bay windows opened onto a huge balcony overlooking the sea. One of the peculiarities of the suite was that it had two doors leading to the outside hall, one in the living room, the other in the bedroom. This double entry delighted Cesare. He would often arrange to have one girl going out of the bedroom while another was entering the living room, or vice versa. He told them all that he had a very jealous wife who would only too gladly shoot any rival she caught with him. The fact was he had been married once when he was twenty-two, but just for six months. He remembered with distaste the dark two-room flat they had lived in outside Paris. It was on a side street of Montrouge, near a truck yard. When the heavy loads went roaring down the street, his bed, the old chandelier, and the paper-thin walls shook like leaves. His love for Colette had not been able to withstand such obstacles. In order to get away from the awful surroundings and a spouse who was letting herself go to seed on the pretext that she was several months pregnant, he didn't even bother packing a bag; he didn't own one. He just failed to come home one night and had never been in touch with her again. Nor had Colette bothered to try to reach him. Had she died? Had she had the baby? If so, what was it? All these questions remained unanswered, even after twenty-five years.

Cesare had never told this story to anyone except one lawyer friend. The lawyer told him that if it was on the level, he was still perfectly legally married. Cesare had given him a great friendly clap on the back, along with a delighted wink.

Ever since, he had been careful never to make the slightest allusion to those old times when he had gotten by on occasional sandwiches and cadged cups of coffee, washed down with cheap red wine. He never mentioned the threadbare hotel rooms to which he accompanied overripe bakers' wives picked up at the tea dances of La Coupole in Montparnasse or the Claridge on the Champs-Élysées.

His handsome Roman profile had taken care of him from there on. The bakers' wives had eventually given way to bankers' wives, and then to those of industrial and political bigwigs. Naturally, his wardrobe as well as his bank account had prospered apace. Today, Cesare was a familiar figure in Parisian café society; he weighed a few more pounds, had a few less ideals, and had long since lost count of his mistresses.

In all the most luxurious meeting places in the world, he was known as Monsieur di Sogno, and if anyone carelessly added the title of Marquis to his name, he never corrected them. In his heart and soul, he felt he deserved it much more than all those little pipsqueak, last-of-their-line noblemen who came licking his boots whenever they or their company wanted a favor from him. For by now Cesare made his living not by selling himself, but by selling hot air.

Hot air carried him aloft, kept him afloat, paid his bills, and allowed him to live a life of ease full of travels, first-class hotels, beauty, fresh flesh, fine wines, exotic foods, tailored suits, and luxury cars. He had learned that on a social level where one's every need was fulfilled, the field was still wide open for one never satisfied proclivity—vanity. Where vanity was concerned, there were always takers. Medals, diplomas, prizes, and decorations were even easier to dispose of than utilitarian items. You could sell hot air, trade hot air, live on hot air. Because he represented only himself, which was not much, Cesare had had the good sense to establish his business on the basis of appealing to the vanity of those who would patronize him.

His very first operation had consisted of printing up a letterhead for the Leader Award, of which he had automatically made himself Executive Secretary. In various European and American reference annuals, Cesare had noted the names of those who carry weight in the world: scientists, philosophers, writers, aristocrats, famous playwrights, internationally known multimillionaires, corporate heads, and politicians currently holding office.

Each of these had gotten a letter from him. "Would you be good enough to favor us by serving on the Honorary Committee for the Leader Award, to be given once a year to that company or individual who has been selected as most dynamic and noteworthy of the year?" Then a string of redundant sentences explained the award in greater detail; the letter was signed by Cesare di Sogno, Executive Secretary, Leader Award. To his great surprise—and with-

out his even having used marquis before his name—Cesare
got back just as many acceptances as he had sent out
requests. The rest was child's play.

He selected a score of the finest and most prestigious
names for Honorary Committee men and had them printed
in the left hand margin of his new letterhead, which now
read, Leader Award, under the sponsorship of (list of the
Honorary Committeemen), Cesare di Sogno, Executive
Secretary.

Without anyone raising any objection, the Leader Award,
originally planned as an annual award, was eventually
presented several times a year, according to Cesare's financial needs. But Cesare was shrewd enough never to ask
for a cent. The Leader Award was strictly a nonprofit
enterprise. Naturally, there were office expenses, staff
costs, dinners, receptions, travel, and so on—all left up to
the discretion and good will of the winner. The winner-
designate would be invited to come to the Award Committee's sumptuous office on the Champs-Élysées. There
he would be received by several magnificent blondes
outfitted in tailored navy blue, and conducted across
deep, plush carpeting into the rarefied sanctuary of the
Executive Secretary, who would greet him with disarming
simplicity beneath a Toulouse-Lautrec hanging on the wall
behind him.

"My dear sir," the winner would be told, "I am happy
to inform you that you have been selected by our international panel of judges as the one most deserving of the
Leader Award. I congratulate you most heartily. Will you
accept the award?"

The new winner, a man of substance, of course, would
take it all at face value. As head of a banking group, an
airplane company, a real estate combine, or a chain of
department stores, he would modestly nod acceptance.
Then Cesare would innocently unreel the schedule of
celebrations to take place: cocktail parties for five hundred
people, candlelight dinners for the power elite among
celebrities and newspeople—never less than two hundred
at a sitting—in the most impressive restaurants of the
greatest cities. Then Cesare would get up and warmly
extend his hand to signify that the business of the meeting was concluded.

The amazed visitor would let Cesare see him to the door, but just before going out would inevitably ask, "What will this cost me?"

Cesare di Sogno would always give the answer which he considered his crowning stroke.

"Cost you?" he would gasp. "Why, my dear sir, the Leader Award is not concerned with money! It won't cost you a cent, sir. Nothing at all. It is we, on the contrary, who are honored."

"But," the businessman would insist, "what you mentioned—five hundred people at Lasserre's, a dinner for two hundred at Maxim's, a charter flight to Acapulco—that runs into money!"

"Don't mention it," Cesare would reply. Then, with a paternally indulgent face, he would add, "Naturally, our committee does incur some expenses..."

"Can't my company help cover them?"

"A limousine will pick you up at the Ritz at six P.M. on the sixth, as we agreed. There will be full press coverage. As for the expenses, you are in no way obligated to share..."

"Oh, but I insist," the honoree would indeed insist. "How much?"

"I really have no idea what expenses may run to. However, we most deeply appreciate your offer to help in our work."

"Well, then give me a general idea. I feel very embarrassed about this. What do other award winners contribute?"

Once again, Cesare would affect his put-upon look. "That depends," he would finally allow, and drop a figure anywhere from twenty to fifty thousand dollars, depending on the size of the honoree's company.

Surprisingly, up to now no one had ever refused to pay. After all, they always got their money's worth. The winning company got to exhibit a fine embossed diploma. The importance of the person honored always insured wide press coverage. And everyone came out of it happy.

The only exception to the rule was Louis Goldman. He had accepted Cesare's proffered prize without any fuss, but had made no offer to share in the costs, even when Cesare, after several discussions, had dropped unmistakable hints regarding the "ceremonial expenses of our fine work." Cesare's sharklike instincts had finally understood why; Goldman was even more of a man-eater than he. So Cesare was left wondering who would pick up the tab? Certainly not himself. Nor Goldman. Then who?

Cesare dismissed his worry. The weather was fine, his white silk spencer fitted him like a glove, and he could see at least two possible victims among the guests invited to the reception—Arnold Hackett and the plane manufacturer, Honor Larsen. When it was time to go downstairs, Cesare went back into his bathroom, looked at himself in the full-length mirror, and threw a light little kiss to his reflection.

"Should we go?" Alan asked.

Norbert was already standing, cap in hand. He let Alan go by him, and followed close behind.

"If you don't mind my taking a minute to clean the car," he suggested.

"Now?" Alan asked with surprise.

"When it's left with the top down, I always find it full of trash," Norbert informed him.

They walked the hundred feet or so to the Rolls-Royce. On the right front seat, the remains of three chocolate ice cream cones lay melting.

"I'll just be a minute," Norbert commented, grabbing a rag to clean up the mess.

When Norbert was finished Alan got into the seat next to the driver and Norbert raised an eyebrow. "I'd rather," Alan told him and the driver discreetly took his cap off.

Norbert got behind the wheel and stepped on the starter. As he cut into the line of traffic with a solid step on his accelerator, he affectionately patted the wheel, saying, "A good car, this. A very, very good car."

A little farther on, he pointed to a restaurant on the left and, said, "Tetou's. They make a good bouillabaisse. Very, very good."

She lay spread-eagle on the bed, trying to reach its far corners with the tips of her hands and toes. Even lying this way, all she had to do was just raise her neck a little to see the sea through the window with the flowered balcony below it.

The sun had left a tiny band of white on the fragment of skin covered by the bikini she wore in the pool. Now her body had three shades: the whiteness in her groin, the light brown of her pubis, and the tender brick-pink of the rest of her, newly exposed to the brilliant sun of the Mediterranean.

She straightened up with a twist of her hips and went over to smell the two bouquets of roses in her bedroom. Why had they been sent to her? At the pool, she hadn't spoken to a soul except for the waiter from whom she had ordered lemon cokes with lots of ice. She inspected the cards attached to the two bouquets, but the name Louis Goldman meant no more to her than the name Cesare di Sogno. She crumpled the cards, dropped them into the toilet, and flushed them away.

She grabbed an apple out of a fruit dish, bit into it, and headed for the suite's kitchenette. In the fridge, there was a bottle of milk from which she took a long drink, wiping her mouth on the back of her hand. She was delighted with everything. Standing on tiptoe, she stretched voluptuously in front of the open window. To the right she could see people diving into the pool. The sound of their bodies hitting the water came to her a fraction of a second later than she saw them.

Still on tiptoe, she went over and opened a dresser drawer from which she took a flowered straw hat and a long pair of black kid gloves.

Having put the gloves on, she set the hat on her head, positioned her ankles against the edge of the bed, and let herself fall forward. Leaning on her forearms, she began doing a series of push-ups, which she kept track of to the tune of a counting rhyme she had learned in nursery school twenty years earlier.

Four miles beyond Golfe-Juan, they got to the edge of Cannes.

"Should I take the Croisette or Rue d'Antibes?" Norbert asked.

"What's the difference?"

"Rue d'Antibes goes through the business district, and the Croisette runs along the beach. The Majestic is at the end of it. It's a little bit longer."

"Take the Croisette," Alan said.

They were nearing a fork in the road. Norbert bore to the left, went past the light under a railroad bridge and then turned sharply right. In the opposite direction, there were hundreds of cars, bumper to bumper.

"People coming back from the beach," he said. "It's worse than in Paris."

With Norbert bareheaded and himself sitting in the front seat beside him, Alan felt much more comfortable. Only the Rolls-Royce now attracted attention, not its occupants. Alan was amazed by the number of girls on the loose. Some of them were piled in bunches on top of tiny jalopies, their breasts scarcely hidden by tiny bits of transparent materials which were hardly more than pasties, their butts well exposed, shouting for joy over the ear-piercing din of blowing horns.

"Is it like this every day?" Alan asked.

"Yes, and at night, too," Norbert assured him.

"Where do they all stay?"

"Nobody knows. Wherever they can. Some sleep on the beach, others camp out, and still others board with locals. Any sleeping space will do: fifteen of 'em pile into a normal-sized bedroom. In July, Cannes has twenty times its off-season population. Do you know Saint-Tropez?"

"No."

"There, it's a hundred times the normal population. And most of them come into town without any money."

"How do they get by?"

"Any way they can. At the end of the season, some of the girls use what nature gave them in order to earn their daily sandwiches. A lot of the boys do, too, you know."

"You mean they prostitute themselves?"

"Well, let's say they take whatever they can get. Try to put yourself in their place. During the season, they get invited out on hundred-foot yachts with all the caviar, whiskey, and cocaine anybody could want. That kicks all their values into a cocked hat. Money corrupts everything, sir."

11

"Well, how was your tea?" Hamilton Price-Lynch asked jovially.

"Okay," Emily answered, looking at him quizzically. "You going somewhere?"

"Down to the bar for a minute. Gohelan wants my advice about something."

"Considering what we pay here, I hope you'll charge him for it."

He gave her a sour little laugh, and said, "Yes, indeed. Should I meet you downstairs or come back up for you?"

"You'll see us down there," his wife replied. "Sarah, what are you wearing? I don't want us both dressed the same."

"I'm wearing the Saint-Laurent white," her daughter called.

"Good, I'll put on my green Cardin."

"I'm going," Hamilton said, and closed the door quietly behind him.

Sarah motioned to her mother to stay put, and then went into the foyer, opened the door slightly, and made sure there was no one outside. She came back into the living room, and said, "I'd like to show you something."

"What?"

"It has to do with your husband."

"I wish you'd stop calling Hamilton 'your husband.' He is your stepfather, you know."

"You want me to call him 'daddy'?" Sarah demanded. "After you see what I have to show you..."

She pulled out a metal briefcase that was hidden in the closet under a pile of Hamilton's sweaters.

"Ever wonder what he kept in this?" she asked.

"Some papers, I guess," her mother replied.

"Yes, papers, but some very special ones."

She took a small flat key out of the pocket of her slacks.

"Sarah!" her mother protested. "How did you come by that key? You have no right to do that!"

"I swiped it, Mother. After all, it's worthwhile knowing what kind of a man you've been living with for twelve years."

"Sarah, don't do that! I forbid you!"

"Just a quick peek. You'll see how interesting it is."

She turned the key in the lock, lifted the lid of the briefcase and dumped its contents onto the couch.

"Girlie magazines! And this, too. You know what it is? A magnifying glass! He looks at them with a magnifying glass!"

Emily turned her head away.

"Sarah, you close that briefcase this minute! I'm shocked that you are such a snoop! Hamilton may be my husband, but I would never have taken it on myself to look into his private papers!"

"That's your business, Mother," Sarah said. "Keep your blinders on if you want. At any rate, no one'll ever be able to say I let some sex maniac steal our money from us!"

"Don't you try mixing into my business!" Emily thundered.

"Well, don't say I didn't warn you!" her daughter replied.

She put the key back into her pocket and returned to her own room. Emily stood motionless for a few moments, her fingers nervously tightened over the small handbag she was holding. Through the bay window opening onto the flowered balcony, she watched flights of sea gulls as they came winging along the facade with strident calls. When her husband died, she had sworn she would never remarry. Who could ever take the place of Frank Burger III?

Three years later, she had married Hamilton Price-Lynch, one of her late husband's associates. The reason she had selected him was precisely because there was nothing special about him, either physically or mentally. She continued giving Hamilton orders, just as Frank had done when he was alive. Naturally, she had felt the same concerns long before Sarah had put them into words. She was leery of weak characters: They were always more devious and dangerous than strong ones. But Hamilton represented no threat to her or to her fortune. She could squash him like a mosquito any time she wanted. At times, when she felt nervous, she ordered him into her bed. He made love to her obsequiously and devotedly, like a servant anxious to satisfy any whim his mistress might have. She could not have cared less what fantasies moved Hamilton to the kind of sexual performance that fulfilled her. Just as long as she was fulfilled. . . .

She had never felt anything when she slept with Frank Burger. He had overwhelmed her with his superior personality. She had lived and breathed only for him, adapting herself to his schedules, his rhythms, his demands, his whims. With Hamilton, it was just the opposite. And now the fabulous Burger fortune was hers, as some day it would be Sarah's.

Her daughter had never forgiven her for marrying Hamilton Price-Lynch. Sarah felt nothing but contempt for him; she never missed a chance to put him down, to claim that he was some kind of danger to the Burger fortune. She cruelly referred to him by the nickname his associates at the bank had pinned on him, Ham Burger. No one saw Emily as the wife of Hamilton Price-Lynch; they only saw him as her husband, "Mr. Burger."

But this time Sarah had gone too far. No one in the world was entitled to search a man's private papers—except his own wife. Emily took the briefcase, carried it into her own room, and opened it with a little flat key that she kept in her jewel case. As she had done a hundred times over the years, she carefully inspected the collection of magazines that Hamilton regularly added to as new issues came out.

With wide eyes and pinched lips, she ogled the vaginas spread by inhumanly large phalluses, which looked nothing at all like the only two penises she had ever seen up close, those of her two husbands, Frank Burger III and Hamilton Price-Lynch.

The Rolls-Royce went along at a snail's pace in the wild traffic jam. Bathers kept crossing the road barefooted to have a drink at the bars across the way. Beach balls rolled under the wheels of the cars.

"We're in Cannes now," Norbert said.

Alan saw a large rococo white building, surrounded by palm trees on the lawn that gave it a kind of noble air.

"What's that?" he asked.

"That's the Palm Beach, the summer casino."

All at once, Alan's worries flooded back in on him.

This very evening he was supposed to go to pass a $500,000 check at the Palm Beach casino. When he thought about it in New York, after a good meal, it had seemed reasonable. It was just the natural continuation of a dream in which you think you can do anything.

But now, face to face with reality, he wondered whether he would ever dare ask for that much credit. He was inwardly cursing Sam Bannister.

"Is the hotel far from here?" he asked.

"Well, this is the Croisette now, and the Majestic is at the other end of it."

Norbert turned into a small side street, then turned left again and pulled up alongside the sidewalk.

"Is this the Majestic?" Alan asked with surprise.

Norbert shook his head. "No, sir, but I'd like to ask a favor. I want to keep my job, and the company has very strict rules. Would you mind letting me put my cap back on and you riding in the back seat, so we can drive up to the hotel that way?"

"But why?" Alan said. "What difference can it make?"

"It's proper," Norbert said. "The Majestic's guests wouldn't be sure which one of us was the passenger and which one was the chauffeur. Do you mind?"

"Okay," Alan agreed.

He got into the back seat. Norbert gravely put the cap back on his head and they drove off for the Majestic Hotel.

Whenever he stopped at the Majestic, John-John Newton, in addition to his seventh-floor suite, rented a living room and bedroom on the second floor. The bedroom was for his amorous conquests, and the living room for his business callers. It happened that at times those in both rooms got along together very well, through accidental meetings that he arranged on purpose.

Depending on who his caller was, John-John would have some gorgeous creature at a given point stick her head out the bedroom door. Pretending embarrassment, he would introduce the girl to his potential customer. After all three had been together for a few minutes, John-John would say he had to go into the next room to make a phone call, and disappear. When he would return half an hour later, full of apologies, he could generally tell at a glance how well his maneuver had worked. Three times out of four, the girl—a call girl hired at top dollar from an exclusive service—had been "seduced" by his caller, who was delighted to be tearing off a piece with the girl friend of so powerful a man as John-John Newton. And also, the caller had been made a bit more amenable to Newton's business propositions.

Since the Newton Company's deals involved millions of dollars, the slightest fraction of a point could mean a fortune. Newton made deals directly and without discrimination with Israeli generals, Saudi Arabian ministers, Chinese people's commissars, or anybody else willing to equip an army, whether regular or underground, with Newton Company's sophisticated electronic gadgetry.

Two years earlier, John-John had tried to diversify by buying into other branches of the industry. He had discussed the matter with several European and American bankers, asking them to let him know if they heard of any promising possibilities. One banker had offered to let him in on an exceptional deal, but it was a deal that required absolutely perfect timing and coordination. In the final analysis, whether it worked out or fell through would hang by the merest thread. Naturally, John-John had wondered what the banker's angle was, and although he couldn't be absolutely certain, he had figured out an answer that he planned to make use of when push came to shove.

Up to now, he had never dared pull his call girl trick on the man who was now coming to see him. Even if he had been dying to get a taste of the morsel, the man was too shrewd and careful to fall for it.

There was a knock on the door. John-John opened it. The little man in the blue cashmere blazer held out his hand, and Newton shook it warmly.

"Come in, Hamilton, come in. What'll you drink?"

"Nothing, thanks. I'll only be here a minute. I'm on my way to a cocktail party."

Newton's face lit up with a smile. "Goldman's?" he asked.

"Know him?"

"Slightly. Enough for him to want to kill me."

"Over what? Woman trouble?"

"Worse than that! I beat him at golf in Florida."

"For big stakes?"

"Except for his vanity, no stakes at all. But his vanity cost him something like twenty-one million dollars."

"Tell me about that!" Hamilton asked.

"Yes, I will, one of these days."

Price-Lynch crossed his hands and said in a serene voice, "Everything has worked out perfectly. As far as I can see, our deal can't miss."

Before Alan could reach for the handle, two blue-uniformed attendants had opened the door for him. At Nice, he had been welcomed with a smile and a rose. In Cannes, he was greeted by a storm of laughter which he did not know the reason for. Through the boxtrees and mimosas surrounding the pool, he could see hundreds of pairs of legs of both sexes, but no faces to go with them. A husky redheaded doorman dressed like a fleet admiral explained to him, "It's a cocktail party, sir. For an award that's being made."

Alan nodded his thanks, not knowing what else to do or say.

"May I show you the way to the desk?" a bellhop asked.

Alan followed him into the lobby, while the baggage-handlers, under the direction of the fleet admiral and Norbert's admonitions to be careful, took his precious luggage out of the trunk of the Rolls-Royce.

The admiral was called Serge. For a quarter of a century, he had been the head traffic manager of the Majestic. So, as can well be imagined, he had seen all kinds come and go in his day. He leaned toward his nephew, a youngster of twenty or so, to whom he was teaching the rudiments of the trade.

"Never be taken in by the wheels," he told him. "They don't prove a thing. What really counts is bearing, ease, natural dignity. Even in a solid-gold Cadillac, a hick is still just a hick."

His nephew asked, admiringly, "But that one wasn't a hick, was he?"

"Not exactly," the uncle replied. "But, in the first place, it's a rented car. Second, the luggage is all new. Third, that's a ready-made suit he's wearing. And fourth, he doesn't know what to do with his hands. You always have to watch their hands! If they don't know what to do with them, chances are they're more accustomed to motels and trailer camps than to deluxe hotels. Everything OK, Norbert?"

"Hi, Serge."

"Hey, Norbert, this is my nephew. I was just telling him . . . Say, what's your guy's name?"

"Pope. Alan Pope."

"Never heard of him. What's his racket?"

"No idea. He's American."

Serge turned to young Antoine Bezard and said, "See?" Then he dashed over toward a young man with swarthy skin who was followed by an entourage of a dozen persons of both sexes, and greeted him, cap in hand, "Your Highness."

Back with Norbert and his nephew, he explained, "Prince Ali, a nephew of King Feisal. He got in this morning from London. Looking to buy an estate here. Every real-estate guy in town is after him."

Antoine Bezard looked lingeringly at the prince, impressed by his faded t-shirt, his frayed jeans, and his worn espadrilles.

"He looks like a bum," he naïvely commented.

Serge paternally patted him on the shoulder, saying, "You're overlooking one thing, boy: class. He's got class!"

Marc Gohelan gazed with irritation at the mountains of caviar and smoked-salmon canapés piled on the flower-bedecked buffet tables his squads of waiters had set up around the pool. He watched with annoyance as the platters were quickly picked bare; it seemed the guests had not eaten in two days, looking forward to this free feast. The night before, Gohelan had seen a TV documentary about a plague of locusts coming down on an African landscape and devouring everything in sight. This party was just like that. He noted with distress that the wine stewards had formed a human chain to pass along the opened bottles of Dom Pérignon, the way firemen set up a bucket brigade at a fire in the country. But this party was just beginning and nothing seemed likely to put the fire out.

Gohelan worked his way through the groups of gossiping guests with difficulty. He was grabbed now by the lapel, then squeezed by beringed fingers. Shaking or kissing dozens of hands, Gohelan would each time find some complimentary comment to make about the person's looks or dress or shape, mentioning his winnings of the night before, congratulating him on his return to form, remarking on another's successful face-lift, the daring of a new hairdo, the elegance of a suntan, the honor of new decorations. He barely made it out of the grasp of three British spinsters, the tallest of whom, dressed in bishop's purple, was madly in love with him, telling him she wanted to include him in her will (failing her ability to get him between the sheets). His necktie askew, his forehead covered with perspiration, Gohelan finally got past the bar into the little room which had been made into the command post for this event. He began to tear into Ettore Markovitch, his head of food services.

"Ettore! You're absolutely crazy!"

"Not quite yet, sir! But I will be soon."

Orchestrating this huge operation, Ettore needed to use both his arms to keep up the steady flow of food-laden trays and bottles of champagne, the corks of which were popping like an uninterrupted string of firecrackers.

"Ettore, how many guests are there?" Gohelan demanded.

"Well, a hundred were invited."

"Yes, but there are more than five hundred out there already and more keep pouring in. Who's gonna pay for all this?"

"Albert said—"

"Gazzoli? Where the hell is he?" Gohelan cut him off.

Then he spotted the bald pate of his head cashier bobbing up and down in the human tide. "Albert! Albert!" Gohelan called. He took a deep breath, gathered his elbows at his sides, and darted into the crowd.

Near the diving stand, Louis Goldman, whose moment of glory was still three-quarters of an hour away, had succeeded in getting into a private conversation with Prince Hadad.

"All this business between Jews and Arabs is just nonsense, Your Highness," Goldman was assuring him. "That's ancient history. They'll all come together around my project, and I think it's only poetically fitting that a Jew—in this case, myself—should have gotten the idea of making what I am convinced will be the all-time classic film of Islam, *The Life of Mohammed.*"

Prince Hadad was nodding mild approval, as he toyed with his glass of Perrier. He was frightfully hung over from all the whiskey he and three of his lieges had imbibed until seven in the morning. Among the four of them, they had performed sexually with no less than eighteen girls, who had appeared in three waves in the two contiguous suites he kept on the fourth floor specifically for such goings-on. During the season, the call-girl services were kept jumping.

The Arabs were exceedingly generous, but made no compromises when it came to the quality of the merchandise. They insisted on tall, handsome amazons with breeding who enjoyed their work and experienced the thrill of it. When they felt they had been satisfied, they did not hesitate to offer diamonds as gratuities.

Unfortunately, even if they repeated their orgies every night for a month, they resolutely refused to have anything to do with any girl they had ever used before. They insisted on new stuff, something fresh to them, every time.

Louis Goldman noted that Prince Hadad's eyes were streaked with yellow as eyes will be after a world-shattering drunk. The Perrier Hadad was toying with was only for effect. In public, these oil potentates drink nothing but water, thought Goldman, but he kept himself informed about what they did in private. He knew the exact number of girls who had been called and how many bottles had been consumed. A great luxury hotel is like a small village when it comes to gossip. The night waiters who went from one suite to another until dawn, the chambermaids, the bellhops and bartenders were the silent witnesses of all the kinkiness that went on. And there was always one who could not resist the temptation to talk. Gossip took it from there.

"There won't be any problem getting the film made,"

Goldman added. "With a fifty-million-dollar budget, it'll be a snap."

Like everyone else, Goldman knew that Prince Hadad's daily income was $3,000,000, money which Hadad was hard put to spend even on the lavish scale by which he lived. Not that he didn't try. And at his rates, no one could say no to him. The room service waiter got a thousand-dollar tip every time he brought him a yogurt, and the same tip went to the masseur and the lifeguard; the servant who pulled Hadad's chair back for him at the casino gaming tables usually got twice as much.

"How does it strike you, Your Highness?" Goldman asked.

Hadad delicately dipped his lips into the Perrier and allowed that it was quite an interesting idea for a movie.

"*The Life of Mohammed*," Goldman went on, "the Prophet's existence hour by hour! The world's best screenwriters, the greatest stars, thousands of extras, filmed against the magnificent panoramas of the desert. It won't take six months to be in the black—and that's just in the Arab world alone! There have been so many superproductions about Christ, a Jewish rabbi, and not one of the Prophet of Allah! Unfair, isn't it? Wouldn't you like to get in on the project, Your Highness?"

A liveried chauffeur stepped up behind Louis Goldman and said, "Excuse me, sir. There's a phone call for you. From Los Angeles."

"You can see that I'm busy, can't you, Leon?" Goldman replied angrily.

His chauffeur was under orders to come and page Goldman every quarter of an hour or so with a so-called urgent phone call from one of the movie capitals of the world. He was rarely called upon to drive the huge Mercedes which Goldman rented for the season. He was paid mainly to take Goldman's constant abuse, and was quite content with his job as Goldman's walking credential.

Leon became valet, private secretary, chauffeur, or butler, according to his employer's needs, but as a result he had entrée to every movie studio in Hollywood, where his boss's name earned him the unfailing interest of all the aspiring young things who hoped to make it on the silver screen. And if it hadn't been for his job with Goldman,

Leon would have been just another mechanic in one of
the automobile factories outside Paris.

He gave his boss a military salute, holding his cap in his
hand, and looked at his watch as he walked away. In
about fifteen minutes, he'd come and announce a call
from Australia.

"Well, here's our honoree now," exclaimed Cesare di
Sogno, giving Goldman an accolade without releasing the
arm of a short, bald man with a hard, weasellike face.

"Later," Goldman grumbled, "not now," as he noticed
the Prince beginning to show signs of impatience.

"Louis," Cesare insisted, "I'm sure you know Arnold
Hackett."

"Of course," Goldman roared. "Please excuse me. I was
deep in conversation and didn't see you. I was looking
everywhere for you a few minutes ago. Your Highness,
may I introduce Arnold Hackett of Hackett Chemicals?
His Highness, Prince Hadad. And Your Highness, this is
Cesare di Sogno, the executive secretary of the Leader
Award."

Cesare winked at the Prince and patted him familiarly
on the shoulder. "Hi, Had," he said.

Cesare immediately rose several notches in Goldman's
eyes.

Some years before, Cesare di Sogno had been the Prince's
principal purveyor of high-class whores. As comrades in
arms—the arms, that is, of the complaisant women which
they had so often shared—there was no need to stand on
ceremony. Especially now, when it suited Cesare's pur-
poses to have Hackett and Goldman see him being buddy-
buddy with one of the world's great potentates.

"Take good care of Louis for me, Had, will you? He's
the one we're honoring tonight, and knowing him, he's
liable to go modest and run out on me," Cesare proclaimed.

12

The doors of the elevator opened at the seventh floor. The uniformed clerk stepped aside, then guided Alan to Suite 758 and opened the door with his passkey.

"This way, sir," he said.

The foyer was dark. The clerk turned the light on in the bathroom as he passed and went to the end of the living room. Alan took in the black marble walls and tiling of the bathroom.

Suddenly, soft evening light filled the living room. Through the huge bay window, Alan caught sight of the sky, which seemed full of seagulls, as the clerk said, "Your balcony . . ."

Alan took a few steps out, struck by the beauty of the view. To his right, toward the west, the sun was setting in a dazzling golden haze. Straight before him, the sea was furrowed by sailing vessels coming into port. He walked to the railing. Immediately below, there was the crowd at the cocktail party he could hear going on by the pool. All around the pool were light-colored parasols, striped with azure blue. They were in sharp contrast to the dark shadows of the palm trees, the slim blackness of the cypresses, the gray of the olive trees, and the red splashes of the tulip beds and solid masses of rose-laurels.

"I'll open the rest of the blinds," the clerk said.

Alan sighed deeply and sat timidly down on the edge of a steamer chair. When he went back into the living room, the reception clerk had gone. There was a bouquet of roses on a table. He bent over and smelled them.

Alan kicked his shoes off, slipped out of his shirt, and unzipped his trousers. Someone knocked at the door.

He went into the bathroom, got into a white terry cloth robe, and opened the door.

"Your luggage, sir," the porter said. "Would you like me to send a chambermaid to unpack it for you?"

"Never mind," Alan said. "Wait a minute."

He pulled a wad of French money out of his pants pocket, tried to figure what it represented in dollars, but gave up. Alan started to give him two hundred francs, but then remembered what Norbert had said, and decided to give him only one hundred francs. No point in spoiling the racket.

Cesare put his arm around Arnold Hackett's shoulders and led him away. Around the pool of heated seawater, the lawns were peppered with exotic-smelling trees—olive trees, orange trees, lemon trees, mimosas, palms, cypresses, giant cactuses, and century-old aloes. The air was sweet and dry.

"Bumping into you is truly an extraordinary coincidence," Cesare was saying. "Only last week, at a meeting of our international committee, your name came up along with several other well-known figures as the leader of one of the most dynamic companies in the United States. Might I ask you a somewhat indiscreet question—which, of course, you are in no way obligated to answer? What is the annual gross of Hackett Chemical? You don't have to give me an exact figure, just tell me whether I'm misinformed. I understand it to be half a billion dollars."

"You're absolutely right," Arnold conceded proudly.

Cesare looked at him with unfeigned admiration.

"That's quite an accomplishment," he said. "What do you attribute it to, Mr. Hackett?"

Arnold concentrated for a few seconds, and finally said, "Enthusiasm, strict management control, imagination, and daring."

"That's wonderful! You know, before Louis Goldman, we last gave our award to the Mercedes company. Would you be amenable to accepting our award next time around?"

"Well, now . . ." Arnold hemmed, biting his lips.

It was all Cesare could do to keep from rubbing his hands together. The old ape was rising to the bait.

"Of course, I'll have to take it up with my board," Hackett hedged.

"Most understandable, indeed. Do you know how I visualize the ceremony? First of all, it ought to be in a distant, warm, and brilliant place—say, Acapulco. We could use two 747s to bring the guests from around the

world, one coming from Europe—Munich, Paris, London—
and the other from the U.S."

Cesare noted Hackett's slight reluctance and wondered
if he had gone too far too fast. No one could build the
fortune this character had without being a pinchpenny at
heart. The trick was not to scare him off, not to let him ask
any questions.

"When would you be able to make it, Mr. Hackett?" he
asked.

"Don't you give your prize around the same time each
year?"

"Arnold—" A woman cut in on them.

"Victoria," he replied. "May I introduce Cesare di Sogno?
This is my wife, Mrs. Hackett."

Cesare nearly broke in two bending to kiss the parchment hand held out to him. At the same time, he tried to
make a sidewalk appraisal of the diamond Victoria was
wearing.

Her providential arrival had saved him from having to
answer an embarrassing question. He could hardly tell
Hackett that the award was given as many times a year as
he could line up a pigeon to accept it. He shook hands
warmly with Arnold.

"Perhaps we could continue our conversation over a
good lunch," Cesare said. "Where will you be tomorrow?"

Hackett glanced at Victoria, who replied, "At the Palm
Beach casino."

"Fine, then be my guests," Cesare said.

At the Palm Beach, Cesare as yet had never been asked
when he was going to settle his tabs, or rather, to the
extent that he had been asked, it had been done so feebly
that he felt they were flattered to have him patronize
them. The fact was, the Palm Beach saw him as a sort of
shill for them.

"I hope you'll excuse me if I leave you now," he went
on. "I have to present the award in ten minutes or so. The
press must be looking for me. I'll see you both tomorrow.
Madame..." Once again, he kissed her hand, then glanced
conspiratorially at Arnold, and went off.

"Cesare!"

"Betty!"

Shown off to finest advantage by a coral outfit against

which shone a single blue-white diamond, no less than
fifty carats in size, Betty Grone was hanging onto the arm
of a huge man wearing great horn-rimmed glasses. Offhand,
Cesare figured he must weigh in at well over three hundred pounds. Betty possessively raised one of the giant's
huge paws and put it into Cesare's hand.

"Honor Larsen, Cesare di Sogno," she said. And she
winked meaningfully to Cesare as she said Larsen.

"Delighted. Absolutely delighted to meet you," Cesare
said, trying subtly to withdraw his hand which was being
crushed in the vise of the huge industrialist's. Many years
before, Cesare and Betty had been lovers simply because
they each had had a free night at the same time. Neither
one had any real recollection of their intercourse, but they
understood one another without words. Cesare sometimes steered his award winners to Betty, giving her a full
rundown, including their financial worth and marital
situation—for, beyond a certain level of fortune, no man
over thirty was ever a bachelor. For her part, whenever
Betty had a promising lover, she would make sure Cesare
got to meet him. It was one good turn deserving another.

"I've been hearing from everyone how you knocked
them dead last night at the Signorellis'," he told her.

"You don't say?" Betty replied in pretended surprise.

With a flick of her eyelids, she let him know this was
nothing to go on about in front of Larsen. She had the
plane manufacturer on the hook, all right, but it still
wasn't too late for him to get away. She was waiting to see
how he acted tonight at the casino in order to know what
he was made of, whether he was really as generous as he
was reputed to be. As for his alleged staying power in the
sack, she couldn't have cared less. She knew she could
convince any man lying alongside her that he was
Superman, Adonis, Casanova, and the author of the Kama
Sutra rolled into one. While she was moaning as if her
whole being were transported beyond earthly sensation,
she would very adeptly be translating the value of her
lover's gifts into Treasury bonds, blue-chip stocks, jewels,
or livestock.

She had once confessed this to Cesare, one morning at
four when they were at loose ends in the Palm Beach
casino. "When they're too ugly, I keep counting how

many head of cattle I'm earning for my night's work. It makes it easier to take."

Betty thought that Honor Larsen looked like an overstuffed pig, force-fed on hormones, but knowing that she had snatched him away from Nadia Fischler made him irresistible. For years, the two of them had covered the same hunting grounds in Cannes, Monte Carlo, Portofino, Las Vegas, Los Angeles, all the magic places where they could bag the big game with the overflowing checkbooks. They never failed to meet, but just as regularly, they pretended not to see one another.

Betty had nothing but contempt for Nadia's passion for gambling; the latter's left hand merely turned back to the casinos what her right had plucked from the pigeons. And Nadia would gladly tell anyone who would listen that Betty used her ass like a fishwife's cash drawer. Well, today the fishwife had turned the tables on the gambling girl, thought Betty. Nadia Fischler was not about to recover from the knockout blow she had been dealt the night before. And Betty felt a voluptuous thrill at the recollection of the admiring silence that had greeted her appearance at the Signorellis'.

Even the most blasé of society people weren't used to seeing several million dollars' worth of jewels laid out on an emerald-green silk sheath.

"Mr. Larsen," Cesare was saying now, "do you know that we spent three hours talking about you at Munich?"

Betty nudged the giant's elbow. "Cesare di Sogno is the man behind the Leader Award."

"Oh, I see," Honor Larsen acknowledged.

"Considering the dynamic upsurge of your company, the committee felt that it was only right to consider you for the Leader Award."

"Do you really mean that?" Betty gasped with delight.

"Oh, Betty," Cesare twitted her. "Don't you know who you're with? Didn't Mr. Larsen tell you he's one of the world's leaders in aeronautics?"

"No, he never said!" she gasped.

Cesare's mother had been a charwoman, and the only thing he remembered of what she had taught him was the saying, You can never lay it on too thick for a jackass. And time had shown that she was right. The power in the

hands of the suckers he manipulated made them lose all
sense of values. Sometimes Cesare himself was embarrassed
by the outrageous things he plied them with. But they
never seemed to be. Other people's opinions, however
outrageously flattering, were always short of their own
opinions of themselves.

"Well now, you certainly aren't comparing me to Marcel
Dassault, are you?" Honor Larsen said.

Cesare gave him a deprecating smile and turned to
Betty.

"Your friend is not only handsome and famous, but
modest to a fault," Cesare said. "Won't you see to it that
we get better acquainted?"

"Monsieur di Sogno, everyone's waiting for you," a
captain called.

"Coming," Cesare called back. "How about our having
a drink after my speech?" he asked them. And then,
turning away, he wondered where Goldman had disappeared to.

Cesare spotted Goldman on the other side of the pool,
dwarfing a little man in a blue blazer, Hamilton Price-
Lynch. Cesare took a deep breath and started to cut
through the crowd massed around the depleted buffet
tables.

Alan walked barefoot out on the balcony that extended
some twelve or fifteen feet in front of his two bay windows.
In a few minutes, the light had completely changed. The
sun had gone down behind the hills, leaving the sea with
a dull dark glow. He thought of taking a shower but
changed his mind. He had something more urgent to do.
He flopped on the bed, picked up the phone, and gave
the operator a number.

"I'll call you back," she said.

He lit a cigarette, looking aimlessly out into the sky,
feeling a strong urge to let himself doze off. The doorbell
brought him to with a start.

He closed the flaps of his bathrobe, went to the door,
and found himself facing a blue-uniformed chambermaid.

"Excuse me, sir, can I take care of your cover?" she
asked.

"My cover?" he replied.

"Well, straighten your room, tidy things up," she smiled.

Alan's eyes bugged out. Over the chambermaid's shoulder, he could see a small man in a bright red blazer walking down the hall. Back home, he had seen the picture of that man hundreds of times. It was Arnold Hackett in the flesh! He felt like slamming the door shut. He was terrified at having this character who had always been an almighty myth now materialize before his eyes.

"Later," Alan muttered to the chambermaid. "Not now."

"Very well, sir."

He closed the door and locked it. He leaned back against the jamb, weak in the knees. The phone rang. It was his call to Sam Bannister.

"What we're trying to do is diversify our sources of financing and open the movie industry to other branches of the business world," Goldman was telling Price-Lynch. *The Night the Sun Died* will be the safest investment since *Gone With the Wind*. It's bound to bring a thousand percent profit to all the shareholders. And when I say a thousand percent, I mean even if we run into the worst of luck."

Ham Burger nodded as if he believed him.

"I'm not one to toss those kinds of figures around, Mr. Price-Lynch. If I can jump three feet, I never set the bar up to five, I assure you. The fact is, it could very well be ten thousand percent before we're through."

"Excuse me, sir, but there's an urgent call for you from South Africa." Goldman turned and looked daggers at his chauffeur.

"Can't you see I'm busy?" he barked.

"I'm sorry, sir," Leon said, backing away.

"Please," Hamilton Price-Lynch cut in, "don't feel you have to stay here on my account."

"Oh, those De Beers people keep driving me crazy," Goldman said. "Everybody wants to get into the act now. But it's too late. I don't owe them a thing!"

"Louis! I've been looking for you high and low!" Cesare called to him. "We're on!"

Pretending he had just noticed Price-Lynch, Cesare continued, "You won't mind if I drag him away, will you?" He stuck his hand out in a spontaneous gesture. "I'm Cesare di Sogno," he said.

"Hamilton Price-Lynch," Ham replied, taking his hand.

"Well, Lou, they'll lynch us if we don't get over there," Cesare quipped. "This way..."

People made way for them with little cries, excited gasps, and applause. One pushing the other, they finally got to the small platform which the Majestic's carpenters had set up for the occasion. Cesare climbed up on it. Hastily, his assistants passed him a parchment scroll. He wiped his brow, cleared his throat, took the mike and tapped it several times with his fingernail to make sure it was working. It was; the clicks of his nail came back from speakers on all sides, loud as thunder. Baring all his teeth—which had cost him a pretty penny—Cesare laughed at the noise.

"Ladies and gentlemen," he called. "May I have your attention, please?"

The noise abated a few decibels.

"If you please," Cesare repeated more firmly, raising his arm to the position of a Roman emperor about to address his legions. "Friends! My good friends, can we have a little silence? Please?"

Progressively then, the guests were able to hear the warm murmur of the waterfall filling the pool and the sharp peeping of the swallows zipping through the sky.

"Thank you," Cesare said. "Thank you very much."

And then he was taken aback by a strange phenomenon. All heads turned to a spot located somewhere behind him. He tried in vain to call for attention again, and looked down at Lou Goldman standing at the foot of the platform. Goldman, too, was staring.

Cesare resisted a second longer, but in view of the amazement he read on the expressions of all those facing him, he had to give in. He slowly turned his head.

At the same moment, the first laughter broke out. What Cesare saw was Nadia Fischler, wearing a simple unadorned black dress, walking quietly among the groups of people, as if she had no idea that all eyes were upon her.

And then came Alice, her chambermaid, walking two paces behind, her eyes cast down, her hair stained a wild red which everyone immediately recognized as a caricature of Betty Grone's. Alice was decked out in a sheath of emerald-green silk literally streaming with a mind-boggling

array of fabulous pieces of jewelry. She was a walking
Christmas tree, ablaze like a torch with the glitter of her
sapphires, rubies, emeralds, and diamonds, all of which
were almost eclipsed by a dazzling tiara with rows of
pear-shaped emeralds and marquise-cut diamonds mounted on gold.

Everyone then swung around to look at Betty Grone,
who reacted no more than if none of this had been aimed
at her. In spite of her sudden pallor, she had the fortitude
to maintain a slight smile on her lips. She slipped her
hand under the arm of Honor Larsen, who winced with
surprise at the strength of her grip, and whispered into
his ear, "All fakes..." Fascinated in spite of herself, she
mentally calculated that there were at least ten million
dollars' worth of jewels on the chubby, cellulite-laden
body of the chambermaid.

"Ladies and gentlemen," Cesare was shouting in a
useless effort to try to get things in hand again.

It was too late. People on all sides were roaring with
laughter, the sound swelling to fill the entire area like a
tide, as Alice and Nadia finished their triumphal circuit
around the pool.

"Well, where are you, Alan? Did you get there? Alan,
say something!"

Alan was speechless, visualizing Sam thousands of miles
away in the stuffy little office where they had spent so
many years dreaming of getting away.

"Okay, get this, Sam," he finally said.

"Where are you calling from?"

"Cannes. Can you hear me?"

"Very well."

"Sam, you won't believe it, but I just saw him!"

"Saw who?"

"Hackett!"

"You saw Hackett?" Bannister gasped. "In the flesh?"

"Just now, wearing a red sports jacket, walking down
the hall."

"A red sports jacket? You sure it was him?"

"Of course, I'm sure. Now what am I supposed to do?"
Alan demanded.

"Keep an eye out."

Alan squeezed the receiver until it almost cracked and barked back, "Keep an eye out for what? Can I stay here for ten years keeping an eye out?"

"Just keep your shirt on. What time is it where you are?"

"Not quite nine o'clock at night."

"All right," Sam instructed him. "The first thing you do is go to the casino. You know what I mean?"

"Yeah."

"Cash the check. Before anything else, cash the check. Get it?"

"Yeah, and then what?"

"Listen, Alan, thank your lucky stars. Here, it's the middle of the afternoon, and everybody is shaking in their boots. It looks like wholesale firings. It's hotter than blazes, I'm soaking wet, and I'm up to my neck in troubles. So, don't you complain! Just shut up and cash that check. Hear me?"

"I'll have a bite and go right over," Alan said.

"Have your bite later."

"Hell, man, I haven't eaten since I got off the plane. You probably just had lunch!"

"Okay, okay, have your feed. How is it?"

"How's what?"

"Everything."

Alan looked around him. The room was pure luxury, but he couldn't find words that might convey what he was feeling just then.

"Well, it's different," he finally said. "Very different."

"I bet it is, you joker," Bannister grumbled. "Anything different would be better than the rathole I'm in."

"Did you talk to Crystal?"

"Are there any broads?" Sam asked.

"I said, 'Did you talk to Crystal?'"

"Yes—that is, I'm going to. Are there any broads?"

"Millions, and all of them naked as jaybirds!"

"You fuckin' liar!"

"Word of honor! If you saw 'em, your eyes'd bug out!"

"Patsy's coming back in. I'll have to hang up. Listen, Alan . . ."

"Yeah?"

"Don't fuck it up, huh?"

"What the hell do you mean by that?"

There were a few seconds of silence.

"Nothing. Just don't fuck it up, that's all."

"I don't know what you're talking about."

"Just remember what you're there for. Keep your head about you, and for Chrissakes don't crack up," Sam urged.

"I'll do my best."

"Okay, tomorrow, same time. But this time, I'll call you. After all, it's not my dough; it's the company phone."

"Whose dough you think I'm using?" Alan quipped.

"Very funny, very funny. Break a leg!" And Sam hung up.

Alan smiled. Good old Sam! Then he remembered how hungry he was. He rang for room service.

"I'm ashamed, madame. Thoroughly ashamed," moaned Alice, her face hidden in her hands as she sat prostrate in a chair.

On the bed lay handfuls of jewels that Nadia had plucked off her chambermaid's dress.

"You were magnificent," she assured the servant. "That Grone bitch'll split a gut over it! Do you have my heart?"

"Yes," she mumbled. "It's in the fridge."

"Well, now don't be upset. I'm going to give you a present."

She glanced over the pile of jewels that were spread on the bed, and spotted a magnificent turquoise ring.

"Here," she said. "This is for you."

"Oh, I couldn't take it," Alice cried, hiding her face again.

"Look at it, or I'll knock your block off! You know how much this is worth? I won it from a produce wholesaler at Rungis!"

Alice sniffled as she looked at the ring. "I could never wear it," she pleaded. "It's much too nice for me."

"Who said you had to wear it? Go ahead and sell it. It's that much they won't take back from me!"

"Maybe we'll win tonight?" Alice suggested.

She so identified with her mistress that when she spoke of Nadia Fischler she often used the first-person plural. Once she had commented about a Lebanese promoter,

"How are we ever going to be able to sleep with that?" At other times, she would say, "We have a headache," or "We lost so much tonight..."

Alice had long since given up the idea of regular wages. Nadia paid her whenever she had money—if she remembered. Alice didn't lose anything by this system. When Nadia had had a good night at the tables, she would sometimes wake Alice at five in the morning to shove a roll of bills amounting to as much as $10,000 into her bag. But when she was down on her luck, Nadia never was reluctant to ask Alice to lend her what she had given her a couple of days earlier. "I need a grubstake," she would say.

Together, mistress and servant lived a gilded life from one luxury hotel to the next, all centered on the green baize tables of the casinos. Filthy rich one night, but deep in debt by dawn, Nadia would then be ready to sell everything, her dresses, her jewels, her furs, her soul and even her ass, because nothing had any value to her, nothing meant anything except the little ivory ball spiraling infinitely around the roulette wheel that spun out the chaotic circles of her destiny.

"Do you think we'll see that big Swede again?" Alice asked.

"Honor Larsen? Who knows?" Nadia answered. "He's so stupid he may not have caught on at all."

"Madame, will you explain something to me? How can men be so rich and still be so stupid?"

Nadia mechanically ran her hand through Alice's dyed hair. "I really don't know. Maybe the two go together. I once knew a man who was really unusually intelligent. And he didn't have a sou to his name. I had to keep him in eats."

"What did he do?"

"Except for being intelligent, not a thing. Go get my heart. I want to look at it."

Alice obediently went toward the living room.

"Hey!"

"Madame?"

"Your ring!" Nadia threw it to her. Alice shoved it down into her bosom and shrugged. "If we don't win tonight, we'll be plenty happy to have it tomorrow," she said.

"Get out my black dress," Nadia told her.

"They're all black. I'll get your heart for you."

She came back a few moments later and handed Nadia a crystal caviar dish. It contained a bloody piece of meat, turning black around the edges.

"What kind of an animal was it?" Nadia asked.

"Fine and fat. It had gray fur."

"You'll find the money in the drawer."

Alice brought her several packets of bills. Nadia grabbed them and rubbed them against the meat in the dish. When she had finished, she said to Alice, "Put it back in the refrigerator, then tell the switchboard to hold my calls. Let them take messages. I'm going to rest now; wake me at midnight."

This was the routine they followed every day.

Nadia had one obsession: The money she was going to gamble with first had to be rubbed against a rabbit's heart to bring her luck. Every morning, Alice went with one of the hotel's valets to the nearest butcher shop. Going with the valet was part of the ritual. Alice had to make sure that it came from a fine-looking rabbit and that the butcher didn't pull a switch, substituting some other heart at the last minute. The valet got one or two hundred francs for this chore, depending on the days. The heart was kept in the refrigerator until Nadia was ready to stash it in her bag before going to the casino.

Nadia would never set foot in a casino without her good-luck charm. It had to be a fresh heart that day from a gray or a white rabbit, and she had to carry it in her purse. One heart had proven so lucky for her that she had wanted to have it preserved. But when she discussed it with Alice, her maid assured her that each charm could only work once. So Nadia sadly threw the lucky rabbit heart into the sea.

Now Nadia took her dress off, went into the bathroom, had a warm shower, and returned to rest, to make herself ready for the night's hostilities. She slept like a baby.

"Did you bring a menu?"

"Here it is, sir. Would you like to order now? We have fresh salmon steak Chambertin, a contrefilet de Charolais du Barry, or jellied duck à la landaise."

Alan glanced over the list of dishes and after having

some of them explained to him, ordered a shrimp cocktail
and baked royal pike.

"Wine, sir?" the waiter asked.

"What do you recommend?"

"I'd suggest a Saran, a blanc de blanc from Champagne."

Alan had no idea what blanc de blanc was, but he
recognized Champagne, despite the way the waiter pronounced it.

He said that would be fine and acquiesced when the
waiter suggested serving him on the balcony. Meantime,
he asked if he could get a Scotch.

"There's a bar in your living room, sir," the waiter
informed him, and left.

Alan got out of his robe, turned the shower on full
force, and checked the contents of his bar. He poured
himself a stiff Scotch and soda, took a swig of it, and
walked under the cold shower holding his drink, amused
at the way the water popped into his glass; as he turned
around under the spray, he suddenly felt relieved of his
fatigue and all his tensions. He dried himself, opened one
of his valises, and got into a shirt and a pair of ducks.
Then he went back out on the balcony. Below, alongside
the flowerbeds, he saw his Rolls-Royce. In fact, he saw
three of them, all with their tops down.

All the tables on the terrace below were taken, as well
as the ones in the restaurant to his left. The pool was now
lighted from below, but the mob that had been crowding
around it an hour before was gone. He poured another
Scotch and soda, sat down on a steamer chair, and looked
at the east facade of the hotel. Without intending to, he
found himself staring into several rooms whose occupants
had not thought to close their drapes. Apparently, they
didn't care at all if anyone watched them. Alan was
completely taken aback, but even though he felt ashamed
of himself, he was so fascinated that he couldn't help
watching one window after another.

One entirely naked young woman was helping another
hook her dress. Two floors below, a corpulent man sitting
on the arm of a chair was having his shoulders massaged
by a woman who was dressed in nothing but a black bra.
To the left, an old lady was coming out of her bathroom,
and her open dressing gown displayed everything that

was left of her anatomy. Alan quickly averted his eyes and looked up at the infinite expanse of starry sky.

But he could not resist turning them back in a quick sweep over the hotel. And, in passing, his eye caught a flash of bright red on the sixth floor. He looked again and on closer inspection there could be no question but that it was Arnold Hackett's red sports jacket. Alan got halfway out of his seat in order to get a better look. Hackett was standing at the foot of a bed and obviously talking to someone lying on it, but Alan could see nothing but the bare feet. At this distance, he could not tell whether they belonged to a man or a woman. Then his doorbell rang. The waiter came in, pushing the serving cart before him. It was loaded down with all kinds of useless utensils which Alan imagined were required for the rich. There was even a bouquet of roses. Whatever was in the dishes was carefully hidden under silver covers.

"Would you like to taste the wine, sir?" the man asked.

He uncorked it and handed a glass to Alan. Alan sipped at it. It was cool and delicious. Then Alan raised one of the silver covers and inhaled the aroma of the royal pike, and dipped a fingertip into its sauce and tasted that.

Just in case it was expected of him, he handed a hundred-franc note to the waiter, who grabbed it with the alacrity of an iguana swallowing a fly.

"Oh, thank you, sir," he said.

"Your tip," Alan said. "What does that come to in dollars?"

"Around twenty-three dollars," the waiter answered.

"Fine," Alan gulped.

He thought of the two good shirts he and Sam Bannister could have bought in New York for twenty-three bucks, and went back out onto his balcony.

The curtains had now been drawn in the window of the room where he had seen Arnold Hackett.

13

"May I close the curtains?" Arnold Hackett had asked.

"Why?" Marina wondered.

She was lying on the bed, wearing a bikini bottom—which was unusual for her—but no halter.

"You might be seen from the other windows."

"So what? You're seeing me, aren't you?"

Arnold cleared his throat. Having paid for her trip to France, he felt he had certain rights over her that didn't belong to the rest of the world. But, he didn't feel he could say that to Marina. She lived on some other planet, where his vocabulary, his reasoning, his logic, simply didn't apply. She had quite unhesitatingly accepted his offer to come to the Riviera, but without her even having had to put it into words, Arnold knew that did not mean he would necessarily get to touch her.

"Are you happy here, Marina?" he asked.

"Oh, you know . . ."

She was looking him straight in the eye, and as usual, this straightforward look of hers discomfited him. When he was about the business of sex, he now needed reassurance, some positive encouragement. The days when he triumphantly mounted anything that wore a skirt were, alas, long past. Nowadays, he needed to be helped, urged along the way Poppy did. But Marina was as unbending as a brick wall. Her eyes threw him for a loop; he couldn't read anything in them.

He awkwardly went over to the window and with one sharp pull closed the curtains. He had gotten a kick out of setting up Marina in the same hotel he and his wife were staying at. In two days, he had only been able to get away twice to see her. Marina had never said that he shouldn't come to her room, but she acted as if he simply weren't there, walking around in the altogether in front of him, going about her most intimate duties, such as using her underarm spray and the like.

"It's really too bad I can't take you with me to the casino tonight—I mean, on my arm."

Marina rolled over on her stomach.

"What difference does that make?" she asked.

"I would have enjoyed it. Wouldn't you?"

"Oh, you know . . ."

"What will you do all evening?" he inquired.

"Dunno."

"Where will you have dinner?"

As she wasn't looking at him, his eyes were able to linger longingly on her rear assembly.

"I'll go out for a walk later," she informed him.

He screwed up the courage to sit down on the edge of her bed. She didn't react. He put his hand out, holding it over her lower back. In spite of himself, his fingers moved down, touching her skin. She merely swung her head around so that their eyes met.

That was enough to make Arnold jump up again. He glanced over at the two bouquets in the crystal vases but didn't dare ask who had sent them.

"I was at this party," he began, trying to make conversation. But she never helped him along. He had to finish all his statements, soliloquizing. "They were giving an award to a movie producer. Louis Goldman. You know of him?"

"No."

"He's a very important man. Asked me whether I'd like to invest in his next film. Are you interested in the movies?"

"No."

"Wouldn't you like to be an actress?"

"No."

"I could make a star out of you."

"Oh, you know . . ."

He desperately tried to find something to say to her. Poppy always was fascinated by everything he said; he could talk about himself hours on end, and he always knew she would understand and appreciate him. This one was different.

"Think you'll come by the casino later?" he asked.

No reply.

"How about tomorrow? You going swimming?"

Her barely audible yes seemed like a precious gift.

"Will I get to see you tomorrow?"

"Oh, you know..."

"Oh, Marina," he said. "I'd like to do so many things for you."

She got up, stretched, went to the closet and got out her flowered straw hat and her long kid gloves. With a twist of her hips, she got out of her brief, which slid down her thighs. Not knowing whether this was meant as an invitation, Arnold felt the blood rush to his head and moved toward her, arms outstretched.

She stopped him cold, saying, "I'm gonna do some push-ups."

"I've got an idea, Marina," he said. "Tonight—very late—what do you say I drop by?"

"No."

"Why not?"

"I won't be alone."

"Huh? Who'll you be with?"

"The first good-looking guy I come across. It's not healthy to live without a man, you know. I have to have my sex every so often."

"Of course," Alan was saying to himself, "to someone who doesn't know me, someone who can't tell I'm scared shitless inside..."

Now he had to go over and face the inquisitive stares of the casino people. He had to act as though it was the most natural thing in the world for him to come to the Palm Beach in his white Rolls-Royce and ask the cashier to give him half a million dollars' worth of chips, presumably to gamble away on roulette.

He stepped away from his bathroom mirror. Another shot of whiskey would buck him up.

He then took a last look at his necktie in the mirror and carefully turned out all the lights. "Poor man's reflex," he told himself. "Sam wouldn't approve."

He closed the door behind him and headed for the elevator.

Norbert had grudgingly put up with Alan sitting next to him, but he absolutely refused to drive without his cap on.

"I'm too well known," he told Alan. "If someone were

to tell my boss that I was seen without my regular uniform, I could get called on the carpet for unprofessional conduct."

They rolled along the Croisette in the stream of other cars. As the Palm Beach came into view, resplendent in its neon lights, the traffic ground to a halt.

"Accident?" Alan wondered aloud.

"No, sir, it's just that they're all going to the same place we are," Norbert explained. "And they only have five or six attendants for the valet parking, so everybody has to wait his turn."

Alan wanted to get out and walk the last short distance, but then he remembered that driving up in a Rolls-Royce was an integral part of the plan Sam had laid out for him. He was horrified to see that there was a row of gaping bystanders on either side of the road watching the passengers get out of their cars. An attendant opened the door for them, and an usher immediately took charge of guiding them inside, while a second attendant got behind the wheel and raced off to leave room for the next arrival.

It seemed the world would come to an end if every one of the cars did not stop directly in front of the door to the casino. His own Rolls-Royce stopped, and Alan pulled his head down into his shoulders and bolted out, so as not to feel the weight of all those eyes staring at him. He hated being the center of attraction. Under normal circumstances, he had to force himself just to walk into a restaurant alone. Now, he practically ran through the lobby, looking neither to the left nor to the right, and headed for the reception desk.

"Is this your first visit here, sir?" one of them asked.

"Yes," he said.

"Do you have some sort of identification, sir?"

Alan took out his passport and gave it to him. The man wrote several numbers down on a pad. "Thank you, sir," he said. "Have a good evening."

The spotter gave Alan a sharp once-over, and he walked into the game room.

"Who's taking your place as cashier?"

"Collard," Ferrero said.

Gil Houdin poured himself a pony of whiskey and downed it in one gulp.

Ferrero smiled discreetly. He knew very well that the boss never drank liquor during the season. In order not to offend any of the hundred patrons a night who asked him to bend an elbow with them, Gil Houdin had some special liquor bottles filled with iced tea, so that he could kill two birds with one stone—keep a clear head on his shoulders and toast everyone who asked him to.

"Do you mind if I have another?" he now asked.

"Go right ahead, *patron*."

Houdin was seated in front of a sort of keyboard that kept him in touch with all the nerve centers of his empire. Including the extra help put on for special occasions, the Palm Beach always had a staff of some 450 people on hand—electricians, carpenters, laborers, gardeners, lifeguards, social directors, musicians, administrators, bartenders, secretaries, chefs, helpers, dishwashers, swimming instructors, sailing stewards, decorators, painters, dealers, cashiers, bookkeepers, private detectives, table bosses, game bosses, spotters, footmen, errand boys, bellhops, and even two unemployed university professors who were in charge of writing publicity copy.

Houdin knew all of them by name and had a gift for keeping them all energetic and on their toes. During July and August, the Palm Beach was always going at top speed, so that everybody had to be alert at all times. There were times when games begun at midnight went on until noon of the next day without any of the players getting up from their seats. They merely had the waiters bring them food or drink at their places. Under the circumstances, there could be no normal hours for the staff. Everyone had to stay on the job as long as required. The tips they collected were such that no one complained. Had anyone ever heard of a gambling dealer going on strike?

Houdin pressed a key on his board. "Paul? How far have you gotten?" he asked.

"To the dessert, boss."

"How was the salmon?"

"Everybody raved about it."

"Good."

Another key. "Jacques, is everything ready?"

"Yes, boss."

"How long will your fireworks last?"

"Nine minutes."

"Fine."

He darted around the keyboard in that way, checking up in turn with the bar, the restaurant, the game room, the kitchen, and his personal secretary. From the heart of the game room to the slightest ramification of the outbuildings, nothing was too small for him to keep track of.

"Okay, Giovanni," he finally said.

Giovanni Ferrero had been the head cashier for the past six years. He gave the boss a sheet of paper. Houdin looked at it. Ferrero leaned over his shoulder. Each time that Houdin said no, he made a red check opposite a name on the list.

"Prince Ali? Who he?" Houdin asked.

"A nephew of King Feisal."

"How do you know? He's got over three hundred."

"I checked with the Majestic."

"Did Gohelan say he had seen his papers?"

"He's got an American Express card in his name."

"How much credit does he want?"

"A hundred thousand to begin with."

"No, end with that. Start with fifty."

"Right, boss."

"And get a check from him. No chits. Let's see how he works out first."

"Right, boss. What about Signorelli?"

"Okay."

"He's asking for a million francs."

"That's okay, he'll lose 'em. He always does."

"On his signature?"

"Does he owe us anything?"

"No, he's always settled whatever he owed."

"How much does he usually take?"

"Half a million, maximum."

"Then let him sign for it. Now, who's this Pastorelli?"

"The little old man who plays trente-et-quarante."

"The white-haired one?"

"Yes."

"He's crazy. How much does he want?"

"Five hundred francs."

"Let him have up to a thousand if he wants it. He's probably celebrating some occasion. How's the chemin de fer doing?"

"It's only eleven-thirty," Ferrero told him, looking at his watch.

"Yes, I know. What else?"

"That's it, boss."

"Okay, go on back and take over. Collard is swamped."

"See you later, boss."

Ferrero went out. Gil Houdin wondered what Ferrero's pallor was due to. Maybe he had liver trouble?

As for Houdin, nothing ever ailed him. At sixty, two hours' sleep a night was enough to keep him trim and fit. He was of medium height, on the stocky side. His short gray hair gave one the impression of a tough efficiency expert. But the minute he smiled, he had everyone on his side. Gil Houdin knew only one other man like himself—a psychiatric administrator friend of his. After all, how much difference was there between running a casino and overseeing a mental institution?

The gaming tables, all of them, were mobbed by people, three and four deep, who placed their bets amidst a buzz of announcements, outcries, clicking of chips, and last warnings from dealers.

Alan swallowed his saliva, took a deep breath, and went toward the cashier's cage with the same tightness around his heart he had felt in New York those three times he had walked into the banks. He had to wait for two people before him to cash their chips before coming up to the pale-faced teller.

"Can I get a check cashed?" Alan asked.

"On what bank, sir?"

"Burger Bank, New York City."

"Do you have identification, sir?"

Alan showed his passport again. And then he felt a presence at his left, turned to see who it was, and at the same moment was overwhelmed by a delightful perfume and two deep-violet eyes.

"May I see your checkbook, sir?"

The woman had high cheekbones, a pursed mouth, and a perfectly shaped, straight nose. She was wearing a very simple black dress, décolleté enough to give a good view of her cleavage. Clipped to the dress was a single huge diamond.

"Sir, your checkbook, if you don't mind," Giovanni Ferrero was repeating, not without impatience.

"Oh, excuse me," Alan stammered, dragging his eyes away from the view.

He put the checkbook on the counter, but immediately looked back at the strange woman whose beauty and style fascinated him. She couldn't be an actress or he would have known who she was. And yet, looking like she did, he couldn't understand how she could be anything else. He noticed that her hands were toying with a small, black, gold-threaded bag.

"How large a check do you wish to cash, sir?"

Except for her involuntary fiddling with the bag, she was absolutely motionless, looking straight ahead. Not once did she seem to notice Alan.

"Mr. Pope?"

"Sorry." Alan came to again.

"I asked how large a check you intended to cash," the cashier repeated.

"Five hundred thousand dollars," Alan said as quickly as he could.

Ferrero's pale face colored slightly.

"In French francs, of course," Alan added. "What rate are you giving?"

Ferrero did some quick mental arithmetic.

"That would be two million, one hundred fifty thousand francs. Would you mind waiting here just a minute, sir? Collard! Take over, I'll be right back."

As he took Alan's passport and checkbook and got up, the woman called to him. "Giovanni, can I see you for a second?"

"Collard, take care of Madame Fischler," he said.

"No, you, Giovanni," she insisted.

Alan noted that her voice became her. It was deep and sensual. In one moment, her face had been metamorphosed, illuminated by a smile, as if the man she was addressing were a god.

"Okay," Ferrero said to her. "I'll be right back." He opened a door behind him and disappeared.

"The most popular man at the Palm Beach casino," Nadia commented, as she put a cigarette in her mouth.

Not daring to believe she was talking to him, Alan looked around. There was no one else there. He pulled his lighter out and offered her a light. Her cheeks sucked in as she took the first drag.

Then she exhaled, turned her violet eyes to Alan, and said with a mocking smile, "It's not that he's so handsome, but he's the one who hands out the goodies."

Alan was speechless, but vigorously nodded agreement and tried to control his hands as he lit a cigarette.

"American?" she asked.

"Yes."

"On vacation?"

"Yes."

"Madame Fischler," Collard cut in. "Can I help you?"

"I'm waiting for Giovanni." She laughed and turned to Alan. "When it comes to taking our money, they're not as picky as when you ask for credit. If I'd held on to what I left with them in the last few seasons, I could have bought this whole place ten times over!"

"Did you lose?" Alan asked.

She shrugged carelessly. "It comes and goes, you know. I got off on the wrong foot this evening. But the night is still young. How about you?"

"I just got here," Alan confessed.

"Have you been here before?"

"No, never."

"Then you'll have beginner's luck."

"Mr. Pope!" It was Ferrero, who had come back. "There will be a small delay before I can get the money for you. Would you mind being our guest for a drink at the bar while you wait? Let me have someone show you the way."

Before Alan had a chance to answer, Ferrero had snapped his fingers and an usher was suddenly, silently, beside him.

"Show Mr. Pope the way to the bar," he said.

Alan didn't want to let his luck slip away, so he asked the lady, "Won't you join me?"

She shook her head, and her silky brown hair danced around her perfect face. "I never drink during the hostilities," she replied.

Alan bowed to her. "Later, perhaps?"

"Perhaps."

Regretfully, Alan turned to follow the usher.

Nadia turned her attention to the cashier. "Who's the good-looking Croesus?" she asked Ferrero, but he merely shrugged.

"How much do you want?" he asked.

"Ten big ones."

"Ten thousand, Nadia? Come on, Gil Houdin said five was to be your ceiling, and you've hit twenty already."

"So what? Does it come out of your pocket?"

"Fortunately not, but I'm the one who gets rapped on the knuckles."

Giovanni Ferrero was the Palm Beach casino's last defense against the madness of the gamblers. He and Nadia had faced off against each other for years, each with his own weapons. His were chilly refusal and calculated risk; hers were charm, feigned anger, unfeigned indignation, and her insatiable passion for gambling.

"Come on, goddamn it, Giovanni, let me have it!"

"Would you like to see a record of what you owe?" he asked.

"In an hour I'll pay it all back. Come on, give!"

"No, I can't."

"Giovanni!" Her violet eyes were now childlike and begging, those of a young defenseless virgin.

"The boss'll can me!"

"Come on, hurry. I feel my luck coming on!"

He shrugged, wrote a figure on a pink chit, and spread five large oblong chips on the counter. "Sign here," he said.

"How much?" she demanded.

"Five. And I'm bending over backwards."

Nadia swept the chips up, signed the chit, and took three steps, before turning around and snarling at Ferrero, "Cheapskate!"

Gil Houdin's tactic was to wear down the gamblers who kept pestering him for additional credit. He pretty well knew what their resources were and how far he could go without endangering the casino's cash flow. Giovanni Ferrero had strict orders on the subject. And he met all temptations that arose with a great stone face.

On some losing days, women supposedly above reproach would gladly have serviced him standing up behind a door if only Ferrero had been willing to give them some extra leeway.

Nadia Fischler was not one of those women, but she was a daily problem to Houdin. Her passion for gambling and her international celebrity were in themselves an attraction for the other patrons. On the other hand, considering her excessive losses and winnings, she seemed too much to look upon the Palm Beach casino as her own private bank. Houdin had to handle this problem, playing it by ear, meeting each situation as best he could. On the one hand, he didn't want to lose her, because if he did, the money she got from her many amorous conquests would go into the till of another casino. But on the other hand, he couldn't give her too much rope, couldn't let her get too far into debt. He had said to Ferrero, "She'll be asking for ten. Play hard to get and then let her have five."

"What if she loses?"

"Come and check with me."

He carefully examined the passport and the check that Ferrero had just given him. They weren't fakes. Who could this stranger be who asked for half a million dollars without blinking an eye? He told the switchboard to put him through to a number in New York. It was almost midnight in Cannes, so it was the end of the afternoon over there. The banks had been closed since three o'clock, but the staff usually worked until at least five. He ought still to be able to reach someone.

"Burger Bank?" he asked when the call went through. "Let me talk to Abel Fischmayer. This is Gil Houdin calling."

Fischmayer was one of the three top executives of the bank, and an old habitué of the Palm Beach casino. But Houdin certainly was not about to let him know that the information he wanted was involved with gambling.

"Abel," he shouted cordially into the phone, "how are you, old man? This is Gil . . . Yes, yes, just wonderful! The water is seventy-seven degrees here. What are you waiting for? . . . Well, I'd enjoy that, too . . . Yes . . . Of course . . . Say, old man, I'd like to ask you for a bit of information for some friends of mine who are real estate agents. They'd like to get a line on how good a risk one of your customers is, a man by the name of Pope, Alan Pope."

Houdin poured himself another glass from his special bottle.

He knew that bankers hated the idea of their customers gambling. Although they themselves gambled all day long with their customers' money, there was a big difference. What bankers do is perfectly legal and at least appears to be moral.

"Yes, Abel, I hear you very well . . . Oh, good . . . Sure . . . Yes, I understand . . . No, they haven't concluded anything yet, of course. They just wanted to know what kind of person they're dealing with. Yes . . . Just routine . . . But, tell me, Abel, it's no small amount; it's half a million dollars . . ."

He listened carefully to the answer, and then said, "Is that so? Well, I'm delighted to hear it. Thanks, Abel, and my friends thank you . . . That's just fine. I'll tell them. And don't forget, Abel, fix it up so you can get away. We're all going to die sooner or later, and you know what they say—you can't take it with you. So . . . Yes, sure . . . I'll see you soon, and thanks again."

He hung up, pressed a button on his board and was connected to the cashier.

"Ferrero, that Alan Pope out there can go ahead. His credit is A-1."

14

Nadia Fischler had been the whole show for the last quarter of an hour. The roulette table she was playing at had been mobbed by all those who wanted to watch her unbelievable run of luck. Placing her bets wherever her hunches led, going for numbers ending in 6, 7, or 9, she had had nothing but winners since she sat down.

"No more bets," the croupier called out.

He was holding the ivory ball between the thumb and

first finger of his right hand while with his left he spun
the wheel. The ball went spinning in the opposite direction.
Two hundred pairs of fascinated eyes watched it on its
course.

When it started coming down toward the pockets of the
wheel, Nadia announced, "All the nines and twenty-nine
every which way, straight, squares, and splits."

Most pathological gamblers waited until the last second
to let on what they were betting. Several overlapping
voices came in calling bets to the croupiers, who obeyed
every manual and visual order from the table. Bosses
seated on their high stools, kept a careful eye on the
delicate betting operation. The green baize was literally
drowned in chips.

"Closed!" the croupier yelled, as another rain of chips
came down on the table accompanied by a flood of calls.
"Closed absolutely, gentlemen!" And he angrily shoved
back a ten-thousand-franc chip that had been placed on
red by a man in a green tuxedo. The croupier ignored the
bettor's protests and stretched out his arms to protect the
playing field from any tardy entries.

Silence suddenly fell on the magic surface. The ball
bounced several times on the partitions of the wheel,
jumping from one number to another, and hesitated for a
moment between 7 and 18 before finally coming to rest in
the spot between those two numbers.

"Twenty-nine!" the croupier proclaimed. "Black, odd,
and high!"

All those standing around watching let out a long roar.
Nadia Fischler had won again. The croupiers' rakes
descended on the table, sweeping up the losing bets.
Even for those who weren't involved, it was fascinating to
see the huge sums that changed hands in a few seconds.
In order to achieve such a shift of fortunes in ordinary life,
it would take time, investments, ideas, work, pains, and
patience. But not in gambling. Here, there was no time
lapse. There was only the intensity, the shocking sensation,
the yes or no that came as confirmation to pure chance.
Those who benefited from chance believed they were
God's chosen people, that the world would accept their
orders and love them besides. And this occurred no less
than thirty times every half hour.

From where he stood, Alan had a three-quarter view of

Nadia's face, surrounded by a sea of heads. Her lips and
eyes were aquiver with something that was both impatient and cruel, something akin to sexual orgasm. He felt a
sudden urge to possess her, an urge more violent than he
had ever felt for any other woman. He was squeezing the
ten ten-thousand-franc chips which Ferrero had given
him, assuring him that they had opened an additional
credit line for the full amount of his check.

So far, Sam Bannister had been wrong in only one detail
of the plan. After two or three days of pretending to
gamble, Alan was supposed to collect the full amount
from the cashier. Obviously, Sam had never set foot inside
a casino. They used heavy oblong chips. Alan knew that if
he was supposed to get two hundred and fifteen chips,
he'd never be able to carry them all.

Now there was nothing left on the table but Nadia
Fischler's bet. The croupier was shoving a huge pile of the
heavy chips in her direction with his rake.

"Three hundred four thousand, five hundred francs," a
skinny blonde lady said to her escort.

"Wouldn't be my luck to hit it like that," he answered.

Nadia stuck a cigarette between her lips. Ten lighters
immediately were held toward her. She took a puff without thanking anyone, her violet eyes never leaving the
pile of chips the croupier was shoving toward her. As was
customary when a number played straight had paid off,
her original bet remained where it was: twenty-nine,
straight, all the squares and splits.

"Place your bets," the game boss called. "Gentlemen,
place your bets!" And once again the chips began to fall
on the table, as the buzz of calls grew louder and louder.

"No more bets!" the croupier announced as he spun the
wheel.

Nadia's hands were flat on the table in front of her.
Alan was devouring the sight of her iconlike face.

"Finished, gentlemen!" the croupier called.

"Absolutely finished," repeated the stentorian table boss.

They repeated the announcement several times, so as to
make sure that all the bets were placed. The field was
already completely covered with chips.

"No more bets!" the croupier called once more, and
sent the ball on its rounds.

Nadia's hands tensed ever so slightly. Alan found himself praying that she would win. As if in reply, he heard, "Twenty-nine, black, odd, and high!"

There was a wild din. People got up from other tables to come and see what was going on, and word spread through the whole casino that Nadia Fischler had just hit a number twice in a row. She collected her new winnings without showing any reaction, impervious to the wild curiosity from other tables as well as to the respectful silence now surrounding her table.

"Gentlemen, place your bets!" came the call.

"May I ride piggyback?" the man in the green tux asked Nadia. Alan noted with satisfaction that she ignored him. The man tossed a ten-thousand-franc chip on the 29, calling "Twenty-nine, straight."

"Impossible, sir," the table boss said. "The maximum straight bet on one number is fifteen hundred francs."

He signaled the croupier, who shoved the chip back with the tip of his rake.

"What's the matter? Isn't my money any good?" the green tux protested.

"Only fifteen hundred on the nose, sir."

"That's an outrage!"

"Your bets, gentlemen, your bets!" the croupier repeated.

Gamblers were in the habit of piggybacking those who had been having a run of luck. But no one was crazy enough to plunge on a number that had come up twice in a row. So, all that remained on 29 was Nadia's chips.

"Finished, gentlemen, finished!"

Alan's throat caught as if it were his own money. His hands squeezed his chips even harder. Except for an occasional poker game with some of the fellows from the office, he had never gambled. But he knew enough about it to know that miracles happen only once.

The ball spun again.

Around the table, everyone held his or her breath. In decreasing spirals, the ivory ball knocked against the partitions between the numbers, bouncing from one to another. Then, in a dead silence, the croupier finally called out:

"Twenty-nine, black, odd, and high!"

Strangely, the silence continued for several seconds. Then, with groans of happiness, the gapers spread through the hall like a flight of sparrows going to proclaim the unbelievable good news.

Nadia made a discreet signal to an usher. Without waiting to be paid off, she got up from the table and left her pile of chips behind her.

Petrified, Alan saw her walking toward the grill room, which meant she was going to go right by him. He watched her approach, and started to step to one side so he would be in her path.

Her eyes, which seemed to see nothing else, came to rest on him. She smilingly pointed to the chips he was holding.

"I hope you rode along," she said.

Alan was speechless. He shrugged contritely.

"I'm hungry," she said. "Want to come along?"

And she walked on without awaiting his reply. He fell in beside her, his heart thumping. People stepped aside for her, whispering. She turned toward him and dazzled him with a smile, as she said, "Whenever I win, I get ravenously hungry. Don't you?"

Once again he was at a loss for words.

"But then, maybe you've eaten?" she inquired.

"No, oh, no!" he hurried to reply.

Nadia negotiated the two steps from the game room into the grill. Three captains rushed toward her at record speed.

"A table, Madame Fischler? Right this way!" they offered in chorus.

Nadia and Alan were barely seated when a wine steward opened a bottle of Dom Pérignon that had not even been ordered.

She looked squarely into Alan's eyes with an amused smile on her lips. She peered for a moment at what she saw, and then asked, "What's your name?"

"Pope," he answered with a dry throat. "Alan Pope."

"Alan Pope," she repeated. "I'm Nadia. Nadia Fischler. May Nadia Fischler ask what Alan Pope is doing at the Palm Beach casino in Cannes on this night of July twenty-fifth?"

He wriggled in his chair. "Watching you," he mumbled.

"And in order to watch me, you came from where?"

"New York."

"Okay. Now that you've seen me, what do you want?"
she asked, without taking her eyes off his.

Alan thought to himself, I want to take you in my arms.
But he said nothing.

She kept gazing into his eyes and went on, "Really? So
do I."

She burst out laughing, and he joined in. For the first
time since they had met, he relaxed a little, carried away
by her scent, her presence, her voice, her eyes, and the
fact she seemed to read his most intimate thoughts.

"What would you like to have?" she asked. "Are you as
hungry as I am? Be my guest!"

"Certainly not!" Alan protested, laying his chips on the
table.

Once again, she smiled ironically, and said, "Mr. Pope
might feel emasculated if a lady treated him to supper. Is
that it?"

"No, not at all, but..."

"Caviar? Broiled lobster? Ham sandwich on French bread?
Bread and butter? Coffee? What'll it be? Take your pick!"

"I'll have the same as you," he answered.

"Fine. Mario, spaghetti for two."

"Very well, Madame Fischler, I'll order them right away,"
the captain replied. "Do you want it as usual, with very
crisp lardoons?"

"Do you like your lardoons very crisp?" she asked
Alan.

"I like everything," he said.

"He's easy to please," she whispered to Mario. "We'll
have the lardoons. Mr. Pope loves lardoons!"

She nodded toward his chips. "Planning to frame them?"

Alan looked at her, perplexed.

"I didn't see you at the tables," she went on. "Do you
like gambling?"

"I don't know. I never have," Alan confessed.

"You haven't?" she exclaimed. "Then what did you get
the chips for?"

"I thought I'd give it a try," he said, and gulped.

"What do you want to lose them at?"

He felt trapped. She was already on her feet. "Come
on," she said, grabbing his hand.

Without letting go, she dragged him to the opposite
corner of the room which was reserved for chemin de fer.

Here, there was a special kind of silence, the kind of silence that goes with championship meets. Alan knew that this game was for keeps. Furtively, he tried to wriggle free.

Nadia gripped his hand even tighter, grabbed the chips he was holding, pushed him into a chair and whispered in his ear, "Fifty-fifty."

"Banco for fifty thousand," the dealer called. "Fifty thousand."

"Banco!" Nadia said.

His hands clammy, Alan looked up at the banker, registered a severe shock, and had to muster up all his courage not to jump up and run. It was Arnold Hackett!

Alan worked on keeping his body from shaking, as Nadia disgustedly threw down the two kings she had been dealt. With a sly smile on his face, Hackett turned up his four of clubs and deuce of spades.

Alan felt like vomiting as he saw his five oblong chips get away. The croupier's paddle was shoving them over to Hackett who immediately grabbed them with his mottled hands. It seemed like there was some kind of higher justice. By pure chance, Hackett was getting back in Cannes what the Burger Bank had given to Alan in New York.

New deal.

"A hundred thousand for banco," the dealer called. "A hundred thousand." Nadia squeezed Alan's hand and said, "Your turn."

"What am I supposed to do?" he mumbled.

"Say 'Banco!' "

He took a deep breath and heard himself call, "Banco!" But his voice had been so soft that the dealer had to ask again, "Who said 'Banco'?"

Unable to repeat the two syllables, Alan merely raised his hand. To the left, his chips neatly stacked in front of him, Arnold Hackett nodded politely and dealt him two cards. Alan palmed them, then raised only their corners, looking noncommittally at them. Hackett turned his up.

"The bank has eight," the croupier announced.

"The old crab is stuck," Nadia whispered. "Show yours."

Alan turned up a five of diamonds and a four of clubs.

"Nine to the punter," the croupier said.

Two fifty-thousand-franc chips landed in front of Alan.

"The bank passes," the croupier announced, moving the shoe over to Alan.

"Take the bank," Nadia whispered.

He gave her a panicky look. "Take it," she said.

She spread their whole stake out in front of him, two fifty-thousand-franc chips and five ten-thousand-franc chips.

"Banco for a hundred and fifty thousand," the croupier called. "Gentlemen, place your bets."

"Banco!" Hackett called right back.

"Give him two cards, and you take two," Nadia whispered.

Alan shoveled them out awkwardly. The croupier got them with the end of his paddle and moved them in front of Hackett.

"Card!" Hackett called.

Alan dealt him another. Hackett looked at it distrustfully before peeking at it. Then he turned his hand up. "Seven."

"Nine!" Nadia crowed.

"Nine for the bank," the croupier called.

He shoved two chips over to Alan, one worth 100,000 francs, the other 50,000 francs. Instinctively, Alan protected them behind his forearm. Nadia grabbed them from him and put them back on the table with the others they had won before.

"Banco for three hundred thousand," the croupier called.

Alan quickly figured in his head that he had close to $70,000 riding on one deal. His forehead got wet with perspiration.

"We'll kick the heart out of them!" Nadia whispered to him. She was having a wonderful time, but Alan could barely swallow. Arnold Hackett, his weasel face sticking out above his bright red jacket, seemed hesitant.

"Banco for three hundred thousand," the croupier called again. "Gentlemen, three hundred thousand . . ."

"Banco!" Hackett finally said with determination.

"Banco followed," the croupier said.

Alan dealt.

"Seven for the punter," the croupier announced.

"The bank has eight," Nadia proclaimed with delight.

The croupier shoved the three hundred-thousand-franc chips toward Alan. Added to what he had already, it made six hundred thousand—something like $140,000.

It occurred to him that he wouldn't earn that much in six years of working for Hackett—and he suddenly felt an overwhelming desire to be anywhere but here.

"They're beginning to break," Nadia crowed.

Alan watched helplessly as she shoved all of his chips back on the line.

"Six hundred thousand francs for banco, gentlemen, six hundred thousand francs," the croupier routinely announced.

Hackett leaned over toward Hamilton Price-Lynch and whispered something in his ear. Ham Burger took a closer look at the young man who, according to his chauffeur, was supposed to have an account at his bank.

"Banco," Price-Lynch said.

"Banco followed! Cards," the croupier said.

With sweating hands, Alan dealt two to Price-Lynch and two to himself. "Card," Price-Lynch said.

Alan shoved it toward him. Nadia peeked at their hand. Alan queried her visually. She gave him a noncommittal smile. Price-Lynch turned up a ten of diamonds and a six of clubs.

"Six," the croupier announced.

"Seven," Nadia peeped.

"Seven for the bank," the croupier said.

He raked six hundred-thousand-franc chips from Price-Lynch's pile and nonchalantly stacked them in front of Alan.

Nadia burst out laughing and made sure everyone saw all their chips on the line. "Now we'll see what stuff they've got below the belt!" she muttered.

"A million, two hundred thousand for banco, gentlemen," the croupier went on, "a million, two hundred thousand."

Alan turned away, praying that no one would be crazy enough to take the bet. He noticed that by now there was a huge mob outside the red velvet rope surrounding the gaming space.

"Gentlemen, a million, two hundred thousand," the croupier repeated again, totally unimpressed. Arnold Hackett and Ham Price-Lynch pretended to be absorbed in conversation.

"One question, Nadia," Lou Goldman put in. "Who's playing—you or him?"

Alan felt like going through the floor.

"We're partners, dahhling," she said. "You feel like committing suicide?"

Goldman laughed. All he had in front of him was three fifty-thousand-franc chips. He took a check from his pocket, wrote a figure on it, and handed it to an usher who ran over to the cashier, and then came back, whispering something to the game boss.

Two other ushers immediately appeared with a million and a half francs that they set down in front of Goldman. He let his dead cigar fall on the carpet, then lit a fresh one after taking a swig of champagne. Conscious that all eyes were upon him, Goldman looked first at Nadia, then at Alan. With a sarcastic little cluck, he called, "Banco!"

Afraid that his trembling hands would give him away, Alan merely moved the cards out in front of the shoe. The croupier pushed over to Goldman the ones that belonged to him.

"Card," the producer called after checking his hand.

Alan slipped another one out for him, and sneaked a look at his own. Inwardly, he thanked God.

"Nine," Goldman announced.

Alan's face fell. There was a great stir among the kibitzers.

"Nine for the punter," the croupier confirmed.

Alan turned his hand up.

"Nine for the bank. Standoff," was the call. The mob groaned with delight.

"One more hand, please," the croupier announced.

Alan wiped his forehead with the back of his hand.

"Want to try it again?" Nadia purred to Lou Goldman.

But before the producer had a chance to answer, a soft voice cut in. "Mr. Goldman, if you don't mind . . ."

Alan felt his heart was going to burst inside his chest. The crazy character who had cut in was a man with a refined face and a short black mustache.

Goldman waved deference. "As you wish, Prince Hadad," he said.

Goldman had just pulled off a double coup. He had gotten 1,500,000 francs out of the casino by sheer chutzpah, and he had publicly acted as grand seignior with Prince Hadad.

"Thank you," the prince replied. He turned away from

Goldman and began to stare at Nadia with insolent irony. Alan felt like killing him.

"Banco," Hadad said, still eyeing Nadia.

"Deal," she whispered to Alan.

He slipped the cards from the shoe. The croupier pushed Hadad's over to him. With a sign, Hadad indicated that he had enough. Terrified, Alan dared a peek at his own. He felt a sudden flush of hope and turned them up.

"Eight," the croupier said. "Eight for the bank."

The prince nonchalantly flipped his over.

"Seven," the croupier called. And he had to go back for a second pile with his paddle to get Alan the twelve hundred-thousand-franc chips he had coming.

"Gentlemen, this game is over."

Everyone got up. Hadad came around the table, bowed to Nadia, and said to her very courteously, but with a bite in his voice, "My congratulations, madame. I trust you'll give me a return match."

"Anytime you wish," she replied coldly. Nadia took Alan's arm and said, "Come."

At no time had the Prince deigned even to look at Alan.

Alan couldn't help lunging toward the chips that were piled up on the table. Nadia smiled at him.

"They'll be there when we get back," she said. "The game starts again in a quarter of an hour," and she led him back to the grill room.

"Mario!"

"Yes, Madame Fischler!"

"May I tell you something in strict confidence?" she asked.

"Of course, Madame Fischler."

Nadia wearily shoved her fork into the spaghetti, and said, "Your spaghetti is just lousy."

"But, Madame Fischler, just say the word. I'll get you another plate immediately."

Mario never tried to understand what made customers complain. It wasn't the food, but their moods, their winnings, their weariness, or their losses. All gamblers were psychological cases, subject to moments of depression, mania and caprice. The only thing to do was to agree with them, never contradict what they said, no matter how outrageous, and always see that they got their way.

"Mario!"

"Yes, Madame Fischler!"

"This plate is cold."

"You're quite right, Madame. Would you like some caviar while I'm having some more spaghetti heated for you?"

"No, I don't want anything, Mario. Thanks just the same."

With a firm but discreet gesture, Mario signaled his host of waiters and helpers to make themselves scarce. He himself bowed to her and left. Nadia looked into Alan's eyes. He had sat through this scene without saying anything.

"You still want spaghetti?" she asked.

"Well...," he began tentatively.

"Say yes or no," she demanded.

"Sure, if you want some."

She got up and tossed her napkin on the table. "Let's try some other joint. I know a trattoria that really knows how to make pasta!"

"Here in Cannes?" Alan asked.

"No, in Rome," she said.

He thought she was joking, and he smiled politely.

"Mario!" she called.

"Yes, Madame Fischler!"

She slipped him a wad of bills, which he quickly put into his pocket.

"Please phone Alberto's on Via Livornio in Rome right away," she said. "Tell them I'll be there in less than two hours, and that there'll be two of us. I want to have some fettucini."

"Very well, Madame Fischler."

"Now call Rent-A-Jet in Nice."

Mario looked furtively at his wristwatch, and Nadia's eagle eye caught his gesture.

"What do I care?" she said. "Wake them up!"

"Of course, madame."

"I want a Falcon Ten for the round-trip," she said. "Have my chips picked up at the roulette table and the shimmy. Take the money for the trip from that. Mario!"

"Yes, madame?"

"I want that plane ready to take off no later than half an hour from now!"

She turned to Alan and said, "Of course, you have a car."

"Yes," he said.

"Good. Let's get going," she answered.

She took his arm and led him toward the door.

"You happy you won?" she asked.

"Oh, yes," he said.

"Well, you haven't seen a thing yet," she assured him. "On a good day, I'm capable of breaking their goddamned bank. I've done it before! Where's your buggy?"

A parking attendant ran up the steps to the entryway and called into a loudspeaker, "White Rolls-Royce, number one-two-seven."

"One-two-seven, that's a lucky number," Nadia said happily. "How do you break it down? One and twenty-seven, or twelve and seven?"

The Rolls-Royce screeched up at top speed and stopped in front of the steps. Two attendants had the doors open before Norbert could get out of his seat. Nadia got in the back.

"Put the top back up," she instructed him. "I don't like to get windblown. Take us to the Nice airport, quick as you can!"

"Yes, madame," Norbert said, as he put the top back up.

They took off.

"The expressway or the coastline?" Norbert asked.

"The coastline," she said.

Nadia took Alan's arm again and leaned her shoulder against his.

"Now, I'm really hungry," she said. "You know Alberto's?"

"No."

"Ever been to Rome?"

"No."

She laughed and squeezed closer to him.

"What do you do in New York?"

"Business," he averred prudently.

"Real estate? Stock market? Manufacturing? Banking? Or what?"

"A bit of everything . . ."

"You seem depressed," she said. "Are you tired?"

"No, not really. It's just—well, I just got in today. And I haven't had any sleep in twenty hours."

"You know how long I can go without sleep?" she
asked.

"How long?"

"Most I've ever done was seventy-two hours. Right
here at the Palm Beach. That was some game, believe
me!"

"Did you win?"

"Lost my shirt! Wiped out! Do you know the people we
took tonight at our table?"

"No."

"Those first two cheapskates were Arnold Hackett and
Hamilton Price-Lynch," she said.

"Hackett?" Alan asked innocently.

"Yes, Hackett of Hackett Chemical. Almost seventy-five
years old and still going strong. And the other one, that
was Hamilton Price-Lynch. They call him Ham Burger; he
married Emily Burger, the widow of Frank Burger, the
banker."

Even with the top up, Alan could feel his hair standing
on end. "Burger? You mean, Burger Bank?" he asked, as
he instinctively felt his pulse to see how fast it was going.

"Yes, Burger Bank. Crooks!"

"Do you bank with them?" he asked.

"Sooner or later, I did, do, or will bank with every
financial institution on this planet through the good offices of my various lovers."

She burst out laughing, leaned toward Alan's ear, and
pointed to the back of Norbert's head.

"What's that cowboy of yours called?" she asked.

"Norbert."

She leaned forward and tapped him on the shoulder.

"Hey, Norbert, step on it, will you? Our spaghetti's
going to get cold!"

The car zoomed forward. Alan had to steady himself in
his seat, still unable to believe that the two people he had
whipped at chemin de fer could really be his big boss and
the owner of the bank he dealt with.

"The big fat guy with the cigar, that was Lou Goldman,
the movie producer. And I bet you don't know who the
last one was either, do you? The Arab? That was Prince
Hadad. If he felt like it, he could buy the casino, the city
of Cannes, the Riviera, in fact all of France. They say his

oil income is ten thousand dollars a minute. What would you do if you had that kind of money?"

"I don't know," Alan said.

Nadia leaned toward him and kissed him lightly on the brow.

"I'll tell you what," she said. "You'd do just what you're doing right now. You'd take a pretty woman to Rome with you to eat a dish of fettucini!"

On the right, he saw the sea, and its soft murmur reached him despite the speed at which they were going. On the left, he saw a series of bars, cafés, restaurants, from which bits of music could be heard from time to time. A little farther on, Norbert turned off toward the airport.

A man, wearing a blue uniform with the wings of Rent-A-Jet on it, was waiting for them. He saluted Nadia and Alan, and said, "The plane is ready."

"Should I wait for you, sir?" Norbert asked Alan.

"No, thanks," Alan started to say, but Nadia cut in.

"Of course, you must. We'll only be away for three hours, no more. You can take a nap in the car."

Escorted by the plane rental man, they got into a car that drove them out to the end of a runway. Alan saw the plane, a most impressive private jet. Nadia got into it with a laugh, helped aboard by a man who said he was the plane's radio operator. Climbing the steps behind her, Alan admired the fine turn of her ankles, finding it hard not to grab them between his thumb and index finger.

The radio operator locked the door behind them.

"We'll take off immediately," he said. "Please fasten your seat belts."

He smiled to them and disappeared into the pilot's cabin. There were five large seats on the plane. Nadia took one near a window, lowered the back of the seat and stretched out. Alan did likewise, although he was excited to be alone with her. She reached out and turned off the ceiling light.

For a few seconds, Alan was conscious only of her scent wafting toward him. Then his eyes got used to the dark. Even without light, he could see her perfect profile against the slightly luminous halo of the window behind.

She took his hand. "You okay?" she asked.

He pressed the tips of her fingers. "Just fine," he sighed.

The plane's jets started to hum.

15

"Arnold, you lost!" Emily Price-Lynch quipped with a sprightliness she was far from feeling.

"Yes, a little," Hackett admitted, "and you know how I hate that!"

Emily gazed sharply at her husband, but without losing her smile, and asked, "Did you play too, dear?"

Ham Price-Lynch slunk down into his chair and chaffed, "Just one or two small hands to keep Arnold company."

Emily could not stand the idea of his gambling. But since she was not able to forbid him to go to the casino, she constantly nagged about it. "What do you call a little hand?" she asked.

Hamilton had made Hackett promise that he wouldn't mention the joint, losing challenge they had put up against Nadia Fischler.

"Oh, nothing of any consequence," he said jovially. "Just a few chips..."

"I was there," Sarah put in, without looking up from her glass. She was delighted to have her stepfather over a barrel. He knew that she tattled to her mother about every little thing he did.

"Incidentally," Sarah went on, "who was that gigolo teaming up with Nadia Fischler against you two?"

"Gigolo? You won't find any gigolos in my establishment," volunteered Gil Houdin, who had just joined them.

He gallantly kissed the hands of Victoria Hackett and Emily Price-Lynch, patted Sarah on the back of the neck, and snapped his fingers to attract Mario's attention.

"Champagne!" he called.

"Do sit down and join us, Gil," Hackett said.

Houdin did as he was invited, saying, "Now, Sarah, tell me what this is all about."

"I was talking about the fellow who was with Nadia. Between them, they took Hamilton and poor unlucky Arnold here to the cleaners at baccarat."

"Well, you know what they say about being unlucky at cards," Arnold commented, never one to pass up a cliché.

Sarah had spotted Alan at first glance. His pallor and his obvious self-consciousness were very attractive to her. She was never comfortable except with men she felt superior to. She always did her best to gain the upper hand over everyone, a trait she had inherited directly from her mother.

"I wonder how that gold digger manages to get people to stake her all the time," Emily said with a vicious smile.

Victoria Hackett was delighted. She would have given almost anything to be able to come up with a barb like that.

Houdin, of course, knew that Emily was well aware of his friendly relationship with Nadia. She might even have known that in times gone by he had slept with Nadia. But, then, who hadn't slept with Nadia? Emily hadn't intended to be too nasty; she had just wanted to prick him a little. He decided to scratch back.

"She's very attractive, my dear Emily," Houdin responded. "She has an animal magnetism that men go for."

"Let's say certain kinds of men," Emily amended, with an involuntary pinch of her lips.

"Arnold," Victoria asked with imperturbable seriousness, "is it true that men are attracted to loose women?"

"Come now," Gil Houdin answered with a gravity equal to hers. "You know very well that virtue alone has charm."

And he noted the disapproving look that Emily Price-Lynch was giving him. He had thrust home.

They had crossed Rome in a car Alberto had sent to Fiumicino to meet them. Via Livornio was absolutely empty. Not a light, not a soul. Only the restaurant was awake. Alberto stood in the doorway, awaiting them.

"Nadia, como va?" he asked.

She hugged him.

"Alberto, you old cutthroat! I've missed you!"

"And I've missed you, Nadia, truly I have. You're about to eat the best fettucini you've ever had in your life."

"Alberto, this is Alan Pope. Alan, Alberto."

Alberto shook Alan's hand as if they had been lifelong friends. Alan glanced about the restaurant. In one corner stood a table with a bouquet of roses and three candles on its white tablecloth. Two waiters rushed forward to hold their chairs for them.

"I got them up specially for you," Alberto said. Then, turning to Alan, "In Rome, you know, anyone would get up in the middle of the night for Signorina Nadia. You're a lucky man, signor."

He poured some light, cool wine into their glasses, and then they heard a song, accompanied by the strains of a guitar. Alan was amazed to see the musician standing nearby.

"It's Enrico," Alberto told Nadia. "I got him over here for you. I know how much you love his songs."

Alberto then seized Nadia's hand and kissed it fervently. "Nadia, cara mia," he intoned, "I'll serve you at once."

He rushed to the kitchen and a nonplussed Alan stared at Nadia. She sympathetically took his hand.

"Hungry?" she asked.

"I'm not sure anymore," he confessed.

During the flight, the radio operator had opened a bottle of champagne for them and joined them in toasts to Cannes, to Rome, to America, to the casinos. Alan had inwardly cursed him. He wished he had been alone with her. Perhaps on the flight back, he speculated.

"Are you okay?" Nadia asked.

"Just fine," he said.

"I really like this place. I feel at home here," she said. "What do you like?"

"Being alive."

"But more specifically."

"Being free."

"Aren't you?"

"No."

She laughed in his face.

"You look like a little boy who just robbed a bank," she teased. "Did you really rob one?"

"I wouldn't know how. I'd have gotten caught."

"Are you married?"

"I was."

"So was I," she told him. "Several times."

"What conclusion do you draw from that?"

"It's just as impossible to live alone as it is to live with someone."

"So, what's the answer?" Alan wanted to know.

"Change partners as often as you change toothbrushes. That way you're never alone, but you never get bored with them."

"Fettucini!" Alberto proclaimed, as if he were ushering a king into their presence, and then started heckling the help. "Hot plates! Quick! Subito! What about their glasses? How come their glasses haven't been refilled? What are you waiting for?"

He seemed to be going in all directions at once, and to Alan he looked like the ringmaster of a surreal circus.

Alan lifted his glass and toasted Nadia with his eyes. Thanks to her, he was part of something that was truly out of this world.

"Please start," Alberto was begging them. "It will get cold. Costa! Bring another bottle! Nadia, how do you like it?"

"Mmm-hmmm," Nadia commented, her mouth full.

"Signor?"

Alan shook his head in vigorous approval. He was eating, even though he wasn't hungry. Nadia's presence made him feel weak in the knees with a hunger that wasn't for fettucini.

"Now, tell me, Alan, what about this bank?" she was saying.

His fork was halfway to his mouth, but Alan stopped stock still. "What bank?" he asked.

"You know, the one you robbed . . ."

In the time that it took to get from his table to the telephone operator, Hamilton Price-Lynch had turned around twice. Emily or Sarah might very well be right behind, spying on him. He had excused himself to go and wash his hands.

"Miss, how long does it take to get New York on the line?" he inquired.

"No time at all. We dial direct," she told him.

He scribbled a number on a piece of paper. "Where should I take the call?" he asked.

"In Booth One. You'll hear it ring."

In order not to have to get into any conversations with

passing acquaintances, Hamilton pretended to be absorbed in the displays of the world-famous jewelers around him. The lobby was crowded, with the ceaseless comings and goings of people. The ones who were leaving usually reflected the fact that they had been cleaned out, and the new arrivals appeared full of hope, well-stocked with chips and systems, ready to conquer the casino.

"Sir, New York is on the line now," the operator called to him, and Hamilton rushed into the booth and took the receiver.

"This is Hamilton Price-Lynch," he said, in the commanding voice he used at the office. "Who is this?"

"The switchboard operator, sir."

He looked at his watch. It was 1:00 A.M. in Cannes.

"Is Abel Fischmayer still in his office?" he asked.

"I'll try him, sir."

In a second, he heard Fischmayer pick up. "Yes. What is it?"

"Hello, Abel," he said. "This is Hamilton."

"Mr. Price-Lynch!" Fischmayer answered. "Where are you calling from?"

"Abel, I need some information. Does a man named Alan Pope have an account with us?"

"Alan Pope? Why, yes, sir, but this is certainly an unusual coincidence, Mr. Price-Lynch. Gil Houdin phoned me from Cannes not an hour ago to check on the man's credit. And just this morning I had a run-in with Vlinsky about him."

"Why, Abel? What was wrong?"

"That stupid Vlinsky pulled a boner! He had Pope listed for an overdraft!"

"Wasn't he overdrawn?"

"Not at all. His account runs somewhere in the neighborhood of a million and a half dollars..."

"You don't say."

"Yes, I'm quite sure of it."

"How long has it been there, Abel?"

"Would you like me to check on that, sir?"

"Yes, I would, Abel."

"Is anything wrong, Mr. Price-Lynch?"

"No, not at all. I just need the information for a friend."

"I'll get it right away, sir."

"Wait a minute, Abel. I'm having dinner with some

people, so I have to get back to the table. Look up Pope's account and make a note of everything, the current balance, recent deposits, any other activity, and wait for me to call you back. You don't mind waiting around a little longer, do you?"

"Not at all!" Fischmayer assured him enthusiastically. "Absolutely not!"

"I'll call back in less than an hour. Is that all right?"

"Certainly, sir. Certainly."

"Thanks again, Abel. I'm sorry to put you to the trouble, but I appreciate what you're doing. You sure you have the name right?"

"Yes, sir, Pope. Alan Pope."

"That's correct, Abel. I'll call back in a little while."

"Whenever you're ready, Mr. Price-Lynch."

Hamilton was a bit confused when he came out of the phone booth. How could it be that he had never heard of Alan Pope, if Pope had a seven-figure account at Burger Bank?

Was he losing his touch?

The plane took off with a roar, gained altitude, banked to the right, then flew straight ahead. Through the window, Alan could see the flickering lights of nighttime Rome. He sat back firmly in his seat, determined not to bother himself with questions for which he had no answers or worries which would in no way change the course of events. As they left the restaurant, Nadia had given Alberto a handful of bills without counting them, just as she had done to the maître d' in the Palm Beach grill room.

"Nadia?"

"Yes."

There was no light in the plane cabin. Nadia had told the radioman not to disturb them.

"Do you always live this way?" Alan asked.

"Yes, always."

"Aren't you ever scared?"

"Of what?" she asked.

He couldn't tell her. He had never met such a beautiful woman. Nor such a wild one. She seemed totally out of touch with all things material. Money meant nothing to her; she recognized no normal standards; she was as much at home in her life of excesses as others were in their quiet desperation.

A small voice inside Alan was telling him that tonight's stroke of luck at the casino would never happen again. The best course for him now would be to retrace his steps, let the bank know about the computer error, return the money that he should never have been given in the first place, and take the first plane back to New York. He'd be richer by half of the money that Nadia and he had won at chemin de fer—almost $300,000 for his own share!

Three days earlier, he wouldn't have dreamed that he would find himself with such a fortune. If he knew what was good for himself, as soon as they got back to Cannes he'd head for the casino, cash in his chips, get out of this madhouse, and start again from scratch. His mind was made up, and he sighed with relief.

Nadia suddenly stuck her hand down the front of his shirt.

"You know why I like you?" she asked.

He felt an electrical charge surge through his body. She came closer and breathed practically into his mouth.

"Under that playboy exterior of yours," she said, "you're really just a country boy. I like country boys, because I'm just a country girl. Do you like me?"

"Very much," Alan succeeded in saying, his voice all choked up.

The plane was pushing ahead through an inky sky. Far below, he could see myriads of tiny specks of light. And right here against him was Nadia with her heady scent and her hoarse voice. It was a perfect moment. He was overflowing with tenderness, with warmth, and he wanted to take her in his arms.

She stopped him short and asked in a panting voice, "Do you want me?"

"Oh, yes, so much, Nadia, so very much..."

"Well, what are you waiting for? Fuck me!"

Nonplussed, he saw her pull her dress up, and he looked away from her white thighs.

"Here, look! Look!" she commanded.

She opened the flaps of her blouse and freed the luscious globes of her bosom.

"Come on, fuck me, you bastard! Fuck me!"

He was struck still as if cold lead had just been injected

into his veins. She lowered her head, opened his belt, unzipped his fly, and slid his pants down along his thighs. Then she took his cock in her mouth, licking it furiously, while at the same time playing frenetically with herself.

Alan felt chilled; his body was not responding readily to her caresses. He had never imagined that this was the way things would be. He made a violent effort not to think about it, to drive the chill out. Then, in a rage, he pushed her off, grabbed both of her wrists in his left hand, threw her back on the seat, knelt over her thighs and savagely drove into her. At the height of his pumping, just as he was about to explode, he saw her face, lighted by a ray of moonlight. It was taut, hard. Her eyes were wide open, dilated, staring at some imaginary spot that she would never be able to see. Until his last second of consciousness, Alan kept gazing intensely at her, expecting to see a repetition of the look of utter transport that she experienced when she was gambling. But he saw nothing of the kind.

He knew then that the only orgasm Nadia Fischler could ever get came from the turn of the wheel of chance.

Hamilton Price-Lynch was a dangerous man because he was a weak man. Abel Fischmayer knew Hamilton was totally in the grip of his wife. With her, Hamilton was not much; without her, Hamilton was nothing at all.

Sometimes Abel dreamed of getting Hamilton into a corner. All he would have needed was enough data in hand to discredit Hamilton in Emily's eyes—perhaps a nice little case of extramarital involvement with compromising pictures, dates, addresses, and sworn testimony. Then it would have been Abel Fischmayer who would have had full say over the way the bank was run; neither Emily Burger nor her daughter Sarah understood the first thing about banking.

"Is Vlinsky still on the premises?" Abel inquired on the phone.

"I'll try ringing him, sir."

Fischmayer's only worry where Hamilton Price-Lynch was concerned was that some day he might call him Ham Burger without thinking. But now he wondered why Hamilton, too, was interested in this Alan Pope.

"Oscar? This is Fischmayer. You mentioned an account

a couple of days ago—a man named Pope, Alan Pope. Get his file and bring it into my office, will you? . . . Yes, right away."

When Vlinsky walked in, Fischmayer did his best to mask the scorn he felt for the frail accountant. His trousers were too short, his tie was too thin, and his myopic eyes looked like two underfried eggs in which the yolk had run over the white.

"Sit down, Vlinsky," he said. "Now, what about this Pope?"

Abel took the file from Oscar's hands, and glanced quickly over several sheets in it.

"I see he's had the account for four years. He works for Hackett; that's good. Regular salary increases. No other apparent source of income. Medium-level job."

Oscar Vlinsky made a gesture, and cut in, "He's been overdrawn on several occasions, Mr. Fischmayer."

Abel froze him with a look and mumbled on to himself. "Net monthly take-home . . . Withdrawals . . . More withdrawals . . . Credit notice."

Abel stopped, as if an alarm had rung.

"Credit notice of one million, one hundred seventy thousand, four hundred dollars. Vlinsky!"

"Yes, Mr. Fischmayer?"

"Shut up! This sum was credited to Pope's account on the morning of July twenty-second. Where did it come from, Vlinsky?"

"I don't know, sir."

"What do you mean—you don't know?"

Oscar seemed to dissolve within his clothes. "All I did was notify the accounting department that this account was overdrawn."

"Vlinsky, go and get me that check. This very minute!"

"Where from, sir?"

"How should I know? From wherever it is. Find it, for Chrissakes. What is this, a bank or a goddamned garbage dump?"

"Yes, sir, I'll get it right away. But may I remind you that I told you about the overdraft in the amount of—"

"Go get it!"

Vlinsky came back a few minutes later, so shaken he was transparent. Unable to say a word, he handed a small piece of paper to Fischmayer, while spasmodically shaking his head with a look of utter desolation. Abel grabbed the check from him and held it up against the light.

"Well, it's our own transfer order. From the Hackett account. And Oliver Murray signed it."

Vlinsky weakly waved his hand to attract his boss's attention.

"Well, what is it Vlinsky?" Abel demanded.

"Look at the figure, Mr. Fischmayer. Look at the figure."

Abel looked at it: $11,704.00. Suddenly the blood that had drained from Oscar's face seemed now to reappear in his own.

"You see, sir, I was sure there had been a mistake. Remember when I mentioned it to you? You told me this account was to be given our A-1 special treatment," Oscar defended himself.

"I told you that? You're dreaming! I told you nothing of the sort!"

"It's just awful, sir," Vlinsky went right on. "Two extra zeroes were added."

"Who? Who could have done it?" Fischmayer thundered.

Vlinsky came back with a shrug of desperation.

"The only explanation I can see, sir, is that the master computer played a dirty trick on us."

Alan felt bitter. He had possessed nothing but a shadow. Nadia's body lent itself to him, but it had never been given. In the wild fury of their sexual encounter, each of them had merely endeavored to use the other. Yet, Nadia seemed happy and satisfied. With her eyes closed, she was resting against Alan's shoulder, a relaxed smile on her lips. He was afraid to move for fear he might wake her.

The Falcon circled once over the landing field. Alan could see the lighted runway alongside the sea and the nearby splashes of spray as the waves broke upon the sands. He wished he could remain here, suspended between sky and earth, until the end of his days. But the wheels of the plane had just touched down.

"Are we landing?" Nadia asked sleepily.

She turned on the overhead light, took a mirror out of her handbag, and checked the state of her makeup.

"You look just fine," Alan assured her.

He did not add that she looked as if nothing had taken

place between them. Besides, was he sure that anything really had taken place? He glanced surreptitiously at her high cheekbones, the well-fleshed line of her mouth, the arch of her eyebrows. Everything was just the way it had been before. But for some mysterious reason, it no longer added up to the same charm. Alan now felt devoid of any feeling for her.

As they stepped out of the Falcon, Nadia made her usual sower's motion. The pilot had come out to say good-bye, and she shoved a roll of bills into his hand.

Norbert was sleeping in the Rolls-Royce, snoring in cadence with a rock tune that was playing on the car radio. It was 5:00 A.M. In the east, the sky was beginning to lighten into the wide band of day.

As the car door slammed, Norbert awakened with a start and instantly became the formal, liveried chauffeur again.

"To the hotel, sir?" he asked.

"No, to the Beach," Nadia answered.

"You want to go back to the Palm Beach at this hour?" Alan asked her.

"This is the time to do it. They'll all be nervous and worn out by now, and that's when they make mistakes. You'll see. We'll be able to take them for a few more million!"

She dug into her bag and pulled out a ball of facial tissue which she carefully opened.

"Look, Alan," she said, holding out a small black lump that had made some brown spots on the tissue. "My good-luck charm," she went on. "As long as I have this, we can't lose."

She was completely crazy. He planned to go and get his chips at the Palm Beach, redeem his check, then get out as fast as he could. Now he understood why, after having made love in the plane, they had not carried on any further conversation. They had nothing to say to one another.

"It's the fresh heart of a fine, gray rabbit," Nadia told him.

Alan turned away so as not to show his disgust. In the east, behind him, the light band was edging out the darkness of the night sky. Soon, it would be daylight. The fun was over.

"I'll bet you ten to one that Prince Hadad is still there waiting for us," Nadia said. "He knows I'll come back. No one has ever challenged me without my taking him up on it!"

Keep talking, Alan thought, as if I care... In half an hour, he'd be sacked out in his room. All this was too rich for his blood. He'd had his fill. And Sam Bannister be damned!

16

"What? Would you say that again?"

Hamilton Price-Lynch was gasping. The phone booth was not ventilated and he tried to wave away the smoke from his Muratti. Through the glass, he could see a parade of evening gowns, tuxedos, and red, sunburned complexions.

Emily had given Hamilton a strange look when, for the second time in less than an hour, he excused himself to go and wash his hands.

Abel Fischmayer's voice was now coming through, muffled, broken with transatlantic static and other interference.

"Alan Pope is just a minor clerk, Mr. Price-Lynch," Abel was saying. "That money was credited to him by mistake."

"What kind of a mistake, Abel?"

"Over a million dollars, sir."

So Pope had been gambling against him with the Burger Bank's money. In other words, thought Ham, he was using my money!

"The transfer was ordered on July twenty-one by Hackett Chemical. And the computer made a mistake. The two zeroes that came after the decimal point were put in front of it. He was supposed to get eleven thousand, seven hundred and four dollars. Of course, there's nobody at Hackett's at this hour, so I haven't been able to find out why that money was being credited to his account. I'll check in the morning..."

Hamilton could sense someone watching him. He turned around. Outside the phone booth, Emily was staring at him, her eyes hard and icy. She was pathologically jealous, not out of love, but because she couldn't stand the idea that anyone who was supposed to belong to her might so much as breathe without her permission.

"Just a second, Abel," he said. "Hold the wire . . ."

His wife had already opened the door to the booth, and was demanding, "Who are you talking to?"

"Abel Fischmayer," he replied, his hand over the phone.

"You don't say! Well, let me have the phone. I'd like to say something to him myself."

She grabbed the instrument from him, a defiant glint in her eye. Hamilton deliberately tried to look guilty.

"Hello," she said. By the look of disappointment on her face, he could tell she had just recognized Abel Fischmayer's voice. "Why, Abel, how are you? . . . Yes . . . Yes . . ."

Choking from the smoke inside the phone booth, she began to cough violently. Hamilton opened the door. She gestured angrily for him to close it again.

"Yes, Abel, yes, indeed. I'm delighted to have had a chance to hear your voice. Here's my husband again . . ."

Hamilton watched as she walked off into the crowd.

"Are you still there, Mr. Price-Lynch?" Fischmayer asked.

"Yes, Abel."

"I guess I'd better report this to the police right away."

Price-Lynch shrugged. "Report it to the police? What the hell for? Are you out of your mind?"

"But, sir, we have to report it and press charges. That money has been transferred to his account. What if he writes checks against it?"

"Honor them."

"Mr. Price-Lynch, I don't understand. It's our money that he'll be taking!"

"Well, if anyone has done anything wrong, it's us and not him. Would you rather have this thing get into the papers, and have everyone know that Burger Bank can't be trusted?"

"But, a million dollars . . ."

"I'll take care of that! If any of his checks come in, just see that they're honored. Tell Vlinsky to keep his stupid mouth shut, and don't any of you do a thing. Hold everything until you get new instructions from me. Is that clear?"

"Yes, Mr. Price-Lynch."

"And not a word to anyone about this, you understand?"

"Yes, sir."

"Very well, Abel. I'll be in touch with you again tomorrow—that is, later today—I mean, tomorrow your time."

Hamilton hung up, wiped his brow, and lit another Muratti from the butt of the one he was smoking. For a moment, he stood pensively inside the booth, then it was all he could do to keep from jumping for joy.

He started back toward the gaming room. With a little luck, he had just discovered how he could avert disaster for himself. By the time he reached his table, he had already worked out the general lines of his plot.

The Rolls-Royce pulled up to the steps of the casino.

"Here we are, sir," Norbert said.

It was 5:30 A.M. A parking attendant opened the door for Nadia. She got out, stretched, and let the first rays of sunshine bathe her face.

"I guess I'm one of the rare people in the world who see the sun go down and come up every night of their lives," she commented.

The long night had had no effect on her. There wasn't the slightest shadow over her limpid violet eyes.

"I think I'll turn in," Alan excused himself.

Norbert took a few steps to the side in order to yawn discreetly. Like everyone else on the Riviera, Norbert knew all about Nadia Fischler, and he felt it was too bad that she had so quickly gotten her claws into his temporary employer. Pope didn't seem to be a bad guy, for all his naïveté. Unfortunately, with Nadia Fischler at the helm, Pope would soon be down to his shorts, and lucky if he didn't lose those.

"Alan, you must be kidding!" Norbert heard Nadia reply.

"I'm pooped," Alan said.

"You can't run out on me just when things are getting the most interesting," she insisted. "Norbert!"

"Yes, madame?"

"Park the car. And wait for us!" And she shoved a
lavish tip into his hand. Norbert pocketed it and obediently
said, "Certainly, madame."

She grabbed Alan's arm and led him into the casino
lobby.

"We'll just go for three hands. Double or nothing!
Banco! You have to strike while your luck's running high,
you know!"she assured him.

They went in past the full complement of checkers and
spotters. Don't those people ever sleep? Alan wondered.

The game room was still fully lighted. According to
Houdin's standing instructions, the curtains always remained
drawn in the gaming rooms. This way, the clock was
stopped, as it were, and the patrons could remain as long
as they wished in that artificial night which teemed with
dreams, poets, and madmen.

Nadia led Alan over to the cashier's desk. Even paler
than usual, Giovanni Ferrero raised an inquisitive eyebrow at her.

"This is a stickup, Giovanni," she called out good-
naturedly. "Give us the dough!"

"All of it?"

"And how! I'm going in there to break your goddamned
bank!" She had suddenly become sensuous and seductive,
full of fire.

"Alan, do you want some coffee?" she asked.

Ferrero pushed an impressive pile of chips toward them.

"I deducted the cost of the chartered plane," he said.
"Would you both be good enough to sign the receipt?"

"I'll sign for it!" Nadia stated, initialing the pink slip.

Ferrero turned to the back of his cage and busied
himself with whatever he had to do there. He knew that
the poor guy in her clutches was unlikely to be able to get
out of there. She would gamble what he had and lose it
all. And Ferrero was sick at the idea.

"Come on!" he heard her urge Alan.

With more chips in her hands than she could hold, she
was rushing toward the chemin de fer table. She had no
idea what the current ante was, yet, her nostrils dilated,
she was rushing into the fray, already calling, "Banco!"

"Banco followed!" the croupier called in echo. "Gentlemen, banco for two million francs!"

Alan stopped short, as if he had been shot in the solar

plexus. He stood where he was, halfway between the cashier's cage and the table, thunderstruck. Nadia had already grabbed the cards dealt her by the banker, and was turning them up.

"Six to the punter," the croupier announced.

And Prince Hadad showed his holding.

By five in the afternoon, Romano's was going full blast for the cocktail hour, but by seven there were usually only a few latecomers remaining, those who had no home to go to or those who were too drunk to care. So Tom kept a wary eye on Sam Bannister and a fellow he didn't know, sitting at a table in the rear.

The other guy looked like a born-again, hymn-singing football player; he had iron-gray hair, and wore plain glasses. His name was Cornelius Grant. Long before he had become a lawyer, he and Sam Bannister had gone to school together. Sam had never outgrown the habit of calling on him whenever he had any ticklish legal problem to unravel.

"This isn't anything that's actually happened, Corny," Sam was saying, "but tell me what the hypothetical consequences would be."

"Well, that's very iffy," Sam's friend replied, "but give me the gist of it again."

"Okay. Suppose that through some kind of a mistake for which he had no responsibility whatsoever, a guy were to receive a check from a big company."

"You mean like Hackett, for instance?" Grant supplied, without appearing to get specific.

Sam suddenly looked up at him; Cornelius wasn't even watching him.

"Okay, let's say like Hackett, for instance."

"And how big was the check?"

"Oh, a big one. Something like a million bucks, or maybe a little more."

"Representing what?"

"Well, that's just it. Nothing. A simple mistake."

Grant looked at him irritably. "Stop putting me on, Sam. Nobody sends anybody a check for no reason at all!"

"All right, already. Let's say the guy gets fired, and they owe him severance pay and vacation pay and stuff. The amount coming to him is supposed to be a hundred

dollars, but he gets ten thousand. The bookkeepers make
a mistake and add two zeroes, get it?"

"Sure. So what?"

"Well, say it's me, and I've got this check. What am I
supposed to do?"

"Don't touch the damned thing with a ten-foot pole.
Give it right back," Grant counseled.

"You mean, don't cash it?"

"Absolutely not."

"Why?"

"Because you might be in big trouble."

"Tom, let us have the same," Sam called out, as he
finished his drink. He bit his lips, and looked down,
depressed. Ever since Alan called, he had been feeling
worried and wondered whether his own envy had driven
him to get his friend involved in something that was sure
to end up badly. With a few hours of consideration, the
plan he had devised for Alan seemed pretty lousy, and
not very likely to work for very long.

"What you're really asking me," Cornelius summed up,
"is whether it's a swindle to take advantage of a mistake
of this kind, a mistake that you haven't in any way
brought about."

"That's it exactly," Sam concurred.

Tom brought their drinks and made a point of looking
at his watch.

"Sam, just between the two of us," Cornelius said, "are
you the person who got this check?"

"No," Sam said.

"Well, I'm relieved about that anyway."

"Why? What's wrong with it as long as the person who
got the check was not the one who made the mistake?"

"But he knows that there was a mistake. Now let me in
on it. Who was it that got the check?"

"A pal of mine," Sam finally conceded.

"Did he cash it?"

"He didn't even have to do that. The bank let him know
that it had been transferred to his account. The money
was already there in his name, you get it?"

"Did he draw on it?"

Bannister wiggled around, more and more uncomfortable,
and then said, "Yep."

"You know what I'd advise your chum if he asked me? Give the dough back!"

"What if he's already spent some of it?"

"That's the least of it. He could say he didn't realize, that he in turn made a mistake... But don't kid yourself, and don't let him kid himself about it, Sam. Sooner or later they'll catch up with him and press charges. Even for a million dollars, I wouldn't want to take that chance!"

Bannister tossed a ten-dollar bill on the table. Corny and he were boyhood friends. Yet, Sam didn't have the guts to admit to him that he was the one who had put Alan up to what he was doing.

Corny got up and clapped Sam on the back. "Don't knock yourself out worrying over it," he said. "After all, the responsibility for a mistake can be said to lie with the party who commits it."

But Sam was no longer listening to him. His only worry now was how he could get in touch with Alan and tell him to forget the whole idea.

Alan's legs gave way under him, and he had to sit down. The gold antique chair creaked under his weight. He was some thirty feet from the chemin de fer table, close enough so he could hear everything that was shouted, but not close enough to read the faces. On one turn of the cards, Nadia had just lost two million francs to Prince Hadad!

Alan forced himself to get back on his feet. Fascinated by the horror he had just witnessed, a horror which had happened to him, he moved toward the gaming table. With a slight, amused smile on his lips, Prince Hadad had just staked again the two million francs he had won from Nadia.

Hadad watched her with the greedy expression of a cat watching a mouse. She didn't blink.

"Two million in the bank," the croupier called. "Gentlemen, place your bets!"

The cathedrallike silence lasted for a moment, and then was broken by Nadia's tense, cold voice.

"Banco!"

The croupier took a sharp glance at her and announced, "The bet is covered. Cards!"

The prince, both hands flat on the shoe, made no move to deal. "Madame," he said, looking straight at Nadia.

She knew very well that she had to have the amount of her punt clearly in view on the table. And all she had in front of her was four hundred thousand francs.

"Just a second," she said.

She looked toward Alan, her deep violet eyes boring into his. "Don't let this man humiliate me like this! I know you have a half-million-dollar credit with the casino. Go on and get it!"

Unable to make a sound, Alan merely shook his head. He noted with terror that all eyes were on him.

"Go get it!" Nadia repeated.

The prince drummed his fingers impatiently on the green baize, well in view of all those around.

"I'll return it to you in a little while. You're not running any risk! Go on!" Nadia said. Then turning toward the prince, she arrogantly stared him down, saying, "Just a minute..."

She dug her fingers into Alan's arm and dragged him over to the cashier's cage.

"Giovanni, put down whatever he has in his account!"

Ferrero looked questioningly at Alan.

"Do as I said!" Nadia commanded. "He's willing!"

Once again the cashier eyed Alan silently.

"Giovanni!"

Ferrero sighed and then spread the oblong chips out on the counter. Nadia swept them up, paying no attention to Alan, and returned to the table.

Ferrero turned his back on Alan, who looked for the closest chair and went to collapse on it. He was inwardly cursing his own weakness. In a cottony fog, he heard someone call out, "Cards!" Paralyzed with terror, he closed his eyes and sent a silent prayer heavenward. He tried to banish the image of Sam that was in his mind: If Bannister were seeing this, he would drop dead on the spot!

The Duchess de Saran exposed herself only to the very early morning sun, and even then only through veils that covered her body. The moment the Palm Beach opened for the day, her chauffeur dropped her off in front of the swimming pool that opened on to the sea. She had a season's reservation for one of the private cabanas that overlooked the beach, protecting their occupants from the eyes of other bathers. One could do whatever one wanted in a cabana, eat, drink, strip down, take a shower, make love, or go to sleep.

Her husband the duke usually didn't come down to join her till about noon. Early in the morning, the place was all hers.

The swimming instructors had set up little camp beds which customers would vie for with larger and larger tips in just a few hours. Mandy had tried two or three of these athletes to see what they were like, but she had never felt that their sexual prowess measured up to the promise of their muscles. Besides, they were too healthy and wholesome looking to appeal to her. Suntanned, strong, and straightforward in their embraces, she found them quite devoid of imagination.

With her beach bag dangling from her arm, her face protected by a huge black straw hat and dark glasses, the white veils floating around her slim body with its delicate skin, Mandy walked along the beach to get to her cabana.

And at that moment, from the empty restaurant between the gaming rooms and the pool, she saw a young man come out. His face looked haggard, it was unshaven, and his eyes were blinking in the bright light of the morning sun. She stopped and stared at him in fascination. He stank of nightlife. He looked exhausted, his face full of shadows.

"Monsieur!" she called.

Alan looked around to see whether someone was really calling to him in French. He was tottering with weariness, trying desperately to get it through his head how Nadia not only had lost what they had won the night before, but also how she had convinced him to give her the $200,000 in travelers' checks he had in the safe-deposit box at the Majestic, to say nothing of his half-million-dollar cash credit which had gone in just a couple of bancos.

She had been truthful with him on only one point. "I'll play three hands, just three hands, that's all!" They were three losing hands that to him were a death warrant.

Seeing that he did not respond, the duchess called to him in English, "Sir?" Alan turned around. "Could you help me?" she asked.

He started toward her, but did not say anything. He

was still too distraught, too dazzled by the sun. Inside the
casino, the game was still going on. Nadia had not even
noticed when he left.

As he left the lobby, through a half-open curtain he had
seen some blue water shining in the sunlight. He had
slipped through a French door and gone into the huge
ballroom, now bathed in sunlight, with its many tables
and hundreds of chairs. To his right, there was a big
bandstand with musical instruments on it. Beyond the
ballroom was the pool, and beyond that, the sea and the
sky with vertical stripes of ships' masts across them. And
now here was this pale, faceless woman, covered by
transparent veils.

"Just come with me. It's right near," she was saying.

Dulled with fatigue, he fell in behind her. His only
thought was to dive into that cool water, to bury himself
in it, to let himself be carried toward infinity, to be washed
clean, to drown in it. He mechanically eyed the supple,
dancing walk of the unknown woman, who was saying,
"Here we are."

He followed her into the cabana with the straw walls.
There were two folding beds, a table, two chairs, a shower,
a beach umbrella. Mandy put her beach bag on the
ground, knelt and took a bottle of suntan lotion out of it.
Alan watched her, strangely intrigued by what she was
doing.

He saw her throw the veils up over her head and reveal
her body which, to his amazement, was spotted with a
great many black-and-blue marks. She noted his surprise
but felt no need to explain to him that these were souve-
nirs left on her skin by a passing plumber.

She handed him the lotion. She lay down on her belly
on one of the beds, opened her brassiere and slipped her
G-string down her thighs without taking off either her hat
or her glasses.

Alan had no idea what her name was. He was just
conscious of the fact that she had stripped down to the
buff. And he thought no more of it.

"Rub some of the oil on my back," she said.

He opened the bottle, and poured so awkwardly that
half its contents ran down into the small of her back.

"Massage me," she instructed.

He started to knead the skin of her back so as to spread the oil more smoothly.

"Harder," she urged.

Though his hands were full of oil, he thoughtlessly untied his necktie. Immediately his shirt was marked with oil, too.

"Harder," she hissed. "Don't be afraid to hurt me!"

Now she was beginning to tauten, to twist and turn under his ministrations. She hung on to the edges of the cot, and emitted a long, low moan that sounded animallike. From the depths of his fatigue, Alan could feel a surge of heat bubbling up inside him. His hands were now gliding down inside her thighs, slick with the brown oil.

She suddenly turned over, swung her legs, and threw herself around his waist. She took the bottle of suntan oil and poured the rest of it inside the front of his shirt. He felt himself flooded all the way down. She pressed herself tighter against his belly, and began caressing his body, her long hands, her expert fingers exploring the most intimate parts of his skin.

Alan looked straight up into the sun, and everything went dark. Panting, he let himself fall back on the bed. His mind was empty; all of him was empty.

He grabbed a pair of swimming trunks hanging on a hook, pulled off his lotion-soaked clothes, got into the trunks, and rushed out of the cabana without even looking at her. He was running like a madman down a wooden staircase toward the beach, aware of the animal sensation of his bare feet sinking into the burning sand.

He hit the sea like a bomb, and disappeared into it.

17

He couldn't sleep. It was three A.M. and Sam Bannister was still slumped on the living room chair, absorbed in his doubts and worries. After his consultation with Cornelius Grant, he had come to the conclusion that all this could only have a bad ending. Out of spite against Hackett Chemical, he had sent his best friend off on a fatally hopeless wild-goose chase.

He poured himself another drink, and once again asked himself the same questions: How do I get the chestnuts out of the fire? How do I put an end to the whole mess? How do I back away from it all?

If he could borrow some money, he might be able to cut his losses before they got too great, pay back what already had been spent. Then he'd go and see Murray, get him to listen to reason and not press any charges against himself or Alan.

"Sam?"

He was so startled that he spilled half the glass of whiskey in his lap. Crystal's voice was surprisingly sweet. And it immediately put him on his guard. Since the evening he had told her off, they had exchanged only two sentences.

"I'm leaving you," he had said to her.

"Go on! You can go to hell!" she had answered.

Since then, he had slept in the guest room, leaving her alone in their bed. They took their evening meal together, but opened their mouths only to swallow the food she had cooked.

Now she hesitantly sat down in the chair facing his.

"Sam?"

"Yes?"

"How many years have we been married?"

"I don't know," he confessed. "Twenty-five? Twenty-six?"

"Twenty-five," she corrected. "I wanted to say..."

She bit her lip, then looked down at the floor. "I'm sorry about what happened the other night. Really, I am. I should have realized how worried you were about your friend Alan. But I guess I was on edge..."

Sam looked sharply at her, trying to figure out whether this unusually conciliatory tone was hiding a trap or leading to a renewal of hostilities.

"Oh, it doesn't matter," he assured her.

"Yes, yes, it does. It was all my fault. I should have been backing you up, trying to help you. And instead..."

"Don't worry about it, Crystal. It doesn't matter anymore." He could feel that he was beginning to soften.

"Aren't you sleepy?" she asked.

"No, I've been thinking," he said.

He had promised Alan that he'd go and join him. But now, he was going to have to ask Alan to come back.

"He got kicked out on his ass, you know," Sam said.

"Yes, I know, and I'm sorry," Crystal answered.

Then, just as naturally as could be, he heard himself say, "I've got to let you in on a secret, Crystal. I've been fired from Hackett's, too."

Alan came out of the water, took a few steps across the sand, and pulled the small chain that released the shower water. The hard, cold stream took his breath away. He forced himself to stay under it for several minutes.

He had swum quite a way out. The sea had cleared his head of all the miasmas of the night before. Unfortunately, that meant that his mind was now clear enough to see the full extent of the mess he had gotten himself into. How would he ever be able to tell Bannister what he had done? He shivered, saw a bath attendant walk by, and asked whether he could have a cabana.

"Sorry, sir. They're all taken."

Alan looked at the fellow as if he didn't believe him.

"It's only ten o'clock," the attendant went on. "Most of the patrons aren't out yet. But they reserve the cabanas from one year to the next. Would you like me to set a folding cot up for you next to the pool?"

Alan nodded. He didn't want to go back to the hotel. The artificial light in his room would be too reminiscent of the last few gruesome hours. He could stay outside, get some rest in the sun, and decide whether he should go and turn himself in. What with the time difference, he wouldn't be able to reach Sam before four o'clock in the afternoon, anyway, so he'd wait at least until then.

He walked down a ramp to the dressing rooms. At the desk, there was a pretty, young blonde in charge. Off a rack, Alan selected a pair of dark glasses and a pair of dark blue swimming trunks.

"That's two hundred and eighty francs," she said.

"Listen," he began, not knowing what he really wanted to say. He had lost so much last night at the casino that his subconscious was now absolutely refusing to spend another franc.

"My name is Pope," he finally said. "Alan Pope. My

driver will come by later and pay you." And he went back out into the sunlight.

He had a few francs left in his pants pocket, but his pants, like the rest of his oil-stained clothes, were in the cabana of that sex maniac who had raped him. He thought he'd rather forget about the money than have to face her again. On the other hand, he felt he ought to return the trunks he had borrowed from her. He went back down to the dressing rooms, took off his wet trunks and got into the new dry ones, then went back toward the pool.

"Your cot, sir." It was the pool attendant, holding out a towel for him. "Do you wish an umbrella, sir?"

"No, thanks very much," Alan said. "Say, I have a car with a driver out there. You think you could get my chauffeur to come in here to me?"

"Of course, sir. What kind of car is it?"

"A white Rolls-Royce convertible," Alan confessed with some embarrassment. "The driver's name is Norbert."

"I'm on my way, sir."

"Oh, and could you get me some strong black coffee and something to eat?" Alan asked.

"No trouble at all," said the attendant. "What would you like, sir?"

"Some ham and eggs, and maybe a jug of orange juice."

"Coming up, sir."

Carrying the wet trunks, Alan headed toward the cabanas. They all looked alike to him. He suddenly remembered that each one had a short mast on top with a flag flying from it. Atop the cabana he had been raped in, he recalled seeing a red flag with a white cross on it. He went as close to that flag as he could, tossed the wet trunks up over the bamboo fence, and ran back toward his cot.

Prince Hadad kept three suites year-round at the Majestic Hotel. In season, he added fifteen more on several different floors, so that the various social castes and groups that he had business with or felt like seeing would not have occasion to run into one another. This delicate job of segregation was carried out by his private secretary, Khalil. Acting in turn as procurer, privy councillor, or ambassador extraordinary, Khalil's special function was to guess what Prince Hadad's wishes and desires would be before the prince had expressed them.

Five of the suites on the fourth floor were reserved for the prince's temporary guests. These guests were high-class call girls, paid top dollar, who when it came to class, manners, and unobtrusiveness, could have given lessons to the wives of diplomats. Hadad, being lazy and disliking unsatisfactory experiences, often asked Khalil to test the girls' accomplishments for him, and the secretary was never loath to do so. The girls were paid merely to stand by, or perhaps more precisely, to lie by. Hadad, whose nights sometimes did not end until noon of the next day, often felt like a bit of food and some sex before going to sleep.

The fifth-floor accommodations were for the last of his legitimate wives, their children, and the flock of nurses, tutors, and other retainers.

On the seventh floor were the Prince's own quarters, and those occupied by Khalil and Gonzalez, the prince's private hair stylist. Gonzalez was on call seven days a week around the clock. He was also a great gourmet, and since he never went out, he was entitled to unlimited room service. He spent his days lying in the sun, eating, drinking fine wines, watching television, doing the hair of Princess Aïcha, entertaining the children, manicuring Khalil, or sometimes brushing the glorious hair of one of the call girls if he found her especially appealing.

All of the advantages that went with this job were, of course, balanced by the drawbacks. The prince would not tolerate anyone of his entourage not being at his beck and call the minute he got back from the casino. Khalil consulted his watch; it was 9:00 A.M. He stifled a yawn and turned toward the four girls dozing on the divans.

"You'd better be ready for action. The prince will be back any minute now," he informed them.

He had tried three of the four, but despite his devotion to his job, he hadn't yet tested the fourth. She was called Karina.

"Karina! On your toes! Did you hear what I said?" he barked.

She was a very tall, slim blonde, who had come in in a stunning white linen suit. She smiled to him, stretched, and in so doing made her nipples stand out. Khalil watched her closely, somewhat intrigued.

"What's the matter?" he asked. "You exhausted?"

"Sort of."

"Here," he said, throwing a roll of bills toward her.

She leaned down, picked up the roll, and licked her lips with a gluttonous look of enjoyment.

"Mmm mmm, good!" she said.

"Good enough to eat?"

"And how!" Karina answered.

"I dare you," he retorted.

"I'll take the dare," she said. "What's the ante?"

"What do you think?" Khalil asked the other girls.

"For every one she eats, you give her one like it to keep," one girl suggested.

"But only big bills," said another.

"Five hundred francs or over," Karina specified.

Khalil took an enormous wad of folding money out of his pocket.

"Shall we start?" he asked.

"Okay," Karina said. "I'm ready."

"Eat!" Khalil commanded, as he handed her the first bill.

Karina laughingly grabbed it, stuffed it into her mouth, and swallowed. "There you are!"

"Was it good?"

"Delicious! More, more!" Karina laughed.

She opened her handbag wide to collect the matching reward for each swallowed bill.

By the time she gobbled ten of the bills, Karina had changed her technique a little. Now she was chewing them up. By the fifteenth, she was beginning to turn green, but she doggedly swallowed it. She took a swig of champagne to wash down each succeeding banknote. Her forehead was running with perspiration.

"Twenty," one of the girls proclaimed.

With a light of pride in her eye, Karina squeezed the next bill, took a mouthful of champagne, threw her head back and tossed down the bill between her wide open lips.

"Twenty-one!"

At the twenty-fifth, her face lost all its color, and she turned and ran into the bathroom where she threw up everything she had forced down her throat.

Khalil shrugged.

"And when I tell people that money doesn't feed you," he said, "they won't believe me."

"Did you send for me, sir?"

"Yes, Norbert," Alan said, opening his eyes. "I had a bit of trouble with my clothes. Somebody spilled a bottle of oil on them..."

"And you'd like me to go to the hotel and bring you something to put on, sir. Is that it?" Norbert asked.

"Yes, if you'd be so kind," Alan replied. "All I need is a shirt and a pair of slacks, and some shoes. You'll find them all in my closet."

"Nothing else, sir?"

"Well, I came out without any money. You might ask the desk to give you an advance and put it on my bill," he suggested.

"How much, sir?"

"A thousand francs."

Norbert took two five-hundred-franc notes out of his pocket. "If you'll allow me, sir," he said.

Alan, nonplussed, was reluctant to take them.

"Perhaps you'd like more, sir?" Norbert offered, reaching into his pocket again.

"No, no, thanks. This'll do just fine," Alan said.

"Very good, sir. I'll be back shortly."

Norbert smiled, put his cap back on his head, and turned on his heels. The night before, he had won eight thousand francs playing poker with the chauffeurs of the other two Rolls-Royces.

Alan pensively watched Norbert walk away. All that Alan had left to his name was the $20,000 that Sam had forced him to withdraw for "pocket money." Not so long ago, that would have been a small fortune to him. But here in Cannes at the rate things were going, it was barely enough to cover a day's tips.

The chef's helper who had been keeping watch came running back into the kitchen.

"Here he comes!" he yelled.

The slumbering crew suddenly woke up. Mario checked his bow tie and went back into the game room.

It was 10:00 A.M. At a distance, he saw the prince

waving to him. Whenever the game was over, it was
always the same. Hadad would be hungry, he would
order some food, but through some caprice of his own, he
would insist on being served in his suite at the Majestic.
Four men were kept on in the kitchen to be ready to cook
for him. They did not feel exploited for having to spend
these sleepless nights. With the tips they got from Hadad
while he was there, they made out very well the rest of
the year."

"Prince?" Mario asked.

"What do you suggest?"

"Fish or meat, Your Highness?"

"Fish," Hadad decided. "Plain broiled fish—and some
crepes."

Mario mentally thanked his stars that the prince had
not opted for a soufflé.

"Some fruit, sir?"

"Yes. I'd like to eat in fifteen minutes."

"But, of course!"

Mario ran across the empty room, dashed into the
kitchen, and called out the order. Everyone started working.
There was a pickup truck at the ready outside the kitchen
door. When the food was done, it would be loaded,
steaming, onto the truck to be conveyed and served to the
prince at the Majestic. Naturally, Gil Houdin did not bill
this kind of service. For his big-spending customers, everything at the casino was on the house. It would have
seemed niggardly to present a one-thousand-franc tab to a
man who sat down in July for the summer's gambling
with $4,000,000 worth of chips in front of him.

Hadad, of course, was not even aware of this kind of
detail. When Mario brought him the meal in his suite, he
regularly gave him ten thousand francs. The maître d'
scrupulously split that sum among his host of staff members,
doling it out according to a complicated system of accounting that allowed for each person's rank and seniority.
Since Mario never knew how many people would be
sharing a meal with Hadad, all the dishes ordered were
prepared to serve a dozen guests.

Hadad was feeling fine. In a few bancos, he had taken
the last franc away from Nadia Fischler. Last year he had
sent Khalil to invite her to sleep with him. To his amazement,
she had turned him down! Rebuffed sexually, he had

sworn to himself that he'd screw her someday—in some other way.

On his way to the hotel, Hadad decided to make a detour by way of the swimming pool. Nothing made him happier than to watch his three youngest children playing in the cool water. When the kids spied him, they came running over, shouting with delight.

"Father," the eldest one said, "make us some paper boats!"

Hadad searched happily through his pockets. For ten minutes each day, before returning to his meal, his sex, and his sleep, there was nothing sweeter than being a good father to his offspring.

Alan gradually emptied his lungs, and let himself sink to the bottom of the pool. With ten feet of water above him, he lay down on the blue tile bottom, and stayed there as long as he could. Then he came back up to the surface, limp as seaweed. He took a deep breath, holding on to the rim of the pool. His eyes were closed, and he could hear some children laughing close by. His hand went out to push away some pieces of paper that were rubbing against his face. The kids laughed twice as loudly. He opened his eyes to see what was going on.

The spot where he had ascended was covered with little, folded-paper boats which three kids, the oldest of whom could not be more than ten, were splashing along across the surface. One of the little boats bumped squarely into the bridge of Alan's nose. Alan shoved it away, glancing thoughtlessly at it. As his mouth fell open, he got a mouthful of pool water—like the rest of the little flotilla, this boat was made from a folded up five-hundred-franc note!

"Ahmed!" Prince Hadad scolded his son.

"Please excuse him, sir. I do apologize!" Hadad went on, as Alan pulled himself up with difficulty onto the edge of the pool, shook his head, and briefly lost his footing. In order to keep him from falling, the prince grabbed Alan's hand, then slipped himself, and ended up with both arms around Alan's shoulders. To the gaping bystanders, the prince seemed to be embracing Alan long and affectionately.

"Incidentally, congratulations on your winning banco

last night," Hadad said, recognizing Alan. He did not let go of his hand, however.

"Unfortunately," Hadad went on, apparently most distressed, "I won the return match. I got every bit of it back from your partner."

"Well, that's the luck of the draw," Alan said, as if he were a lifetime habitué of the casinos.

"My name is Hadad," the prince said. "Prince Hadad."

"Alan Pope," Alan introduced himself.

"I'm delighted to make your acquaintance," said the prince. "And I'd be delighted to let you have another crack at me."

Alan heard Sam's words echoing in his mind: "Remember, behave as if you were very, very rich."

"Thanks," Alan replied. "Why not? Any time you say."

They shook hands once more. Alan returned to his cot without noticing the girl who with the tips of her toes was pushing away one of the little paper boats that had drifted near her.

Prince Hadad, however, immediately caught sight of the streamlined shape of her gorgeous legs. She was sitting at the edge of the pool, dangling her feet into the water. She raised her face to get the sun on it, and Hadad got the shock of his life. He could have sworn it was Marilyn Monroe!

Prince Hadad never directly addressed a woman. If he wished to meet her, he sent an ambassador, usually Khalil.

For the first time in his life, Hadad broke one of his own princely regulations. He went over to the unknown girl whose back was to him, leaned down over the nape of her neck, and said, "I am Prince Hadad. Do you like my little paper boats?"

Maybe it was the voice that woke him, or maybe it was the shadow that fell across his face.

Alan opened one eye and saw a tray with the breakfast he had ordered on a small metal table next to his cot. He raised one of the silver covers hiding the dishes and tested the eggs with his fingertip; they were still nice and warm. That meant he had not dozed off for too long.

"Don't you recognize me?" the man's voice was saying. "We played against each other."

Squinting in the bright sun, Alan made out a faded pair

of Bermuda shorts and a tennis shirt above it, topped by a
turkey neck at the end of which was the face of Hamilton
Price-Lynch. He started to jump up.

"Oh, don't bother getting up," the banker indulgently
said. "Please, don't let me keep you from your breakfast.
Your eggs will be getting cold. My name is Hamilton
Price-Lynch, and I'm delighted to meet you."

"Pope," Alan replied. "Alan Pope."

"An American, eh?"

"Yes."

"From the East Coast?"

"New York," Alan said.

"Well, so am I. Please, do eat your breakfast. Go ahead."

Alan took a bite of the eggs, and began chewing it as if
it were a mouthful of tough meat that he couldn't swallow.
The fact was, at the moment he couldn't.

"On vacation?" Price-Lynch asked.

"Yes," Alan stammered, trying his best to get the mouthful of fried egg down.

"Beautiful place this, isn't it? I've been coming here
every year for the last ten years with my wife. Where are
you staying?"

"At the Majestic."

"What a coincidence! So are we!" And then, after a
slight pause, "When did you get here?"

"Yesterday," Alan told him. And he wondered whether
there were cops hidden somewhere nearby, ready to pounce.

"What line are you in, Mr. Pope?"

Trying to keep his hands from trembling, Alan set about
pouring himself some coffee, and inwardly cursed Sam
Bannister for not having foreseen that kind of a question.

He drank the coffee as Hamilton repeated the question.
"What line did you say you were in, Mr. Pope?"

Alan kept his eyes on a slice of toast he was buttering,
and mumbled, "Investments..."

Hamilton looked truly interested, and said, "Why, that's
fascinating." After which he added, "I'm in banking myself.
You may have heard of my bank. It's Burger Bank."

Alan nearly choked on his coffee, as the banker continued,
"We have over thirty branches in New York City."

Alan dipped his toast into the remains of the fried egg
on his plate and moved it around to soak up what was
left. In order not to have to look up, he ferociously

speared it with his fork, and wiped the plate as clean as possible.

"The French certainly do know how to fry eggs, don't they?" Hamilton Price-Lynch commented happily.

Inwardly, Alan wondered how long this stupid game was going to go on. Come on, Price-Lynch, cut the bullshit, he wanted to say. You want to have 'em take me away? Bring on your goons. I'm ready.

But Price-Lynch said, "I've got to hand it to that partner of yours. She certainly showed guts last night. And it took a helluva lot of courage on your part to keep going along with her. You know, everyone here says she has a death wish, that she really plays to lose. Do you play to lose, too, Mr. Pope?"

Alan had no answer to that one, but that did not faze Hamilton Price-Lynch.

"I don't," Hamilton said. "Believe you me, I play to win!" And he got up and waved good-bye to Alan.

"I was really delighted to bump into you like this, Mr. Pope, and I'm sure we'll meet again at the gaming tables or somewhere else. I hope you enjoy your stay."

He moved away, stepping gingerly around the cots, most of which were taken by now. The sun was beating down hard as it approached its zenith, but Alan put the towel around himself. He felt a great chill pass through him.

"Did you see the morning paper?" Cesare di Sogno was asking Louis Goldman, as he proudly showed him a copy of *Nice-Matin*.

On page four, there was a three-column cut of the two of them up on the platform at the Majestic. The caption read, Cesare di Sogno Presents Leader Award to Louis Goldman.

"This is only the beginning of it," he assured his honoree. "Wait until you see the Paris dailies and the magazines."

Cesare had had the misfortune of bumping into Marc Gohelan as he came out of the Majestic, even though he had gone out of his way to use the side service entrance.

Very courteously, Gohelan had inquired of him whether the bill for the reception was to be charged to his account or to the producer's.

"Goldman's," Cesare had answered, without blinking. But he wondered what would happen when Goldman was asked the same question.

"It was a triumph, Lou, a real triumph," he was assuring Goldman in the meantime. "Do you have a table reserved for tonight?"

"How about you?" Goldman asked.

"Oh, I've been invited by so many people, it's just awful. I don't want to offend any of them. Who's going to be sitting with you?"

"A bunch of people," Goldman muttered, noncommittally.

"Couldn't we make one party of it?"

"Who with?"

"The Hacketts, the Price-Lynches, the Duke and Duchess de Saran," Cesare suggested.

"You know the duke?" Goldman asked in surprise.

"Yes, he's an old friend, and of course I've known Mandy longer than it's gallant to admit!" Wanting to get Goldman back on the hook, Cesare added, "Why don't you and your wife, and whatever friends are with you, join us? As my guests, naturally."

This was the occasion Goldman had been hoping for. He was anxious to get to the pharmaceutical magnate and the banker with his proposition for *The Night the Sun Died.* "Since you insist, I'll see if I can work it out. Thanks for the invitation."

"Wonderful," Cesare said. "See you tonight." He walked off toward the bar, looking suave in his all white outfit, his tennis towel around his neck. The problem was, Cesare hadn't been invited by anyone for tonight.

Alan was running over the green roulette table, hopping the dozens, skipping around Odd, feinting from Red to Black, and desperately trying to avoid the croupier's rake which was trying to catch him and toss him aside onto the pile of large pink chips. But it was too late. He came to rest on the zero, which seemed to be his foreordained number, and waited there to be raked in . . .

"Hello," said a voice again.

Alan tried to come out of the haze of his nightmare.

"You're beginning to turn a nice, bright red," it said.

It was an appealing voice, and it spoke English. Without knowing whose voice it was, Alan was grateful to its owner for having gotten him out of that frightful dream. He put his hand over his eyes to block out the light. The sun was too bright for words.

"My name is Sarah, Sarah Burger," the voice said, and his muscles tensed up. "Oh, don't move," she went on. "They've sent me here as an ambassador."

Alan succeeded in sitting up on the edge of his cot. "My name is Pope. Alan Pope."

She sat down beside him.

"I know," she said. "The two families asked me to come as their emissary and invite you to tonight's benefit."

"What two families?" Alan stammered.

"Why the Burgers and the Hacketts," she replied.

She was very attractive, yet there was something not quite right about her looks. Taken separately, all the parts of her anatomy were perfect. There was nothing wrong with her legs or her large brown eyes or her slightly mocking mouth, her hands, or the slope of her shoulders. But somehow the overall picture didn't quite work. Something in nature had made it impossible for all those perfect parts to match up with one another.

"So, is it yes?" she demanded.

Alan had difficulty imagining himself sitting in the place of honor between Arnold Hackett and Hamilton Price-Lynch, the two men who, quite unknowingly, were responsible for his being in Cannes.

"I have to confess to you," she was saying, "that charity affairs are not my favorite kind of entertainment. All those fat ladies with their lapdogs turn me off. Do you like dogs?"

"Only big ones," Alan said.

"How about old ladies?"

"I can't say I know too many."

"You ought to get to. They find ways of being mean to people that the rest of us can't even imagine. Seeing other people being young makes them physically ill, so they dream up the most brilliant ways to get even. I respect that. At least you know where you stand.

"I like you," she went on. "You seem nice. You seem kind of harmless. Hamilton says that you're probably the most important middleman the Saudis have working for them. But I don't believe a word of it. Yet, Prince Hadad certainly seems to have a high opinion of you. You don't catch him embracing everybody the way he embraced you!"

Behind his dark glasses, Alan's eyes were bugging wide.

"Of course you know Hamilton," she said.

"No," Alan ingenuously replied.

"Oh, come on. He's the one you took to the cleaners last night at chemin de fer. And you were having a conversation with him right here not more than ten minutes ago. You know, the little fellow, the one who's my mother's toy poodle. She thought she was doing something smart when she married him. She thinks she's an iron woman in a velvet corset. What all was he telling you?"

Alan shook his head in ignorance.

"Oh, he had to be telling you something. Hamilton never talks to anyone unless he expects to get something out of it. Please tell me, Mr. Pope. What can Hamilton be expecting to get out of you?"

"I'm damned if I know."

"He's a bastard. The worst son-of-a-bitchin' bastard that ever set foot on this earth," she spat.

Alan suddenly felt uncomfortable, and changed his position.

"Take your glasses off," she asked. "I'd like to see your eyes. Come on, take 'em off."

Alan did as he was asked, and blinked against the brightness of the light.

"You have sweet innocent eyes," she said. "You want a good piece of advice? Anything my stepfather may propose to you, just turn it down. Tonight, I'll hold you by the hand, so he won't be able to gobble you up."

Alan put his glasses back on.

"I'm not free tonight," he said.

"You're fibbing!" she came back. "We'll expect you at nine o'clock in the lobby of the Majestic. Then we can all go over together. Thanks so much for joining us, and don't be late, will you?"

She walked off, full of self-assurance. Completely taken aback, he dragged himself over to the pool and let himself slide down into the water.

18

"Vlinsky, you're a jackass!"

"Yes, Mr. Fischmayer."

"You have just committed one of the most unpardonable of professional blunders."

"I did?"

"Yes, you did," Fischmayer thundered at him. "And I can tell you right now that I don't know what kind of a future you may have in this bank!"

"But, Mr. Fischmayer—"

"Keep still, you! Here you go crediting over a million dollars to a customer the money doesn't belong to, and you don't even realize it! Is that any way to run a railroad, I ask you? What do you think we're paying you for?"

"Excuse me, Mr. Fischmayer," Vlinsky pleaded his case, "but I was the one who called your attention to his overdraft."

"You did nothing of the kind, you fool! Never!"

"Oh, yes, I did, sir. I swear it to you. Right here in your own office, I reported that he was three hundred and twenty-seven dollars overdrawn."

"Three hundred and twenty-seven dollars," Fischmayer snorted. "What difference could you think that made?"

He suddenly realized that the phone had been ringing for a full minute or more. He grabbed it viciously, while shaking a threatening finger at Oscar Vlinsky.

"I'm not in," Abel yelled into the mouthpiece, and hung up again, still staring at his erring underling.

"You have the chutzpah to tell me you caught a three hundred dollar overdraft after you let more than a million dollars slip right through your fingers? To someone named Pope, a man you don't even know. What kind of a fool are you? Didn't you think that looked funny?"

The phone rang again. "I just told you—" Fischmayer yelled into it.

Vlinsky saw him suddenly freeze in his chair, concentrating on what was coming in over the phone.

Fischmayer put his hand over the receiver and hissed across the desk, "Vlinsky, out! Out! Get out of here!"

"Just one more thing, Mr. Fischmayer—"

"Get out, you jackass! What's the matter with you?"

Although never too quick on the uptake, Vlinsky could tell from Fischmayer's red face that this was not the time to try and plead his case. He made his way out silently, on tiptoe, and quietly closed the door behind him.

"Well, how are you, Mr. Price-Lynch?" Fischmayer was saying into the phone in a totally calm tone.

"Fine, Abel, just fine. Did you discuss that matter with Vlinsky?"

"Yes, Mr. Price-Lynch. As a matter of fact, we were just thrashing it out."

"Good. Do you think we can depend on him to keep his mouth shut?" Hamilton asked.

"Oh, beyond any doubt."

"Have any checks come in yet on the Alan Pope account?"

"No, sir, not since the ones he cashed in New York."

"Well, when they do come in, you know what to do about them, don't you, Abel?"

"Yes, Mr. Price-Lynch. We will honor them, just as you instructed."

"Fine, that's just what I want. Now, Abel, listen to what I have to tell you. There are some other things I want you to keep in mind concerning this account..."

Abel Fischmayer listened carefully to his instructions. In surprise, his mouth fell open and he gasped aloud.

All the tables were reserved for lunch. The captains were already wheeling around the serving carts with food on them. Some old ladies were wading in the shallow end of the pool, while expert divers were somersaulting off the high tower.

It was supposedly forbidden to go around bare-breasted near the pool, but the fact was that all the healthy women between sixteen and fifty had shed their halters and were displaying their bosoms for the world to see. Many of the mammaries—thanks to plastic surgery—remained at a ninety-degree angle to their owners' bodies regardless of what position the women got into. When they lay down, their breasts pointed skyward as true as missiles; when they stood up, gravity seemed to exert no downward pull.

The entrance onto the Palm Beach's sand was through the dressing rooms, from which one came right out into the full sunlight on the level ground in which the olympic-sized pool was dug. So everyone arranged to make the entrance that most suited his or her personality. All eyes were turned to each new arrival. The less daring bathers came in wrapped in robes which they shed only when they got to their own places. Others, proud of their physiques, strode in like conquering heroes.

The romantic pairings that occurred here were extremely flexible. Everything happened at a speeded-up tempo. Infatuations that had begun during the evening often ended in good-byes before morning had appeared. Passions were short-lived, heartbreaks were not considered proper, and no one tried to overdramatize the depth of these passing summer loves.

So, when Norbert made his entrance in his black uniform, it did not go unnoticed. Apart from the waiters, he was the only man around with a tie on.

He walked majestically around the pool, quite impervious to the gawking of those who were naked about him. "Sir," he said, as he bent over his employer, and then, bending further, he realized Alan was asleep.

"Mr. Pope," he said somewhat louder, now removing his cap.

"Yes?" Alan answered, with a slight movement of his head.

"Everything has been taken care of, sir. I left your clothes in the dressing room and, I took the liberty of settling your tab there.

"Thank you, Norbert. You're very thoughtful."

"Not at all, sir. But, if you don't mind my saying so, sir, I don't think it's a good idea to fall asleep out here in the sun. Wouldn't you rather go back to the hotel and get a good nap?"

"What time is it?" Alan asked.

"Eleven o'clock."

"You think it would be all right if I took a dip first?"

Norbert smiled politely, and said, "I'll be waiting for you in front of the door." Then, with the same dignity as he had coming in, he made his way back out around the pool.

"Hello there, Mr. Pope," Alan heard a voice call. "Did you get over last night all right?"

Alan saw that he was being addressed by a fat man who displayed his bulging belly with just as much satisfaction as he seemed to get from the dead cigar he was sucking on.

"Louis Goldman," the man introduced himself, as he grabbed Alan's hand and vigorously shook it. "You really had a close call in the casino last night. I was worried about you. How did it finally turn out?"

"Not too well," Alan had to admit.

"May I?" Goldman asked, as he sat down on Alan's cot without awaiting an answer. "You know, that Nadia Fischler is crazy," he went on. "Have you known her long? Oh, what a career she could have had if she had only worked at it. All of us producers got down on our knees to try to get her to stay in pictures. But she just wasn't interested."

He hailed a passing waiter.

"Do you have some cold lobster?" Goldman asked, adding to Alan, "I suddenly feel an urge. Won't you join me?" And then, to the waiter again, "Bring us a nice cold bottle of Dom Pérignon, too."

Like everyone else, Alan had heard a good deal about Louis Goldman, although he wasn't quite sure what movies he had produced lately. But he wondered how Goldman knew his name.

"Are you just getting up, or haven't you been to bed yet?" the producer inquired.

"Haven't been to bed yet."

"That's not a good idea, young fellow," Goldman clucked. "If you plan to go back to the tables tonight, you'd better get some rest. You know, gambling is pretty much like boxing. If that's your game, you've got to keep away from women and booze, and get plenty of rest and exercise. What line are you in?"

"Business," Alan said.

"You certainly seem to be on good terms with Prince Hadad," Goldman commented. "They say he's a tough man to deal with. Have you ever?"

"No, not really," Alan said.

Goldman went on asking him harmless questions, talking

to him about the film industry in general and his own plans in particular.

"With the kind of guts you showed in the casino last night, you'd have made one helluva producer. Didn't you ever consider making pictures? . . . Oh, thanks, just set it there," he said to the waiter, who had arrived with his order.

The waiter uncorked the champagne and set the tray with the lobster on it on a small table. In a few huge mouthfuls, Goldman did away with the lobster, and then he offered Alan a glass of champagne.

"Do you have a good table for tonight's benefit?" he asked.

"I'm not going," Alan replied. "I just got here yesterday, and I haven't slept a wink since I left New York."

Alan was still holding the full glass of champagne in his hand, but he noted that the bottle was already more than half-consumed. How could Goldman drink that fast? he wondered.

"Well, why don't you get some sleep this afternoon, and join us at the gala tonight? My wife will be delighted to meet you. We're entertaining quite a party, so please be our guest."

"No, thanks," Alan told him, "I don't think I'll be up to it."

Goldman helped himself to one more glass of champagne, and then got up.

"If you change your mind, you'll be most welcome," he assured Alan again. "I'll have my chauffeur drop by and see whether you won't come." And waving to Alan, he walked away.

By now, all the cots were occupied. There was a waterfall that fed the pool. Before going out to Norbert and the car, Alan felt like swimming under it. As he started toward it, he bumped into the waiter who had taken Goldman's order.

"I beg your pardon, sir," he said, "but Mr. Goldman said to put the Dom Pérignon and the lobster on your bill."

Duchess Armande de Saran had not bothered to throw out the oil-stained clothes left in her cabana by the man whose name she did not know. She was lying there, her body entirely covered by her veils, except for her pubic mound which was exposed to the sun. Twice a week she took a pubic sunbath, ever since she read in a beauty magazine that exposing the genitals to ultraviolet rays activated the blood flow to them and thus increased their sensitivity.

Her memory was short on faces and names. But on the other hand, it recorded and brought back to her like a photographic negative every one of the blows she had ever received. The most sensational beating she had ever had was at her own townhouse near the Bois de Boulogne in Paris at the hands of two young hoods who had tied her to the bidet in her bathroom with electric wires. The fact that one of her arms had been broken in the process was only incidental. But the $2,000,000 worth of jewels they had stolen from her had given her a bit of a hard time. The insurance people, smelling a rat, had threatened to have her private life thoroughly investigated if she insisted on trying to collect the whole amount of what she claimed to have lost. After consultation with her husband, she decided not to sue, but to accept a modest settlement so as to avoid the publicity. But since she wanted the insurance people to know just how she felt about such a vulgar lack of breeding, she then transferred her coverage to a rival company.

Ever since, all she wore were fake copies of those stolen jewels. Everybody knew that that was the case. Her reputation for elegance, of course, had perhaps suffered some as a result, but her security was much better—no one was going to hold her up to steal cheap imitations. Only she and the duke were aware that her alleged fakes were the real thing.

"Mandy," her husband said, coming into the cabana.

"Hubert," she replied without moving, "you're early."

"Whose clothes are those?" he wanted to know.

By way of reply, she merely gurgled a little laugh.

"Mandy, answer me," he demanded.

Whenever he sensed that his wife had just had another sexual experience, the duke's metabolism underwent a deep and immediate transformation.

"Who was it, Mandy?" he urged.

"Someone. I don't know who. Just don't get excited."

"Mandy, please," he begged, "now, give me that blow job!"

"The only two beautiful women around the pool who aren't exhibiting their charms in monokinis!" Cesare di Sogno exclaimed with a smile on his lips, as with the tips of his fingers he threw a kiss to Sarah Burger and her mother Emily.

Then he shook hands with Arnold Hackett and Hamilton Price-Lynch as if they were his best and oldest friends.

"Do you two have some secret for staying so slim? Let me in on it. Do you go without food, or do you get a lot of exercise?"

He kissed Victoria Hackett's hand. She alone was not in a swimsuit.

"Madame Hackett," he said, "your husband is just magnificent. Every woman in Cannes is envious of you."

"Would you care for a drink?" Hamilton asked.

"Never before lunch," Cesare replied. "I presume you have your table for tonight's benefit? Just as I thought. Well, you can cancel it. I want all of you to be my guests!"

"Mr. di Sogno!" Victoria protested.

"Oh, yes, absolutely," Cesare insisted. "I want to bring together all the nicest people here. You know my friends the Duke and Duchess de Saran? They'll be delighted to be spending the evening with you."

"Well," Hackett said hesitantly, looking over toward Emily Price-Lynch. "You see, we made a reservation for six. We have an additional guest for tonight."

"The more the merrier!" Cesare exclaimed joyfully.

"We would be delighted to join your party," Hamilton put in, "but there is really no reason for us to be your guests."

"Don't complicate things, Mr. Price-Lynch. You'll make me extremely happy by accepting."

"I agree with Hamilton," Hackett said. "We'll all make up one big party, but only on condition that you and your friends join us as our guests."

"My friend Goldman will be along," Cesare said, "as well as his charming wife, Julia, if that's all right with you. Let me go over and tell the Duke and Duchess what we've worked out!"

Cesare strode quickly off toward the cabanas.

"I can't stand that character," Sarah said.

"Neither can I," her mother agreed.

"Why not?" Victoria inquired, tenderly rubbing the back of her hand where Cesare had so gallantly and continentally kissed it. "He's so attractive! And so well mannered, my!"

"He looks just like a kept man!" Sarah commented, looking slyly over toward her stepfather.

"Sarah!" her mother reprimanded.

"He knows everybody in the world," Hamilton said to Hackett, paying no attention to Sarah's insinuations.

"And that Leader Award of his certainly gets a lot of recognition," Arnold said.

"Well, I've got a confession to make," Victoria straightforwardly told them. "I think this is the opportunity of a lifetime. I've never before spent an evening with a real live duke and duchess!"

"I think you look like anything but an Arab."

"Is that so?" the Prince said. "Why?"

"Because you have blue eyes," Marina told him.

Hadad chortled with delight. Not only did this girl look just like Marilyn Monroe, but she spoke her mind in full candor to boot. A child's soul in the body of a woman. Hadad had possessed so many children's bodies that had old, worn-out souls...

The limousine was gliding smoothly along the Croisette. Marina had one of the five-hundred-franc sailboats on her lap.

"Are you in Cannes alone?" Hadad asked her.

"Yes."

"What do you usually do?"

"Nothing. I don't know how to do anything. How about you?"

"Just like you," he answered. "Nothing. Did you come here with friends?"

"No," she said, "just an old guy who treated me to the trip."

"An old guy?" he queried. "What do you mean by old?" And he wondered whether she might be just another whore after all.

"I dunno, maybe seventy or eighty," she told him.

"Looks like a dirty old man to me. He keeps a girl friend of mine, Poppy."

"In that case, how did he happen to bring you here instead of her?"

"Oh, it was all kind of an accident. It just happened. You see, sometimes Poppy lets me use her apartment."

"What's the matter with your own?"

"I don't have one," she told him.

"Well, then where do you live?"

"Oh, here and there, wherever I can. It depends on the fellow I'm going with," she confided. "I got sore at Alan, so I went off with Harry. But then I got sore at Harry, and I went back to Alan's, but the water was cut off. So, I just went over to Poppy's. And that's where I met the old guy. He sent a ticket over for me."

"Just like that?"

"Yep. Just like that."

"Why did you say he looks like a dirty old man?"

"Because he likes to watch me when I'm working out."

"At what? Tennis? Golf?"

"No, doing push-ups," she said. "I like to do push-ups."

"Where is that old guy now?" the prince asked.

"Here at the Majestic Hotel. With his old lady."

"And I suppose he's going to pay your hotel bill?"

"Well, they're sure not gonna get me to pay it," Marina said in a guffaw. "I don't have any bread."

"I haven't been to bed yet, Marina," Hadad said to her. "I'm on my way to have a bite with a few friends. Would you like to break bread with me?"

"No, all I want to do is get my hat," she answered. "I forgot it in my room."

"There's a charity gala on tonight," Hadad countered. "Would you like to go with me?"

"How would I have to dress?" she asked.

"Formal. Long dress."

"Then, I can't," she said. "All I've got is a short black dress and some jeans."

"Well, that's easy enough to remedy," the prince told her. "My secretary Khalil will take you out to the stores. You can buy anything your little heart desires. Don't worry about a thing."

"You mean that?"

"Yes, I do. Do you have any jewelry?"

Marina burst out laughing. "What would I do with jewels?"

"Don't you like jewelry?"

"I don't know. I never really thought about it."

"Well, this time you can get the finest jewels you see. Go to Van Cleef's, Cartier's, wherever you want to go. I want you to be more beautiful than a queen when I take you out tonight."

He seized the tips of her fingers and kissed them.

"It's strange, haunting," he murmured, "your uncanny resemblance to Marilyn Monroe."

"Not you, too!" she exclaimed. "That shit's beginning to bug me. They all say the same thing!"

Cesare knocked discreetly at the door of the cabana.

"Duchess?" he called. "It's Cesare di Sogno. Are you people all exposed? Or can a person come in?"

"Come on in," she answered.

"Just a second!" Hubert called out. He hurriedly covered his wife's body with a scarlet robe.

Mandy shrugged. "Cesare knows my body better than you do," she said.

"Well, that's no excuse," her husband irritatedly answered. "Come in."

"The handsomest couple on the Côte d'Azur!" Cesare beamed at them. "My dear Duke, I've known you for ten years now. And every year you become two years younger. As for Mandy, well, no need to say..."

He gave her a friendly squeeze on the back of the neck.

"You'd be surprised to know how many women are jealous of you just because you're so beautiful," he assured her. "You're the most beautiful one of all!"

"Really, Cesare? Who's jealous? Who? Tell me."

"I'll tell you tonight. You'll be at the benefit, won't you?"

"Yes, we're going to be in the Signorellis' party."

"Oh, no, Hubert, you can't mean that! You'll have a terrible time. They're the world's greatest bores."

"What did you have in mind?" Mandy asked.

"Can't you guess? I'm getting up a party of the fun people who are here."

"Give us a for-instance."

"Louis Goldman, the movie producer."

"He's Jewish, isn't he?" the duke worried.

"Nobody's perfect," Cesare said. "It's not catching, and he's a genius, and at least he's white. There'll also be the Hacketts, the Price-Lynches, and that aviation tycoon, Honor Larsen."

"It's really too late for us to get out of our date with the Signorellis."

"Oh, Hubert," Mandy twitted, "we see them all year wherever we go. I'd really like to see some new faces. You could tell them that I have a headache," she suggested.

"And then have the Signorellis be at the table right next to us?" the duke countered.

"Life is short, and it's summertime, so who's going to take offense?" Cesare pleaded. "Hubert, do you want me to handle the whole thing for you? I'll explain to them that you'd forgotten we had a long-standing date for this affair. They'll understand."

"Very well, Cesare, if you say so," the duke reluctantly agreed. "But only on one condition. You must allow me to host the party."

"Never in the world! Rather than that, I'm afraid I'd have to forego the pleasure of your company."

"My lord, you are old-fashioned, Hubert," the duchess chided. "What difference does it make who picks up the check? The main thing is to have some fun!"

"The duchess is right," Cesare said. "Is it all right for me to go ahead and tell the Signorellis?"

"Yes, yes, yes," Mandy assured him.

She hopped up and got under the shower stark naked. Out of deference to the duke, Cesare averted his eyes.

"Yes, all right," Hubert de Saran conceded. And then, lowering his voice, "But I want your word of honor that you'll let me pick up the bill."

"I have no word of honor," Cesare laughingly confirmed.

"You must promise, Cesare!"

"Tonight at nine-thirty," Cesare concluded. "I'll be looking for you in the main lobby. Mandy!"

And he walked out without looking back. The duchess was not his dish at all. Every time they had made love, he had felt that his male prerogatives had been taken away from him. Besides, beating up on a dame was not his idea of kicks. What he liked was tenderness, voluptuousness, sweet surrender.

He walked behind the diving tower, waved to a group of people he knew as he passed by, crossed the terrace, and headed straight for the table where Betty Grone was having lunch with Honor Larsen.

"Mediterranean Sea dace," he announced, as he appraised what they were eating. "Imported from Dieppe up north. That is, it's originally from Dakar in Senegal, but it comes by way of Dieppe in refrigerator ships. How are you enjoying it?"

He gave Betty a kiss on the forehead, and held his hand out to Honor Larsen.

"I swear that everything I just said to you is phony. Besides, everything here is phony anyway. Some days I look at myself in the mirror and wonder whether I am real. Betty, you'll be at my table tonight, that goes without saying. I won't take no for an answer. All my other guests agreed to sit with me only because I told them that you'd be there with Honor. There'll be the Duke and Duchess de Saran, Louis Goldman, Arnold Hackett, Hamilton Price-Lynch, with their wives, of course, and all the rest. How have you been feeling, darling?"

Betty had a whispered exchange with Larsen.

"Honor is happy to accept," she told Cesare, "but only on condition that it be his treat. He wants you all to be his guests."

"Out of the question! This one is on me!"

She gave him a look and made a face.

"Don't give Honor a hard time, Cesare."

"Not at all! It's just that—"

"Okay, forget it," Betty cut him off. "Where do we meet?"

"In the lobby of the Palm Beach at nine-thirty. Does that suit you?"

"Just one more thing, Cesare," Betty whispered in an icy tone. "In case Nadia Fischler is shameless enough to put in an appearance tonight, I'm warning you that I'm going to make a scene!"

"So'll I," Cesare seconded her vigorously.

Everything was turning out just fine; his guests were all fighting to pick up the tab. He swiped an olive, took a small fork and speared a bit of dace off Betty's plate, and took off. "See you tonight," he called back.

"A very, very nice man," Honor told Betty after Cesare was gone. "You and he must be old friends, eh?"

"Well, we keep turning up in the same places. But not necessarily with the same people. He's fun to be around."

"Do you think I ought to accept his award?" Larsen asked.

"It's quite an honor to get it, Honor. Oh, I made a joke!" She laughed heartily.

An hour earlier, Betty had seen Prince Hadad embracing the fellow that Nadia had picked up last night at the casino.

"Honor, do you see that young man over there?" she said. "I want you to ask him to join us at the benefit tonight."

"Do you know him?" Larsen asked in surprise.

"No, of course not. But he's a very close friend of Prince Hadad's. He's involved in some of the biggest deals in the Middle East. I was only thinking that he might be useful for you to know, Honor."

Larsen put down his napkin, which in his huge hands looked like a dainty pocket handkerchief. He rose to his full, impressive height, then bent over and kissed the tips of Betty's fingers.

"You are wonderful, Betty," he said. "You think of everything. I'll go right over to him."

The swim had done him good, but now Alan was beginning to feel really pooped. If he stayed here at the Palm Beach a minute longer, he knew he'd fall asleep and not wake up for a week. He picked up his towel, and got ready to head for the dressing room where he would find the clothes that Norbert had brought for him. A huge shadow barred his way.

"I'm Honor Larsen," the shadow said, grabbing his hand.

"I'm Alan Pope," Alan answered mechanically, as he tried in vain to get his hand out of that vise.

"We have a mutual friend, Prince Hadad," Larsen said. "Will you be coming to the benefit tonight?"

"No, I won't. I really have to get some sleep."

"Nobody sleeps on the Riviera, Mr. Pope. People even die here standing up. The only time they ever lie down, they tell me, is to tear off a piece!" And he laughed uproariously, delighted with his own wit.

"Would you do me the honor of being my guest tonight?"
he went on.

"Honor, won't you introduce me?" said Betty, who had
come up behind him.

Alan was amazed at seeing the gorgeous redhead.

"Alan Pope," Larsen said. "Miss Betty Grone."

She was wearing a violet sari that sculpted all the
perfect curves of her figure. Alan had never seen anything
quite like her huge green eyes. Except perhaps Nadia's
violet eyes.

"I absolutely insist on your joining us tonight," she
said, as those eyes looked intensely into his.

"I would very much like to. But unfortunately—"

"We're going to be with a group of very enjoyable
friends," she insisted. "Please don't deprive me of the
pleasure of your company. You'll see, there'll be some
very pretty women in our party. Where are you staying?"

"At the Majestic."

"Would you like my chauffeur to come for you?" Larsen
asked.

"No, no," Alan sputtered.

"Well, then, let's say about nine-thirty in the lobby of
the Palm Beach, okay? Can I count on you?"

"But I was just telling Mr. Uh—" Alan stammered.

"Then it's all settled, Mr. Pope. We'll meet you here.
Honor and I are delighted that you've accepted to dine
with us. Are you coming, Honor?"

After they had left, Alan tottered away, wondering
whether he was surrounded by lunatics. In New York, he
got fired, his girl walked out on him; here in Cannes, they
were falling all over one another to have him as their
guest!

Marina was as happy as a child. She would point to
something, and the salespeople would immediately rush
to get it and wrap it up. At Khalil's orders, two gorillalike
bodyguards who were along handed the packages to the
chauffeur who put them in the trunk of the black limousine.
It was like a fairytale! Marina couldn't have cared less about
owning anything at all. What fascinated her was to be at
the center of all this activity. Each time she selected a
dress, Khalil suggested she take several more like it. She

didn't need them, would never wear them, but it was such fun to be getting them all handed to her. Every haute-couture house on the Croisette had treated her as if she had been the Queen of England.

Now at Van Cleef's, she didn't really know what to choose. The manager was trotting out cases that contained jewels of which she knew neither the price nor the use.

"Look at the beauty of this diamond necklace, madame," he was saying. "Such pure stones! And then there are matching earrings to go with it."

Marina made a face. She was sitting on a Louis XV armchair upholstered in faded turquoise that just about matched her jeans. And she was wearing her flowered straw hat.

In a semicircle around her, the entire general staff of the store stood by, watching attentively, ready to move at the slightest blink of her eyes.

"Don't you have anything that's more fun?" she asked.

"Fun, madame? Would madame explain what she means by fun?"

"I know," one of the salesmen exclaimed. He was wearing a sober black suit. "If madame will wait just a moment..."

He leaned over toward the manager and whispered something in his ear, as he clapped his hands in joy and anticipation. The manager gave his approval.

"Yes, get it," he said. "This is the most recent of our original creations, madame. I do think it will appeal to you."

The salesman returned, and set a jewelry case down on the counter.

"Why, it's a—" Marina exclaimed with delight.

"Yes, madame, that's just what it is, a dog collar. Made of twenty-one diamonds set in platinum. May I?"

He put it around Marina's neck. Three salesmen immediately held up mirrors so she could see it from every angle.

"I'll take it! That's terrif!" she crowed.

"Very well, madame. Now, if you'll let us show you our rings?"

Khalil discreetly motioned the manager aside.

"His Highness will really like that dog collar," he told him. "Do you have the leash to go with it?"

When he got back to his room, Alan collapsed on his bed and went to sleep. The phone rang and rang. He finally awoke sufficiently to reach for it, and looked at his watch. It said four o'clock. A.M.? P.M.? He had no idea.

"Hello," he mumbled sleepily.

"Alan, is that you? This is Sam."

"Sam! What time is it?"

"It's ten in the morning here in New York. Are you still asleep or are you drunk? Listen to what I have to tell you, this is very important, Alan. I've thought it over. We're calling the whole thing off."

It took several seconds for Sam Bannister's words to get through to him.

"Calling what whole thing off?" he asked.

"I talked to a lawyer, an old friend of mine. He says we really fucked up. It's best to quit before we get in any deeper. We'll try to pay back what you've already spent, one way or another. You follow me, Alan?"

Alan felt as though lead had just been run into his veins.

"If we return the money to the bank," Bannister went on, "we're off the hook. They can't do anything to you! All you do is report that they made a mistake, and everything is jake. We'll find you a job some place and pay back what we owe. And then the slate'll be wiped clean."

"There's just one thing wrong with that picture, Sam," Alan answered in a toneless voice. He paused, then lowering his voice, he said, "I don't have the money anymore."

"What was that?" Bannister asked.

"I said I don't have the money anymore," Alan shouted into the phone. "So, it won't work. I can't give it back. Now, do you get it?"

"No," Sam sputtered.

"Sam, I'm broke, washed up, cleaned out. Remember you told me to cash my checks at the casino? Well, I did, and they got it all from me!"

"Alan, you're kidding. Why are you trying to scare me?"

"I'm not. I don't have a dime left."

"Alan, I don't believe you. Alan, swear to me—"

"Oh, shit!" Alan said.

"Alan, I'm taking the first plane over!" Sam screamed.

"Go take a flying fuck for all I care!" Alan answered, and slammed the phone down.

There was a knock at the door. He jumped out of bed, cursing Sammy, cursing Nadia, and especially cursing himself. He dashed over and opened the door.

"Hello," said Betty Grone. She had changed from her sari to a pair of black slacks and a white tailored shirt with nothing underneath.

"May I come in?" she asked.

Alan stepped back to let her in, and as she went by he got a whiff of her intoxicating scent.

"You look like somebody who just got some bad news," she said. "Or am I wrong?"

Alan closed the door, and they were immediately enveloped in the conspiratorial darkness of the room. That, along with her scent . . .

"I told Honor that I was going to the hairdresser's," she confided, and let herself down on his bed. Sitting back, she took her knees into her arms.

"Come sit near me," she said. "I like you. I hope I'm not bothering you."

"No, not at all."

"I live one floor below. Honor'll be getting back soon. I don't have too much time."

She straightened out, stretched, and lay back completely. With amazement, Alan saw that she was wriggling out of her slacks.

"Want to give me a hand?" she asked.

Awkwardly, Alan tried to help her undress. At one point, their heads rubbed together. Betty pulled him violently to her and greedily sought his mouth with hers. At the same time, she took his hand in hers and guided it down between her thighs. She had apparently meant it literally.

19

Abel Fischmayer didn't care much for Oliver Murray. Murray was short, while he was tall. Murray was petty, while Abel considered himself generous. On the few occasions they had had lunch together, Fischmayer had been hard put to hide his distaste at the poor table manners of Hackett Chemical's chief of personnel.

Hackett Chemical was one of the Burger Bank's principal accounts. And on the eighth of each month, Abel and Oliver had to get together to determine the salary payments due to the sixty thousand people on the pharmaceutical company's payroll. Close to $120,000,000 was involved each month, vouched for and approved by Abel Fischmayer for Burger Bank and Oliver Murray for Hackett Chemical. So Fischmayer had to shake hands with Murray on those occasions. With a slight revulsion, he dialed Murray's number.

"Oliver, how are you?" he asked with feigned warmth. "Abel Fischmayer here. I wanted to get some information from you about one of our accounts which seems to be out of line. Do have somebody working for you named Alan Pope?"

Murray's rasping voice put Abel's teeth on edge. "No, I don't have, Mr. Fischmayer. But I did."

Not only was the man as mean-spirited as a truant officer, but he insisted on addressing Abel as Mr. Fischmayer, as if to put him in his place.

"What do you mean, 'you did'?"

"We dropped him from the payroll four days ago. On July twenty-second to be precise."

"You don't say, Oliver," Fischmayer said. "Any reason?"

"Retrenchment. He was just the first of what'll be quite a list of layoffs. May I ask why you're so interested in him, Mr. Fischmayer?"

"Just routine, Oliver, just routine. Incidentally, how is your good wife?"

"Fine, thank you."

"What did this Pope do at Hackett?"

"He was assistant to the head of one of our claims departments."

"Hmmm, I see. I wondered at so big a deposit as eleven thousand, seven hundred and four dollars turning up in his account all at once."

"That's what he got on being let go. You know our policy. That covers his severance pay, accumulated vacation, and other fringe benefits."

"Thanks very much, Oliver. That was all I needed to know. How are things otherwise?"

"Just fine, Mr. Fischmayer, just fine."

"Very good, Oliver. I'll see you soon, and thanks again."

Abel hung up and told the switchboard to get him the Majestic Hotel in Cannes, France. Now let Hamilton Price-Lynch worry about what kind of a nobody had been given that huge hunk of Burger Bank overpayment!

Alan had always loved women. And at times they had reciprocated. But even when women had been the ones who had made the advances, Alan had never felt that he was merely a sex object in their hands. On the other hand, the three brief affairs he had had since his arrival in Cannes had left him with a bitter taste in his mouth. Nadia Fischler, Betty Grone, and the unknown woman in the Palm Beach cabana had all challenged him to a sexual duel. These three females had assumed male prerogatives—deciding, taking, rejecting. There had been no abandon, no tenderness about any of it.

He glanced around his disheveled room, still impregnated with Betty's lingering fragrance. The sheets were dragged over the floor, the mattress was stripped bare, and pillows and cushions had been tossed every which way. Their stormy encounter had traveled from the bed to three couches and two armchairs before Betty, whose outcries must have been noted by the hotel's security service, was finally fulfilled.

Bone-weary, scratched, and bitten, his lips raw, Alan had collapsed after that tornado had passed. But strangely, he did not feel sleepy any longer. He went into the bathroom, took a long shower, returned to the bedroom

and lay down again, trying in vain to get some shut-eye.
He lit a cigarette and tried to take stock of his situation. At
this point, he had no control over what was happening, so
he might as well let himself be carried along by events.
Under the best of circumstances, he could look forward to
being arrested in a few hours. It wasn't hard to foresee
what the charges would be: swindling, passing bad checks—
of course, Burger Bank would refuse to honor the ones he
had signed—and fraud. That being the case, it didn't
much matter whether he was apprehended here or somewhere else, so why not just go along until the cops caught
up with him?

He got up and went out on his balcony. It was five in
the afternoon, and the sun was still very high in the sky.
He took a good daylight look at this landscape in which
he was about to spend his last few hours of freedom.
What he saw was beautiful, harmonious, the very essence
of life as it ought to be. As far as the eye could see, the
beaches were teeming with bathers, passersby walked
nonchalantly along the Croisette, children were laughing
in the swimming pool as the sun reflected off the shimmering
swells raised by the bodies of divers, and countless sails
dotted the indigo sea.

Suddenly, he rushed back into the bedroom, got into a
pair of trousers and a shirt, and dialed the garage on the
housephone.

"Garage?" he asked. "This is Alan Pope, Suite 751. Will
you please have my car brought out front? Thanks."

Why not take advantage of the Rolls-Royce while he still
had it? His next ride might be in a paddy wagon.

The hotel lobby was full of beautiful women, their pet
dogs, old men dressed for yachting, and young men in
expensive, but slovenly jeans.

"My name is Serge, Mr. Pope," the doorman said.
"Would you like me to phone for your driver?"

Alan put on his sunglasses, got in behind the wheel,
and said, "No, thanks. That won't be necessary."

"Mr. Pope!"

Alan turned to see who was calling to him.

"My name is Marc Gohelan. I'm the manager of the
hotel," the man said to him. "I haven't had a chance to
welcome you to the Majestic before this.

"If you need anything at all," he went on, "please don't hesitate to ask. Our only aim is to make your stay here as enjoyable as possible."

Alan thanked him with a nod, smiled, and slipped the Rolls quietly into gear. He cut across the road, turned left, and drove along the Croisette, delighted with the animal enjoyment he was getting from being behind the wheel of this silent machine. With all the troubles that lay ahead, he wondered how he could really be enjoying such a pointless pastime. He went by the Palm Beach casino, followed the coast road, and turned right at a sign that read Juan-les-Pins.

Beautiful, young, tanned, half-naked girls turned to look as he went by. If only they could know! he thought.

Despite the heat wave, the messenger was wearing a formal gray uniform. The flaps of the collar bore an ornate letter *B*.

"What does that *B* stand for?" the super asked him.

"That's *B* for Burger Bank." The messenger held out a letter. "This is to be delivered to Mr. Alan Pope, personally."

"Okay, I'll give it to him as soon as I see him," the super promised.

The messenger saluted smartly and hopped back into the car he had double-parked outside the building.

It was July twenty-sixth. Pope still had not paid this month's rent, nor had the super seen hide nor hair of him since the twenty-third. He was beginning to think Pope might have skipped. In view of that, the super decided the safest thing to do was to find out what was in this hand-delivered letter. Going indoors to his kitchen, where a kettle of water was boiling for tea, he held the envelope over the steaming spout long enough to loosen the flap so he could open the envelope. He unfolded the sheet of paper, fairly certain of what it must say.

The super read the bank notice through once, without understanding it. Then he read it again. Suddenly, he leaned against the kitchen table as if a horse had just kicked him in the gut.

There were a dozen or so of them lying in the shade of some tall parasol pines. One of the fellows, a tall redhead with a red scarf tied around his forehead, was strumming a guitar. Another was beating time with the palm of his hand on an empty can that he held on his stomach. Some of the girls were humming. All of them appeared to be between eighteen and twenty-five. From time to time, passersby would stop for a moment to listen to the music. The Riviera was overflowing with students like these, who had come from every corner of Europe to bask in the sun. Bread was fairly inexpensive, and so were fruit and tomatoes. They could sleep out in the open. The view, sea and sky, belonged to everyone.

"He's trying to bug us," a Dutch fellow said, pointing to the white topless Rolls-Royce that had just pulled up a few meters away.

"Some nouveau riche," his girl yawned.

"Bull twaddle!"

"Would you dare ride around in a thing like that?" she asked.

"What do you think I am?" he pouted.

"When you're forty, you'll kiss some boss's ass to be able to afford one."

"Screw that! I'd rather cash in my chips right now," he said.

"You got your bomb with you, Hans?"

"In my haversack."

"Hey, you two," a neighbor chimed in, "let's not have any of that shit, huh? What the fuck do we care about him?"

"It'd be some beau geste," the girl answered.

"Hell, we were having a nice quiet time. What we need that kind of shit for?"

"Hans, go and get it," she persisted.

Hans pulled out a can that looked like an aerosol of shaving cream.

"What should I write?" he asked.

"Capitalist, go home!"

"Stupid, he's home right here. Besides, that's too long; I don't feel like it."

"How about 'filthy rich'? That wouldn't be bad."

Hans knelt down alongside the Rolls-Royce. The black paint squirted out of the can onto the lily-white car. All of the kids started to laugh uproariously. Some of the passersby stopped to look.

Hans was a graffiti specialist. At night, he was in the

habit of going out and leaving derisive statements on the walls of public buildings, denouncing various political parties, pollution, atomic energy, and all officeholders.

"I'm a retired colonel and I protest what you're doing!" said a pompous-looking Frenchman who was passing by.

"It's our own car," the guitar player lied. "What right you got to tell us we can't paint it, huh, colonel?"

They all laughed twice as loudly. Hans had finished the *R*, and he handed the aerosol can to a tall girl with ash-blonde hair.

"Here, Terry, you finish it. I'm pooped," he said.

Terry carefully completed the word, her tongue sticking out. There was applause on all sides, from their group as well as from one passerby who grabbed the can from Terry, and on the still unsullied fender added the word *PIG*. Hans walked over, stood squarely in front of the man, and gave him a military salute. The man acknowledged it, then stepped back as everyone cheered him, returned the can to Terry, opened the door of the Rolls-Royce, and slipped in behind the wheel. He put the key in the ignition, turned the starter, and drove off.

All the laughter died in the throats of the young demonstrators. Suddenly there was silence, and all one could hear was the peeping of the sparrows, the muffled cries of locals playing boule, the hubbub of the nearby town, and the familiar noises of people leaving the beach.

"I'll be goddamned!" Hans said, coming back to his senses.

Some twenty yards ahead, the Rolls-Royce had come to a stop, then gone into reverse, and backed up to where they were standing. Speechless, and still holding the aerosol can, Terry heard the driver hail her.

"How about hopping in?" he said.

She looked around at her friends, but they were all expressionless. Alan opened the door for her.

"What's the matter? You afraid?" he asked.

Never one to refuse a dare, Terry got in beside him.

"Hey! The bastard's taking her away!" Hans commented, as he instinctively made a mental note of the car's license number. The Rolls-Royce was already at the end of the square, turning a corner at breakneck speed.

"What's your name?" Alan asked.

"Terry," she said.

"English? American?" he asked.

"What's it to you?"

"Nothing."

He was speaking in a neutral, colorless voice. She tried to get a good look at him, but behind the dark glasses she could not make out his eyes.

"Where we going?" she asked.

"I don't know."

He had driven through Juan-les-Pins, reached the main highway, and turned right.

"You think you're funny?" Terry demanded.

No reply.

"I want out," she said.

"Who's stopping you?" he asked, increasing his speed.

She shrugged and hunkered back against the leather upholstery.

"You're not funny," she said.

He turned sharply to the left onto a side road that went up the side of a hill.

"What have you got against my car?" he asked.

"It's horrible! A typical sign of conspicuous consumption. How come? You're not all that old."

The landscape was marked off by clusters of rose laurels. Here and there below, hidden by masses of verdure, there could be seen the ocher roof of a private villa.

"We going much farther?" she asked.

He put a cassette into the stereo deck.

"Listen," she finally exploded, "your little joke has gone far enough. Okay, so we wrote something on your damned car. Big deal! Anybody who can afford a car like this can afford to get a new paint job. So stop and let me out."

Alan braked the car, pulled over to the shoulder, and turned the motor off. She jumped out. He didn't try to stop her. She set off briskly walking back down the hill they had just driven up. He started his motor again, made a U-turn, drove about a hundred and fifty feet beyond her, and then stopped and got out. He leaned back against a low stone wall behind which there were tufts of mimosa. The air was perfectly clear.

In the distance, the sea was shimmering behind the foothills that rushed down to it in soft, rounded cascades, dotted with the shades of grays, mauves, and greens. As

Terry walked by him, she looked the other way. In a leap, he was alongside her, taking her by the arm.

"Now, suppose I were to give you a good spanking?" he asked.

"You just try!"

He shook her furiously, because he was not really able to feel as angry at her as he might have wished.

"Who's going to pay for the damages?" he demanded.

She gave him a venomous look.

"Okay, okay, you'll get your lousy dough. Forget it!"

"When?" he wanted to know.

Suddenly, she was frightened. What was wrong with him? Was he crazy? Was he a gangster? A rapist? Or what?

"Let me go!" she shouted.

He let go of her wrist, took off his glasses, rubbed his eyes with a gesture of weariness, and then turned and went to lean against the parapet again.

She rubbed her freed wrist and stood there watching him, and wondering. She now saw that he couldn't be more than twenty-five or thirty. He took a cigarette out of a fresh pack, and lit it. He did not look at her.

"Hey, you," she called.

But he didn't turn.

"Listen," she said, "I'm really sorry about what happened. You know, we didn't mean any harm by it. It was just supposed to be a gag."

He shrugged and puffed at his cigarette.

"You angry at me?" she asked.

"Why on earth would I be?" he replied with a tight half-smile.

She was watching him carefully. "I guess after what we did, you don't especially want to drive me back there, do you?"

"No, I don't especially," he said.

"Okay, I'll walk." She shifted from one foot to the other. "What's your name?"

"Alan."

She sat down near him on the parapet and looked out in the same direction he was looking.

"You know, you really don't look like you belong in that kind of car at all," she said. "Riding around in a tub like that at your age—it's sick!"

He didn't answer.

"Isn't it?" she persisted. And then, "You American?"

"Yes."

"What do you do for a living?"

"Stuff," he said. "A little bit of this, a little bit of that."

"I'm a student," she informed him.

"What are you studying?"

"Life."

"They teaching a course in that this year?"

He turned to look at her. She was dressed in a pair of jeans and a man's khaki shirt that was several sizes too big for her. Her ash-blonde hair harmonized perfectly with the gray of her eyes. She had small, delicate hands, a child's hands.

"Can I have a smoke?" she asked.

"I don't have any joints with me," he replied.

"Why would you say something like that to me?"

"On account of your friends back there."

"Look, they're about the same age as you, but they think a lot younger," she told him, nodding toward the Rolls-Royce.

He looked at her, lighted a cigarette from his own, and gave it to her. She took it from him, and their eyes met. He could see his face reflected in her eyes. He turned away.

"Should we go?" he asked.

He opened the door for her and she got in.

"What do you plan to do when you grow up?" he asked.

"Stay young. How about you?"

He went into first gear, took off from the shoulder, and said, "I'm gonna try to live to a ripe old age."

"Well, you've practically got it made already," she said. "I imagine you have a chauffeur for this bus?"

"Naturally."

"And you've got a big suite in one of the deluxe hotels in Cannes?"

"Obviously."

"And at night you go to dinner with a bunch of old bores?"

"In a tuxedo, of course."

"And you enjoy it?"

"Bores the shit out of me."

She burst out laughing. "Then why in the world do you go on doing it?" she wanted to know.

"Do you always do only what you want?" he asked.

"Always," she said.

"You're lucky," he sighed, making a face.

"Not lucky. Just gutsy enough to try. There's a difference."

"Or maybe lucky enough to have the guts to try," he said.

"Don't you?" she asked.

"Not usually."

"And right now?"

"Not at all."

She tapped on the dashboard. "Get rid of this claptrap," she said. "Ditch your boring old farts and decide to do something else!"

Alan made a hairpin turn.

"Where are you staying?" he asked.

"At Golfe-Juan. I have a room with a girl friend."

"A six-foot girl friend with a beard?"

"She weighs a hundred and fifteen pounds and has a thirty-six inch bust, if you must know. How about you? You being kept by some rich old widow?"

"Yes," he said, playing along. "She's a hundred and three years old and very jealous. First thing every morning I have to take her lapdog out to pee."

When they got into Golfe-Juan, he was amazed to discover that in less than an hour she had made him forget what a hell of a spot he was in. While he was talking to her, he had bathed in a cool spring which washed away all of his worries. He remembered with surprise that he had even laughed several times.

"Do you have a phone?" he asked her.

She looked at him as if he had lost his mind. "Why not a marble bathtub? We have a cold-water tap out on the landing. And it's kind of temperamental about whether it works or not. Wanna see?"

"Yes, I'd like to," he said.

He parked the car on a quiet little street of Golfe-Juan. Some kids who were playing ball laughed with delighted merriment when they saw the graffiti on it. Terry pretended she hadn't heard them. Alan simply paid no attention.

"This is it," she said.

They went through a doorway right next to a little restaurant called Chez Tony.

"Twenty-seven-franc prix fixe," she informed him. "Fresh fried sardines, salade niçoise, cheese, and fruit."

She looked at him sarcastically. "What else can poor people expect?" she asked. "My room's on the fifth floor. You think you can make it?"

"I'll try," Alan agreed.

She led him up the winding stairway. Her feet landed on the steps so lightly that she seemed to be dancing up, rather than climbing.

"I'm quite concerned about this, Your Highness. My government is insisting that I tell them what the shipping date will be within the next forty-eight hours. The authorities don't want to keep the shipment on a military airfield any longer than they have to."

"Just what is the shipment made up of?" Prince Hadad asked.

"A hundred planes. Forty Drakens, thirty-five Viggers, and twenty-five 105s." Honor Larsen detailed to him. "We just can't let eight hundred million dollars' worth of aircraft stand by indefinitely."

"Couldn't you have the transaction carried out by one of your own corporations?"

"No, Your Highness. We're under very strict government supervision, and not only from the Swedes!"

They were meeting on the fourth floor of the Majestic, in one of the several suites that the Prince kept reserved. Hadad and Honor Larsen had known one another for a very long time, but never had made the fact evident in public. The kind of business they had with each other required the most absolute discretion. Politics and economics were so intimately connected that it had become impossible to make a deal under normal conditions.

According to the terms of the agreements made with the United States government, Hadad was not permitted to buy military materiel for his army anywhere except in the U.S.A. Unfortunately, in view of the American government's support of Israel, it could not easily make direct deliveries of armaments to an Arab emirate. So Hadad had to go shopping in France, Sweden, Great

Britain, or Italy. But even in those countries, there was a problem. Alliances and sworn principles forbade their selling to Hadad's emirate what it had already been refused by the United States. This made it impossible for his acquisitions to be made officially between one government and another. The way they got around this difficulty was that Hadad had an active go-between to handle his deals. That way, business could go on as usual, and political ethics remained intact. Up to now, the deals for aircraft between Sweden and Hadad had been handled by the late Erwin Broker.

"I really can't understand what could have happened to him," Honor Larsen muttered darkly.

"He blew it, that's all," the Prince answered, without any intention of being funny.

"Yes, but why? Who would have had an interest in tying him to the fireworks deck with a stick of dynamite strapped to his belly?"

"What commission was he getting?" the Prince asked.

Honor Larsen looked sharply at him. "Two percent."

"Well, that makes sixteen million dollars," the prince pointed out.

Larsen did not go on to point out that Hadad's commission was eight percent, or the mere sum of sixty-four million dollars for the purchase under discussion. The big airplane man was gauche and childlike only where women were concerned.

"I'm afraid we're really in a bad way here, Your Highness. Broker's death has led us up a blind alley with no way out. Do you have anyone else you can turn to?"

"No. How about you?"

"Me neither," Larsen concurred.

Each of them racked his brain. It was impossible to find a dependable go-between in a matter of two days. The risks involved were much too great for a transaction of this magnitude.

"Your Highness, are you still in touch with the people who originally got you together with our late friend?"

"Absolutely not," His Highness lied blandly.

He did not want Cesare di Sogno involved in his affairs in any way whatsoever. The man was too conspicuous, too much in the public eye, and most especially too loose a talker. The fact that Cesare had introduced Erwin Broker to Hadad four years earlier was just a lucky coincidence. But now that Broker had been murdered, Hadad decided that Cesare might be very handy when it came to finding good whores, but in business he'd never touch him again with a ten-foot pole.

"That's too bad," Larsen sighed. "By the way," he added, "are you going to tonight's gala?"

"It is a charitable benefit," the Prince piously answered.

"One of your friends is going to be sitting at my table," Honor said.

"Who is that?" asked the Prince, who knew very well that he had no friends.

"Alan Pope," Larsen told him.

Hadad frowned.

"I was told you were very close," Larsen went on. "Just this morning everyone saw you congratulate him at length down at the pool."

The Prince tried to remember what Larsen was referring to. Then he remembered grabbing the man who almost slipped on the edge of the pool. It was the same fellow who had joined Nadia Fischler in several hands of chemin de fer against him the night before.

"I don't know the man at all," he stated. "What point did you wish to make, Mr. Larsen?"

Honor made a knowingly resigned face.

"None at all, Your Highness. I'm just racking my brain, trying to find some way out. After all, if we don't come up with a solution in the next forty-eight hours, an eight-hundred-million-dollar deal goes down the drain."

"Watch out for the beam. Duck!"

Alan bent down. Terry was closing the door behind him. Over the antenna-dotted roofs, a tiny bit of glimmering sea could be seen through the window between the scarlet flowers of two potted geraniums. The whitewashed walls of the room were decorated with posters of rock stars. On the table, there was a fruit bowl with a banana, two apples, one grapefruit, and three oranges.

"Which is yours?" Alan asked, nodding toward the two quilt-covered beds.

"The one on the left. The other one is Lucy's. You want me to make you some coffee?"

"Can you?"

"If you don't mind instant," she said.

"I didn't think your water was running," he quipped, and somewhere in the back of his head he remembered that the water was off in his New York apartment, too.

With a dramatic gesture Terry pulled back a royal-blue curtain, revealing a tiny space in which there was a shower with a small tub under it, a washbasin, and a small gas heater.

"Did you really believe me?" she asked.

"This looks like a painting—a Matisse, I think."

"What does?"

"The whole thing—your room, the colors, the open window."

"Well, isn't that something? You've actually heard of Matisse! So rich and so cultured all at the same time. You're quite a guy!"

"What did you think I was, an idiot?"

"As a general rule, money takes the place of culture, charm, politeness, and wit. Come on, don't stand there like that. You're making me nervous."

"Where should I sit?"

"On my bed," she said, as if that was all too obvious.

"If I do, I'll stretch out," Alan said.

"Who's stopping you?"

"I haven't had any sleep since God knows when," he told her.

"Take your shoes off," she suggested. "You'll be more comfortable."

Alan wondered whether this was going to be another fast come-on like he had had with Nadia, Betty, and that sex maniac in the Palm Beach cabana.

"You make a night of it last night?" she asked.

"Yes, I went to Rome."

"For business?"

"No, for spaghetti," he told her candidly.

She put two teaspoonfuls of powdered coffee in a cup, added hot water, and stirred.

"Sugar?" she asked.

"Yes, please. One. Aren't you having any?"

"I hate instant," she answered. "Lucy likes it. But I go down to the corner bar to get espresso."

She handed him the coffee, looked him in the face, and laughed.

"What's to laugh about?" he asked.

"You. You look like a schoolboy who's been given a detention. What's the matter? You still angry about the car?"

He watched her as she moved about, watering the geraniums with water from her toothbrush glass. She was young, limber, wholesome, and natural. Beautiful, too. He suddenly felt that he had come across something rare, something precious, something he would never get to know any better because he was no longer master of the things that fate held in store for him. She took a yogurt off a shelf, rinsed the coffee spoon, and sat down on Lucy's bed.

"Why are you looking at me like that?" she asked.

Their eyes were locked; she had stopped her spoon in midair. The silence between them resounded with the cries of children playing in the street below, music coming from the house across the way. But still, it was a real silence—for the words that might have broken it could only have confirmed what their eyes were telling each other, both of them equally amazed that this could happen between them so fast and without their having willed it.

"Terry?"

"Yes . . ."

Life, which had been suspended, resumed its course after that brief arrest, that hole in the tissue of time. Alan wanted to ask her whether she had felt the same thing he had. She turned her eyes away.

"I'd like to come and see you tomorrow," he said. "You think we could go for a swim together?"

He knew she was going to say no. And even if she said yes, he probably would not be free to keep his date with her. His unbelievable reprieve could expire at any moment.

"What time?" she asked.

"Ten o'clock?"

"Fine."

"Here?"

"I'll be waiting."

Birds weren't the only ones who could fly. As Alan went down that winding staircase, he was practically gliding over it.

He lovingly wiped away the remains of chocolate ice

cream cones that the kids had squashed on the front seat of the car. In the back, the same little darlings had smeared part of a pizza with anchovies, tomato sauce, and olives. With the graffiti on the side, his fancy car now looked much more like a garbage pail than like a luxury Rolls-Royce.

20

Lucy came tearing up the stairs, unlocked the door, and flung it open.

"Good, you're home!" she yelled to Terry. "I was so scared you'd be out."

Terry smiled vaguely at her. She was lying on her bed, both arms folded under her head, a cigarette dangling from her lips, her feet propped up on a pile of laundry.

"Get up and get ready," Lucy went on. "We're on our way in just a minute."

Into her big straw bag, Lucy threw a toothbrush, an apple, a tube of toothpaste, a swimming suit, and a T-shirt.

"It's the most gorgeous house you've ever been in! There's a fantastic swimming pool surrounded by olive trees and cypresses, bedrooms with big arched ceilings, a special stereo room, and a kitchen. Get going now. They're waiting for us down by the wharf in their car."

Lucy realized that Terry hadn't moved.

"What's the matter?" Lucy continued. "We've gotta hurry. We're invited to sleep over at the MacDermotts'! The people who live on the mountain above Saint-Paul, remember? I told you about them. Come on, Terry, they're waiting for us. Terry? What's wrong? You sick or something?"

"I can't go," Terry finally said. "I have a date here tomorrow morning."

"Who with?"

Terry took a long drag on her cigarette. "A fellow," she said, turning her eyes away.

"A fellow? What fellow?"

"Alan."

"Do I know him?"

"Nope." And then, as if the better to savor the name she had just said, she repeated it languidly, "Alan."

"Well, that doesn't make any difference, Terry," Lucy replied. "We can have dinner at the MacDermotts', spend the night there, then come back early tomorrow. They're all dying to meet you. I came back on purpose to find you. Their place is hardly more than an hour away, and it's terrific! You'll see. What a collection of artwork they have! Klees, Mondrians, Mirós, Chagalls, and Giacometti sketches. Come on!"

She jumped on the bed and shook Terry, who made no effort to protect herself.

"Go without me, Lucy. I don't feel like it."

"No such thing! I give you my word that you'll be back on time tomorrow morning. Come on, Terry! Hurry up!"

She ran over to the little alcove where the shower was, and threw Terry's toilet articles into her own bag.

"Come on, hop to it now!" she commanded. "You can tell me all about him on the way there."

Lucy shoved her roommate onto the landing, pulled the door shut, but didn't bother to lock it. The only thing they had worth stealing was their youth, and nobody could take that away from them.

The first person Alan saw when he drove up in front of the Majestic was Norbert. He could see his chauffeur standing there open-mouthed, but he did not realize why Norbert looked so amazed.

"Why, sir," Norbert stammered as he opened the door for Alan, "did you see what the car looks like?"

"What do you mean?" Alan asked distractedly.

Now Serge, the doorman, had also come up and was inspecting the vicious inscriptions that had been painted on the side.

"What bastards!" he said. "To do that to a defenseless car!"

"I'm gonna get in trouble for this," Norbert said.

"It happened in Juan-les-Pins," Alan explained, "during the few seconds it took me to go in and buy a pack of cigarettes."

Norbert didn't dare tell him that company rules were that nobody except the chauffeur was to drive the Rolls-Royce. Letting a customer take the wheel was one of the worst infractions a chauffeur could commit, although in this case there was a mitigating circumstance. Alan Pope certainly had not asked him whether he could take the car out.

"You can't be seen in a car like this, sir," Norbert said. "I'll take it into the garage to get the damage repaired."

"I'll be responsible for any cost involved," Alan said. He was torn between the realization that he had done something wrong and the urge to get to his suite so he could dream of Terry before he fell asleep.

"Oh, we're insured for that, sir," Norbert told him. "But I'm afraid it may take a little time to get a new paint job."

"Oil paint!" Serge was saying indignantly, as he scratched off some of the graffiti with his nail. "You'd think they'd at least have the decency to use watercolors! This is some age we live in!"

"What should we do, sir, if the garage doesn't have another car of the same type available for you?" Norbert asked.

"I'll phone them," Serge volunteered, as he headed for the outside wall phone.

"I really can't tell you how sorry I am that this happened, Norbert," Alan apologized.

"Don't let it worry you, sir," Norbert replied. "Things could be worse."

That statement was certainly appropriate to the situation. It perfectly described Alan's most pressing problem—the threat of having his bluff called and being arrested. The only thing he was hoping for was that that might not happen before his date with Terry the next morning. Provided he had a chance at least once to take her in his arms, let the world fall in for all he cared! He clapped Norbert reassuringly on the shoulder and walked through the lobby to the elevators to go up to his room.

Hans wore the standard counterculture uniform at all times: jeans of undefinable color, a once-blue T-shirt, a frayed shirt-jacket that more or less matched the jeans, and high-heeled cowboy boots. In his haversack, he carried his spray can of paint and an extra pair of socks. He was twenty-two years old and one of the best students at The Hague's school of architecture. What upset him was that his talent would be put to use in the service of a society he considered rotten and decadent. What need was there to study the architecture of the Quattrocento, ancient Egypt or Greece, if one would eventually have to build concrete rabbit warrens for the fat, soulless pigs who financed them?

He wanted to build radiant cities in which people, at last equal, could develop to their fullest, far from the degrading demands of assembly-line jobs. He dreamt of pyramids, Babylonian hanging gardens, music rooms in space, brotherhood, and individual liberty. And Hans sensed that he was being had. Once he earned his degree, he would have to say "Pretty please" to those in power in order to get commissions for lousy country villas or functional office buildings paid for by taxpayers.

The alternative was to blow it all up, smash the system. And he didn't have much time left in which to do that. So, whenever Hans got a chance, he and others who were disgusted with their prospects, got even by vicious graffiti, acts of vandalism, making noise, rioting, demonstrating, and outraging the bourgeoisie in any way he could, thus venting his fury at having been born in so weak-kneed and stupid a period. Hans knew that the only feeling inside himself was the terrible hatred he felt for all those who represented what he feared he would turn into some day.

Then Terry had come along. She had appeared one day in his group, which claimed to have no regard for any property. And her gray eyes had cast a spell on him. She had let him hold her hand and lay his head on her shoulder, and one evening she had even let him kiss her. But when his hands had tried to explore her hips, she had firmly pushed him away, leaving no doubt that sex was off limits.

When he had seen her let herself get carried off by the phony jerk in that Rolls-Royce, Hans felt as if a knife had been stuck through his heart. Triumphant, shameless display of wealth, pretentiousness, self-satisfied smugness— the guy either had to be a bastard or a pimp.

Hans climbed up to her landing and knocked on the

door. By the very sound of his knuckles on the wood, he could tell there was nobody home. He remembered that Lucy had gone off to visit some friends and he wondered if Terry had gone with her. He was piqued in his jealousy and sat down on the landing, deep in thought, determined that, come what might, he would not budge until Terry had come home.

"Why," Alan was wondering, "didn't I ask her to come with me tonight?" He felt certain that the time at his disposal was very limited, and that he had probably just wasted the one chance he had to get to see her again.

His eyes heavy with sleep, he came out of the bathroom, drying himself off. The huge, low bed attracted him like a magnet. He let himself down on it, closed his eyes, and tried to recall every feature of Terry's face. Immediately the faces of all the other women he had ever known before were swept right out of his mind. He realized how foolish and empty his life had been, how futile the dreams of grandeur that Sam Bannister had filled him with. Terry had blown through his life like a great salutary wind.

He got up, walked over to the bar, and poured himself a glass of whiskey which he sipped deliberately, sitting on the edge of the bed. He looked at his watch. It was eight o'clock.

Elsewhere throughout the hotel the guests must have been getting themselves ready for tonight's benefit. But everything that had happened since he got to Cannes now seemed somewhat unreal. Had he really gone to Rome last night? Did all those people who had invited him to tonight's party really exist? As soon as any of these ideas took lasting shape in his mind, Terry's gray eyes appeared and drove them right out. Her image overwhelmed everything else. His glass slipped from his hand. He was about to doze off again. The telephone rang.

"This is the concierge, sir," a voice said. "There's a gentleman here asking for you. May I put him on?"

"Who is it?" Alan inquired in a semi-comatose state.

But the concierge had not heard him. Now, there was a different, rough voice on the wire, speaking to him in atrocious English.

"Mr. Pope? I am Captain Le Guern. Your yacht is ready for you now."

"Yacht?" Alan croaked. "What yacht are you talking about?"

"The *Victory II*, sir, the one you rented as of July twenty-sixth. This is July twenty-sixth, and I am awaiting your orders to set sail, sir."

Alan was floored; he couldn't answer. The whirlwind that had engulfed him since his arrival in Cannes had made him totally forget the fact that he had chartered a yacht.

"Did you hear me, Mr. Pope?"

"Yes, Captain."

"Everything is ready for you, sir. Would you like the crew members to come and get your luggage and move you aboard? I took the liberty of having the chef prepare dinner for you."

Alan almost yelled yes at the top of his voice. To get on board, sail away, and forget his troubles . . . He tried to remember whether he had paid in advance for the yacht charter in New York, but he couldn't recall.

"Where are you docked, Captain?" he asked.

"In the Old Port, sir, just opposite the Winter Casino at the end of the pier. It's the *Victory II*. I can have a car bring you right down."

"Listen, Captain . . . ," Alan started to say.

But his sentence hung unfinished. He could hardly tell the man that he hadn't had any sleep for days and days. And yet . . . A yacht! The idea of having a yacht all to himself! He was dying to see it.

"I'll be right down, Captain," he said.

"I'll be waiting for you in the lobby, sir."

Staggering, but inexplicably excited, Alan slipped into a pair of trousers.

"Hi, there," Sam Bannister said to the super. "You recognize me? I'm a friend of Alan Pope's."

The super gave him a very strange look.

"He asked me to come by and pick up his mail," Sam told him.

"Why? Did he go away? I hadn't heard."

"He had to go on an unexpected business trip," Sam improvised. "Probably didn't have a chance to let you know."

"Will he be away long?"

"Just for a few days. Is there any mail for him?"

"Look, if you're his friend," the super said, "maybe he gave you the money for his July rent."

"Why, did he forget to pay it? You really mean that?"

"Yes, I do," the super insisted. "And here it is the twenty-sixth. Not that I don't think Mr. Pope'll pay it, but I could get in trouble if the landlord knows how late he is."

Sam took out his checkbook. "I'll take care of that right away!"

Considering the mess he had gotten Alan into, this was the least he could do. Just one thing, though: He wasn't sure he had enough money in his account. Crystal never let his paycheck get out of her hot little hands, and she kept him on a very short tether.

"Whatever I take will be that much less for you to spend in saloons," she would tell him.

The super watched attentively as Sam made the check out. When Sam gave it to him, he checked the amount, folded it, and put it in his pocket.

"There is one letter," he said in a very noncommittal tone. "It was delivered by messenger, to be given to Mr. Pope personally. It's from his bank."

Bannister's blood beat against his temples like a blacksmith's hammer. He grabbed the manila envelope, said thanks to the super, and walked out. He went as far as the corner, turned, and ducked into a doorway. With trembling hands, he tore the envelope open. He read the two lines of text in it, then had to lean back against a wall in order not to collapse.

"Have you charted a course, sir?"

La Guern could not know that a cruise was out of the question, so Alan played along with him.

"Not yet. What would you suggest, Captain?"

"Well, we could remain in the Mediterranean, sir—Corsica, Sardinia, Portofino, Rapallo, Santa Margherita, or else Capri, if you prefer. Or the island of Elba. Will you have many guests aboard?"

Alan looked obliquely at him.

"No—uh, that is, not right away," he said.

Le Guern looked like a stereotype of the old sea wolf

with his blue eyes, gray hair, deep wrinkles, and deeply tanned skin.

The car turned onto the Quai Saint-Pierre.

"Where have you just been, Captain?" Alan asked.

"Corsica. We did a lot of deep-sea fishing."

"Much of a catch?"

"Monsieur d'Almeida filled practically all our food requirements with what was caught. This is it."

He pulled the car up facing the gangplank.

"This evening, I'm just going to give her the once-over," Alan said, averting his eyes from the yacht.

He was living one of those rare moments in a lifetime when a human being is confronted with his dream come true. Subconsciously, he was afraid he'd be disappointed. He took a deep breath and turned to look at *Victory II*. She was superb!

The yacht was white, sleek and solid-looking where she lay. She was even more handsome than he had dreamed! Two sailors stood at the head of the gangplank to welcome him. He shook their hands and stepped onto the rear deck.

Passersby walking along the dock looked enviously at the yachts that were berthed there. Alan understood that what separated the privileged from the poor, the wealthy from the mediocre, reality from imagination, was no more than the length of the gangplank. On land were those who dreamed of cruises. On deck, one gangplank away, were those who went on them.

"This is the saloon," Le Guern said, standing aside to let him through.

Its woodwork was of dark mahogany, and it had a bar, low tables, a tv set, and seascapes on the walls.

"The dining saloon is on the upper deck. Would you like to see your cabin?"

Alan passed a chambermaid and two stewards in white uniforms, who greeted him as he went by.

The sight of the cabin took Alan's breath away. The bed had to be larger than any he had ever seen. The furnishings were overwhelmingly luxurious. The cabin itself was spacious enough to ride a bicycle around in it.

"How many other cabins are there?" he asked non-committally.

"Six, sir. Two of them very large, the balance smaller."

"How big is the crew?"

"In addition to me and my second in command," Le Guern informed him, "there are eight men and two cooks."

"Pretty self-contained, isn't it?"

"It could circle the globe easily," Le Guern smiled to him. "This is a very good ship."

All you needed was a little money; then anything became possible. One's dreams would all come true. But was it really as simple as that? Alan wrenched himself away from the illusory dream that was seducing him.

"I have to get back now, Captain," he said. "I'm expecting some calls. We'll meet again tomorrow."

"At your command, sir. But it's too bad to lose a day of sailing," Le Guern commented pointedly.

The captain drove Alan back to the Majestic. Alan went up to his suite, feeling ill at ease with all the contradictory sensations he had. There was his highly volatile situation, his anxiety, his sudden love for Terry, the fabulous toy he had just visited which was his for the moment, the fortune that had melted away through Nadia's fingers, Sam Bannister, Norbert, Hackett, Hamilton Price-Lynch, the pomp and circumstance. He kept meeting these people who seemed to live on some alien planet where all the laws of behavior he had learned to live by no longer applied.

There were too many shocking new things to put up with. He felt it would be weeks before he could sort it all out in his mind, analyze it, figure out what was going on. Others, unlike himself, had enjoyed these privileges all their lives. Did they, he wondered, take advantage of them as much as people who had merely dreamed about them?

He shut the curtains, took off his clothes, and got into bed. Maybe, if he slept a little more . . .

The phone rang.

"Well, are you ready?" a voice asked. "This is Sarah. It's nine o'clock, you know."

"I can't, Sarah, it's really out of the question. I'm sorry to do this to you, but I can't help it."

"Did I hear you correctly? We have a place for you at our table, you know. You're sitting on my right."

"Listen, Sarah—"

"I'm warning you, Alan," she cut him off. "If you're not down here in the lobby, all dressed and ready to go in ten minutes, I'm coming up to break down your door. And don't think I won't do it!"

She hung up. Alan didn't know too much about her, but from her tone of voice, he believed that she might mean what she said. Discouraged, knowing he was licked, he rang for the floor waiter.

"Let me have a double espresso as soon as possible," he said, "and make it as strong as you can."

He went into the bathroom, looked forlornly at his reflection in the mirror, then hopped under the shower, alternating hot and cold water to try to get himself going. He took a white raw-silk spencer out of his closet and slipped it over his naked torso, but then shook his head, took it off, and started to dress.

The phone rang again.

"Mr. Pope, New York is calling you, sir."

Alan gritted his teeth.

"Alan, don't hang up, this is Sammy," he heard.

"Drop dead!"

"Don't do this to me, Alan," Sam begged. "I can't make heads or tails out of what's going on."

"You think I can?" Alan yelled back.

"I'm at my wits' end! I just went by your place to see if you had any mail. Know what I found there?"

"The FBI?"

"Hold on, Alan," Sam warned. "There was a letter from Burger Bank."

Alan tightened up; this was it!

"They've credited more money to your account, Alan! I think I must be going crazy. They've credited another two million dollars to you!"

"You're lying," Alan answered. "You're scared shitless and you're putting me on."

"No, I'm not, Alan, I swear to you," Sam said. "Two million bucks. I have the notice right here in my hand."

"Throw it in the wastebasket," Alan told him. "I don't want any part of it."

"Alan, listen to me. It's on the level!"

"Bullshit, man! Why don't you shove it?" Alan hung

up, and grabbed his head in both hands. Everything was topsy-turvy; nothing made sense anymore. And he was frightened.

The phone rang again.

"Alan? It's Sarah! I'm on my way up for you."

He heard himself say, "I'll be right down."

"Well, then hurry," she demanded.

The waiter rang the doorbell, and entered Alan's suite. "Your coffee, sir."

Alan gulped it down as if it were medicine. Then he tied his bow tie and slipped into his shoes.

The phone again.

"It's the concierge, sir. You're expected in the lobby."

"I know, I know. I'll be right down," Alan answered irritatedly.

Still wondering what the hell that call from Sam Bannister could mean, he poured himself a shot of Scotch and downed it quickly, then slammed the door behind him as he went out.

There were several people in formal evening attire waiting for the elevator. Alan was the last one in, and he was struck by the pervasive scent of perfume in that padded steel cage.

The hotel lobby was alive with people. He looked about to see where Sarah was, but did not find her. He stepped out onto the front step. Serge the doorman rushed up to him.

"Ah, Mr. Pope, here you are, sir! All of these gentlemen are here for you . . ."

Alan saw a huge gunmetal-gray Mercedes bristling with antennae, and three Rolls-Royce convertibles, two white, and one garnet-red. The four uniformed chauffeurs came toward him in unison. Of the four, he knew only one: his own.

"Sir," Norbert said to him, "there must be some kind of misunderstanding. All of these drivers say they are here to pick you up. They have been sent by Mr. Price-Lynch, Mr. Goldman, and Mr. Larsen."

Alan noted that each chauffeur had left the back door of his car open, ready for Alan to get in.

"Did you get it repainted?" he asked Norbert, nodding toward the two white Rolls-Royces.

"No, sir. There was another available just like it."

"Ah, here he is at last!" Sarah announced, grabbing him by the arm. "Who says it's always the women who keep everybody waiting?"

And, as if it were the most natural thing in the world, she shoved Alan into the Price-Lynch Rolls-Royce.

The small restaurant was overflowing with its youthful customers. Tony the owner called a few orders to his waiters, who were scurrying among the tables. He dried his hands on his apron, put both his fists on the table, and leaned over to talk to Hans.

"I was able to trace it for you. The Rolls-Royce is a rental from Carlux, an agency on Rue d'Antibes. It was rented by an American named Alan Pope. He's staying at the Majestic."

Hans shoved his chair back.

"Keep your shirt on, young fellow," Tony advised. "Nobody kidnapped your Terry on you. You told me yourself that she got in willingly."

"Thanks, Tony," Hans yelled back, paying no attention to the restaurateur's counsel.

He rushed out and jumped on the back seat of a huge motorcycle that was idling noisily out front.

"Go, Eric!" he shouted. "We're heading for Cannes!"

The cycle reared, then took off like a rocket. Hanging on to his friend's shoulders, the wind whistling in his ears, Hans was consumed with a desire for destruction. After sitting around for two hours on Terry's landing, he had decided it was time to take things in his own hands.

Tony knew everybody on the coast, and having been the local *pétanque* champion gave him an in with people that most others didn't have. Before opening his restaurant, Tony had also been a policeman for a couple of years, so he still had access to help from the force.

Hans had given him the license number of the Rolls-Royce, which he had made a note of at Juan-les-Pins. It had taken only three phone calls for Tony to get all the facts about it.

"Step on it, Eric!"

Hans had dragged him away from his table, saying, "I'm gonna need your wheels. You coming along?"

Now the two of them were out for blood.

They had met a few days earlier at the Juan-les-Pins

Jazz Festival. Hans had had no trouble at all in finding recruits to join him in spelling out on the walls what was wrong with the world.

The cycle tore down Rue d'Antibes, and turned left onto the Croisette.

"Let me off here," Hans said. "I'll be right back."

He straightened his windblown hair, using his fingers as a comb, and walked the last few yards to the Majestic.

He walked with self-assurance through the open-air courtyard and stared insolently at all the old farts dressed in monkey suits so that their old ladies could show off their fine jewels. What a waste! Why was it that all the great cars had to belong to characters who didn't deserve them? He made his way through the mob of tuxedos and evening gowns. The overworked concierges hardly even noticed him.

"Alan Pope, please," he asked at the desk.

"He just left for the charity ball at the Palm Beach, sir."

"Alone?"

"No, with a lady."

The attendant in the blue uniform had answered the questions without really paying any attention to who had asked them. He was busy answering ten people at once, in as many different languages.

Hans left the hotel fuming with jealous rage. The lady he had taken to the Palm Beach couldn't be anyone but Terry! Just because he was in a Rolls-Royce, she was available.

"Where are we going now?" Eric wanted to know.

"Back to Juan."

"How about your bird?"

"Don't ask. Just get going."

"You find her?" Eric insisted.

"Some bastard took her to a shitty charity ball. We're going back after the gang. Those bastards want to have some fun? Well, we'll go have some fun too!"

"Where?"

"At the Palm Beach."

21

Sarah clung to Alan's arm. The photographers' bulbs were popping on all sides, and the parking attendants, drenched in sweat, were quickly jumping behind the wheels of empty cars in order to clear the circular driveway of the bottleneck of waiting vehicles. Despite the heavy security service, dozens of gapers and gawkers had made their way past the metal guardrails that were supposed to hold them back, and were now edging closer to the arriving guests. Almost every one of the latter corresponded to a name, the figure of a huge bank account, or a famous product trademark, which the onlookers often chanted in a friendly singsong.

A hefty brigade of ancien-régime footmen escorted the guests of the gala until they were safely past the first shock of the crowd. Sarah, like many other female guests, was wearing a diadem of precious stones in her hair, and was now holding it in place with her hand as she entered. Some twenty yards beyond in the lobby of the Palm Beach casino, there was a quiet zone, away from the human whirlwind outside. The lobby seemed endless as it stretched between its marble basins filled with floating aquatic blossoms.

At its end was the doorway of the ballrooms leading to the Terrace of the Iron Mask, with another terrifying bottleneck of people. There the casino employees tried to verify the printed invitations in the light from torches carried by additional ancien-régime footmen.

Never in his life had Alan made so gaudy an entrance anywhere. Inclined to stand back rather than push himself, he let Sarah take charge. Holding his hand firmly in hers, she led the way, forcing a passage through a tide of tanned bodies emblazoned with precious jewels, shouldering aside evening jackets that clanked with the medals decorating them. They finally cleared the last obstacle, darted ahead, and came out on the terrace which was illuminated

233

by thousands of candles on the flower-draped tables,
around which circulated a Brazilian band playing bossa
novas. Waiters and captains were rushing around in all
directions, their arms full of magnums of champagne.

"Your table, Madame."

A waiter led them down the aisle, while hundreds of
pairs of eyes gaped avidly at them. Sarah, heiress to the
Burger Bank fortune, was considered one of the most
attractive catches on earth. Who could that be with her?

"You haven't made any comment about my dress," she
said to Alan, paying no apparent attention to the curiosity
their entrance had aroused.

She was holding his arm again and moving forward
with a determined step, thrilled by the pleasure of seeing
and being seen. She greeted certain celebrities as she went
by, her smile in each case measured according to the
importance of the person it was addressed to. Alan felt
terribly embarrassed, as if he were her dachshund being
lead in on a leash.

"Do you like it, or don't you, Alan?" she demanded.

Not knowing what to say, he made a face that was
supposed to be a smile.

"Always last!" Cesare di Sogno jovially greeted her.

He had risen to greet Sarah, and as he bent in two to
kiss her hand, he added, "Just like the stars."

To his extreme distaste, Alan had to go around the
whole table and be introduced to every one of the other
guests. When Arnold Hackett enthusiastically shook his
hand, he had to control himself in order not to turn and
run in terror. But Cesare had a solid grip on him.

"I'm sure you know all of our friends," Cesare had
said, as he introduced them in turn. "The Duke and
Duchess de Saran, Mrs. Hackett, Hamilton Price-Lynch
and Mrs. Price-Lynch, Honor Larsen, of course, Miss
Betty Grone, Julie and Lou Goldman. Well, I guess that's
everybody. I didn't miss anyone, did I? So, why don't you
take your seat, and let's all have a good time."

His hands clammy from having shaken so many other
hands, Alan sat down on the chair he was shown. Sarah
was on his left, and on his right the Duchess de Saran.

She sensed that he was looking at her. She smiled
mysteriously at him, as she whispered, "I sent your

clothes to be cleaned. They'll be delivered to your suite tomorrow morning."

Alan blushed to the roots of his hair. Not for a second had he realized that this ethereal, sophisticated creature could be the black-and-blue-marked man-eater who had jumped him that very morning in her cabana. Instinctively, he glanced over toward the duke who, as it turned out, was staring at him. Alan quickly looked away, only to have his eyes meet those of Hamilton Price-Lynch, who was also eyeing him with interest.

Caviar was served.

"People today are absolutely crazy!" Arnold Hackett commented, as he spread a half-inch-thick slab of caviar on a slice of toast. "They make revolutions, and protest, and don't want to work anymore! Working people think they ought to be in charge, and the poor think the world owes them a living. A good war might not be such a bad thing!"

He bit off half of his canapé with one healthy clamp of his dentures.

"We have the same kind of troubles in the film industry," Goldman concurred. "Extras today all want to be stars the first time they're in a movie. Every stagehand thinks he's another Orson Welles!"

Hackett pointed his finger at Alan.

"Let me tell you something, young man, because I've seen a lot more of this world than you have. You know how I go about keeping the people in my company on their toes? Every year when summer rolls around, we let a few heads roll. Scares the hell out of everybody! A few dozen get the gate, and then you should see how hard the others work!"

"His bark is worse than his bite," Sarah whispered. "Why aren't you eating?"

"When I was twenty," Hackett was orating again, "believe me, it took some true grit to make your way in the world."

"Arnold, you are and always will be twenty," Cesare said, as he lifted his glass. "Let's drink a toast to all those who know how to retain a twenty-year-old heart!"

"Are you going to be staying here long?" Mandy de Saran asked with feigned indifference.

"A few days, I guess," Alan said.

"You absolutely must come out on our yacht with us," she told him.

"Alan, shall we dance?" Sarah cut in, having already started to stand up.

As he pushed his chair back, she grabbed his hand, and led him out onto the floor.

"Look me in the eye," she said as they danced. "I asked you a question a little while ago. I don't like it when people give me evasive answers. What color is my dress? Do you even know? No cheating now! You just looked at it. Do you like it? Or are you one of those men who claim they never see what the woman in their arms is wearing?"

She held him tighter, rubbed her cheek against his, and whispered into his ear.

"Do you know that you're a very handsome man? The duchess couldn't take her eyes off you. They say she drops her pants as readily as her glasses. And as you can see, she doesn't wear glasses. Hah! Poor Hubert. He's one of the most noble of all French noblemen, but he's like a dummy in the hands of that tart."

With the tips of her nails, Sarah was teasing the back of his neck.

"Have you ever been married?" she asked.

"Yes," Alan said.

"Long?"

"Long enough not to want to be."

She noticed that he was looking at something behind her back, turned her head, and saw that Betty Grone was eyeing him.

"You like her?" she asked.

"Who?"

"That woman you were staring at. The one dancing with Larsen. Betty Grone."

"I wasn't staring at her!" Alan protested.

"Fibber! She has gorgeous eyes and a lot of other things that used to be gorgeous. They say she's been selling it for the last twenty-five years in order to build up a cattle holding. And she either owns all the cattle in Australia by now, or else she must be giving discounts. You like that kind of love for sale? We're having lunch at the offshore islands tomorrow. I hope you'll be on time."

"I'm not free," Alan told her.

"Oh, I adore you," she said, as she buried her head against his chest. "You act just like a young girl who's sweet sixteen and afraid to be raped. Have you ever been raped, Alan?"

"Yes," he said.

She snuggled even closer to him.

"I'm not surprised," she answered. "What's it like to have all the women in the world trying to get into your pants?"

At this point, a company of whirling gypsy dancers and violinists invaded the dance floor. They spread around the terrace in a bewildering flow of Slavic music. The guests who had been dancing were driven back toward their tables with a great clanking of precious gems.

"I'd like to dance," the duchess said a little later to Alan.

Sarah put a possessive hand on Alan's arm. "He's already promised me the next one." Her smile was viciously polite.

"Sarah, won't you do me the honor?" Hackett asked.

"Arnold, what about my lobster?"

"Sorry, twenty-year-old hearts come first!"

She got up unwillingly, gave a knowing, possessive look to Alan, and then let Hackett lead her off in his stiff, jerky dance rhythm. Once again, Alan noticed that Price-Lynch's eyes were upon him. He felt uncomfortable and turned his head away. His eyes met those of Betty Grone, who was discreetly giving him the come-hither.

"You enjoying yourself, Mr. Pope?" Larsen asked, as he sat down in Sarah's seat. "Just what kind of business was it that you said you were in?" he asked without waiting for an answer to his first question.

Alan made an inconclusive gesture. In order to gain some composure, he took a gulp of champagne.

"Have you ever been convicted of anything?" Larsen asked.

Alan choked on the wine, and had trouble not spitting out what was in his mouth. Larsen gave him several friendly claps on the back which felt like so many blows of a battering ram and only made him cough the more.

"Never!" he finally succeeded in getting out.

"Good. Do you know who I am?" Larsen asked him politely. "I am the largest stockholder of Sekandier

Aeronautics. I'd like to have a private conversation with you. Could we arrange that? The sooner the better."

"Honor, do I get my seat back or do I have to sit on your lap?" Sarah asked, as she returned.

Larsen quickly got up, leaned over Alan, and whispered to him, "I'll be in touch with you during the course of the night."

"What were you two plotting together?" Sarah wanted to know. "Was he asking your advice about how much he ought to let Betty take him for? Hackett, that old klutz, nearly trampled my toes off."

"Sarah!"

"No, thanks," she answered Cesare di Sogno dryly.

Then she started in on her cold lobster.

"Inedible. I don't want any more," she said, pushing her plate away.

"Wherever you go, you seem to be the center of attraction," she said to Alan. "How do you do it?"

Alan was going to answer, but Hubert de Saran was gallantly kissing Sarah's hand, saying, "I love these slow fox-trots. I know you won't turn me down."

Sarah danced off with him.

"I'd like to dance," the duchess said once again.

Alan got up and led her to the floor. She was almost as tall as he, but danced so lightly that he could barely feel her in his arms.

"Did you like it?" she asked.

"What?" he replied.

"This morning."

Her body rubbed against his.

"Your husband is watching us," Alan warned.

"I tell him everything I do," she said. "When this dance is over, I'll go out to the ladies' room. Come and join me."

He thought he must have misunderstood her. There was a haughty, aloof smile on her lips. She was carrying herself very straight, majestically. Only her mound, pulsating with a life of its own, was rubbing in insistent waves against Alan's crotch.

"I'll be waiting for you," she said, without changing her cool, faraway expression.

Alan accompanied her back to the table. She took her gold-threaded bag and walked toward the ladies' room without paying attention to anyone. Lou Goldman grabbed

Sarah's arm as she was returning to her seat. Hamilton Price-Lynch immediately made a beeline for the chair that the duchess had left empty.

"I have to talk to you, Mr. Pope," he said.

This, thought Alan, is the end.

"Here?" he mumbled.

"Be in your suite sometime during the night. I'll call you."

He smiled dazzlingly at his wife. She had not taken her eyes off him while pretending to listen to the small talk she was hearing from Victoria Hackett.

Suddenly, all the lights went out. The men instinctively hugged their partners—not out of affection, but to keep unseen hands from taking advantage of the darkness to snatch their jewelry. Gil Houdin appeared in a debauch of spotlights.

"Mr. President . . . Highnesses . . . Ladies and Gentlemen . . . ," he announced.

"The circus is going to start," Sarah whispered to Alan. "What was my stepfather saying to you?"

Cesare was kissing the hand of Julia Goldman, whom he had just taken back to her seat. Alan thought derisively of Mandy de Saran waiting for him in the ladies' lounge.

"Alan, what are you thinking about?" Sarah asked.

" . . . so wonderful of you not to forget them, to be ready to help them with your great, generous hearts . . . ," the voice of Gil Houdin was going on, " . . . appreciate your generosity . . . auction . . . I thank you in advance on behalf of those in need. Thank you, one and all!"

For the first time, Alan now looked Sarah in the eye. He had lost everything, so there was no longer anything to worry about. Sarah didn't scare him anymore—neither she, nor anyone else.

The voice of the auctioneer was droning on.

" . . . A major work by Chagall . . . Fifty thousand dollars for the good of the cause. Do I hear sixty? Sixty, on the right. Who says more? Seventy? Thank you, Mr. President. Eighty? Ninety! Any museum in the world would be delighted to get it. A hundred!"

Sarah took Alan's hand under the table.

"You know, Alan, you're a strange man," she said. "Hard to figure out."

"A hundred and twenty thousand from the President...A hundred and fifty thousand. Thank you, Princess!"

"A hundred and sixty," Hackett called out, even though his appreciation of art hardly went beyond the nude pinups on office calendars.

Betty nudged Honor Larsen. "Your turn," she whispered.

He looked at her, not getting her drift. "It's for charity," she said. "Bid something."

"How much?"

"Two hundred."

"Two hundred!" Honor Larsen called out, raising his arm.

"Two hundred," the auctioneer roared back. "Who'll top two hundred?"

There was a commotion near the main entrance. Surrounded by a vast entourage of friends and sycophants, Prince Hadad was making his appearance. All eyes turned toward him.

"Come on, gentlemen, is that all I am offered for this superb Chagall? Two hundred thousand? Two hundred thousand once! Does anyone say two ten?"

"The sheik of Araby," Sarah snorted.

Like everyone else, Alan had turned to see this group of late arrivals. Hanging on to Prince Hadad's arm was a ravishing creature in a white gown, glittering with diamonds and precious stones. Alan's heart skipped a beat. It was Marina!

At the same moment, Hackett was adjusting his glasses, unable to believe that his eyes were really seeing Marina.

Following a group of torch-bearing footmen, the prince and his entourage were nearing the huge table that had been reserved for them. Alan was sure he had to be dreaming, but when Marina was ten yards away from him, he impulsively raised his arm to hail her. Immediately, the spotlight picked him out and blinded him.

"Two hundred and ten thousand," the auctioneer was shouting breathlessly. "Two hundred and ten thousand right here before me!"

"Are you really that crazy about Chagall?" Sarah said to Alan to hide her surprise at his bid.

"I beg your pardon?"

Marina was passing right by him, without seeing him.

"Two hundred and ten thousand, gentlemen. The last bid is two hundred and ten thousand dollars."

No more hands went up. In a blink of the eye, the auctioneer had taken in the whole of the Hadad party which was settling down at its table, with much squeaking of chairs on the floor. This contretemps had completely broken the spirit of the auction. It was very hot, and he felt this was the last place he wanted to be.

"Then, if there is no further bid on the Chagall, gentlemen, it is two hundred and ten thousand once, two hundred and ten thousand twice, sold to the gentleman there for two hundred and ten thousand dollars!"

There was a roar of applause throughout the terrace.

"Please, sir. If you don't mind, sir. Would you come up here," Houdin was urging. "Do come up, please."

Sarah nudged Alan sharply with her knee and said, "Well, what are you waiting for?"

"What?" he asked, truly perplexed.

He couldn't understand why he was suddenly in the limelight. Two blond hostesses in blue uniforms were at his sides, each taking one of his arms. Totally nonplussed, but still caught in the beam of the light, he was firmly shoved up onto the stage.

"My congratulations, sir!" Houdin said to him, as he gave him a hearty accolade.

There were ten mikes in front of him, and Houdin had a firm grip on him. The two hostesses were holding the Chagall up for everyone to see. Houdin stepped back, and Alan stood in the spotlight, holding his painting which they had just handed him. Everyone applauded and cheered him. The girls took the painting back from him, and Houdin said in a low voice:

"Write your check now. I'd like everyone here to see it!"

Alan looked at him as if he had lost his mind. And at just that moment, three motorcycles came roaring onto the terrace with an earsplitting racket.

The guests all thought this was a staged gangster act, and they began to applaud, the bejeweled dowagers waving their hands in delight. Simultaneously, ten other cycles came up from the other side, onto the stage, crossing it like bombshells and gliding on down onto the nearest tables, smashing glasswear and dishes. The whole terrace began to reek of acrid motorcycle exhaust. One cyclist, grabbing a huge, chocolate cream cake from a waiter, hurled it onto the face and the immaculate stiff shirt of a fleet admiral.

The guests now realized that they had actually been invaded.

"Quick! Call the police!" Gil Houdin shouted to his captains.

Countless cycles were now circulating madly among the tables, driven by a ragged horde whose peaked helmets made them look like medieval warriors. In a breathtaking, nightmarish whirlabout, they shouted obscenities as they smashed and destroyed anything they could reach. The passengers riding on the back seats pulled at the tablecloths, bringing down in a shower of glass and clatter of silver everything that was on them, including the flower vases, pastries, and the magnums of champagne.

"Bring the gypsies back!" Houdin was ordering. "Music! Music! On with the dance!"

Half the cycles took off with a shattering whistle, rushing into the hallway and going through the main entrance, brushing aside the lobby attendants like tenpins.

Around the gaming tables, there was a panic. Everybody was trying to grab his ante and—if possible—rip off the next player's at the same time. The croupiers were defending the stacks of chips with their rakes, and waiters were throwing whatever they could lay their hands on at the attackers—trays, pots, piles of dishes, hams, anything heavy enough to knock a man off his motorcycle. Some of the more athletic footmen jumped the riders and wrestled them to the ground.

A number of the cycles went behind the bar, knocking down the rows of bottles, then rode into the kitchens, where servers, dishwashers, and cooks' helpers, armed with spatulas and vat tops, had fallen back behind a huge buffet stacked with pastry to await the onslaught. A furious fight took place, as the cycles began skidding around on the currant jelly and icing. Hand-to-hand combat was soon taking place in the midst of an overturned vat of whipped cream.

Out on the ravaged terrace, the battle was still going full blast.

"Start the fireworks!" Gil Houdin was yelling.

The sky was suddenly filled with a whirlwind of white suns that lighted up the casino like daylight. Their tuxedos in shreds, the toughest of the guests had formed a square in order to block off the exits with overturned tables.

"Cops!" someone yelled.

The sirens of the police cars could be heard. The motorcycles reared up, climbed over the devastated tables, roared back up the steps to the podium leading to the stage, flew out of the hall of honor into the main lobby, came out of the game rooms and the grill room to disperse in all directions.

On one of the cycles, Hans could be seen. He had found no trace of Terry at the Palm Beach casino. The rodeo he and his friends had put on had not exhausted the fury that was boiling within him, waiting to be vented.

He whistled through his fingers to assemble his riders.

"On to Monte Carlo!" he yelled. "Let's smash the works!"

BOOK IV

22

"I'm going to bed," Emily announced.

"I'll be right there, darling." Hamilton Price-Lynch smiled sweetly at her. "I'm just squeezing your orange juice for you."

This was a ritual. For fifteen years now, he had to squeeze two or three oranges for her, so she could have fresh juice for a nightcap. He also had to hold out a light for her the minute she placed a cigarette between her lips. Hamilton opened doors for her, kept still when she was speaking, pretended to be concerned about her when she was silent, soothed her endless headaches, approved of all selections she made for her wardrobe, silently put up with the poisoned arrows that her daughter Sarah aimed at him, and in every way modeled his behavior on his wife's. In exchange for this, as prince consort he was entitled to the external signs of power and glory.

"Well, Hamilton, what are you waiting for?" Emily demanded.

"Just go to bed. I'm coming," he replied.

They had succeeded in standing off to the side while

the melee was going on. It had been, after all, a matter of everyone for himself.

He watched as she went toward the bedroom. At fifty-five, Emily still had a young girl's figure. Hamilton knew that more than one of his male business contacts found her positively attractive. As for himself, she had never been his cup of tea.

When Emily was the wife of Frank Burger III, Hamilton was merely an executive in the bank. Today, he was its managing director and chief executive officer, but only on condition that Emily approved of what he did. And even then, only until Sarah could get him kicked out, or at least aside, so that she could take over.

This was the highly tentative and truly uncomfortable situation that had led him to the decision to make a move, regardless of the fact that he might lose everything by it.

He opened the refrigerator door, took out three oranges, and juiced them into a glass. After making sure there were no pits in the juice, he tiptoed forward and peeked through the partly opened door into the bedroom. Emily was sitting at her dressing table, putting revolting brown cream on her face. He quickly stepped back into the living room, took three pills out of a little box in his pocket, and dropped them into her orange juice. With a spoon, he stirred briskly until they were dissolved.

"Hamilton!" she called.

"Here I am, dear!"

Emily hated to be kept waiting. He carried the glass in to her. She was wiping the excess cream off her face with a tissue.

"Aren't you coming to bed?" she asked.

"I have some papers to go over," he said, as he put her drink down on the night table.

"At three A.M.?" She raised an eyebrow.

"Fischmayer needs an answer right away," he replied. "It'll only take me twenty minutes or so. You weren't too upset, were you?"

"By what?"

"Those hoodlums who ransacked the Palm Beach," he said. "They were enough to upset anybody!"

"I do feel nervous, Hamilton," she conceded.

She slipped between the sheets, took the glass of juice, and swallowed it in one long draught.

He sat down on the side of the bed, took her hand, and kissed it tenderly.

"Very nervous," she repeated.

He knew very well what she was getting at. And it was to be able to meet her physical requirements that he traveled with his briefcase of erotica. It was his connubial shot in the arm, so to speak.

"I'm coming to bed, my love," he said.

He patted her forehead, went back into the living room, and settled himself on the divan with a look of concern on his face. Two days earlier, John-John Newton's money had been received in New York. In order not to have his staff smell a rat, Hamilton had left it in the hands of Chase Manhattan, from which he had demanded—and gotten—twelve percent on the short-term deposit. It was for four days, if everything went off as planned. Unfortunately, Erwin Broker had thrown a monkey wrench in the works. Hamilton had finally decided the man had to be rubbed out only because he saw no other solution to what had developed. Broker was trying to bleed him white. He had threatened to drop a word to Emily about their deal. Hamilton could see that his whole carefully worked-out scheme would soon collapse. He had concocted it for the purpose of getting rid of his wife, inheriting her money, and gaining control of Burger Bank before Sarah had a chance to lay claim to it.

He heaved a deep sigh, and realized what a ludicrous situation he had got himself into. In a few hours, John-John Newton would be asking him for an accounting. If Hamilton was unable to give him the name of the go-between, Newton would pull out, and Hamilton would be facing catastrophe. His last chance to make it work out now depended on that glorified claims clerk who had thought he was going to be able to swindle them out of the fortune erroneously credited to his account!

He looked at his watch. In five minutes, the sleeping powder which Emily had unknowingly swallowed would take effect. Then he would be able to go and see this Alan Pope.

"You were magnificent, Alan," Sarah said.

"Oh, come now, I didn't do a thing," he countered.

"You knocked off one of those motorcycles."

"All I did was pull the tablecloth while he was riding over the table. He skidded."

"If that had been my stepfather instead of you, he would have used my mother as a shield," Sarah assured him.

As soon as the police arrived, Sarah had dragged him away from the Palm Beach commotion. Leaving her car and chauffeur where they were, she had taken him by the arm, and they had walked along the Croisette, surrounded by the clanging of fire engines and the wailing of ambulances.

"Why do you despise Hamilton so?" Alan asked.

"Because he's petty, pretentious, and a perfect phony."

"I don't imagine your mother feels that way."

"He's just her doormat. He hates the very sight of her!"

They were passing Chez Félix. It was a balmy night. On the deserted terrace, two girls and a fellow, astride their chairs, were beating out a blues rhythm on the bongo drums. Alan thought with bitterness that this young woman hanging on to his arm with just a touch too much possessiveness was the heiress to one of the wealthiest private banking establishments in the world, the one through which all of his misfortunes had come about.

"Have you ever been married, Sarah?" he asked.

"No."

"How come?"

"I've never found anyone who could be my master."

Out of the corner of her eye, she could see Alan smile. "Is that so funny?" she asked.

"It's just that you seem to conceive of marriage as a struggle for control."

"Well, isn't it?"

"Not when people trust one another."

"Do you trust people?" she asked.

"Yes."

"And you don't live to regret it?"

"Yes. Almost always," he conceded.

"And still you go right on doing it?"

"I guess it's just the way I'm made," he said. Was Hamilton Price-Lynch going to have him locked up tonight or tomorrow? He was wondering.

He blessed the intrusion of that band of motorcyclists who had saved him from the auction—one more grotesque situation! Eventually, he was going to have to write a check with money he no longer had, for a painting he had not even bid on. It was just seeing Marina on Prince Hadad's arm that had gotten him into trouble!

A few hours earlier, such an encounter would have left him weak in the knees. But in the interim, he had met Terry.

How could it happen, he thought, that a pair of gray eyes and a luscious head of ash-blonde hair could come into one's life and, in just a few hours, sweep away everything that had gone before?

But then how could Marina show up dressed to the nines at a charity benefit in Cannes when only a week before she had never been out of Greenwich Village, didn't seem to know that France even existed, and had almost no clothes at all to her name?

"Caught in the act, Alan," Sarah said. "What were you dreaming about?"

"Nothing," he said.

For just a second, he felt tempted to spill his guts to Sarah, and ask her to help him out of his mess. He no longer knew where it was going to lead, didn't understand what was going on, and wondered what he had gotten himself into. Across the dark harbor, he could see a lighted cruise ship setting out for the high seas. Back in New York, Sam Bannister was probably ready to get into bed and was just watching the late news. Alan felt sorry that he had been brusque with him. All Sam was guilty of was wanting to see his friend do the things that Sam had always wanted to do, but couldn't.

Sarah squeezed his arm.

"Going to buy me a nightcap?" she asked.

He wondered whether Larsen and Price-Lynch had tried to reach him in his room yet.

"I'm awfully tired, Sarah. I'm likely to die if I don't get a few hours' sleep."

"Oh, you'll die sooner or later anyway," she reassured him.

They had crossed the driveway of the Majestic, where one car after another was returning from the Palm Beach casino, delivering its load of rattled millionaires. Hearing them talk, it sounded like every one of them had beaten the gang off single-handedly. Some of them were proudly displaying black eyes or bruises they had gotten during the fray, relating the event with much embroidery to the bemused concierges and desk clerks.

"Alan? How about it?"

"No, Sarah, I really can't." He was firm. "I'm falling off my feet. I hope you don't mind too much."

She gave him one of her mocking smiles.

"No, I don't. But don't you forget. Tomorrow we're having lunch in the islands. I'll meet you in the lobby at eleven o'clock."

And she walked off toward the elevators without even looking back. Alan thought to himself that if he had lunch at all tomorrow, it would probably be in the local lock-up.

While Crystal was fixing supper in the kitchen, Sam went into the bedroom to decide what clothes he was going to take along. It wasn't an easy selection to make: he had never been on the Riviera before.

He listened to the familiar, reassuring sound of pots and pans and dishes rattling. Ever since the evening Sam told her that he had been fired, Crystal had not nagged him about it once. He had continued sleeping in the children's room, and she had gone right on acting as if nothing had changed. Yet, there had been that moment of truth between them, a moment in which they broke a silence that had lasted for twenty-five years. How would she react now on discovering that he was going to go?

"Sam?" she called.

"Yes?"

"It's on the table."

"Here I am."

He checked the lock on his valise one last time, and went into the kitchen.

"You can sit down," she said. "Everything's there."

"Smells good," he said.

He concentrated on his roast chicken leg, with the corn on the cob and broccoli on the side.

She sat down opposite him, opening a can of beer for him and a Coke for herself.

They ate in silence, having nothing to say to one another. But the longer they were silent, the more Sam wondered how he should go about breaking the news of his trip to her. He cleared his throat.

"Crystal . . ."

"Yes?" she asked without looking up, continuing to nibble on her ear of corn.

"I talked to Alan Pope this afternoon. He's in a bad way. Very bad . . ."

She showed no reaction. He poured half the can of beer into his glass.

"I feel sort of responsible, you know," he went on.

"Why should you?"

"Well, he's younger than I am. And I was kind of a big brother to him at Hackett's."

She was carefully pulling the meat off her chicken wing.

"I think he really needs some help," Sam said.

"So the lame will go to the help of the halt," Crystal remarked acidly, barely opening her clenched teeth.

The pact between them was broken! He might as well go whole hog, he felt.

"I'm going to have to go away for a few days," he said.

"Just when you got fired yourself?" she inquired.

"I've got a week's vacation coming," he said.

She flung the half-eaten ear of corn across the table and roared at him. "So where are you going to take it? And who with? With me? No, of course not! With Pope! Pope! Always that Alan Pope! Are you secretly married to him or something?"

"Crystal, it's just that—"

"In no time you're gonna be an unemployed and maybe unemployable fifty-year-old, your wife'll be left without a cent, and you're going off on a vacation with Pope! Don't you think I have a week's vacation coming, too?"

Sam put his napkin down on the table.

After Alan had hung up on him, Sam had had Patsy reserve a seat for him on a plane to Nice. The Burger Bank letter crediting an additional two million dollars to Alan's account had worried him more than all the rest.

Whatever else Crystal might still say to him, he was going to leave the next day, come hell or high water.

"Listen to me, Sam," she warned him. "If you're not here for dinner tomorrow night, don't bother coming back at all. Because I'll be gone."

He realized he was hoping that she meant it.

*   *   *

Alan had long since reached that stage of fatigue when it is no longer possible to sleep at all.

He sat sprawled in an armchair, a highball in his hand. He was truly at the end of the line. Hamilton Price-Lynch would come in at any minute to sound the knell.

There was a knock at the door. Alan opened it. It was Price-Lynch.

"I won't keep you long, Mr. Pope. May I sit down?" he asked.

He was no longer wearing his tuxedo, but had a black cashmere jacket on over an open shirt.

"You don't know who I am," he said to Alan, "but I know very well who you are. You are thirty years old, you've just been fired from Hackett Chemical, and you're having a helluva fling in Cannes with money that was paid to you by mistake by my own bank, the Burger Bank. To be exact, the mistake was one million, one hundred seventy thousand, four hundred dollars. Correct me, if I'm wrong."

Alan didn't make a move or say a word. The tension of the last few days had been so gruesome that he was almost happy to see it coming to an end. In a few more hours, he'd be locked up. He wouldn't be able to see Terry again.

"You didn't really think I was going to let you get away with stealing my money and coming to the Riviera to carry on like a millionaire, did you?"

Alan turned his glass in his hand. The only sound was the clink of the ice cubes in his drink.

"Is that all you have to say to me, Mr. Pope?"

Alan shrugged wearily.

"You know that I could have you arrested any time I want, don't you?" Price-Lynch went on. "I could have you taken from this suite directly to a prison cell."

Alan still did not answer.

"Now, note that I said I *could*. I didn't say I *would*. You see, I think it would be utterly foolish for a young man your age to spend the best years of his life rotting away in some prison. Perhaps there is a better way out of this."

Alan looked up and saw the man's eyes, icy behind a set phony smile.

"I've tried to figure out what you thought you were

doing," Hamilton went on, "tried to put myself in your place. I wondered how an intelligent man could do something so utterly stupid. Stupid, you see, because it inevitably had to turn out badly for you. It was just a question of time. And I could only find one answer, Mr. Pope—spite and rancor. You felt you had been unfairly discharged, and here was a chance to get even. That was it, wasn't it?"

There was a look on Alan's face that Price-Lynch pretended to take for agreement.

"Unfortunately, while you were trying to get even with Hackett Chemical, I'm the one you took it out on. In case you didn't know it, the mistake that was made in your favor was made by my bank. I've been wondering. Had you ever even met Arnold Hackett before last night?"

"No," Alan finally said.

"He's a hard man, one who isn't given to humane considerations. The only thing that counts for him is the bottom line. I can very well understand how people might hate him. I'm not trying to justify your dishonesty, of course, but only trying to figure out what might have motivated it. Now, here's another question: Do you still want to get even with him?"

"No, I don't," Alan humbly admitted.

"In spite of everything Hackett has done to you?"

"He doesn't even know I'm alive."

"Yes, but what would you say if I gave you a chance to pay him off in his own coin?"

"I don't care about it," Alan said.

"What? A man who fired you from your job? Who drove you into a life of crime?"

"Don't dramatize it like that. Just call the cops. It's all the same to me."

"Oh, come now, Mr. Pope."

He looked around and then answered the silent question that he had read on Alan's face.

"Yes, thanks, I'd be glad to have a drink. Considering what you've done to me so far, standing me to a drink is the least you can do." Hamilton laughed.

Alan stared at him, then went to the bar and got the Scotch and some ice.

"Here's to you, Mr. Pope," Hamilton toasted cheerfully. He drank a long gulp and licked his lips.

"What would you say if I told you I came here as your friend?" he asked Alan.

Alan was stock still. Hamilton crossed his hands and tried to concentrate, feeling heartsick at having to risk his plan on such an insignificant, mediocre person.

"Wouldn't you like to ruin the man who so mistreated you, Mr. Pope?" he asked. He took another gulp, in order to let his words sink in to Alan.

"I am making you a very serious proposition, Mr. Pope. I want to give you a chance to get your revenge, and at the same time, wipe the slate clean of what happened between you and Burger Bank. Obviously, before I go into any further detail, I have to know if you are in full agreement. Do you understand what I am trying to tell you?"

"Yes, I do," Alan said, suddenly torn between the desire to forget this whole mess or grab the glimmer of hope that was beginning to emerge.

"Does that mean you agree?"

Alan bit his lips in embarrassment.

"Very well, Mr. Pope. Let me fill you in on everything. This morning I had another two million dollars credited to your account with Burger Bank in New York."

So, Sam had known what he was talking about!

"You'll have to admit that in doing such a thing, I don't seem to be acting like your enemy."

"Why did you do that?" Alan stammered.

"You're in very bad trouble, Mr. Pope. Very, very bad trouble. And I would like to help you out. Besides, I am trying to negotiate a deal unofficially with a man who has a certain financial standing."

"Negotiate what kind of a deal?" Alan asked.

"A deal that should prove to be a lot of fun for you."

"What would I have to do?"

"I want you to buy up control of Hackett Chemical," Price-Lynch informed him.

Alan jumped up as if he had been struck.

"What's that?" he gulped.

"You are going to buy control of Hackett Chemical," Hamilton Price-Lynch repeated in a perfectly calm tone.

"Are you crazy?" Alan gasped.

"Decide that for yourself."

"But Hackett must be worth at least two hundred million dollars!"

"You'll have whatever money it takes," Ham said.

"Nobody will ever believe that I could suddenly be in a position to buy control of the company. I was only a minor employee there until I got fired a few days ago!"

Price-Lynch's mirthless laugh had the rasping sound of a rusty rattle.

"If you can come up with the cash, what anyone believes is completely beside the point, Mr. Pope. No one cares any more about what you used to be than about where your money comes from."

"But what about Arnold Hackett? You think Hackett would hold still for this?"

"That's no concern of yours," Price-Lynch assured him.

"Your deal just won't work," Alan said.

"Not my deal, Mr. Pope, your deal. And it's very simple. Tomorrow, you'll make an announcement with a public tender to buy up all outstanding Hackett stock."

"But, Mr. Price-Lynch," Alan countered, "even if all the small stockholders were ready to sell their shares, it wouldn't do you any good. Arnold Hackett owns the controlling shares of his company. He has sixty percent of all the voting stock. Everybody knows that!"

"Mr. Pope," the banker dryly replied, "if you knew as well as I do what everything is worth and who owns what, why you'd be the chief operating executive of Burger Bank, not me. And I'd be where you are, which is not exactly in clover, you'll have to admit. For the moment, all I want you to do is do what I tell you, and for God's sake, don't try to do my thinking for me. If you do this job for me, you'll come out of it with twenty thousand dollars clear when the whole thing is over. In fact, you can hold it back right now from the one million plus which you are going to return to me."

Alan's face lost its color.

"There's just one problem to that, Mr. Price-Lynch. I don't have that money anymore."

"I beg your pardon?"

"What do you think I was gambling with the other night?"

"Why, you won!" Hamilton indignantly replied.

"Against you, yes. But not against Prince Hadad."

"You mean to say you played against Hadad?" he demanded.

"Not me. My partner. Nadia Fischler. She lost the whole kit and caboodle."

"And you expect me to believe that?" Hamilton asked.

"It's the truth. Everybody who was at the casino knows it. Just ask."

"Why, you thief! You robber! You're lying! I demand that money!" he shouted. "Don't think you can get away with this!"

Hamilton Price-Lynch was standing now, his fists clenched, his eyes bugging out of his head.

"I'll turn you over to the police!" he yelled. "I'll see that you get ten years at least! I'll give you until ten o'clock this morning to return that money that you swindled out of us. Ten o'clock, do you hear me? You work it out any way you want with that high class whore of yours. And let me give you some good advice. Don't get it into your head that you can take a powder. I'm already having you watched!"

He knocked over his empty glass with a swing of his hand and stormed angrily out of the suite. Petrified, Alan stood still and waited for his pounding heart to stop beating so wildly.

He tried to think things through, to make sense out of what had happened. Price-Lynch had given away too much of his scheme. Alan was now in on a secret that was a very dangerous secret to be in on. Hamilton's last words rang in his ears: "I'm already having you watched!"

The best way to test what it all meant was to call Price-Lynch's bluff.

Alan tossed a pair of jeans, a few shirts, and some toilet articles into a traveling bag. It was 3:30 A.M. In a little less than seven hours, he would go knocking on Terry's door. The only thing that mattered to him was to keep his date with her before he got locked up. The time he spent with her would be something no one could take away, whatever happened to him afterwards.

He decided to sneak out of the hotel and find a place to spend the rest of the night. Suddenly he remembered that he had chartered a yacht! Who would think of coming to look for him on a yacht? He walked to the door, and started to grip the handle. Somebody knocked three times on the other side.

The Duchess had given him plenty of occasion to get used to her escapades, but now Hubert de Saran was really worried. Mandy had been alongside him at the height of the riot, when he swung an empty magnum of champagne, trying to throw it at one of the motorcyclists. By the time he let go of it—and missed his target, worse luck!—she was no longer there. In the mad melee that had followed the arrival of the police riot squad, no one had noticed the duchess's disappearance. Everyone was taking care of his own wounds and bumps, checking on what jewels had been lost, how badly their clothes had been torn.

Figuring that Mandy had probably made a connection with one of the motorcycle brutes and gone off for a quickie, the duke felt the better part of discretion was to return to the Majestic. He had then taken a shower and gotten into his pajamas and silk robe with the family coat of arms on it. Now, sitting by the telephone, he was wondering whether he should call the police.

He heard the key turning in the lock. By the time he turned to the door, the duchess was already inside the suite.

"Mandy! What happened to you?" Hubert called. "I was scared to death for you!"

He was not unduly surprised to see that her black chiffon dress was in tatters, that a heel was missing from one of her shoes, that her wild, unkempt hair was full of grass.

"Mandy!" he called again.

She motioned him to be quiet. She leaned back against the wall, closed her eyes, and breathed evenly through her nose with a kind of hissing sound. Her chest was heaving in convulsive waves. He went over to her.

She smelled of motor oil and axle grease.

"Mandy, what did they do to you?" he asked.

"Let me catch my breath, Hubert," she said.

He looked at her more closely. She had marks on her neck that looked suspiciously as if someone had tried to choke her.

"That's not the half of it," she said in a voice that didn't sound like her own. "Look at this..."

She raised the folds of her tattered dress. The duke blanched as he saw the red welts across her skin.

"They whipped me, Hubert," she said.

His eyes bugging out of his head, he could not tear himself away from the sight of those long nacreous thighs marked with red lines from which drops of blood were oozing.

"Did they rape you?" he asked, tremulously.

She nodded.

"How many of them?" he asked.

"I can't remember."

"I'll call the police," he said.

"Oh no, don't, please, Hubert," she said, feebly.

She was staring fixedly at a spot somewhere behind the duke's back.

"It was terrific, Hubert . . ."

Honor Larsen's gigantic figure blocked the whole doorway. He saw Alan holding a suitcase in his hand.

"Were you leaving?" he asked.

"No, of course not," Alan said.

Larsen was still in his tuxedo. Alan had seen him trading punches with the cyclists who had invaded the Palm Beach. But he still looked unruffled.

"I realize this is a strange hour to come calling," Larsen said. "But you know as well as I that some business deals just won't wait."

He looked interestedly toward the bottle of Scotch.

"With ice or without?" Alan asked.

"Without. Ice just spoils the liquor."

Alan was upset. Every minute that went by made it that much harder for him to make a getaway. He looked inquisitively at Larsen.

"Mr. Pope," the large man said, "I'll come right to the point. I want to offer you a deal, but before I do, I'd like to ask you several questions. Are you an American citizen?"

"Yes."

"Where do you live?"

"New York City."

"Do you own a corporation?"

"No."

Honor Larsen looked surprised. "I thought I had understood you to say you were in business."

"I have been without occupation for the last three days," Alan confessed.

"Wonderful!"

Alan looked at him, perplexed. The man surely wasn't coming to see him at this time of night just to make fun of him!

"What are you driving at, Mr. Larsen?" he asked.

The giant hesitated for a moment. "How would you like to act as a go-between, Mr. Pope?"

He mistook Alan's amazement for lack of interest. "Oh, you would get a very good commission," he assured him quickly.

"Would you be more specific? A commission on what?"

"On an order of supplies."

"What kind of supplies?"

"You know very well what line I am in, Mr. Pope," Larsen said.

"Airplanes?"

"Precisely."

"You want me to buy some of your planes?" Alan stammered.

Honor nodded.

"And what would I do with them?"

"All you have to do is lend your name to the deal."

This was the second time in half an hour that he was being asked to become a front man.

"What made you think of me for this deal, Mr. Larsen?"

"Because my usual go-between doesn't happen to be available right now. And the deal has to be concluded within the next forty-eight hours. I have no one else at hand. Would you be interested?"

"How many planes are involved?"

"A hundred."

Maybe exhaustion is finally getting the better of me, Alan thought. He felt his legs giving way under him; he sat down.

"All you have to do is sign the purchase order, Mr. Pope. The planes will be delivered to your name in a foreign country where your customer will have them picked up. You won't have to be involved in any part of it. And for your trouble—if I may put it that way—you would get one-half of one percent of the total amount involved."

"Which comes to?" Alan asked in a dead voice.

"Eight hundred million dollars." Larsen gave a nervous little laugh. "Your commission would be four million dollars."

Larsen was not about to explain that if Alan played hard to get, he was ready to go as high as two percent commission. Otherwise, he'd pocket the difference himself, a mere $12,000,000. It would let him stay a little longer on the Riviera and buy a few more trinkets for Betty.

"Interesting," Alan commented, while trying to sound unimpressed.

A volcano had just erupted inside his brain. The man was offering him $4,000,000! Enough to start over from scratch, pay back everything he owed the Burger Bank, wipe the slate clean, and end this whole nightmare! But would Hamilton Price-Lynch give him enough time to get the cash and pay him back? Would Hamilton accept a promise, when he had given Alan until ten o'clock this morning as a final ultimatum?

"When could the deal be consummated, Mr. Larsen?" Alan asked.

"The sooner the better. Today, I hope."

"Very well, Mr. Larsen. Could we seal the bargain by having you deposit a down payment to my account at a New York bank?"

"Certainly! Would you consider half your commission to be a satisfactory assurance?" And then, so there could be no misunderstanding: "That is, two million dollars."

"I would like to have that down payment credited as soon as the papers are signed," Alan ventured, growing bolder. "Please send instructions for it by telex a little ahead of time. And then, when would I get the balance?"

"As soon as the buyer takes delivery of the shipment," Larsen told him. "Let's say in two weeks. You would be the first to know, since the quitclaim could not be executed without your signature."

"What time could we sign the purchase instructions?" Alan asked.

"Would eight o'clock this morning suit you?"

"That would be fine, yes. Four hours from now. But I'd rather it was outside the Majestic, if you don't mind."

"Where would you like to do it?" Larsen asked.

"Why not aboard my yacht?" Alan said. "It's anchored

right across the way, in the Canto Port. It's called the
Victory II."

23

"How about the Empire State Building, could you buy
that, too?" Marina chortled.

"What would I do with it?" Prince Hadad answered
quite seriously.

"Oh, aren't you the one though," she said.

And she started to giggle. Marina was at that disquiet-
ing state where liquor changes one's view of things without one being actually drunk. It was a long time since she
had had as super an evening as this one, especially with
the excitement of the motorcycle gang coming in and
putting the Palm Beach casino to rack and ruin.

Her beautiful new dress had fallen victim to the onslaught.
It was now lying at the foot of the couch, all spotted with
red wine, torn and shredded, alongside the high-heeled
shoes she had kicked off the minute she got into the
Prince's suite.

"I thought that Arabs weren't allowed to drink liquor,"
she commented.

Hadad raised his glass to her. "We never do in public,"
he said.

He was eyeing her with sincere admiration. She had
nothing on, her whole body entirely free, as if she were
unaware of its power or even its very existence. Hadad
had been speechless when she returned the jewels to him
that had been bought for her that afternoon.

"I don't want these. I don't want anything against my
skin," she told him. "Take them back." Such a lack of
greed was something new to the prince.

He was so fascinated by her that he had not yet gotten
around to exacting the reward due him for what he had
spent on her. At no time had he tried to get near her, even
to fondle her.

He watched her pour champagne into her glass, then

lick the edges of it with little darting moves of her pink tongue. She put it back on the table, and swirled her finger in it.

"It's nice and cool," she said. "I could bathe in it."

Hadad picked up the phone.

"Room service? Please bring ten cases of Dom Pérignon up to my suite immediately. This is Prince Hadad."

He covered the mouthpiece with his hand, and asked Marina, "Do you care what year it is?"

"The year doesn't matter. All champagne tastes the same to me," she told him.

"Fine, if that's the way you feel about it," he said to her, and into the phone, "You can decide on the vintage yourself. I'll be waiting for it."

"You sure are a funny one!" Marina said after he hung up. "Oh, boy! Day is breaking. I better start doing my exercises. You gonna wait for me?"

"Where are you going?" he asked.

"I'll be right back up," she said. "Gotta go to my room for my gym clothes."

Hadad didn't quite trust her. "I'll send my secretary to get them for you," he offered.

"No, why should you?" she protested, as she walked toward the door, an irresistible wiggle to her backside.

"Marina! You can't go out into the hall looking like that!" Hadad called to her. "At least put your dress on."

"It's just one floor up," she answered. "Who cares what I'm wearing?"

And she went out, whistling between her teeth.

Twenty seconds later, a squad of floor waiters arrived, bringing the cases of champagne.

"Empty them into the bathtub," the Prince ordered.

Without so much as blinking, the waiters did as they were instructed. Corks popped like machine-gun fire. When they had finished decanting all the bottles of champagne, the tub was three-quarters full. Just as they were leaving, Marina reappeared, wrapped in one of the hotel's white terry cloth robes, and wearing an old straw hat.

She walked in front of Hadad with a very determined look on her face, and sat down on the bed.

"You'll have to do everything I do," she said to the prince, as she put on a pair of black kid gloves. "Okay?"

"Okay," Hadad agreed, with an amused smile.

She dropped the robe. His throat tightened.

"Well, what are you waiting for?" Marina demanded.

"First tell me what we're going to do," he insisted.

"Push-ups," she said. "Hurry up. Get undressed."

He immediately got out of his clothes as he was told. She planted her feet firmly against the foot of the bed, then let herself fall forward, balancing herself on her hands.

"Okay, now you," she said.

The prince tried to do as she had done. He hit the carpet hard and rolled over; he hadn't had any physical exercise in years. Marina burst out laughing and started doing her push-ups. At thirty-five, she collapsed.

"Time for a bath!" Hadad said.

He could not hide the fact that her exercises had turned him on. He took her by the hand, led her into the bathroom, leaned over the edge of the tub, and took a deep gulp of the amber liquid in it.

"Have a taste," he told her.

Reluctantly, she dipped her tongue into the tub.

"Wow! Champagne!" she shouted, clapping her hands.

She stepped into the tub, let herself down into the champagne, and enthusiastically started lapping it up.

"What time is it?"

Those were the first words that Alan pronounced when he woke up, even before he had opened his eyes. A delicious smell of coffee was tantalizing his nostrils.

"It's seven-thirty, sir."

Alan saw that a young lad in a light blue uniform was standing there.

"Who are you?" he asked.

"Costa, sir. Your personal waiter."

Alan sat up on the bed, rubbed his eyes, and looked around the huge, luxurious cabin. Then it came back to him. He was aboard the *Victory II* and, unless he had been dreaming, Honor Larsen was due there at eight o'clock with a contract for him to sign.

When he had arrived in the middle of the night, Alan had had a bit of trouble convincing the crewman on watch to permit him to come aboard. The sailor had gone to wake Captain Le Guern, who had fallen all over himself with apologies and personally led him to his quarters, where Alan had immediately fallen into a dreamless sleep.

"Just in case, I took the liberty of having the chef prepare some bacon and eggs for you, sir," the waiter told him now. "Would you like them?"

"Yes, please, Costa," Alan said.

He saw that there was a huge tray which, in addition to the coffee he had smelled, had orange juice on it as well as toast, croissants, brioches, jam, butter, and his bacon and eggs.

He had slept less than four hours, yet he felt strangely energetic, all fired up, ready to take on the world. He plowed into the breakfast tray as if he hadn't eaten a thing in a week, then went into the marble-tiled bathroom and took a good, long shower. Through the porthole, he could see the sides of a black sailboat and, beyond that, the quiet waters of the Old Port splashing against the sun-drenched Quai Saint-Pierre.

Alan went back into his cabin, which was on the upper deck, pulled back the curtains, the opened the large bay windows. He stretched, and filled his lungs with the cool morning air.

At 7:55, he was in the main saloon of the yacht. And at 8:00 A.M. on the nose, a crewman led Honor Larsen into his presence.

"You have a very fine yacht here, Mr. Pope," the plane magnate said. "Is it yours?"

"Do you have the papers?" Alan said, ignoring his query.

Larsen put a heavy attaché case down on the table, and took a sheaf of documents out of it.

"Just look them over, if you would," he said. "All you have to do is sign them."

Alan set about reading them.

It turned out that he was about to become the nominal owner of a hundred Cobra helicopters, forty Vikings, twenty-five 105s, and thirty-five Victors.

The shipment was to be sent via freighter to offshore Dakar, outside Senegalese territorial waters.

"What happens after that?" he asked Larsen.

"The buyer's representatives will check on the contents of the shipment, and once they have okayed it, it will be forwarded to its final destination."

"Which is?"

Larsen chuckled good-naturedly.

"What you don't know won't hurt you, Mr. Pope," he said. "All you are supposed to do is purchase the planes and then sell them again."

"But I have to know," Alan insisted.

"May I ask why?" Larsen countered, getting a look of dark concern on his face.

"I'm supposed to get another two million dollars when the final delivery is completed," Alan said.

"And you will."

"How can I be sure of that, if I don't know where and when the delivery is due to take place?"

"You may have my word on it, Mr. Pope. Don't forget, I've had to accept yours," Larsen told him. "Don't ask too many questions."

Alan glanced over the papers once more, and took the pen that Larsen was holding out to him.

"Mr. Larsen, we agreed that I was to get the first two million dollars on signature, right? Now I'm about to sign. Do you have the two million dollars?" he asked.

Once again, Larsen neighed.

"I was ready for that question, Mr. Pope," he replied.

He took a wrinkled document out of his pocket and handed it to Alan.

"Here is the telex from Citibank in New York. It just came in," he said.

Alan read it and nearly burst a gut at this wild new development. He was now the proud owner of a two-million-dollar account at Citibank in New York.

"I could have had the money credited to you in a Swiss bank where you might have had less tax problems, but you said you wanted the money in New York. And as you requested, it was done by certified check. May I ask why you insisted on the certified check, Mr. Pope?" Larsen asked, with a slight tone of complaint. "I've trusted you completely. You are free to spend that money this very minute, if that's what you want to do."

Alan cleared his throat, and asked the question that he was burning to get out. "Why have you trusted me completely, Mr. Larsen?"

The Swede gave him an exquisitely affable smile.

"I am certainly not one to put a price on a human life,"

he told Alan. "But on the other hand, I know that no one's life, not even yours, is worth eight hundred million dollars."

Alan lowered his eyes, looked down, and signed.

Hamilton Price-Lynch couldn't sleep. He got out of bed silently, and looked at Emily. She was dead to the world. He wondered whether he had gone a little too heavy on that sleeping powder.

He went into the living room, got into a pair of ducks and put a tie on his shirt, wondering how he could ever face John-John Newton after last night's fiasco. How stupid it had been of him to lose his temper with that Pope character! Now, he was in a jam. Newton wouldn't let him hold on to the funds for that tender any longer. He looked disgustedly at himself in the antique mirror. He looked like hell, and what's more, his idiotic fit of temper was going to jeopardize his position, his marriage, and cost him $70,000,000.

It was too late to look for some other way out. He was going to have to contact Pope again and convince him to go along on the deal, whatever it might cost to bring him around. Anyway, Pope wouldn't have any choice in the matter. Since he had gambled away the bank's money, it was obvious that he wouldn't be able to return it. Therefore, Price-Lynch had him just where he wanted him.

But the bile flowed up into Hamilton's mouth. By the same token, that lousy Pope now had him in a tight spot, too. All Pope had to do was tell what he had been offered during last night's meeting, and Hamilton Price-Lynch's situation would become untenable. Erwin Broker had died for having tried just that kind of blackmail on him. Now, he had just given Pope exactly the same leverage!

Hamilton put his jacket on, walked out into the seventh-floor corridor, very quietly closing the door to his suite, and walked down two flights. On the fifth floor, he waited until a waiter who was carrying off a breakfast tray was out of sight.

It was eight A.M. He knocked on John-John Newton's door. Panic-stricken though he was, Hamilton tried to put on the countenance of a man who was the bearer of good news.

Newton greeted him with a big smile. "Well, how are things? Is everything settled?" he asked.

"Everything," Price-Lynch lied. "I just need a day or two to work out a few minor details."

Newton gave him a look that froze him to the spot.

"Mr. Price-Lynch," he said, "I've been perfectly happy all these years without having a controlling share in Hackett Chemical. You seem to be running into some snags. If that is the case, I'd appreciate your making a clean breast of the matter to me. Otherwise, I'm ready to pick up my marbles and go home."

"Why, there's no snag at all," Hamilton hurried to reassure Newton.

"You were supposed to let me have the name of that front man over a week ago. Do I have to remind you of the amount of money I've put at your disposal without interest?"

Hamilton smiled a soothing smile. "I can understand your feeling edgy," he said, "but just put yourself in my shoes for a moment. Here I am in Cannes with Arnold Hackett himself. I'm his company's banker. That puts me in a very delicate position, and I can't afford to make a misstep. I have to weigh every little detail before I set the mechanism in motion. Don't you see that?"

"Yes, but this delay was not part of the arrangement that we made. I'm going to have to ask you to pay me interest on the loan for any time during which the money is not used in the manner we agreed upon."

"You certainly don't think I've been putting your money out at short-term interest, do you?" Hamilton demanded.

"Well, I don't like deals that drag out. I'm a man of action. If I don't see an announcement of your tender in the financial pages within the next forty-eight hours, I'll have to pull out."

"John-John," Hamilton wheedled with a honeyed smile, "you very well know that everything'll be settled before that."

"I certainly hope so, for all our sakes," Newton replied coldly.

Hamilton left the interview white as a sheet. He walked back up to the seventh floor by way of the service stairs, and rang several times at Suite 751. Alan Pope was not in.

* * *

Clean-shaven, spick-and-span, his cap pulled jauntily down over one eye, Serge the doorman took a couple of steps toward Arnold Hackett.

"Would you like me to call your car, Mr. Hackett?" he asked.

"No, thanks," Hackett said. "I'm just going out to sit on the terrace."

"Boy!" Serge called to one of the bellhops. "Show Mr. Hackett to a table on the terrace."

It was a glorious day. Children were already at play in the wading pool, under the watchful eyes of nannies and bodyguards. Hackett found a spot between two tables occupied by some British ladies who were enjoying their morning cuppa. He was wearing a gray-green shirt-jacket, the tails of which flapped against his mauve-checked Bermuda shorts. As long as he could remember, Arnold Hackett had always gotten up at six in the morning, even when, as had happened this night, he did not get to bed until four. He opened the *International Herald*, still redolent of printer's ink, and cast a longing look at a tall Nordic blonde in a beach robe and oversized dark glasses who was heading toward the swimming pool. Victoria had fallen asleep with a migraine headache. She wouldn't be up until noon.

He looked toward the west facade of the hotel, counted the floors until he located Marina's window, and saw that it was wide open. Even more than the riot caused by those hoodlums on their motorcycles, seeing Marina come in on the arm of that Arab had been an intolerable shock to him.

Had she spent the rest of the night with that man? he wondered. If that was so, why shouldn't the Arab be the one to pay her hotel bill? His thoughts went back to his dear Poppy, alone in New York and missing him. Poppy had told him a hundred times how bored she was whenever he wasn't around. This Marina acted as if he didn't even exist.

He ordered a tomato juice, and since Victoria wasn't with him, he added, "With just a dash of vodka."

One of the English ladies nodded toward him and called over, "How is the news today?"

Women over thirty left Arnold completely cold. This one had to be at least seventy-five.

"Bad," he told her. "Very bad."

As soon as Larsen was off the yacht, Alan was overwhelmed by the reality of his new situation. He was a rich man; he had no more financial troubles!

Not only could he now return the money to the Burger Bank, but that would still leave him with over $800,000 in his account at Citibank, to say nothing of the second $2,000,000 he was to collect in a couple of weeks when Larsen's delivery was completed.

Under the bemused eyes of the crewmen, Alan dashed down the gangplank, jumped onto the wharf, and started sprinting back to the hotel. Inasmuch as he now could pay back those ill-gotten gains of his, he no longer had any reason to hide; he could square everything and look everyone in the eye.

"Do you have a telex here at the hotel?" he asked the concierge.

"Of course, sir."

He rushed over to it, and scribbled a message for the operator, telling her it was to go to Citibank in New York. It read:

TRANSFER FROM MY ACCOUNT TO ACCOUNT OF BURGER BANK NEW YORK CITY THE SUM OF ONE MILLION, ONE HUNDRED AND SEVENTY THOUSAND, FOUR HUNDRED DOLLARS. (SIGNED) ALAN POPE, HOTEL MAJESTIC, CANNES, FRANCE.

He felt as though he were walking on air. He blithely bounded up the stairs, not even winded when he got to the seventh floor. He rushed into his living room, picked up the phone, and dialed Hamilton Price-Lynch's suite.

"This is Alan Pope," he said.

"Where are you?" Hamilton answered. "I have to talk to you."

"So do I. Can you come to my suite?"

"I'll be right there," Hamilton said.

Half a minute later, he appeared. And before Alan could say a word, Hamilton shook his hand vigorously.

"I am so sorry about what happened last night, believe me!" Price-Lynch was saying. "I was exhausted, and after the way those hoodlums had roughed us all up, I guess I lost my temper with you, and I do apologize."

Somewhat taken aback, Alan shook the man's hand in return.

"I have good news for you, Mr. Price-Lynch," he said. "I have just returned the money that Burger Bank erroneously credited to my account."

"I beg your pardon?"

"I don't owe you anything anymore," Alan repeated. "Citibank just transferred $1,170,400 from my account there to your bank."

Price-Lynch blanched.

"Why, that's impossible! You yourself told me you had lost that money gambling," he gulped.

"That's true," Alan agreed. "But I was able to work out something else. Now we're even. It's only nine-thirty, and I wanted you to know before the ten o'clock deadline. No hard feelings."

"Just a second, Mr. Pope. I couldn't be more delighted than I am to hear this news. That means that nothing now stands in the way of your coming in on the deal I offered you."

"The Hackett deal?" Alan asked.

"That's right."

"Sorry, Mr. Price-Lynch. But it's not up my alley."

"Oh, come, come now," Hamilton said with his most engaging smile. "I may have said a few harsh words to you last night, but as I told you, I didn't really mean them. You know, my offer of twenty thousand dollars still holds."

At exactly ten o'clock, Alan was supposed to be in Juan-les-Pins to keep his date with Terry. He got a little bit hot under the collar.

"No, I assure you," he said. "I'm not interested."

"Please, Mr. Pope," Price-Lynch countered, "the situation has changed completely. Yesterday, you owed me over a million dollars. Now you tell me you've paid it back."

"You can check for yourself," Alan said.

Hamilton raised a deprecating hand in protest.

"I believe you. I know you've paid it back, if you say so. And just because of that, I'm ready to raise my offer to you from twenty thousand dollars to thirty thousand."

Alan sneaked a look at his watch. If he hit any kind of traffic jam, he might be late for his date.

"Thanks, but no thanks, Mr. Price-Lynch," he said. "I wouldn't consider it even for a hundred thousand!"

"I'll meet that!" the banker said, terrified at the idea that Alan might not be bluffing.

He knew it was unwise of him to keep after Alan, but he had no choice. He had already told him much too much.

"A hundred thousand dollars—tax free, if you want—and you get even with old Hackett!"

He noticed that Alan was observing him sharply. Hamilton tried to treat the matter lightly.

"You told me during the night that you were willing to go along on this deal, don't you remember?" he said.

"Listen, Mr. Price-Lynch," Alan said, "I'm late for an appointment."

"Yes, but you can well understand that it's inconvenient for me to have you outside this deal after everything that I told you last night. This kind of negotiation requires the utmost discretion."

"You have my word—" Alan started to say.

"You've already broken it; you agreed to go along last night, and now you're backing out," Price-Lynch quietly reminded him. "So, why should I believe it now?"

"Look, I haven't the slightest interest in the world in Hackett Chemical or all the tenders you might put out against it," Alan answered irritatedly. "I've turned my back on any grudge I might ever have had against the company. And now, if you don't mind, I have to get going."

Price-Lynch's face suddenly turned into a stone mask. "What's your price?" he barked.

Alan looked at him in stupefaction. "I already told you—"

"Your price!" Hamilton shouted. "Every man has his price. I want to know what yours is!"

"I told you I'm not having any of this!"

"It's too late for you to back out on me, Mr. Pope!"

"Too late? What do you mean?" Alan demanded.

"I'm not going to endanger the existence of my bank on your whims, Mr. Pope."

"Your bank—hell! I don't give any more of a fuck about your bank than I do about Hackett Chemical! I'm finished with all your hanky-panky. Now get out of here!"

"For the last time, how much are you asking for?" Price-Lynch persisted.

Alan shoved him out of the way, rushed into the bathroom to get his swimming trunks, and ran out, leaving the nonplussed banker in the living room of his suite.

"Mr. Pope!" Hamilton screamed.

He went out into the hall, but at the landing he could see Alan's figure dashing down the stairs. For a few seconds, Price-Lynch felt paralyzed. Not only had his deal fizzled, but now that little jerk had just signed his own death warrant!

Sam Bannister was tired of lying in the dark with his eyes open. He turned on the bed lamp. He felt guilty toward the whole world, first and foremost toward Crystal and Alan. Yet, his intentions had been to do what was best for them. He turned over in his bed, cursed the fact that it was three in the morning. He realized he wasn't going to be able to get any more sleep.

His plane was due to leave at seven. He got up, padded barefoot into the kitchen, and drank a tall glass of water. Then he tiptoed back into the bedroom so as not to wake Crystal, got his suitcase out of the closet, and checked the clothes packed in it. When he was done, he sat on the edge of his bed, his arms dangling at his sides. He wished he didn't have to leave his wife with the harsh words they had exchanged the night before; he would have liked to hear her agree that he should go and help Alan out of the mess he was in. He found Crystal harder and harder to take these days, yet he was heartsick at the idea of being separated from her. Twenty-five years of married life had given him some very bad habits.

He wondered once again whether that additional $2,000,000 in Alan's account was a Burger Bank computer error. If so, how long would the machine continue pouring out its manna? He pensively went to the window and looked out. It was a dark, suffocating night. He felt overwhelmed.

Sam went into the bathroom, shaved, took a quick shower, got dressed, and made sure his passport and plane ticket were in his jacket pocket. Then, unable to stand the heavy silence any longer, he grabbed his valise, and quietly closed the apartment door behind him. He figured he'd call Crystal from the airport later to say good-bye to her. He rang for the elevator, pestered by remorse, but he wasn't quite sure why.

"Can you go a little faster? I'm very late."

The taxi driver looked back indulgently over his shoulder.

"Look, just as sure as my name is Albert, you don't have to get yourself in such a sweat about it! Either she doesn't give a hoot about you and she's gone already, or else she loves you and she'll wait all year for you."

Because Alan's T-shirt and jeans made him look very boyish, the taxi driver had assumed Alan was a lovestruck student on the way to his first date.

With a sigh, Alan glanced out at the Croisette where, early this morning, he had been walking with Sarah. He felt it was better to go to see Terry in a cab than in the Rolls-Royce. She wouldn't have approved of his arriving with a chauffeur. Then he thought of that last, hate-filled look Hamilton Price-Lynch had given him, and he thanked his lucky stars that he had finally gotten out of the nightmare in which he had been blindly wandering these past days.

But the banker's insistence kept coming back to him. Alan had no special regard for Arnold Hackett, but he felt there was something unseemly about Hackett's own bank being about to double-cross him. If that was what it was like to be rich, he'd a thousand times rather stay poor.

"Where do you want to go in Juan?" the driver asked.

"Just follow the road along the shore, and I'll tell you where to stop. Will you wait for me for a few minutes?"

"Where do you want to go afterwards?"

Alan didn't know the answer to that one. "I'm not sure yet. We'll see," he said tentatively.

For hours now, Alan had been haunted by the thought of his date with Terry, the day they were going to spend together, their perfect day in the sun. What would it lead to? he wondered.

Cesare di Sogno opened his eyes and was surprised to see a woman lying beside him in his bed. He had no idea who she was. He could see she was a blonde, so he peeked under the sheets to find out whether she was a real blonde or a fake. She was real.

Little by little, stray, hazy bits of memory were coming back to him. When the Palm Beach had been invaded by that gang, he had taken his cue to duck out before calm was restored and bills were brought around for signing. He had gone on to other nightclubs, all of them filled with people he knew, and had drunk an endless series of ungodly mixtures.

He certainly must have met a lot of people, he thought, if he didn't even remember the name, the face, or the figure of the woman he had finished the night with. Where the hell had he picked her up?

He shook her gently. "Hey, there," he murmured.

She grunted, turned her back on him, and hid her head under the sheets. Cesare tapped her persistently on the fanny.

"Time," he said softly.

The voice that came to him from the depths of the bedding was not an unpleasant one. "Time for what?" she asked.

"My name is Cesare," he said.

"What the hell do I care?" she replied.

That left him wondering.

"I'd like some coffee, orange juice, and eggs with very crisp bacon," the voice under the sheets went on.

"What's your name?" he asked.

"Marion."

"Do we know each other?"

"How should I know?" she said. "I haven't seen you yet."

"I might point out that this is my bed that you're sleeping in," Cesare informed her.

"Look, be nice, and get me some coffee, will you?" she asked.

"How about getting up and having it in a café," Cesare replied impatiently. "I'm in a hurry. I have a flock of appointments today. You'll find the bathroom right over here."

"After I have my coffee," she said. "I've got to sleep some more. I'm still tired."

He walked over to the bay window, opened the blinds, and let the sun stream into the bedroom.

"Really, Marion, I have to have my room back. I'm expecting some people here to see me."

He pulled the sheets off of her. On seeing what her body was like, he figured he must have had a pretty good night of it. He only wished he could remember what they had done together.

He grabbed her chin between his fingers and forced her to look at him. No, he could honestly say he had no recollection of ever having seen her before.

"Let me sleep. I'm pooped," she sulked.

The telephone rang, and it startled him.

"Cesare?" the voice on the phone asked.

"Yes."

"You know who this is?"

"Hamilton Price-Lynch!"

"Right," the banker said. "I wonder if you could do me a favor."

"Let me hear what it is."

"Like the last one. You know what I mean?"

Cesare took a deep breath, and allowed a pause.

"Yes," he finally conceded.

"He was at our table last night. The modern-art lover. You know who I mean?"

"Yes, of course. When?" Cesare asked.

"Immediately. The sooner the better."

"I'll take care of it," Cesare assured him. "You can depend on me."

Cesare hung up. He was in the middle of dialing a number when he noticed Marion moving into a corner of the bed. What had just happened in the last twenty seconds was so important that it had made him totally forget that she was there. He grabbed the black chiffon evening gown that he saw on the chair, a pair of gold high-heeled shoes, and a black, transparent, postage-stamp-sized bra and panties. He rolled them all into a ball and tossed them at her.

"Here. Take your clothes, and get going!"

"Coffee," Marion moaned, as she stretched.

Cesare grabbed her roughly by the arm and threw her off the bed.

"Now, get your ass out of here! I've got work to do!" he yelled.

Marion now opened her eyes wide, rubbed the elbow which had bumped against the foot of the bed, and looked at him with fear in her eyes.

"You crazy or something?" she asked.

"Fuck off!" he snarled. "I tried to say it to you nice, but you wouldn't listen."

"You bastard!"

She got up and slipped into her gown. Without taking her eyes off him, she sat down to get into her shoes.

"You can finish dressing out in the hall," Cesare grumbled. He grabbed her hand, pulled her into the foyer, opened the door, and shoved her out.

When he got back to the bedroom, he picked up the phone again.

"Marco? Cesare here. I have another customer for you. He's staying at the Majestic . . . Name's Alan Pope . . . Yes, today . . . No time to waste. Lemme know when you're done."

24

There were still a grapefruit, three apples, and two oranges in the ceramic fruit bowl. Through the window, in between the ocher roofs, Alan could still see the same little patch of sea, half-hidden by the scarlet petals of the potted geraniums. And there in front of him, standing in the center of the room, was Terry, wearing white duck slacks and a large man's shirt. She was holding a book.

"Well, come on in," she urged. "And watch your head."

He took a hesitant step forward. He closed the door behind him, his throat constricted.

"You're on time," she said. "I was wondering whether you were going to forget."

A flood of contradictory assertions crowded up behind his lips, but died there without a sound coming out.

"What are you reading?" he finally succeeded in saying.

"The *Diary of Anaïs Nin*. Ever hear of it?"

"No," he admitted.

She tossed the book down on the patchwork cover.

"Want some coffee?" she asked.

"No, thanks."

"Did you finally get a good night's sleep?"

"Not really. Only part of one."

"You seem to be having an exhausting vacation," she mocked.

He made a despairing face.

"Look, I've got a proposition for you," Terry said. "I've got a boat. That is, it's not really mine. It belongs to Lucy's friends, but they're not using it today. Like to go out on it?"

"Terrific!" he said.

"Got a swimsuit?"

"Under my clothes," he laughed.

She shoved a few things into a straw tote bag.

"The boat's moored in Cannes at the Canto Port," she informed him.

"I have a taxi waiting downstairs," Alan said.

"Then, what are we waiting for?" Terry replied.

They flew down the stairs.

Seeing Terry appear, the savvy French cabby gave Alan a triumphant wink, and commented, "See? What did I tell you?"

"We're going back to Cannes," Alan told him, ignoring his remark. "To the Canto Port."

"What did the driver mean?" Terry asked Alan as the cab got under way.

"On the way over here, he was giving me some French theories about women and the patience they have."

"Meaning?"

"I was explaining to him," replied the cab driver, who had obviously been listening, "that when women don't run out on a guy, they'll stay around and wait ten years for him. Miss, was I right or wrong?"

"Absolutely right," Terry concurred.

"You really believe that?" Alan wanted to know.

"Not at all," she said. "Lucy stayed at the MacDermotts'.

They have a super villa in the hills. You feel like staying there and never leaving. Aren't you getting sick and tired of New York?"

"Yes," he admitted.

"What good does it do you to be a millionaire? Why do you have to stay in New York?"

Alan was reminded of the miracle that had just happened. He was out of debt and had over $800,000 in his Citibank account.

He smiled at Terry. "No reason to stay in New York at all, anymore."

"This is the Canto Port," the cab driver announced.

"How do we go about finding the boat?" Terry wondered aloud.

"What's it called?" the driver asked.

"I don't know."

"You know the owner's name?"

"MacDermott."

"We'll go ask the harbor master." He headed the cab along the quays.

"Just wait a minute, please," the driver said. And he went into a building.

Alan looked at Terry. She seemed lost in thought as she stared at the yachts. He didn't dare tell her that he had one of his own. He was afraid it would put her off like the Rolls-Royce had, and that she'd look down on it as more conspicuous consumption.

"You know what it's called?" the driver said, as he returned. "*La Fête*, which means 'The Good Time,' and it looks like that's what you're going to have on it!"

He started up again, and stopped some two hundred yards away in front of a large outboard craft painted white with broad red stripes. A sailor was busy in the cockpit. As soon as he saw them, he jumped ashore to greet them.

"We're friends of the MacDermotts'," Terry said.

"I know. I've been expecting you. Name's Gwynn," the crewman told her, and he nodded to Alan, who was busy paying the cab driver.

The cabbie gave a delighted whistle at the size of the tip he got. "Thanks, sir," he said. "If ever you need me again, I always park right outside the Majestic. Just tell 'em you want Albert."

With one leap, Alan was alongside Terry on the gun-

wale of *La Fête*. She had wasted no time in getting out of
her outer garments, and now Gwynn was releasing the
ropes that kept the Baglietto moored to the wharf.

"Where would you like to go, Miss?" he asked.

"Out to sea," Terry answered.

Gwynn smiled broadly, took the helm, and started the
engine.

"Has your dear little husband gone out to do his jogging?"
Sarah asked offhandedly. She was grinding fresh pepper
onto her fried eggs and buttered toast.

It was late morning. Breakfast was being served on their
balcony on a table with a sky-blue tablecloth protected by
a striped ultramarine umbrella. Emily Price-Lynch, her
face partly hidden by her heavy dark glasses, was pouring
herself some tea. Her daughter's constant sniping at her
husband was getting on her nerves. Not that Sarah was
unjustified—there was more than a grain of truth in her
remarks—but it seemed to be the only subject of conversation Sarah had.

"I'm going deep-sea fishing today. I'll take the boat. Are
you going to the Palm Beach?" Sarah asked.

"I've got a killing headache," her mother told her.
"That riot last night was just too much."

"I thought it was rather amusing," Sarah replied. "That
gang of motorcycle hoods busting in on a charity affair
was like something out of the movie *Hair*. Where else but
in Cannes could you expect to see something like that?"

"Oh, there are hoodlums everywhere," her mother
said.

"That's true, but there aren't too many charity galas
anymore. Alan Pope walked me home from it."

"Who?" Emily asked absent mindedly.

"Pope," Sarah said. "You know, the young man who
was sitting across from you. I'm sure you must have
noticed him. He was the only one at our table who wasn't
over the hill."

"Oh, that one," Emily replied, scanning the edges of
the pool seven stories below. Where could Hamilton be?
she was wondering.

"Are you listening to me, Mother?" Sarah asked.

"Yes, of course."

"Is this conversation upsetting you or something?"

"No, no. I heard everything you said. Pope. Alan Pope. So what? What's so special about him?"

Sarah quietly and deliberately tore the petals off a rose, looked at her mother challengingly, and in a lowered voice announced, "I'm planning to marry him."

They both lay on their stomachs at the stern of the boat. The wind whipped over their bodies. They were so far out by now that their eyes could take in the whole coast from Cannes to Nice. The craft was heading straight out to sea at high speed, leaving a great wake of snow-white spume over the indigo water. They had passed many sailboats cruising near the offshore islands and outraced other outboards.

"Wanna swim?" Terry yelled over the roar of the engine.

"Yep," Alan yelled back.

She climbed over the layer of mattresses and tapped on Gwynn's shoulders. The boat seemed to dive into the water when he cut the motor. It scooted ahead a few seconds on its momentum and then came to rest in a swaying movement of the wavelets. The shore was no more than a gray stripe barely visible on the horizon. They felt as if they were alone in the world, cut off from everything. Gwynn turned his back on them and quietly lighted a smoke.

Terry dived in first. Alan watched her swim off in several smooth strokes, then he dived in after her. The water was warm. He let himself go under, opened his eyes, and could see Terry's orange-colored body, outlined in a fringe of foam. He surfaced alongside her. They both started to laugh.

"What if Gwynn were to take off without us?" she asked.

"I hope you'd be able to grab hold of me and tow me in to shore!" he said.

She went under head first. For one second, as she was going down, her legs formed a perfect arrow. Where she had just been, there was now nothing. For the one second, Alan felt a void.

Suddenly, two hands gripped his ankles. He just had time to take a short breath before he was pulled under. They played like two happy animals, enjoying the freedom of their bodies, straddling one another in the midst of silvery splashes, softly swimming side by side, bumping and rubbing, skin to skin. At one point, they were facing one another, their faces streaming water, and their lips met in a salty kiss. Terry took Alan's hand and tenderly squeezed it. Then she swam back toward the boat, and swung herself aboard in one lithe movement.

"I'm hungry," she said.

Gwynn made a gesture of powerlessness. "Mr. Mac-Dermott didn't give me any instructions about provisions," he said.

"There must be a restaurant in the islands, isn't there?" Alan asked.

"Sure. But it's mobbed."

"Oh, well," Terry said. "We'll eat after we get back." She looked meaningfully at Alan. "I don't feel like being with people, anyway."

"If I might...," Gwynn hesitantly suggested. "I did bring a few sandwiches along. Do you think you'd like to share them? I have a couple bottles of wine, too."

Terry and Alan glanced at one another, and then both burst out laughing.

"Fine and dandy," Gwynn said, joining in their merriment. He opened a compartment in the fore part of the boat and brought out a bottle of wine.

"Would you like to go over to the islands?" he asked.

When he turned to serve them, he noticed that both of them were holding their glasses out to him stiffly, quite unaware of him. They had turned to stone, a smile creeping over their lips, and each one's eyes were pinned irrevocably to the other's.

Marco came out of the Majestic lobby. His customer wasn't in. He thoughtfully considered the limousines at the entrance, as they took on their precious loads of walking bank accounts.

Cesare di Sogno had given him until evening to get the job done. But how was he to do it if the victim was invisible? He went over to Serge.

"I've been looking for one of my friends, a Mr. Alan Pope," he said. "He doesn't seem to be in."

"He left a little while ago," Serge told him, as he rushed

over to separate two elderly ladies' dogs. He untangled
the leashes and came back over to Marco. "I remember
calling a taxi for him," he said.

"Any idea where he went?"

"You might check at the taxi stand across the way.
Albert was the one who had the fare."

"Thanks."

"At your service, sir." Serge saluted politely.

The two dogs were at each other again, barking and
growling while their mistresses shouted and cursed.

Marco turned and crossed the Croisette, then walked
up to the first taxi in line.

"I'm looking for Albert," he said.

"That's me," Albert said.

Marco smiled gratefully at him. "Seems this is my lucky
day," he commented. He took a fifty-franc note out of his
pocket and handed it to the cabby.

"The doorman told me you picked up one of my friends
this morning—Alan Pope," he said.

"I sure did! He was the only fare I've had so far, at least
from here. I just set them down at the Canto Port. They
went out on a boat. A great big red and white outboard
with a funny name, *La Fête*."

"Thanks a million," Marco said. "The only problem
now is how do I find a boat like that out at sea?"

"They probably went to the offshore islands. No one in
Cannes goes anywhere else."

Marco thanked him again and was off. A hundred
yards away, Salicetti sat waiting for him at the wheel of a
cream-colored Dodge convertible.

"We're going to the ship shed," Marco instructed him.
"And make it snappy!"

The Dodge screeched away in a stench of burning
rubber. There was not too much traffic to be concerned
about; at this time of day, all the summer people were
lying in the sun somewhere, getting tanned. The car
gathered speed, went around the basin of the Canto Port,
and followed the shoreline. Marco lighted a cigarette.

"We going fishing?" Salicetti inquired.

"Yes," Marco mumbled. "For a real big fish."

"Fishing is kind of dangerous in broad daylight, isn't
it?" Salicetti said as he concentrated on his driving.

"Bah! During the season, there are so many accidents

on the water. All these crackpots sail their boats every which way."

"Yeah, that's true enough," Salicetti agreed.

He suppressed a little laugh.

"Like I always say, boats and fireworks are the two most dangerous things of all!"

Marco slowly exhaled his cigarette smoke through his nose.

"We'll try not to make quite as much noise as we did with the fireworks," he commented.

Ten minutes later, the Dodge pulled up in front of the iron gate of a house that was built right into the rock formation below it. No one could see the house from the road. Marco opened the gate, then closed it again after the Dodge had gone through. Dug out of the solid rock beneath the house was a boat hangar with a padlocked door, which Marco swung back.

Salicetti came to his side. "Boy, I never saw one as big as that!"

The outboard was a Riva that had been fixed up especially for smuggling on the high seas. No police launch was fast enough to keep up with it. Its hull, totally devoid of metallic ornamentation, was painted dark blue on the sides, deep green on the surface between the gunwales. Even in broad daylight, it was impossible to make it out against the water at anything more than a hundred yards. Forward, its keel was plated so that it was capable of smashing a tree trunk at seventy-five miles an hour; when going full speed, its motors easily carried it along at more than ninety miles per hour.

"Get in," Marco instructed Salicetti, after which he himself took the helm and turned on the ignition. A raucous panting sound filled the underground shed.

"Undo the ropes," he said.

Salicetti swung them through their rings.

"Where we going exactly?" he asked.

"Taking a little jaunt out to the islands," Marco said.

He gave it a little gas. The menacing snout of the Riva slid out of its grotto.

The sun was playing over Terry's body. She was lying at the stern of the boat, her arms crossed, an expression of quiet happiness all over her face. Alan could not get enough of looking at her. Lying next to her, he was hesitant to repeat the fleeting movement that had made their lips join out at sea. Terry's hand lay motionless only a few inches from his own, yet he dared not reach for it.

Along with Gwynn, who was now engrossed in a comic book, they had devoured the sandwiches which they washed down with red wine, diving into the sea between bites, then coming back out to dry in the sun. The narrow arm of the sea between Sainte-Marguerite and Saint-Honorat was jammed with boats of every type and description.

The water was totally transparent. Twenty-five feet straight down, one could see tiny nacreous shells around which small silvery fishes swam incessantly, darting quickly and unpredictably. From some of the neighboring crafts, tunes could be heard, coming in over transistor sets. There was peace, warmth, light...

Alan's hand gradually crept closer to Terry's. There was something perfect about this instant. Alan was afraid he might destroy it. But his impulse won out: With the tips of his fingers, he softly grasped hers. Their hands found each other, joined, wove together, embraced, suddenly linked one to the other by a skin-to-skin kiss which was endless.

Neither one of them was aware of the green-and-blue outboard that passed near them, barely fifteen feet away.

"Gwynn," Terry asked without letting go of Alan's hand, "would you take us around to the other side of the island for a swim?"

The sailor put his comic book down, shook his head to rouse himself, and turned on the ignition. He steered a slow course through the multitude of yachts swaying on the limpid, shimmering surface of the calm water. Once he was out of the inlet, he turned left in a sudden spurt of foam.

On the Riva, Marco put his hand on Salicetti's arm. "Wait about five seconds, and then take off after them."

At 1:00 P.M., Alan still had not come down into the lobby.

Sarah phoned his suite again. The phone rang and rang. No answer.

She walked over to the doorman, who now had a large bandage on his hand from the last dog fight.

"Serge, have you seen anything of Mr. Pope's driver?" she asked.

"Norbert?" he replied. "Yes, Miss. He's right there."

"Are you Mr. Pope's chauffeur?"

"Yes, madame."

"It's Mademoiselle. Did you see him this morning?"

"No, Miss. I'm here waiting for his instructions."

"Was there anything on the schedule?"

"No, Miss."

"I see. Thanks very much." She moved onto the terrace, which was full of patrons protecting themselves from the sun beneath the table umbrellas.

Alan was nowhere to be seen.

She went around the pool. To the left, hidden behind some clumps of boxwoods, bare-breasted women were sunning themselves in spite of the rule against it. Sarah nodded to a few acquaintances, turned down ten luncheon invitations, crossed through the bar, went to the elevator, and pressed the button for the seventh floor.

She had never done anything like this before. Usually she put off the men who tried to press their suit with her. Every declaration of love seemed to her suspicious mind only a front for some scheme to lay hands on her fortune. Sex to her was mostly in the mind. Sometimes she indulged in a one-night stand, just by way of having an outlet. It was rare that there was ever a repeat with the same man. The screen of her millions always set up an insurmountable barrier.

She got out of the elevator and knocked at Suite 751. Could he still be asleep? she wondered. She knocked harder, and rang the bell.

"There's no one in there, madame," a chambermaid said to her. "I made the room up very early this morning, and the gentleman had already gone out."

Sarah smiled icily. Alan really had not made any promise to her when she suggested they go for a sail today. Her heart tensed at the recollection of their long walk along the Croisette. She had held his arm, the night had been warm. She remembered the exact moment when she had been smitten. They had just gotten to the hotel, and she had suggested to him that they stop for a nightcap. He had answered, "I'm awfully tired, Sarah. I'm likely to die if I don't get a few hours' sleep."

At that moment, he had looked like a lost little boy. And she had known that Alan was the one. He was so different from the others!

But this morning, her mother had told her she was crazy, when it finally dawned on her that Sarah wasn't joking.

"Why, you don't even know anything about him," she had said.

"He's the one, Mother."

"Just another fortune hunter who thinks you look like a good catch."

"Not everyone is as rotten as that jerk of a husband of yours!"

"Sarah, I forbid you!"

"I'm going to ask him to marry me this very day," she had replied. "And I'd like to see you stop me!"

Sarah returned to the lobby, and decided to go to the Palm Beach casino and have a look. Maybe Alan was there. She called for her chauffeur.

"A penny for your thoughts," Alan said.

Terry put her head down in the hollow of his shoulder.

"I was just thinking how nice it was not to be thinking any thoughts at all. I was just looking at the sky."

"What did you see in it?"

"Not a cloud."

Alan rolled slightly toward her and grazed her lips.

"How about now?" he asked.

"Not a thing. My eyes are closed."

With the tip of her tongue, she was reaching for his lips. They were lying in a tiny sandy cove protected from the sea by a rampart of sharp rocks. Three hundred yards away, *La Fête* was swaying in the slight swells. Gwynn was asleep on board.

"Funny that the two of us should be out here together," Terry sighed.

"Funny?" Alan queried.

She took his face in both her hands and devoured him with her eyes.

"Yes. Because you represent everything in the world that I detest."

"Such as?"

"The establishment. The system. Status symbols. The

Rolls-Royce, the suite at the Majestic, the charity balls, gambling, money, money, money..."

"How would you know?" he said, and he was dying to tell her the truth, but somehow was afraid to let his mask fall.

"Look," she told him. "I know how unhappy a lot of people can feel underneath the moneyed fronts they put on. It was because I had a feeling about you that I rode along in that goddamned luxury-heap of yours. And that's why I'm here today. How old are you?"

"Thirty," he said.

"Strange," she commented. "You don't seem so dried up at all. Money dries people up."

"Especially when they haven't got any," he countered.

"You talk about it like someone who has too much, a man who owns too much. People don't ever enjoy what they own."

"What do they enjoy then?"

She gave him light little kisses all around his lips.

"Well, that, for instance. That doesn't cost a red cent! You must have been awfully poor once to have wanted so to be stinking rich!"

Once again, Alan was on the point of telling her.

"How old are you?" he asked, instead.

"Twenty-two."

"What do you plan to do with yourself later on?"

"Just what I'm doing now. I plan to be happy."

"Are you really happy?"

"Yes," she said.

"So am I."

"Alan..."

"What?" he muttered, as he buried his face in her wet, salty-smelling hair.

"Nothing." She put her arms around his neck, hugged him to her, and with eyes closed, spoke his name several times.

"Alan...Alan...Alan..."

A hot wave swept over him, a wave of intense desire but a feeling of tenderness, too. He slowly ran his hand up and down her thigh, each time getting just a tiny bit closer to the inside. She let him go on for a moment, then pulled away and looked him squarely in the eye.

"I want you, Alan, just as much as you want me. But

not here. Not this way," she said. "You'll have me, don't worry about that. I want you, too."

"When?"

"Tonight. That okay?"

"Yes," he said, hoarsely.

She quickly jumped up and in three strides was into the warm water. He watched her swim away, heading for the boat with big, powerful strokes. He dived after her, and stayed under in order to calm down, then surfaced again and started to float, trying his best to regulate his breathing, for he had been dazzled by her, by that moment, by an electrifying burst of happiness.

He turned over on his stomach again and saw her swing herself up onto the gunwale of La Fête. He started swimming toward her.

The sea was dense with sails, white flakes that danced against the azure of the sky. His eye caught sight of Terry with her head thrown back, smoothing her hair, and Gwynn who was pulling up the anchor, and the big rough rock over to his left which stuck up a couple of feet above the bluish mirror of the sea.

He was barely twenty yards from the boat when he heard the roar. He looked up and saw the huge outboard bearing down, its colors so close to those of the waves that it was hard to distinguish. He was startled by the ferocious roar of its motors running all-out, as it cut its way through an immense geyser of silvery spume.

On board La Fête, he heard Terry shriek and saw Gwynn jump up with his arms waving, yelling words that he could not make out. For a fraction of a second, Alan was paralyzed by the sudden noise and his fright. The helmsman of the outboard had obviously not seen him! He frantically raised his arms in the hope of catching the man's eye. But the outboard did not change its course by so much as a hair. Alan looked desperately toward that protective rock, then dived with a swing of his hips and started swimming toward it under water, his lungs burning as if they were about to burst. The people on that outboard had to be crazy!

The roar became thunderously, apocalyptically loud. Alan was suffocating. But if he surfaced, he would be sliced in two. He clung to just one idea: to survive!

Through the clear water, he could see the dark wall of

the rock. He grabbed it, and then, in a hysterical leap, he jumped to the surface of the water, gasping for air. He stayed there, half-suffocated, trying to breathe, and turned his head out toward the open sea. The outboard was only a trace of foam disappearing on the horizon. Gwynn, with arms outstretched, was shouting curses after it. When Alan reached the Baglietto, Gwynn reached down and pulled him aboard in one heave. Alan collapsed on the deck like a bunch of wilted algae.

Marina opened her eyes with difficulty; they hurt. She didn't recognize the room or the bed she was in. She was wearing a white terry robe, which surprised her since she always slept in the nude. She wrinkled her nostrils, and sniffed suspiciously at the back of her hand. She stunk of booze!

She grabbed her left foot with her right hand and bent it up to her nose. It had the same awful stench, too.

She hopped out of bed, and walked over her white dress on her way to the bathroom. The bathtub was full of a pale yellow liquid that smelled suspiciously like wine. She tested it with her finger. No doubt about it, that was where the smell on her body came from. She sucked the end of her finger and frowned. It was champagne!

She released the plug and watched the flat champagne begin to run out of the tub, wondering what the hell she could have been up to during the night. She discovered the answer in the form of a small package at the bottom of the now-empty tub. It was sealed in a sheet of plastic wrap. Inside was a jewelry case containing a magnificent bracelet set with precious gems. Under the bracelet, a handwritten note read: *For Marina, In memory of a wonderful night of love.* It was signed, *Hadad.*

Damned if she could remember a thing about it!

She sat down on the edge of the tub, a whole night lost out of her life.

"Boy, did you see those bastards!" Gwynn was saying, as he had been for the last ten minutes. "Every year, people like that cause accidents. I'm going to report them to the authorities. They're madmen! Absolutely crazy! It ought to be against the law to let scum like that get their hands on a boat!"

"They couldn't see me," Alan said, trying to placate him.

He was sitting next to Gwynn, a towel over his shoulders. Snugged against him, Terry had her arms around his body.

"But that's just the point of it," Gwynn replied. "Don't they know that there's a speed limit in near the beaches? I thought they were going to slice you in two."

"So did I, Gwynn, but now it's over. Let's forget it."

"Never!" the sailor said in a voice vibrant with indignation. "As soon as we land, I'm turning them in to the harbor patrol."

Alan nudged Terry and smiled. She was still drained of all color.

"You know how?" he asked, nodding toward the tips of the water skis sticking out under her feet.

"Yes," she said, "but not right now."

"Don't you feel like it?"

"I wouldn't be steady enough on my feet for it."

"Gwynn," he called.

"Yes, sir?"

"Can I go waterskiing?"

Gwynn immediately killed the motor, and said, "If I was you, I think I'd be too shook up."

"That's just it. It's what I need to make me snap out of it!"

They were three hundred yards out to sea. Alan dived into the water, and came up. Gwynn handed him the skis. He got onto them and winked to Terry.

"Ready when you are!" he shouted.

Gwynn released the rope and threw it to him. Alan grabbed the wooden handle at its end. With the motor in low, Gwynn began a slow swerve around Alan, then straightened out the nose of the craft until the rope was in a taut, straight line. He nodded questioningly at Alan.

"Go!" the skier called.

Alan felt a sudden jerk forward, steadied himself on the skis, and then let himself enjoy the powerful tug that was dragging him forward across the water. His face was whipped by the wind and the foam; his mind was dazzled by the light, the speed, and the noise. His skis whistled against the sea, which seemed to be undulating beneath his weight, keeping up with the rhythm of his hip movements, sending him diagonally away from, then back across the foamy wake with the speed of an arrow.

He had learned how to water-ski when he was a kid. He noted with pleasure that his body had forgotten none of the intricacies of the sport, despite all the years he had been away from it. In the stern of the boat, Terry kept her eyes steadily upon him. Alan saw her face against the light, a golden halo around it, splashed with the spume of the waves. He did several maneuvers, delighting in the muscular reflexes that recalled those formations even before the idea of them had formed clearly in his mind.

That was when Terry screamed, as she pointed to something behind him.

Frozen with terror, Alan turned and saw no more than thirty yards away, the powerful keel of a huge outboard craft heading directly for him. He instinctively knew that it was the same boat that a little while before had almost decapitated him. Gwynn, alerted by Terry's shriek, made a quick left, giving it all the gas he could, and steered toward the open water. The Riva followed suit, picking up speed, and passed them with ridiculous ease. Alan gritted his teeth and clung to his wooden handle. If he stopped, he'd be at their mercy. If he went on, his legs would very soon give out on him.

Now he was flying across the face of the water at breakneck speed. Gwynn deflected the boat back to the right at an unbelievable angle. Their last hope was to be able to get in to the beaches. But this was just what the Riva was waiting for. After a wide swing, it came back quick as lightning toward the Baglietto, trying to get at it from the side and cut Alan off. In a couple of seconds, the Riva was on top of him. With a desperate swing of his hips, Alan leaned hard to the right.

Plowing the sea with its screws, the Riva missed him by not much more than a yard, coming by in a fantastic wake of spume that nearly knocked him off balance. Terry was screaming. Gwynn was heading toward shore as fast as *La Fête* would go. The Riva came roaring back to attack at the top velocity of its engines. This time Alan realized he would not be able to dodge it. He crouched, waited until the very last second, and then spun up into the sky over the outboard in an absolutely inhuman spring. He was now only a hundred yards or so from

shore. The Riva headed out to sea and disappeared.
Gwynn made a sharp turn. Alan let go of the handle, shot
forward like a torpedo right up along the jetty of the Plage
Sportive, barely missing the heads of some bathers who
were paddling about near it. Out of breath and finally
slowing down, he grabbed hold of one of the pilings,
doing his best to get his wind back. A sharp pain was
stabbing him in the chest.

He looked back. *La Fête* had stopped some ten feet
behind him. Terry was sobbing convulsively on its deck.

His face curiously bloodless beneath his deep tan, Gwynn
said in a trembling voice, "Those people were trying to
kill you, sir."

25

Sam Bannister jumped out of the taxi, paid what he owed,
and went into the lobby, looking for the desk.

"Mr. Alan Pope?" he asked.

"His key is on the rack, sir," the concierge replied. "He
hasn't come back yet."

"My name is Bannister, Samuel Bannister," Sam said. "I
just got in from New York. I'm his friend and associate;
he's expecting me. Will you please give me his key?"

"I'm afraid that's not possible, sir. Mr. Pope left us no
instructions to that effect."

"Well, in that case, it can only be because he forgot. I'm
tired and I want to rest a while. Are you going to give me
the key or not?"

"I'm truly sorry, sir, but I don't see how we can."

"I just told you I'm his friend and associate. But if
that's the situation, let me have a room of my own."

"Out of the question, sir," the concierge said. "We're
booked solid until the end of August. Wouldn't you like to
go into the bar and wait for Mr. Pope to come back?"

"No, I wouldn't," Sam answered exasperatedly. "I'm
tired and hot, and I want to take a shower."

His tweed jacket had turned out to be the wrong thing

to wear for Cannes. But he knew that insufferable arrogance was what set the deluxe hotel patron apart from the bulk of ordinary mortals.

"Are you giving it to me or not?" he growled.

"I just told you, sir—"

"Very well, then!"

Without hesitation, Sam walked over to one of the huge armchairs in the main lobby, sat down and started unlacing his shoes, then took them off, pulled off his tie, opened his shirt, removed his socks, and unzipped his fly and began taking off his trousers. People passing through the lobby stopped open-mouthed and watched his performance, for it was perfectly clear that Sam intended to strip right there in full sight.

"Quick! Go get Mr. Gohelan," the concierge yelled to one of the bellhops.

"Who is that?" Mandy de Saran asked with feigned indifference.

The duke was out playing golf. She had just come back from shopping. Her muscles, still aching from the beating she had gotten the night before, hurt deliciously.

"It's someone who claims he's a friend and associate of Mr. Pope's, Duchess. Unfortunately, we're not authorized to let him have the key to Pope's suite."

The sight of Sam Bannister's big hairy thighs was beginning to turn the Duchess on. The man was so ugly, so common looking, and yet at the same time so utterly defiant, that she felt a desire rising within her to be taken by him just as soon as possible. Besides, he had a horsy face. And, from as far back as she could remember, the idea of being mounted by a horse had been one of her most obsessive and erotic fantasies.

She was about to take matters into her own hands when Gohelan appeared on the scene, followed by a bellhop carrying a terrycloth robe. The bellhop covered Bannister with the robe as the bystanders burst out laughing. Gohelan was most embarrassed; he decided the better part of valor was to let the man have his way.

The bellhop picked up Sam's discarded clothing, took Alan's key from the concierge, and led the way to the elevator as Bannister, now draped in the robe, followed with the dignity of a toga-clad emperor.

Mandy watched thoughtfully.

"What is Mr. Pope's room number?" she inquired.

"Seven fifty-one, Duchess," the concierge told her.

She took another elevator, went up to the seventh floor, and passed the bellhop on the landing. The door to Room 751 was ajar. She opened it and went in.

"Hello," she said.

Sam looked at her in amazement. "Hello," he answered mechanically.

Mandy didn't give him a chance. She walked over to him, shoved him back up against the wall, stuck her tongue into his mouth, while her hand slipped under his robe and down into his briefs.

"Fuck me!" she murmured passionately.

"Madame, swear to me that it's true," Alice said to Nadia Fischler.

"You little idiot, of course, it's true," her mistress said.

Alice grabbed her forehead in her hands.

"Good Lord in heaven! We've won three million dollars!"

"And I'll swear something else to you," Nadia replied. "This time they're not going to get it back. I've just bought the Villa La Volière."

"The one at Cap d'Antibes?"

"Yes, you remember? I told you that someday it would belong to me. Well, now it does. I paid two million dollars for it!"

"Oh, madame, how wonderful! How magnificent!" Alice said, "We'll be so safe and comfortable over there."

"You can go over there right away," Nadia told her. "I want to let everyone know about this. This time it'll be my turn to get even. Tonight, I'm going to give a party such as they've never seen anywhere on the Riviera. That lousy Betty Grone will turn green with envy!"

"But, madame, it's too late to make arrangements."

"What do you mean?" Nadia demanded. "Everything's been arranged already. Ten bellhops from the hotel have gone out delivering the invitations. And since La Volière means The Aviary, the theme for my costume party is birds. The party will go on from midnight to noon. We'll serve breakfast to the survivors tomorrow morning at my private pier down on the ocean. And there'll be ten bands playing! Come on, now, get going! The chauffeur is waiting for you!"

Alice started to trot away, but Nadia called her back.

"Aren't you even interested in who I won all this money from?" she asked.

"Who, madame?"

"Hadad."

"He deserved it. I sure hope you didn't invite him."

"Of course, I did. Although I'm not all that sure he'll come. And aren't you going to ask me what you're supposed to do at La Volière?"

"What am I to do when I get there?" Alice patiently inquired.

"Well, you're going to be in charge of receiving everything that's been ordered. The movie studios at La Victorine are going to send over tons of feathers, costumes, beaks, and rhinestones. And another batch of costumes will come in at nine-thirty from the studios in Paris. I've ordered the full stock of three costume houses. All the disguises are to be laid out in the entrance foyer. None of the guests will be allowed into the ballroom without first having put a bird's headdress on. Understand?"

"Yes, madame. But who's going to do the hairdressing for all those people?"

"Alexandre. He's coming into Nice by the late plane. And bringing his own feathers and fifteen of his helpers!"

The Plage Sportive, sometimes known as Muscle Beach, had a crowd of excessively handsome young men on it who did nothing to hide their interest in Alan. He meanwhile took Terry by the hand and led her over to a quiet spot behind the buffet.

"Listen to me, Terry," he said. "You go on home. I'll call a taxi and have you dropped off there. Lock yourself in your room, and don't budge out of it until I come for you. Okay?"

Her big gray eyes still reflected the terror of the moments they had just lived through.

"Do you hear me, Terry? he insisted.

"What about you?" she said.

"I think I know who's behind all this nonsense," he told her. "But I have to find out for sure. As soon as I do, I'll take care of the matter and get right back to you."

"When?"

"As soon as I can. Not more than an hour or two from now."

He was afraid for her. He didn't want her to be seen with him any more than necessary. He had thought about stashing her away on his yacht, but then he figured that the killers had probably already connected it with him.

It hadn't taken Alan long to figure out who was behind this: Hamilton Price-Lynch. Alan recalled the banker's veiled threats when he had refused to play along, and he felt an overweening urge to grab the guy by the neck and beat his head against the wall until it split open.

"Just stay put in your room," he urged Terry.

He went over to the bar, called for a taxi, and came back for her. She was trembling all over.

"Just don't worry about anything," he said.

She clung to him, paying no attention to the gaping looks of the handsome beach boys, who were fascinated by such a fine-looking fellow wasting his time on a girl.

"I love you, Terry. I love you," he was whispering into her lovely hair.

And he was amazed to hear the words come out of his mouth; he had never before spoken them so reverently to anyone.

"Alan! Alan darling!" she replied, as if in echo. "I do love you!"

"Okay, mister, here's your taxi!"

"Go on," Alan instructed her.

Terry pressed his hand one more time, took a last frightened look at him, and went up the wooden stairs leading from the sand to the Croisette.

Alan waited a few seconds for her to get away, then ran up the stairs himself, and dashed as fast as he could toward the Majestic. His lips were taut with contained fury, his face livid, his fists clenched tight.

"My key!" he barked to the concierge as he approached the desk.

"One of your friends has taken it, sir," he was told.

"My friend? Who?" Alan shouted back.

"A Mr. Bannister from New York. We did everything we could to refuse to give it to him, but he stripped down to his undershorts right here in the lobby."

"Sam Bannister!" Alan gasped. Things had been going

at such a pace in the last few hours that he had completely forgotten about Sam.

"Alan, whatever happened to you?" Sarah ran over to Alan, nuzzled up to him, and kneaded his arm with her hand. "I've been looking all over for you. We had a date for one o'clock this afternoon. And you stood me up!"

Alan tried to free himself from her grip without being too rude or brusque.

"You'll have to excuse me, Sarah, but something unexpected came up," he said. "I'm terribly sorry about the whole thing, but right now I have to get upstairs."

"I'll go with you," she offered.

"Impossible. There's somebody waiting for me up there."

"Let them wait," she said petulantly. "I have to talk to you."

"Really, Sarah, this isn't the time for that!"

"Alan, what I have to tell you is terribly important!"

"Later, Sarah, please. Try to be patient with me."

Alan turned on his heels and rushed toward the elevators. Sarah ran after him.

Three huge dogs held on leashes by one little girl came tumbling out of the elevator.

"This is urgent, Alan! It's a matter of life and death for me—and you, too!" Sarah insisted.

He was suddenly all tangled up in the leashes, caught between the dogs, Sarah, and the little girl.

At the same instant, Marina walked into the lobby. She was totally surprised to see Alan, fighting to free himself from a maelstrom of mastiffs and skirts. Without even stopping to wonder what sort of miracle could have made him appear in this place, Marina rushed toward him.

Arnold Hackett, who had been watching Marina's window for hours from the bar, saw her enter the lobby. Forgetting his age, his dignity, his social position, and the fact that he was a respectably married man, Arnold came tearing out toward her.

In the meantime, the three huge dogs were merrily dragging the little girl who by now was lying flat on the marble floor of the lobby, Marina and Arnold saw the elevator doors close in their faces.

Alan and Sarah started to ascend.

"Alan! Will you at least let me talk to you for a second?" Sarah demanded.

"No," he said.

"Alan!"

"Look, I said no and I mean no! Now leave me the hell alone!"

"Why, you nasty man! I'm going to speak my piece anyway!"

The little girl had pushed every button in the elevator on her way down, so it stopped at every floor as Sarah and Alan went up, and despite his curses, there was nothing Alan could do to change that.

"I'm going to marry you, you hear?" Sarah said.

Alan steadied himself against the wall.

"What are you saying?" he gasped.

"You and me. We're going to get married!" And then, as he seemed to be struck stone dead, she added, "I've already told my mother."

They were at the fifth floor.

"Sarah, you must be completely out of your mind," he finally managed to say.

"Yes, I am—over you," she replied. "You'll never have another worry in the world. My lawyers will draw up an agreement between us. And you can be the one to decide where we spend our honeymoon!"

They were at the sixth floor.

"Alan, I know I'm impulsive," she went on. "But this is the first time I've ever wanted to get married."

"I'm not interested," he said.

"It'll be wonderful..."

"Never."

They were at the seventh floor. The doors opened. So did the doors of the other elevator, and out came Arnold and Marina.

"Marina, I'm entitled to some kind of an explanation for your conduct," the old man was remonstrating.

"Oh, leave me alone, you! All you ever want is explanations!" Marina snarled back. And then, she stopped short.

"Alan!"

The two elevators went back down to the ground floor, leaving the four of them on the landing.

"Marina!" Alan exclaimed.

"How are you, Sarah?" Hackett politely said.

"Alan, who is this woman?" Sarah demanded.

"Why, it's Marina," Alan replied, no longer quite up to sorting out everything that was happening.

"Good afternoon, sir," Hackett said icily to Alan.

Marina threw her arms around Alan and hugged him warmly, completely forgetting that a few days before in New York she had walked out on him.

"What the hell are you doing here?" she wanted to know. "This is super! You know that business with Harry? That's all over!"

"Alan, I'd appreciate the courtesy of an introduction," Sarah was saying as coldly as she knew how.

"Marina, this is Sarah," Alan complied. "Sarah, Marina."

"Where do you know her from?" Arnold Hackett asked warily.

"Did you hear that, Alan?" Marina chuckled. Then, turning to Hackett, she said pleasantly, "As long as you insist on knowing, we used to live together!"

"Alan, is that true?" Sarah demanded.

"Listen," Alan said to the assembled group. "All of you, listen to me..."

He took a breath, in order to be able to say something that would settle everything once and for all. But he couldn't find the necessary words; it was all too complicated. He tore down the hallway, and pounded on the door of his suite.

"Alan!" Marina and Sarah called out in one voice, as they both started after him.

"Sam, open up!" Alan shouted. "It's me! Alan! For God's sake, open the door!"

"Never in my life have I been treated like this, Alan," Sarah was yelling.

"Leave him alone," Marina ordered, as she grabbed Sarah by the sleeve.

"You, shut up! And don't you dare go near my fiancé!"

"Marina," Hackett was roaring, "I demand that you—"

"Oh, get the hell out of here, you old fart!" she replied.

At this point, Sam Bannister's stupefied head appeared in the open door. All that he had on was a pair of undershorts and one sock, and he looked like a punch-drunk boxer after a losing fight. Alan shoved him back into the suite, followed by the others who were yelling and swearing at one another as they tried to grab hold of him.

Once inside, all got a shock: Lying beatifically on the carpet, totally nude, her hair askew, her body covered with bruises and red welts, the Duchess de Saran was greeting them with the same superlatively dignified gesture of her head as if she had been sitting on the throne of France, graciously granting an audience to her vassals.

"Sam!" Alan managed to say.

Bannister helplessly raised his arms toward the heavens.

"Alan, I swear to you on the life of Crystal," he said, designating the duchess with a wave of his chin, "she raped me!"

Looking absolutely aghast, Alan wrung his hands.

"I guess you all know, or want to know, my good friend Sam Bannister," he heard himself saying. "Sammy, Marina, you two know each other already. And this is Mr. Arnold Hackett and Miss Sarah Burger."

Bannister, his jaw hanging limp, reacted to each of the names as if they were so many blows to his solar plexus. Alan then pointed to the duchess, who was peacefully getting back into her dress.

"This," Alan added, "is the Duchess de Saran."

"How do you do?" Sam Bannister mumbled.

Arnold Hackett immediately bowed to her from the waist.

"How good to see you again, Duchess. I do hope you'll excuse me for not having noticed you. Unforgivable of me!"

Mandy unthinkingly held her hand out for him to kiss.

"Alan, I'm still waiting for your answer," Sarah put in.

"What the hell did she ask you?" Marina wanted to know.

"Alan, I was speaking to you," Sarah said.

"I have every right to know what went on between you and that Arab prince," Hackett cut in, darting a vicious look of reproof at Marina.

"I took a champagne bath," she told him.

"Alan," Bannister begged, "could I get something to drink, please? Something good and strong?"

There was a scratching at the door, and a voice calling, "Alan . . ."

It was Nadia Fischler, radiant and triumphant. Paying no attention to any of the others, she gave Alan a long, lingering kiss and said, "I won it all back, darling! Here is your money—all of it!" She waved an envelope under his nose.

Alan started to grab it, but she pulled it back.

"It's all yours—but on one condition. You have to give me your word of honor that you'll come to the costume party I'm giving tonight. It's a housewarming for my new home, La Volière. That means The Bird House. And all of you are invited," she said, turning generously to all of the others. "Promise?"

"I can't, Nadia," Alan said.

"How much is there in the envelope?" Sam whispered to him.

"Eight hundred thousand dollars!" Nadia answered for him.

"He'll be there!" Sam Bannister assured her.

"I want this to be a wonderful, wild, wild party!" Nadia continued as she slipped the envelope into Alan's belt. "It will be the night of the birds. Everyone will be flying. Tonight at midnight. At La Volière, in Cap d'Antibes!"

She threw Alan a kiss with the tips of her fingers and was gone.

"Now, all of you, get out of here," Alan yelled. "Out, come on!"

He firmly shoved Sarah away as she tried to hang on to him.

"Even me?" Sam Bannister piteously asked, as he held up his drawers with one hand.

"My, you sure are edgy all of a sudden, aren't you, Alan?" Marina said.

"I'll see you later, darling," Sarah called as she let herself out. "I'll make the announcement right away."

Hackett stepped back to allow Mandy de Saran to go imperiously by, and then ran as fast as his short legs would carry him, trying to catch up with Marina.

Alan bolted the door, and leaned back against it. He looked long and silently at Sam Bannister.

"Alan, what's the matter?" Sam asked. "What are you planning to do?"

"To go kill a man," Alan replied, pushing Sam out of his way.

Bannister pushed back and shoved Alan against the wall.

"First of all," he said, "I want you to give me some kind

of a rundown on what gives in this lunatic asylum!"

"Sure, as soon as you tell me what you were doing in your B.V.D.s in the lobby of the Majestic," Alan replied.

Then Alan hid his face in his hands. "There's a bar right over there," he said, "with Scotch in it. Get me a drink, will you?"

Sam did as he was asked.

Holding his glass, Alan let himself down on the carpet.

Then, looking off into space, he tried to reconstruct for Sam all the things that had happened to him.

"You're so pale, Terry. You sick or something?"

"No, Lucy, I'm perfectly fine," she replied.

"Doesn't look like it. Did you see him?" her friend inquired.

"We spent the day together on the MacDermotts' boat."

"Swell. Tell me about it. Have a good time?"

"A wonderful time," Terry said, turning her eyes away.

"I saw some of the guys from the gang," Lucy informed her. "Seems they had one wild time last night! They decided to go have a look in Cannes and Monte Carlo. They smashed everything up in the gambling casinos. It was great, they said. Tonight, we're all getting together at the Siesta. You coming?"

"No."

"Why not?"

"Alan's going to come by for me," Terry said.

"Hey, this sounds serious. You falling in love or something?" Lucy wanted to know.

Terry buried her nose in *The Diary of Anaïs Nin, 1947–1955.*

"This the real thing?" Lucy asked.

Without letting go of the book, Terry dropped a lump of sugar in the cup of instant coffee she had just made. She started turning the spoon so as to crush the sugar. But the spoon was stirring outside the cup, on the oilcloth covering the table.

"What ever made you think such a thing?" she asked.

Bannister was drinking his sixth Scotch, Alan his second. Considering what was ahead, he felt he had to keep a clear head on his shoulders.

"Let me have another one," Sam said.

"You trying to get drunk?" Alan asked.

"No, but I'm trying to get my bearings," his friend replied. "I don't seem to recognize you anymore. It's like you've turned into a different person."

"You think a person can spend three days in this atmosphere and not be affected by it? In New York, I was locked into my quiet little job; I had my dreams; I didn't know what the world was like. I thought that working for a living was the way to get ahead. I was a sheep among the sheep, and I thought all the other sheep were honest and nice. I had never seen any of the wolves at work! This is where they share out the catch, Sam. Everyone is trying to bite off a bigger piece than the next fellow."

"Does that make them any happier?" Sam asked.

"Look, you've spent twenty-five years getting your ass kicked, only to be thrown out on your ear like an intruder," Alan said. "We only have one life to live, Sammy, and nobody lives it for us. Even as late as this morning, I was ready to drop the whole business, and try to get someone to give me a nice, quiet twenty-thousand-dollar-a-year job in New York. Which only goes to show that I'm just as much of a jerk as you!"

"But, then there was this Larsen character, Sam. I swear, I wouldn't have believed it if I didn't see it with my own eyes. But when he came up with the dough, then I knew anything was possible!"

"That may very well be," Sam told him. "But I can sleep nights."

"Sure. Because you're dead already, only you don't know it. Socially, financially, sexually—you're dead and buried. You're resigned, and you think that means you're good. That woman you just fucked here in my room—tell me, when was the last time you had a piece like that?"

"Crystal is good enough for me," Sam said.

"You're lying! It's just that you never dared try it before."

Bannister shook his head in embarrassment, then took off his glasses and wiped them.

"Maybe you're right about that. But that's no reason to go and do what you're planning," he said.

"They tried to kill me, you jackass!" Alan told him. "Every one of them tried to take me. You think I'm just gonna say thanks, and let it go at that?"

"Well, look," Sam said with some acerbity, "try to put yourself in my place. I sent away a broken rag of a friend who had just been fired from his job, and five days later I find he's turned into a gunrunning go-between, living the life of the affluent on the Riviera. He has turned his nose up at the heiress to the biggest private bank in the United States of America, but he's ready to swallow up the sixty thousand employees of the company he used to work for, and toss Hamilton Price-Lynch on the junkpile besides. How can you expect me not to feel it's all too much?"

"You're the one who pushed me into it," Alan reminded him. "Everything that you're criticizing is just what you told me I had to go ahead and do. Have you forgotten about that?"

"Talk is cheap," Sam admitted shamefacedly. "Those were just words I was saying."

"What about unemployed? Is that a word? And how about my corpse pickled in formaldehyde in the morgue at Cannes? Is that just a word, too? Could I count on you to take up a collection at Hackett's so there'd be some nice flowers at my funeral? I can see the scene from here, Sam. 'Let's all observe a moment of silence for poor old Alan Pope.'—And then, down to Romano's to tie on a snootful. Right?"

"You're scaring the shit out of me, Alan," Sam said.

"Well, then you shouldn't have filled my head full of those ideas of yours. Price-Lynch is a son of a bitch. Hackett is just as bad. And you think we ought to handle them with kid gloves after what they did to us? Well, it's too late, Sammy, my boy! I'm not giving them any more presents. Believe me, I've had some good teachers!"

Sam was going to say something, but Alan cut him off.

"No more time for words," he declared. "Now is the time for action."

With a slightly twitching finger, Alan dialed three numbers.

"Hamilton Price-Lynch?" he said. "This is Alan Pope. I have to see you right away down in the lobby. Yes, that's right. I'll be right there."

He turned to Bannister.

"Cut out the boozing," he told him, "and wait for me here. I'll be right back."

* * *

Price-Lynch's fingers had tensed around the telephone. "What's that you're saying?" he muttered into it.

"The deal didn't work out," Cesare di Sogno repeated.

Hamilton looked anxiously toward the door. Now more than ever, he felt that Pope had him at his mercy. Unless he was a complete idiot, Pope must have figured out who had tried to do away with him.

"It has to work out," he said into the phone.

"My associates are busy putting another deal together," Cesare told him.

"I hope it'll work better than the first one."

"Look, I'm doing the best I can!"

"That's not good enough! I want this taken care of before tonight—or else!" He didn't really know what he was threatening di Sogno with. Of course, he could turn the man in for any number of other things. But compromised as he himself was, which one would come out of it smelling worse?

"I'll take care of it," Cesare assured him. "It'll work out."

"I hope so, for your sake," Hamilton said as he hung up.

"Who were you talking to?" Emily wanted to know.

He was startled to see that she had come into the living room without his having realized it.

"Wrong number," he said.

She looked at him distrustfully.

"Where did you spend the day?" she asked.

"I was looking for you," he told her. "But I couldn't find you, so I came home."

"You look worried," his wife said.

"No, not at all. Everything's just fine."

She gave him that surly little smile she put on whenever she was about to announce a catastrophe.

"I've got a problem with Sarah," she said. "A real problem."

Hamilton knitted his brow and tried to look worried.

"Don't pretend to look upset," Emily said to him with just a trace of scorn in her voice. "I know that you're probably delighted. Unfortunately, this problem concerns you, too. She's taken it into her head that she's going to marry Alan Pope!"

Hamilton felt the blood drain from his face. The telephone rang. He didn't move.

"Well, what are you waiting for?" Emily ordered him. "Answer it."

He picked up the receiver as gingerly as if it had been white hot.

"Hello?" he said. "Yes, himself."

His face fell. Emily queried him with her eyes.

He shook his head in irritation.

"When?" he said. "Where? Okay. I'll be right down."

He hung up, and said nonchalantly, without daring to look at his wife, "That was Alan Pope, now. He wants to talk to me down in the lobby."

"I'll go," she said.

"Emily, you can't!"

"Why? I can certainly talk to a gigolo better than you can! And Sarah is my daughter, after all."

Hamilton repressed the desire he felt to slug her, smiled instead, and in a very calm tone, said, "Come, Emily. Let's do this with a little class. Let me get the news from him first. Once he's told me, I'll tell him we'll give him an answer later. Then we can decide what you want to do about it. Don't you think that's best?"

"Just don't be too long about it," she told him curtly.

Half the lobby of the Majestic was rented out to jewelers who displayed their finest merchandise in well-guarded windows. With relief, Hamilton spotted a dozen hefty men who were easy to recognize by the bump underneath their jackets and their determination to keep an eye out while looking at no one in particular. They were hired for the season to act as guardians for these precious displays.

Alan Pope was there already, sitting in an armchair beneath a potted palm. If he wanted to kill Hamilton then and there, those gorillas probably wouldn't give him the chance.

"Sit down, Mr. Price-Lynch," Alan said.

Hamilton sat on the edge of his buttocks, all set to leap away if Alan should prove to be armed.

"Is your offer still open?" Alan asked him.

"What? Did you change your mind?"

"Well, I've thought it over. And I don't see why I can't

do the job that you asked me to. Only not on the terms that you outlined."

Hamilton Price-Lynch relaxed a little. Pope was not here to talk to him about the attempts that had been made on his life.

"What did you have in mind?" he inquired.

"You offered me a hundred thousand dollars," Alan said. "I'd want two hundred thousand."

Hamilton's heart leaped with hope of success.

"That's quite a lot of money, Mr. Pope," he said.

"That's not for me to say, Mr. Price-Lynch," Alan replied.

The Hackett Chemical payroll was due for distribution the next day, July 28. It was now a matter of hours. Price-Lynch decided to take the plunge.

"All right. Suppose I accept?" he said.

"I don't deal in suppositions, Mr. Price-Lynch," Alan countered. "I need a yes or a no from you."

Hamilton pretended to be deeply upset. "You put me in a very difficult position," he said with a sigh.

"When would you pay me the money?" Alan asked.

"One half as soon as we reach an agreement, and the other half when the operation is completed," Price-Lynch said. "I would first have to have the two million dollars that I credited to your account transferred back to you again. Naturally, after you turned me down this morning, I gave instructions to have that money withdrawn from your account."

"Naturally," Alan agreed. "But at what bank did you intend to pay me the two hundred thousand?"

Hamilton looked at him with real shock on his face.

"Why, my own bank, of course. Burger Bank," he said.

Alan shook his head firmly.

"No, Mr. Price-Lynch, that wouldn't do at all," he told him. "How could I put my trust in a bank whose computer makes gross mistakes? Or in a banker who is out to double-cross his most important account? You can have the money credited to my account at Citibank. And now, will you please explain to me just what is supposed to happen in this transaction? You can tell me exactly what it is you expect me to do to earn your two hundred thousand dollars. I'm all ears."

Hamilton's eyes were wide with amazement, and he

remained silent for quite a while. Then, folding his hands over his knees, he began to speak.

26

"Well, Murray, how are we coming along?"

"Just fine, Mr. Hackett. Just fine."

"Not too much reaction over the layoffs?" Arnold asked.

"No, they've had a very salutary effect, Mr. Hackett. In spite of the summer season, I must say we've never had such a high level of productivity."

"Very good, very good," Hackett complimented him. "And now tomorrow is the twenty-eighth. Is our cash flow in good shape to meet the payroll?"

"Yes, it is. I'm having the usual payroll meeting at nine o'clock with Abel Fischmayer," Murray informed him. "Incidentally, you might be interested to know that he called me on the phone yesterday. Wanted some information about one of our people who had been let go."

"Well, tell him we're not in the business of acting as informants," Hackett said indignantly.

Arnold was still irritable because of the ungratefulness that Marina had shown him. Not the slightest affection, not a kind word, not even a thank-you. Nothing! If Poppy had been in Cannes, she would have spent her days crouching at his feet, listening to his every word, devouring him with her eyes. She wouldn't have shown up at a big affair with an Arab.

"You don't have to give anybody any information about what goes on within our company," Arnold instructed Murray.

"Well, it just happened, Mr. Hackett, that—"

"That's enough of that," his boss informed him. "You did say it was Fischmayer who called, didn't you? I'll take the matter up with Ham Price-Lynch myself."

"Very well, Mr. Hackett," Murray conceded meekly.

"And don't say yes to everything I say. You sound like a parrot," Hackett barked. "I like my associates to speak their minds to me. I like to be contradicted when it's in the best interests of Hackett Chemical."

"But, Mr. Hackett—"

"I'm gone a week and everything starts going downhill," Hackett complained. "On your toes there, Murray! Don't run the risk of spoiling my vacation!"

Arnold hung up abruptly without saying good-bye. He was sitting on the terrace of the hotel in a beach robe. He hadn't touched the club sandwich before him; the mayonnaise was beginning to make the bread soggy, because of the heat of the sun. Victoria was at her hairdresser's. He could have been having a good time now with Marina. For the hundredth time, he looked up at her windows. They were wide open, and there was no one in her room. Maybe he'd see her tonight at the costume party that Nadia Fischler was giving.

They looked at one another, each unable to tear his eyes away from the other's, unable to make a move, unable to speak. Through the open window, they heard the shrill tweeting of swallows, some bits of conversations between gossipy women on the street, and they could smell saffron and oil from the restaurant below.

"I was so scared you wouldn't come back," Terry said to him.

Alan took the two steps that separated him from her, and gently put his arms around her, burying his head in her hair, breathing in its wonderful scent.

They remained glued together that way, two victims of a shipwreck finding one another in the intimate island of a closed bedroom. Against his chest he could feel the suggestive outline of her breasts, and beneath his hand, the soft curve of her hips.

"I was so scared," she was saying.

"That's all over now, Terry," he reassured her.

He wanted to say something to her, something binding, words he had always considered idiotic when others spoke them.

And she felt it.

"Go on, Alan," she said. "Say what's on your mind. Speak to me. I need to hear your voice. I want to know that you feel the same way I do."

"I do," he said.

"Just as much?" she asked.

"Just as much."

"Then say it, Alan. Tell it to me," she implored.

The lump that was obstructing his throat kept him from answering. He hugged her tighter.

"Tell me, Alan," she repeated.

"I'm not prepared for what's happening to me," he finally got out.

"Neither am I," she concurred. "That's why I'm so scared."

"I didn't know that this was the way it would be," he said. "I imagined I'd jump you and devour you without a second thought. But that's not the way I feel."

She looked at him with an expression he had never seen before, then pulled her blouse up over her head and started to unbutton his shirt. Now he could feel the warmth of her nipples against his skin. He caressed them with the tips of his fingers, and his body thrilled with short shivers as he was overcome by a desire that took his breath away. He wanted to hold her, to keep her, to protect her, to drink in the aroma of every inch of her skin. He picked her up and carried her to the patchwork-covered bed. She did not take her eyes off him.

They lay next to one another.

"I want you to look at me," she said. "I want you to keep looking at me—always."

Their tongues met.

In her wide-open eyes, he was overwhelmed at seeing the reflection of the wild wave of enjoyment that was carrying them off to an unknown planet, millions of light-years away, where time and space meant nothing.

What was Price-Lynch to do now?

If he made the tender offer without being sure that Pope remained alive, it would be tantamount to committing suicide. And so far, di Sogno had not been able to get in touch with the hit men that he had put on Pope's trail.

On the other hand, if he waited another hour before acting, it would be forever too late. In his race against time, Hamilton decided to gamble on the only hope he had left, the hope that Pope was still alive, even if he had vanished as completely as the hired killers who were out to get him.

He called Fischmayer, in order to start the wheels rolling.

"Is that you, Abel?" he said. "Price-Lynch here."

He cleared his throat and assumed his dry, tough, authoritarian banker's tone.

"I'm in a great hurry, Abel," he went on, "so please don't hold me up by asking questions. Just do as I tell you, detail by detail and point by point. Understand?"

"Yes," Fischmayer answered reluctantly.

"Very well, then take this down carefully. Burger Bank is about to make a public tender."

"For whose stock, Mr. Price-Lynch?"

"Hackett Chemical's."

There was a long silence at the other end.

"Did you hear what I said, Abel?" he asked.

"Would you please repeat it, sir?"

"We are making a public tender for Hackett Chemical stock. Are you deaf, or what?"

"But, sir, Hackett Chemical is our biggest account!"

"Fischmayer," Hamilton said, "you've moved ahead most consistently at Burger Bank. My wife and I have even discussed the possibility of making you general manager. If you're not interested in that kind of a promotion, you might as well tell me so here and now."

"Oh, Mr. Price-Lynch, you know that the only thing that matters to me is what is in the best interest of Burger Bank," Fischmayer responded.

"Well, I am Burger Bank, and the sooner you get that through your head the better, Fischmayer!"

"Yes, sir."

"How much are we carrying Hackett for at the moment?"

"Oh, about the same as usual. Forty-odd million," Fischmayer said.

"Representing what?" Hamilton asked.

"Oh, various receivables we've discounted, a bunch of their payables, and some long-term notes. Hackett Chemical made several large investments within the last few months."

"And what figure is the payroll we'll be supplying tomorrow?" Hamilton asked.

"Forty million."

"Which means that by tomorrow night, Hackett Chemical will owe us something in the neighborhood of eighty-odd million dollars. Right?"

"Yes, sir. Exactly. But I would point out to you, sir, that this is a regular, normal occurrence," Fischmayer said.

"I appreciate your point, Fischmayer," Hamilton snarled at him. "Now, tell me, among Hackett's outstanding notes is there one for about half a million dollars?"

"I would imagine so, sir."

"Then buy that up immediately in the name of Alan Pope," Price-Lynch instructed him.

"With what money, sir?" Abel asked in a tight, disapproving voice.

"The principal whom I am representing in this has made a deposit of one hundred thirty million dollars to the Chase Manhattan. Have it transferred to Burger Bank. This money is to be used for the purchase of six and a half million shares out of the ten million shares outstanding. Hackett stock is selling right now at twenty dollars. You will have enough money on hand to pay cash to all shareholders who care to redeem their stock. Do you follow me, Fischmayer?"

"Yes, of course, sir."

"Is there something wrong, Abel?" Hamilton asked.

"Mr. Price-Lynch," Abel replied, his disgust coming through his voice, "this tender is absolutely impossible! Arnold Hackett personally holds sixty percent of the stock in his company. Even if all the other stockholders accept our offer, which you can't be sure of at all, your principal still won't have control."

"Do you think I'm an idiot, Abel?" Hamilton snarled.

"But, sir, do you think that Hackett is stupid enough to sell his own shares and lose control of his company?"

"Fischmayer," Price-Lynch said threateningly, "you don't know all the facts in the case, so you have no way of knowing what Hackett will do. But I have all those facts, and I know what I'm about. Now, yes or no, are you going to do as I have instructed you?"

"Of course, sir. I beg your pardon."

"Now then, let me dictate to you the text for announcing our tender. As soon as you get off the phone, I want you to get it out to all the media—dailies, business publications, news weeklies, tv, radio, the works. I want it to break everywhere tomorrow morning. Are you ready to take it down?"

"Go ahead, sir."

Hamilton dictated what he had scribbled on a pad a few minutes earlier:

Burger Bank today opened a tender for the purchase of all outstanding shares of Hackett Chemical at the going rate of $20.00 per share. This tender is contingent upon the number of shares offered for purchase by Burger Bank reaching 6,500,000 by the close of business on August 3.

Over three thousand miles away, Hamilton Price-Lynch could hear Fischmayer's sigh of resignation.

"What am I to tell the members of the board, Mr. Price-Lynch?" the man asked.

"Nothing," Hamilton shouted. "Let them go on sleeping. By the time they wake up, the whole thing will be signed, sealed, and delivered. Who do you handle the payroll with tomorrow?"

"Oliver Murray, sir."

"Listen to me. You tell him..." And Hamilton explained in detail what was to be said and done, despite Fischmayer's indignation, which grew more and more violent as he learned each new phase of the secret operation.

When Hamilton Price-Lynch finally hung up, he was soaked with perspiration. He wiped his forehead with one of Emily's scarves which she had negligently thrown down on the couch.

The die was cast.

Normally, after making love, Alan felt a need for time, time to be alone with his thoughts.

With Terry, Alan learned something he had never known before: that he could want a woman before, during, and afterwards, that he could just want her to be there with him so he could inhale her, feel her, listen to her, hear her silence. Day had turned into night in her small bedroom, hours had gone by, but Alan, coiled up with Terry, had never felt himself so free, so light. There was total accord between his own senses and the outside world, a perfect harmony in every second.

After the wondrous discovery of Terry's body, the frenzy that had thrown their two bodies together in a wild tumble of love, then the breathing spells had followed, allowing him to savor the intensity that just had been and imagine what the next would be like. Her concentration in becoming his, fully, wholly, so that there was no hollow within her that he could not reach, that she did not offer to him before he even guessed its existence, had surprised him. It was like diving into infinity, a golden spiral dotted with shimmering spots of light. In this wonderful shipwreck, the only reference points were the buoys of her beautiful wide-open eyes that remained forever locked into his.

Within these past few hours, Mabel, Marina, and all the others had receded into the limbo of forgetfulness. After Terry, no other woman could exist. Alan was afraid to admit to himself that without her there would never be another, only the cold emptiness of lifeless space.

"I'm so happy here, Alan," she said.

"What time is it?" he asked.

"I don't know."

"Terry," he said.

"Yes?"

"Put on a dress and come with me."

"Where?"

"We're going to a big private party on an estate. It won't take more than an hour, but I promised I'd go," he said.

"No, let me wait for you here," she replied. "I don't even want to see anyone else looking at you."

"But I want to have everyone see you," he told her. "I want to show you off. We'll come back right away. The hostess is Nadia Fischler. She just did something really magnificent for me, and I gave her my word of honor."

She ran her fingers around the outline of his lips.

"I'd rather wait for you here, Alan," she persisted.

"Really, you'll enjoy yourself. You have no idea what a thing like this can be like," he assured her.

"Go ahead by yourself," she said. "The sooner you go, the sooner you'll get back."

"You sure you won't mind?"

"Of course not. Let the rest of them enjoy you, too."

"You promise you won't move from here?" he said.

"Where do you think I could go?"

"Promise you won't even get out of bed?"

"I'm not up to it," she swore.

He got up, went and looked out into the darkness

through the slits in the shutters. He didn't want to leave her again. Ever. And he knew he'd tell her so when he came back.

In the eyes of eternity, what difference did one hour more or less make?

The entrance was through a huge oak portal that was wide open. The four men on guard merely scanned the faces of the guests whose chauffeurs stopped the cars for a moment to drop them off. Ground lights were set at intervals along the lane leading to the main building, which could be seen only after walking along a long pathway between greenhouses, flower beds, and exotic trees which filled the night with the heady aroma of their rare essences. Attendants carrying torches directed new arrivals toward the few remaining empty spaces where a limousine could still be parked.

Hadad got out of his limousine. "Stay in front of the entryway and wait for me. I won't be here long," he said to his chauffeur.

He was swallowed up in the music of ten bands playing in different places at different distances, and a hubbub of raised voices and noisy laughter. A six-foot-tall turkey passed by in front of him, followed by a pheasant hen. Hadad commented to himself that Nadia Fischler's guests were certainly having a good time on his money.

Three hostesses grabbed the prince by the arms and led him into the main hallway, which had been put into service as a dressing room.

"What kind of bird would you like to be?" they asked.

"A falcon," a voice answered for him.

Hadad turned and saw a magnificent bird of paradise wearing innumerable shimmering feathers. It was Nadia. He took the hand which she had extended to him and kissed it gallantly.

"Congratulations on the wonderful way you are managing my capital," he told her.

"No longer yours," Nadia answered icily. "My own."

"For how long, my dear Nadia?"

"Just as long as I come up against opponents whose nerve gives out on them," she replied with a dazzling smile.

Expert hands put a falcon's skull on his head.

He walked in after her and found himself in the eerie world of a surreal aviary. On seeing Hadad, an overweight turtledove took flight with frightened cooings.

"Heavens! A falcon," she cried.

It was two in the morning. Everyone was drunk. A stilt danced with a disheveled leghorn layer. Drink in hand, a vulture kissed a pheasant squarely on the mouth. A pelican, surrounded by Brahmaputra chicks, was telling a dirty story. A parakeet was lying in the arms of a cockatoo, and a partridge was running after a black swan, calling, "I am your Leda. Don't run away. Come back!"

Dozens of servants wearing sparrow costumes circulated among the guests. They had been instructed to serve drinks from the several buffets that were set up throughout the huge ballroom.

The bands were made up of sea gulls and parrots, and birds of all types danced the farandole. Elbow to elbow, feather to feather, there were ducks, penguins, pigeons, hummingbirds, blackbirds, and jays.

Off to the side a bit, a peacock was defending itself against the onslaught of a crow.

"Where do you expect me to be able to find them?" the peacock was saying. "I've tried everything. They've just made themselves scarce!"

"If they touch so much as a hair of Alan Pope's head, you'll be sorry," the crow threatened.

"But, Mr. Price-Lynch," the peacock argued, "you were the one who gave the contract."

"Call it off, Cesare," the crow answered. "I don't care how you go about it, but you're responsible for Pope's safety. Or else!"

The peacock turned on his heel and ran back toward the telephones. For hours, Cesare had been trying to reach Marco and Salicetti. But no luck.

"What a picture," Nadia commented. "Makes you want to get a gun and go hunting, doesn't it?"

"I hunt only big game," Hadad specified, smiling at her. "You know that everything about this place is a fake," he commented.

Nadia burst out laughing.

"Yes, this like all the rest," the prince told her. "The house, the trees, the statues, the birds—all are just illusion. All of this will fade along with the night!"

"Are you that upset with me for having won money from you?" Nadia taunted him.

"Another illusion," he said. "How do you know that you really did win it from me? When you turned up a five and I threw my cards in without showing them, could you swear that I didn't actually have you beat?"

"You bastard!" she snarled.

"I just wanted to give you another chance to go on believing in your good luck."

He bowed to her, and then added, sarcastically:

"As I believe in my own. To which I am now returning. Good night, madame."

"Oh, come now, come now," the crane said, pushing away the hand that the wild turkey cock had placed in her cleavage. "You are very attractive. But couldn't you take it a little easier?"

"Just wanted to see what would happen," Bannister answered.

A soft coxcomb crowned his head, which was bedecked with plumage that came down to his shoulders. Seeing how disappointed he looked, the crane took his hand and put it back on her breast.

"You like to play?" she asked.

"What, Karina?"

"A real fun game," she said. "One of my specialties. What we do is, you give me folding money, and I swallow it."

"You mean it?"

"Sure."

"I'd like to see that," he said.

"Got any money on you?" she asked.

He shook his coxcomb. "Not on me," he said. "The only thing I could give you to eat is my American Express card."

She placed her long blonde hair against his chest and petted his feathers thoughtfully.

"I've eaten worse," she said. "Maybe we could give it a try when we get back to the hotel."

"Oh, yes, a wonderful idea," Sam said.

A playful old owl joined them. Without letting go of his drink, the owl ceremoniously bent over and kissed the crane's hand.

"Hackett," the owl introduced himself. "I don't believe we've met..."

Bannister was startled. He caught sight of Alan, who, helped by the hostesses, was putting on a pigeon's head.

"Karina," Sam said, getting up precipitously, "tell Mr. Hackett about that little game of yours, won't you? I'll be right back."

He dashed toward Alan. But Sarah suddenly materialized from nowhere and got to Alan first. She was dressed as a toucan, in a shiny black tunic with a huge yellow beak.

"Alan! I've been looking all over for you!" she exclaimed, grabbing him by the arm. "Come along! I have to introduce you to some people!"

Alan sent a pleading look to Sam Bannister.

"Mr. Pope!" The crow, gasping for breath, took hold of Alan's hand and squeezed it as if he were a long lost childhood friend. "How amusing that you should be dressed as a pigeon," he quipped.

"Samuel, may I introduce Hamilton Price-Lynch to you?" Alan said.

The woebegone cock did a double take, but shook hands with Price-Lynch. Sam had had too many shocks in too short a time, and they had knocked him off his pins. He was ready by now to believe anything.

"Delighted, Mr. Burger," he absent-mindedly said.

Sarah was delighted with his gaffe. "Did you say Burger? That's a good one! Burger's my name, not his. But you can call me Sarah," she said.

Hamilton looked daggers at her.

"Come on, Alan," she repeated. "My mother is having a terrible time. She'd like to have a talk with you."

"I just got here," Alan said. "Let me go and pay my compliments to our hostess, and then I'll join you."

"I'm going with you," Price-Lynch declared. Hamilton was now ready to use his own body to shield Alan's from the hit men he himself had hired. Now that the attempt to buy Hackett Chemical was underway, Alan's existence was the key element in it, and Hamilton didn't plan to let him out of his sight. Danger, after all, could come from anywhere at any time. Nervously looking around, Price-Lynch paid special attention to a group of parrots who were sharing a magnum of champagne, passing the bottle from hand to hand and drinking directly from it.

"Hamilton," Sarah yelled, "stop hanging on to Alan like that!" She referred to Alan now as if he were already her property.

Bannister took advantage of her interruption to whisper in Alan's ear. "Guess who's gotten palsy-walsy with me," Sam said. "Hackett! What do you say we stop acting like jerks, huh? I'll come clean with him, and we'll both have our jobs back in no time!"

Alan gave Sam a powerful kick in the shins, and looked around the ballroom. It was a wild party, a barnyard let loose.

Alan realized that he could put this revelry to good advantage. He slipped out a side door, and in a few quick strides, he was well hidden behind a clump of bushes. He bent down, and started running along the edge of a line of shadow. He wanted to see Nadia so he could keep his word to her, and then get away and go back to Terry.

He looked back several times to make sure he had gotten rid of the crow and the toucan. He stumbled over a couple of golden eagles screwing on the grass, apologized, and went on his way.

The moon was beaming playfully through the branches of the pines that swayed softly in the sea breeze. There were couples everywhere, embracing in various positions on the lawns. As soon as a band stopped playing, he could hear the subtle sound of the sea. He saw a brilliantly plumed bird of paradise standing alone, and stopped.

"Nadia?" he asked.

"Alan!"

"You see, I came."

She turned his face to the moon, looked at him, grabbed his hands, and squeezed them affectionately.

"I'm so happy," she said.

"So am I. Did you really buy this estate?"

"Yes, I did."

"It's fantastic. I've never seen anything like it," he said.

"You'll come again," she told him.

He was struck by the unusual calmness in her voice.

"It must have cost you a fortune," he said.

"Only half of what it's worth—two million dollars," she

told him. "I paid cash. I wanted to have something that wouldn't fade away in a casino on a green baize table, something that would last at least for one night, for one full night. But it didn't work."

Alan was thunderstruck.

"What do you mean?" he asked.

"I've just sold it," she informed him.

He felt that lump in his throat again. She was walking slowly, dragging him along with her, holding him by the arm.

"I went back to the casino," she said. "And for the very first time, I forgot to take my good-luck charm."

Several embracing birds went by. This was certainly a magic night, soft and tender, and the whole planet seemed warm and reassuring. He put his arm around her shoulders.

"Hadad set a trap for me, and I lost everything I had," she said. "He came here, and he challenged me. Now I have no jewels, no furs, no cars, no house. Nothing. I can't even buy myself a pack of matches. I got the real estate agency people up in the middle of the night. I needed some cash money in order to go on gambling. They would only give me half a million dollars for this place, and I had paid two million a little while before.

"I lost it all on one banco. At times like that, a person goes completely crazy. Do you understand?

"Hadad was making fun of me. So I came back here. There are hundreds of people on my lawns, drinking my wine and stuffing their faces on my food. Not one of them has held a hand out to me or offered to lend me a sou. They all act as though they think I am kidding. Goldman even laughed in my face. Yet, how many times did I get that faker out of a hole! He's never paid me back. They're bastards, all of them!"

Alan drew her to him.

"Nadia," he asked, "how much do you need?"

At the end of the lawn, a waterfall spun into space. A stairway cut out of the rock led down to the sea below. At the bottom, along the concrete wharf, boats were dancing on the glinting reflections of the moon.

"How much, Nadia? How much?" he repeated.

She took his chin in her hands, and kissed him sweetly on the mouth.

"Nothing, Alan, thanks all the same," she said. "You were the only one."

She pulled away from him, gave him a smile, but her eyes were filled with so bitter an expression he couldn't stand it. Then she spread her huge wings and started running toward the cliff.

"Nadia!" he screamed.

But she ran faster and faster and faster, a magical bird whose feet were no longer touching the ground.

With horror, Alan saw her fly out into space with one final rustling of her feathers. The echo sent back the awful, dull thud of her body crashing below.

27

On the twenty-eighth of every month, Oliver Murray had the same tedious job to do. At nine in the morning, he would go to the main office of Burger Bank to sign the necessary papers so that the sixty thousand Hackett Chemical employees might get paid. He would be ritually received by Abel Fischmayer, who turned Murray's stomach with his huge size, his patronizing manner, his florid complexion, and his affected and paternalistic attitude.

Their meeting only took ten minutes or so, and for that length of time each of them would pretend to be delighted to be seeing the other again. Fischmayer seemed to delight in asking Murray about his health, commenting on his appearance, and inquiring about his wife.

"Mr. Fischmayer is expecting you, Mr. Murray," the banker's secretary said with a welcoming smile. "Just come this way, please."

Murray followed her into Fischmayer's office, every element of which was calculated to impress business callers—the distance one had to walk to get to Fischmayer's desk, the thickness of the wall-to-wall carpeting, the opulence of the furniture, the original art hanging from the burnished steel panels that covered the upper part of the walls, the bar with its rare liquors on display, the woodwork, and especially the stereo system so prominently in evidence.

"Delighted to see you, Oliver," Fischmayer said, standing up and coming around the desk to shake hands with Murray.

Murray felt revulsion, and the minute his hand was free again, he started taking some papers out of his briefcase. He placed them on the banker's desk.

"Well, how's your liver acting these days, Oliver?" Fischmayer asked.

"There's nothing wrong with my liver, Mr. Fischmayer," he replied.

"Are you sure? You look like you need a vacation, seem a little on the peaked side to me. I'll have to take you out for a spin some time. Do you play golf?"

"No."

"That's really too bad. How is Mrs. Murray?"

"Just fine, thank you."

He pointedly nodded toward the papers he had put down. "I don't have much time. Would you mind signing these?" Oliver asked.

Fischmayer walked back around his huge desk, sat down, and said, "Why don't you have a seat, Oliver?"

Murray let himself go into the armchair, so large that his body almost got lost in it.

"I have some distressing news for you, Oliver," Fischmayer said. "Burger Bank is not going to be able to advance the money for your payroll this month."

Murray jumped from the chair as if he had been shot out of it. "I beg your pardon?" he gulped.

Fischmayer gestured pacifyingly to him, although there was no longer the slightest trace of a smile on his lips.

"Your credit with the bank has reached forty-two million dollars," he stated coldly. "Our board of directors has decided that this is as far as we can safely go without Hackett Chemical giving us some more collateral. I'm afraid there's nothing I can do about it."

"You must be joking," Murray hissed, trying to keep his breathing under control. "We've been running this kind of a credit with you for years now. We're your biggest account!"

"Believe me, this was no easy decision for us. But you can readily see that, with forty-two million dollars outstanding, we can't very well approve an additional forty-million-dollar outlay."

"Why, Mr. Fischmayer, this is absolutely impossible!" Murray protested. "We've never had the slightest financial problem of any kind. You're being ridiculous. You know that Hackett Chemical's assets run into the hundreds of millions of dollars."

"Certainly," Fischmayer conceded. "But perhaps you've spread yourselves a little too thin. Your diversification and expansion program is certainly admirable, but this time our board felt that it just couldn't stretch any farther."

"This is some kind of a trap!" Murray yelled, pointing an accusing finger at Fischmayer. "If you decided to withhold funds, then you should not have waited until the last minute to let us know about it. You're putting us in a very difficult position, you know."

"Oh, I'm sure there's nothing basically wrong with the Hackett operation, Oliver," Fischmayer said.

"Stop calling me Oliver!"

Ignoring him, Fischmayer went on, "I'm sure that with your company's reputation, you'll have no trouble coming up with the money to meet your requirements."

"Eighty-two million dollars in three days isn't peanuts, Mr. Fischmayer. And you know that any small creditor can have us thrown into bankruptcy if you cut off our credit, to say nothing of what it would mean to our reputation if we missed a payroll! I can't believe that you are doing this to us. Have you really thought through what you are doing?"

"Our board—" Fischmayer began.

"Your board be damned," Oliver cut in. "I will get on the phone immediately and let Mr. Hackett know how you are treating us. We'll see what Hamilton Price-Lynch has to say about it! In case you didn't know, the two of them are vacationing together on the Riviera. Good day to you, sir!" He turned and walked out, purple with indignation.

Fischmayer made no move to stop him.

Sitting in his limousine, on the way back to his office, Murray glanced at the front page of the *Times*, which he hadn't had a chance to read yet this morning. His eye was caught by a small paragraph referring to a lead story in the Financial Section. It read:

Tender for Hackett Stock

Burger Bank has made a tender for all outstanding shares of Hackett Chemical stock. Page D1.

Murray's complexion faded to a waxy colorlessness. He started to turn to the business pages.

"Get me to the office as fast as you can," he ordered his driver.

With his stomach churning, he read the announcement carried on page D1. Then he began to understand the awful fact that Burger Bank had just lured Hackett Chemical into a trap.

Alan opened an eye, looked around without realizing at first where he was, then saw that he was coiled around Terry. She was sitting on the bed, wearing glasses, reading her favorite book. He closed his eyes again and snuggled closer to her.

"What time is it?" he asked.

"Four o'clock."

"A.M.?"

"P.M.," she answered.

She was naked and warm.

"I've been up for hours," she added. "But I didn't dare move for fear of waking you. You were hanging on for dear life."

"I don't believe you!"

"You were talking to me in your sleep, and kissing me," she told him. "I tried to break away once or twice, but you almost crushed me, you held on so."

"Terry . . ."

"Yes?"

"This is just right."

She leaned over, lightly kissed his lips, and patted his shoulders.

"You want some coffee?" she asked.

"I want you," he said.

"I'll make coffee for you and be right back."

"That's what they all say!" he mumbled.

After Nadia had committed suicide, he had had to stay two more hours at La Volière. The police had come and questioned all those who had actually seen what took place.

By the time he got back to Terry's, Alan was at his wit's end. She had listened to his account and comforted him. He had indeed hung on to her as if she were a lifebelt. He had made love to her as he had never before made love to anyone in his life, deeply, uninterruptedly, violently, and tenderly, all at the same time.

Sleep had overcome him while he still embraced her, his body against hers, his lips to her mouth.

"Did I really fall asleep hanging on to you?" he asked.

"So tight I couldn't breathe," she said.

"That never happened to me before."

"Nor to me either," she laughed.

"Terry..."

"Yes?"

"I want to live with you," he said.

"For three days?" she taunted.

"Forever."

She took his face into her hands and looked very seriously into his eyes.

"Don't say things like that to me," she declared.

"Why?"

"I might believe them."

"You want to?"

She shrugged.

"Terry, do you want to?" he repeated.

They looked at each other again, intensely questioning each other's eyes. The same electric thrill ran through both of them.

"Oh, yes," she whispered.

"You know, what's happening to us is just crazy," he said.

"Crazy," she echoed.

"For the first time in my life," he confided to her, "I don't feel like being somewhere else, or like doing something other than what I am doing. If I had my druthers, it would be to stay here with you, like this, and not have anything change. I feel like there's nothing missing in my life now. Everything is just as it should be. Can you understand that?"

He shivered as her nails ran slowly across the nape of his neck.

"Yes," she said.

"We've had so little time together," he went on. "We've

hardly had a chance to talk. Listen, Terry. I'm going to be very busy in the next few hours. I may have to be busy for a day or two. Will you wait for me?"

"Yes, if you promise you'll never go waterskiing again."

"I promise. I'll explain all about it to you later. There's something wild going on in my life, Terry! A terrific chance, the kind you get once in a lifetime. If it works, I'll be in the chips for the rest of my life."

"Who needs it?" she said.

"Look, you don't really know me," he told her. "I've had my fill of what I was. I was really down on my luck."

"Who needs it?" she asked again.

He laughed, not knowing how to answer.

"It would take too long to explain. And you'd never be able to understand," he said.

She threw herself against him violently.

"Alan," she whispered, "there's nothing to understand."

"I'm phoning you from the lobby. I have to see you at once."

Hamilton Price-Lynch was startled to recognize the voice of Cesare di Sogno.

"Did you catch up with them?" he panted into the phone, nearly crushing the receiver in his hand.

"Yes."

"Thank heavens for that."

Luck was turning his way; Pope was still alive, and would stay alive. Soon Hamilton Price-Lynch would gain control of Burger Bank, dump his penny-pinching wife, spit in the eye of his bitch of a stepdaughter, fire Abel Fischmayer, and finally be free to live his own life, taking orders from nobody.

"I must see you at once," di Sogno was repeating.

Hamilton was offended by the commanding tone this hoodlum was using. He had done what he was supposed to, now all he had to do was get out!

"Not here," he told Cesare. "That's out of the question. I'll contact you later. Good-bye."

"Don't hang up! I only need five minutes—but it's got to be right away!"

"No, impossible. My wife is in the next room."

"That's not true. I just saw her down here; she went off

in a car. I'm telling you, you'd better agree to see me. I'm on my way up."

Hamilton looked at the dead phone in his hand with powerless fury. Cesare di Sogno had had the gall to hang up on him!

He lit his fiftieth Muratti of the day, kicked at the leg of the couch, stubbed his toe, yelled in pain, and then started limping across the living room.

There was a knock on the door.

"Do you want the whole world to be in on the fact that we're working together?" he demanded of Cesare as the latter came in.

"There's so much going on in this hotel that not a soul noticed my coming up here."

"Did you reach them?" Hamilton asked again.

"Yes."

"No more danger?"

"None."

"Then what's the matter?"

"They have to be paid."

"We paid them."

"What are you talking about?"

"We paid after our first deal," Hamilton said.

"But not for the second one."

Price-Lynch raised a haughty eyebrow.

"They didn't do anything, so far as I know," he said.

"I beg your pardon?"

"Pope is still alive," he told Cesare. "Your friends didn't carry out the contract. I don't owe them anything."

A fleeting shadow passed over Cesare di Sogno's handsome Roman face.

"Mr. Price-Lynch, what the fuck are you talking about?" he said.

"I forbid you to use such a tone to me," Hamilton exclaimed.

"You owe them thirty thousand dollars," Cesare informed him.

"Not one red cent!" he yelled back. "Over and done with. Forget it."

Cesare gave him a hard, scornful look.

"It would be better for you if you kept your word," he muttered.

"Get out of here! I'm finished with you!" Hamilton shouted.

"Is that all you have to say?"

"Get out! And don't ever come back!"

"Okay, I'll give them your message. You can settle it with them," Cesare said.

"You do anything at all, and I'll turn you over to the police," Price-Lynch threatened.

Cesare turned on his heels, went to the door, and then, before slamming it behind him, called:

"I wouldn't want to be in your shoes!"

Sam Bannister was at Alan the moment Alan entered the suite.

"I've been trying to find you since last night," Sam said. "Everybody's looking for you. Price-Lynch has been on the phone every five minutes. Sarah must've been here ten times already. I thought something had happened to you. I was getting ready to call the police."

Alan just walked by Sam as if he didn't hear. He had a strange beatific smile on his face, and his eyes seemed to be contemplating something far away. He looked hypnotized.

"Alan," Sam called.

"Hello, Sammy," he replied dreamily.

He went over to the bar, poured himself a drink, and went out on the balcony. Nonplussed, Bannister followed him.

"Are you listening to me, Alan?" Sam asked. "Or are you up in the clouds somewhere."

"I'm going to get married," Alan said, as if that were the most natural thing in the world.

Bannister's face broke into a delighted smile.

"You mean it?" he asked.

"Sure."

"Boy, I knew you would! That's terrific! That'll be the end of all our troubles. The richest girl in America!"

"Rich? Is Terry rich?" Alan asked.

"Who?"

"Terry."

"Terry?" Bannister gasped. "Who the hell is Terry?"

Alan leaned against the rail of the balcony. He was floating in a happy daze. Everything was beginning to fall into place. Time, which had already given him a past and a present, was now adding a wonderful new dimension, the future. He wasn't going to give anyone a chance to take that away from him.

"Just wait till you see her," he said. "She's..." He was trying to find the proper words to describe her. But Terry was just not describable. He shrugged, and sipped his Scotch.

"What does she do for a living?" Bannister asked in a worried tone.

"She's a student."

"Where'd you meet her?"

"Here, at Juan-les-Pins. She was writing graffiti on the side of my car. She has gorgeous hair, and she's a little bit of a hippie—you know what I mean?"

"What's her name?"

"Terry."

"But the rest of it?"

"I don't know. She has beautiful gray eyes."

"You're planning to marry a girl whose name you don't even know?" Bannister exploded. He slammed his palm against his forehead and looked to the heavens as witness.

"The man's out of his mind!" Sam said. "The richest heiress in the U.S. of A. can't keep her hands off his fly, and he goes and falls in love with some nameless hippie! I won't let you do it, Alan! I swear! I'll protect you from yourself!

"While you were gone, Sarah talked to me a lot. She's nuts about you, and she wanted to know everything I could tell her. She filled me in on your plans."

"What plans?" Alan asked.

"The house you're going to live in, your private plane, your yacht, your horses. You'll be managing director of the bank, and she's naming me head of the credit department."

"Congratulations," Alan said.

"I haven't mentioned salary to her yet."

"Oh, I'm sure that won't be any problem."

"I wouldn't think so," Sam agreed in all seriousness. "You'll be spending Christmas at your estate on Cape Cod."

"Will we?" Alan asked.

"Easter in the Bahamas. There's a Burger tradition that they always spend Easter in the Bahamas. Did Sarah tell you about her grandmother?"

"Not that I recall."

"Name's Margaret," Sam said. "A terrific woman. She's ninety-one years old, and is still the elder statesman of the family, so to speak."

There were several sharp raps on the door. A female voice called, "Sam!"

"That's Sarah," Bannister whispered. He began to turn toward the door when Alan grabbed him.

"Listen, Sammy," he said. "And pay attention to what I'm telling you. I'm going to hide in the bathroom. And if you so much as let Sarah guess that I'm here, you'll never see me again. That's a promise!"

"You can't do that to her!" Sam said. "She loves you. She wants you. She's worried over you."

"You heard me, Samuel," Alan replied. "I still need forty-eight hours to get myself out of the mess you got me into."

"The richest girl in America," Bannister was imploring.

"Get rid of her, or you'll be sorry!"

After one last threatening look at his friend, Alan slipped into the bathroom and locked the door.

"Coming!" Bannister called. He checked his looks in the mirror, straightened his shirt, and went to the door.

Arnold Hackett rushed for his box of heart pills and quickly swallowed two. He came back into the bedroom and collapsed on the bed, his face livid, desperately trying to catch his breath. Victoria had gone shopping, and he would die here all by himself. His mouth wide open, he waited for his heart, beating away like a bellows within his chest, to calm down.

What Oliver Murray had just told him on the phone was too fantastic to contemplate: Burger Bank had refused to cover his payroll, when Hackett Chemical had been the bank's best account for the past fifteen years. In fact, Burger Bank was making a tender for all the outstanding shares of Hackett Chemical—the shares in his own company! It was just too much. He felt like getting up, grabbing something heavy that he could use as a weapon, and going down the hall to find Hamilton Price-Lynch, then beat his brains in. Did that nothing of a little banker think that Hackett was going to let himself be eased out of his own company? To think that he had been spending his vacation with a double-crosser!

If what Murray had said was true, Price-Lynch would never be able to wipe away the insult to Hackett, no matter how long he lived. Arnold would ruin him, have him thrown out into the street, buy up his bank if need be, but get him he would, one way or another!

Arnold realized that his breathing was returning to normal. He forced himself to remain quiet for a few more minutes, while he seethed inwardly with hate. But finally, he couldn't stand it any longer. He got up, went out of the suite, and walked the few yards to Price-Lynch's door, which opened just as he was about to knock on it. Out came the double-crosser.

"Why, Arnold, how are you?" Hamilton said.

"Let me by, you scoundrel."

Hamilton quickly stepped into the hallway and pulled the door shut behind him.

Arnold grabbed Hamilton roughly by the lapels of his jacket.

"Your tender! My payroll!" he roared. "What is this all about?"

Price-Lynch tried in vain to break free, but Hackett had a grip of iron.

"Control yourself, Arnold," the banker said. "Let's go down to the bar and talk this over."

"Then it's all true!" Hackett exclaimed.

Some hotel guests walking through the corridor, looked away politely and continued on their way.

"Please, Arnold, let's have a little decorum," Price-Lynch said. "We're among gentlemen here."

"Some gentleman! You swine!"

"Arnold! People are watching. Let's not make a scandal of this."

Still hanging on to his lapels, Hackett dragged Hamilton to the end of the hall and pushed him through the double swinging service doors that led to the dumbwaiter.

"Tell me what this is all about, or I'll knock your block off!" he hissed.

"I didn't have anything to do with it, Arnold," Hamilton contended. "My board of directors simply decided not to extend another forty million dollars' credit beyond the forty-two you already owe the bank."

"And what about that tender, you double-crossing Judas? Who's behind that? And what do you think you'll get out of it? You think I'm going to come to you and sell you my shares?"

A floor waiter stared at them open-mouthed, considered going back where he had come from, but then thought better of it.

"Excuse me, gentlemen," he said, as he went by.

Hackett, who had Price-Lynch pinned to the wall, remained still long enough for the waiter to take some trays out of the dumbwaiter and put them on a serving cart.

"Excuse me again," the waiter said, as he went back out, looking straight ahead, and pushing his cart in front of him as if he were in a race.

"What is all this about, anyway, huh? I want to know that, Price-Lynch!"

"Arnold, you're choking me," Hamilton replied. "You're going to force me to fight back!"

Hackett released his grip, slapped him savagely, then knocked his head back against the wall again.

"Fight back, you miserable twerp," he snarled. "You wouldn't know how! You lousy little gigolo! Everyone knows you're nothing but your wife's kept man! You haven't got the balls of a castrated lizard! Just wait till I'm through with you. You'll be ruined, your bank'll be worthless, and you'll be back where you started—in a manure heap, where you belong!"

Hackett grabbed a dish of tomatoes à la Provençale from the dumbwaiter and slopped it over Price-Lynch's head. A red goo blinded Hamilton and ran down onto his immaculate white suit. He raised his arms to try to protect himself. Hackett grabbed what was left of the tomatoes and squashed them into Hamilton's face, then went back into the corridor, leaving his victim there with the stacks of dirty dishes.

Alan cautiously stuck his head out the bathroom door. "She gone?" he inquired.

"Unless she's hiding under the bed," Sam Bannister answered tartly. "I just can't understand you, Alan. I think the heat here went to your head. Barely a week ago you were ready to end it all, because you had lost your job. Now you've got the chance to be the head of a bank, and you spit on it!"

Alan piled a few of his things into a bag.

"Not on the bank, Sam. Just on Sarah. There's a difference."

"What have you got against her?" Sam wanted to know. "She's very good-looking."

"She's beginning to act like her mother already," Alan said. "And I have no intention of becoming another Ham Burger."

"Where are you going?" Sam asked.

"Out on my yacht."

"Your yacht? What yacht?"

"The one you told me I had to charter so I would impress people, you jerk! I have to get away from all the people who are on my tail. I have some accounts to settle, and some things to do, and I need some peace of mind while I'm doing them."

"Is it a nice yacht?" Sam asked.

"Gorgeous."

"What am I supposed to do? Where do I fit in?"

"You stay right here," Alan told him. "Be my eyes and ears; keep me informed and forewarned about everything."

"What's the name of your yacht?"

"The *Victory II.*"

"Where's it located?"

"In a berth in the Old Port. But I'm warning you, if you do the least thing to attract attention, I'm sailing for the West Indies. I absolutely have to have a free hand for the next forty-eight hours."

"What am I supposed to say if anyone is looking for you?" Bannister asked.

"Tell 'em you didn't see me, you don't know where I am. Tell them I left on a trip."

Sam poured himself a glass of liquor, sat down on the arm of the chair, and glanced sideways at Alan, thinking. Such a change in his friend in so short a time was more than he could comprehend.

"Alan..."

"Yes?"

"This business about marrying the hippie student. That

was a gag, wasn't it? You were just trying to scare me, I bet."

"I'm inviting you to be best man."

"Too bad," Sam sighed. "Here I was thinking I had a chance to be one of the top executives of Burger Bank. It's just like I got fired from my job for a second time."

Alan was closing the bag.

"Alan . . ."

"What is it now?"

"If whatever it is that you're on to succeeds, you think you might be able to use me as your secretary?"

Alan pretended to be outraged by the idea.

"Come on, Sam," he answered. "You don't even know any shorthand."

Oliver Murray hung up once more, dejected. The public announcement of the tender had been enough to sow seeds of panic throughout Wall Street. The most alarming rumors about Hackett Chemical were running rife. The firm was on its last legs, people said, and everyone wanted to pull in their sails while there was still time.

The principal stockholders kept calling to find out what was what. The phones were ringing off their hooks on every one of the eight floors of the Rilford Building which housed the company's main offices. Desperate calls were coming in from branches and representatives in every corner of the United States. The managers, the technicians, the chemists, the medical consultants, all wanted to know what this new development meant for them.

In a few hours, the entire balance of power had been altered. The large banks which generally came hat in hand to ask Hackett Chemical to make use of some of their money, now turned a deaf ear on the quiet SOS that Murray had sent out. None was ready to come up with the money. The sharks were just swimming around waiting to get their share of the prey.

Murray begged Arnold Hackett not to return to New York. There were still two more days in which Murray could find the money and get control back into his own hands.

But Murray no longer believed that was possible. As he saw it, the only way to avert the disaster was to get Hamilton Price-Lynch to change his mind. Price-Lynch was the one who had started the whole thing. He could still call it off, if Hackett played it cute, negotiated, and agreed to make it look as if he had taken a beating. Unfortunately, once the old man's pride was at stake, he became as stubborn as a mule. But if he refused to stoop to conquer, the company would go into bankruptcy within the next forty-eight hours.

In that case, Oliver Murray knew he wouldn't have a job left. With a weary gesture, he now answered the phone for the hundredth time since the start of this deadly morning.

28

The knock-down-drag-out fight between Arnold Hackett and Hamilton Price-Lynch two days earlier was by now well known to everyone at the Majestic, the Palm Beach, and other choice spots up and down the Croisette. Everybody in Cannes had wondered aloud about what might have caused it. And then the newspapers, in prominent stories, had announced Burger Bank's tender for Hackett Chemical stock.

Ever since he heard what was threatening him, Arnold Hackett had moved heaven and earth to try to scare up new funds. But to no avail. He had contacted every banker he could think of, but to a man, they had turned him down.

Washington had turned a deaf ear to his pleas. The Secretary of Labor—an old family friend—had not been the least bit moved when Arnold reached him with his most powerful argument: "If Hackett goes under, that means the loss of sixty thousand jobs!"

"What about your skull sessions, Murray?" he had demanded. "Anything come of them?"

"We're still looking for a way out, Mr. Hackett."

"You're all a bunch of incompetents, Murray! You're being paid to find a way out, not look for one!"

"Mr. Hackett, please listen to me for a minute," Murray pleaded. "If we don't solve this thing in the next four hours, it's all over!"

Despite the thousands of miles between them, each man could hear the other's anguished breathing at the end of the line.

"I'm told the small stockholders are standing on line at Burger Bank, Mr. Hackett," Murray went on. "And here at our offices, there's a real panic setting in. Creditors are coming at us from every direction."

"Tell those ungrateful bastards to wait!" Hackett roared. "We've never been late on a payment to them in over thirty years!"

"But everyone is scared! All kinds of rumors are around. At twenty dollars a share, they're all selling."

"Who do they think holds control?" Hackett roared on. "I own sixty percent of the stock. What the hell is there to be scared of?"

"Mr. Hackett, if we don't find forty-two million dollars right away to take care of what's outstanding, and forty million more for the payroll, this company is bankrupt."

"How the hell can anybody be expected to find eighty-two million dollars in a few hours—and on a Sunday yet?"

"What if you were to sell some part of the shares you hold?" Murray timidly suggested.

"Never!" he thundered.

"They're going to go down in value by the minute. You'd better do something fast, Mr. Hackett!"

"I was right. Not one of you knows his ass from his elbow. I should have come back to New York right away."

"No, sir. Our only hope is there in Cannes."

"Murray, if you mention Price-Lynch's name to me once more, I'll fire you, so help me! I may be facing financial ruin, but I'll be damned if I'm going to crawl to that worm!"

"Mr. Hackett, if Price-Lynch wanted to, he could still withdraw that tender! I beg you, in the interests of the company, won't you go and talk to him?"

"I warned you, Murray. This is it. You're fired."

"I already have been—six times today by actual count."

"Well, then, this is the seventh time. You've done enough damage already. From now on, I'm going to run things myself. Have everybody stay where they are. I'm on my way home."

And he hung up.

"Your heart, Arnold! Think about your heart!" Victoria warned him.

"You, shut up!"

Ever since he had smashed the dish of tomatoes into Price-Lynch's ugly puss, Arnold had been living on his nitroglycerine pills. He had hardly slept a wink. Victoria was driving him crazy; she wouldn't let him out of her sight. It was the first time in years that he really needed her to watch over him—and she was doing it with a vengeance.

"Phone the concierge," he yelled to her. "Here, let me have that phone." He grabbed the instrument from her hands, and dialed himself.

"Concierge?" he asked. "This is Arnold Hackett. I want a chartered jet to stand by at Nice Airport... Yes, right away... A Boeing, if you say so, it doesn't matter. Just be ready to fly me direct to New York."

"It makes me ill to see you carrying on so about mere matters of money," Victoria said.

"They're trying to bleed me to death. What do you expect me to do? Watch myself die, then thank them besides?"

"Take these."

He swallowed the two pills she handed him. But they were not enough to calm the constriction that he felt inside his chest.

"Call Richard," he said. "Have him get the car ready."

She found new courage and put her hands on his shoulders, reestablishing a physical contact they had long ago abandoned.

"Arnold, I was just thinking—"

"What are you thinking now?" he retorted.

"Do you really know what you're going to do when you get to New York?" she completed her thought.

She kept her hold on him, despite the rebuff. He tried to fill his lungs with air, closed in on himself, and stayed that way for a moment, looking into space, thinking. What was being done to him was something he had done a dozen times to others. He wasn't fooling himself with the bravado he was putting on. The fact that he was going back to the office to head up his staff would have no effect whatsoever on the course of events. He was beaten; this time, it was his turn to give in. He could feel the weight of his years, the exhaustion of all the successes he had carried off as a pitiless combatant.

He shrugged wearily, and then said, in somber resignation, "No, Victoria. I don't know what I'm going to do."

"Well, my friend, I've got nothing but good news for you. Everything is going off exactly as planned. In only two days, we've acquired thirty percent of the stock."

John-John Newton met Hamilton Price-Lynch's optimistic report with a skeptical face. "That's a bit short of outright control, isn't it?"

"I promised you that Hackett would have to give in," Hamilton said, "and he will. Before four this afternoon, I can guarantee you that you'll have control of Hackett Chemical. Arnold has no choice anymore. If he doesn't sell, he'll lose the bundle!"

"I wish I could see it as hopefully as you do," Newton said.

"I'm not being hopeful, old man, I'm being realistic."

"Suppose he decides to go down with the ship?"

"He's not that crazy!"

"Do you think he might still get money somewhere at the eleventh hour?" Newton asked.

"I'm afraid he can't. The only place he could get it is from me. But I have to be leaving now. I'll go back to my suite and supervise the final details of the kill. Can I reach you here later?"

"I'll be right here all the time."

"See you later, then. I expect I'll have the victory bulletin for you even sooner than I'd thought."

As he crossed the foyer of Newton's suite, Hamilton wondered who the woman was whose scent was still lingering there. Deciding not to wait for an elevator, he merrily walked up the three flights to the seventh floor. In his living room, the phone was ringing.

He answered it, and delightedly recognized the voice of his pigeon.

"Green light," Hamilton said.

"Okay, I'm on my way," Alan Pope answered.

*   *   *

Arnold was still sitting motionless in his armchair when he saw Victoria come in from the foyer. He hadn't even noticed that she had moved away from him.

"Arnold, can you see Mr. Pope?" she asked.

"Who?"

"Alan Pope. The young man who had dinner with us at the Palm Beach. He says he has some very important information for you about your business. No reason not to see him is there? I'll show him in."

Richard was waiting for Arnold at the wheel of the Rolls-Royce. The plane was standing by at the airport. In New York, the world was coming to an end. And now, ten minutes after making up his mind, Arnold still hadn't budged from his chair. Through the open window, he could hear children shouting as they dared each other to dive into the pool. The door creaked, and Victoria showed Alan Pope in.

"How do you do, Mr. Hackett," Alan said.

With his eyebrows knitted, Hackett looked the young man over. He couldn't be any more than thirty years old. He envied him his youth. And without getting up, he nodded to him. "I'm going off on a trip. All I can give you is half a minute. What did you want to tell me?" he asked.

Alan smiled politely. "I've just heard what's been happening to you, Mr. Hackett," he began, but Arnold was already shaking his head impatiently.

"What's this important information you have for me?" he demanded. "Come to the point."

"I can get you out of your bind in a minute," Alan told him offhandedly.

Arnold was stunned. This fellow was crazy! "What do you mean by 'get me out of my bind'?" he asked.

"Settle those forty-two million dollars' worth of payables staring you in the face, Mr. Hackett."

"Where did you get that figure from?" Arnold barked.

"Every penny-ante broker on the street knows that figure."

Hackett eyed him arrogantly. "And I suppose you have forty-two million dollars?"

"If I didn't, do you think I would have come here to bother you?"

Arnold quickly started mental calculations that were a combination of distrust, hope, and cunning.

"What would you expect from me in exchange?" he asked warily.

"Your controlling shares," Alan coldly stated.

"As soon as I saw you, I knew I was dealing with a madman," Arnold answered.

"That's something we'll soon find out, Mr. Hackett. I'm ready to wipe out your forty-two-million-dollar debt, if you'll give me your six million shares."

"Are you ready to come up with an additional hundred and twenty million dollars?"

"Considering the current situation, do you think any-one would be silly enough to pay twenty dollars a share for them? Hackett stock is burning a hole in everybody's pocket. They're fighting to get rid of their shares, not buy them."

"And you think I'm silly enough to scuttle my own ship?"

"No, but I think you're smart enough to know that in barely four hours more, it'll be too late to sell anything at all. You will have gone into bankruptcy, Mr. Hackett. In view of that, I'm ready to make you a very decent offer. In exchange for your six million shares, I will pay you seventy million dollars."

Mentally, Hackett was reversing their roles. If he had been in Pope's place, he would have started with an offer of thirty or forty million, planning to bargain and settle for no more than fifty.

"That's a ridiculous offer," Hackett threw at him. "I wouldn't think of it."

"Take it or leave it," Alan said.

By the tone of Pope's voice, Hackett could sense that the young man facing him was not going to be bluffed down.

"Sit down, Mr. Pope," Arnold said in a conciliatory tone.

Wearing only her straw hat and black kid gloves, Marina was brushing her teeth over the bathtub. How had she ever stayed stuck in New York, she wondered, when there was a place like Cannes? She rinsed her mouth, went back into her room, and looked around at the bouquets of roses that were crowding it. She wondered how all those people found out where she lived.

She thought she'd do a few push-ups, then decided that it was too hot.

The technique, she realized, was always the same. First they sent flowers, and then they phoned to ask her out. But Khalil always came for her before dinnertime to take her to Prince Hadad's quarters.

Several times a day, Hadad would send her presents—a small diamond, a bracelet, a string of pearls. Marina thought he was real cute. She didn't give a damn about the money or the jewels, but it was nice to have him thinking of her all the time like that. The men she had known before had never treated her that nicely. She could hardly wait to tell Poppy all about it.

She was getting ready to lie down on the bed when she heard someone scratching at her door. She went to open it and stood there dumbfounded.

"My God," she said, "what happened to you?"

"Mr. Pope, my hearty congratulations!"

Hamilton Price-Lynch was lighting his third cigarette in two minutes, and doing his best to control the tics that in his excitement were contorting his face. Up to the last second, he had really been as pessimistic in his heart of hearts as John-John Newton. He had never been able to believe that Hackett would actually capitulate.

"How did the meeting go, Mr. Pope?" he asked.

"Nice and easy," Alan said. "Arnold Hackett could readily see where his own best interests lay."

"Did he threaten you? Or curse you?"

"Not at all. And why should he?" Alan replied. "Wasn't I showing him the way out of this mess?"

Price-Lynch looked up sharply to see whether that last remark was intended as a barb. Alan's face did not reveal a thing.

"In order to convince him, did you use that unpaid note that I had bought back for you?" Price-Lynch asked.

"It wasn't necessary."

"Do you have his agreement in writing?"

"Of course, Mr. Price-Lynch."

Alan took it from the inside pocket of his jacket. Hamilton grabbed it eagerly. His hands shook as he raised it to read it.

Alan walked over to the bar and took out glasses, ice, and some liquor.

"Want a drink?" he asked.

"No. No, thanks. Did you give him his check?"

"Do you suppose that he would have signed that paper without getting a check? He phoned New York first to make sure that it could be certified by the bank and credited to him. Incidentally, do you have mine?"

"Yours?"

"Yes, my check. The hundred thousand dollars," Alan said. Unobtrusively, he took back the signed paper on which Hackett stated he had sold him six million shares for the sum of $70,000,000.

"Here it is," Ham Burger said. "I had it ready and waiting."

Alan took his time in checking it carefully for date, amount, and proper signature.

"How about the other check?" he asked.

"As agreed. You get it as soon as you return from New York. When are you leaving?"

"Right away. There's a chartered jet waiting at the Nice Airport to make a round trip. You'll be getting the bill for it any time now."

"What?"

"I took the liberty of having it billed to you. There's no reason, of course, for me to pay my own expenses. Arnold Hackett had the charter reserved. You're very lucky!"

"What's it going to cost?" Price-Lynch choked.

"How should I know? You'll see when they bill you. I assume you've already made the necessary arrangements for all the creditors' bills to be honored."

"Mind your own business," Hamilton told him. "Just do as I've instructed and keep your nose out of anything else. How long will it take you to get back?"

"Oh, seventeen, eighteen hours. Just the time I need to get to your bank and head back. I presume that everything is set to go off without a hitch. And now, if you'll excuse me, I have to pack for the trip."

Price-Lynch bored into him with a suspicious look. "Try not to make any mistakes, Mr. Pope," he said.

"I'll do my best," Alan replied noncommittally.

After Price-Lynch left, Alan drank his highball in small

sips, thinking hard. He walked out on the balcony. Seven
stories below, he could see Norbert at the wheel of his
Rolls-Royce, parked in front of the hotel entrance. He
made a little face at himself in the living-room mirror, and
muttered:

"Well, it's now or never. Keep your chin up!"

He thought about Sam Bannister, and went down.

"Alan!" Sarah called out the minute he got into the
lobby.

He wondered whether she stayed there day and night,
just to be able to catch him whenever he went in or out.
He cursed himself for having called for his car to be ready
too soon.

"I'm awfully sorry, Sarah," he said. "But I have to catch
a plane."

"Where are you going?" she asked.

"Away."

"With another woman? You know I haven't been able to
sleep for the past two nights?"

"Take a sleeping pill."

"Alan, I demand to know!" she stormed.

He sidestepped her and made a broken-field run between groups of kids and nannies to hop into his car.

"Take off, Norbert, on the double!"

By the time they had turned into the Croisette, Alan
decided to look back: Sarah was running after the car!

"Let's make a short detour by way of Juan-les-Pins,
Norbert," he said. "I'm going to want to drop something
off there."

"Very well, sir. But we'll run into a bit quite of traffic."

"Let's take that as it comes."

He let down a mahogany writing ledge, took out a pen,
and wrote on the top blank sheet of the pad: *I have to go
away. I'll be back here in twenty hours. Wait for me. I love you.
Alan.*

He slipped the folded sheet into an envelope that he
addressed to Terry, put a cassette into the tape deck,
leaned back, and let his mind think about her. Ever since
he met her, things which once had seemed important to
him now had become insignificant.

Whatever he did, wherever he was, Terry's gray eyes
came between him and the rest of the world.

She was the one and only answer to all questions.

"We're in Juan, sir," Norbert said, interrupting Alan's reverie. Alan told him just where to go, guiding him past the restaurant, and having him turn the corner before he parked.

"Watch out for ice cream cones and pizzas, Norbert," Alan warned. "The kids around here are holy terrors."

"I'll stay in the car, sir," Norbert assured him.

Alan went back around the corner, walked through the cool, dark doorway next to Chez Tony and up the three flights of stairs. On the landing, he stopped and gazed at Terry's door. He knew she was away somewhere with Lucy visiting friends. Nevertheless, just for the heck of it, he knocked. No answer. He stuck his note on the door with a thumbtack the girls kept there for just that purpose, threw a little kiss to the envelope, and went back down.

Hans had gone up a flight to hide when he heard footsteps on the stairs. Now he listened to the sound of the steps going down. When he was certain that the person was gone, he ran down the steps to Terry's landing. He stopped to look at the envelope, then pulled it off the door and opened it. Once he had read it, he tore the note into tiny little pieces.

Arnold Hackett was standing before her when she opened the door. He looked even older than usual, scarcely recognizable as the same man.

"Are you sick or something?" Marina asked.

There was such silent pleading in his eyes that she was moved by it.

"Come in, Arnold," she said.

She had him sit down on the bed, which he did resignedly, apparently not even noticing that she was stark naked, except for her straw hat and kid gloves.

"Did you have an accident?" she asked.

He shook his head and tried his best to give her the semblance of a smile.

"I had to talk to you, Marina," he finally said. "I hope you won't mind if I stay a little while."

"Of course not!"

She affectionately patted him on the top of the head. After all, thanks to him, she was here in the first place.

"Tell me all about it," she said.

He was nothing like the randy old goat to whom she had obstinately closed her door in the last few days. Now his breath came in hissing, irregular spasms.

"Is it your wife?" she asked.

"Oh, no."

"Then, what? Tell me."

He tried to find words, bit his lip, and finally said in one spurt, "I just sold Hackett Chemical."

Marina looked at him with amazement.

"Is *that* what did this to you?" she gasped.

"Well, it's like my child just died."

She put her arms around his shoulders.

"Look, Arnold, that's nothing to get upset about. It must be a pretty good thing for you. You have to get out of the harness some day, you know. You've spent your whole life working, and now's your chance to relax and have a good time."

"No, not a good time," he said. "I just got screwed, can you understand that? And I was always the one who did the screwing! I was always the winner! This time, they pushed me against the wall, and I had to give in. It's making me sick."

"Did they ruin you?" she asked.

"Yes."

"You mean, you have nothing left to live on?" she asked, pityingly.

"Very little," he said.

"How much?"

"I had to sell out for seventy million dollars."

"My God! That's a fortune!"

"A fortune?" he protested, coming out of his torpor. "Why, those shares of mine were worth at least two hundred million."

"Seventy million or two hundred million—how much difference does it make?"

"I've lost my business. I'm all alone in the world!"

"You still have your wife," Marina consoled.

"We practically haven't spoken a word to each other for years now. I have no goal left in life."

"Well, there's nothing to keep you from starting another business, is there? With seventy million dollars, you ought to be able to buy out General Motors."

"I'm a broken man, Marina," he moaned. "This is worse than being unemployed."

"People don't die from it. I have a friend who got fired from Hackett Chemical..."

She paused in mid-sentence, amazed. This was the first time it had occurred to her that Hackett Chemical, where Alan used to work, and Arnold Hackett, the pitiful old man who needed her to comfort him, had the same name.

"Boy, that's funny!" she exclaimed. "You mean you're that Mr. Hackett? The Hackett Chemical guy?"

"Didn't you know?"

"Of course not."

"I am Hackett Chemical," Arnold said, almost as if to convince himself of it. "Or, at least, I was."

"Well, you're a real son of a bitch, aren't you, the way you fire people right and left. Do you know my friend Alan Pope?"

Hackett jumped back as if he had just touched a red-hot stove.

"Pope?" he gasped.

"What did Alan Pope ever do to you? He's one of the nicest people in the world. And everybody at Hackett Chemical thought he was doing a very good job. Then, all of a sudden, you went and fired him—without even any reason!"

"What department did he work in?" Hackett said mechanically.

"Claims Accounting."

"In New York?"

"Sure, in New York. He was my boy friend," Marina said.

"Could I have something to drink, Marina? Some water, just some cool water..."

While she stepped into the bathroom, he put one of his pills into his mouth.

She came back, walked around the bed, and put the glass down on the night table.

"We used to live together. But me, dumb cluck that I was, I went off with Harry. He was some selfish guy! Anything that wasn't his lousy painting was just horseshit to him. Even me!"

She lay down on the bed next to Arnold, who was still sitting with his back to her. She was a little bit ashamed of herself for having told him off that way when she knew he was so unhappy. She tenderly scratched the back of his neck.

"You've put in your time, Arnold," Marina said to him. "No reason to take this so tragically. You're not the first person to end up this way. You have to make room for the younger generation, you know!"

She was unconsciously increasing the insistence of her nails as they ran up and down the back of his neck and over his scalp. She could clearly feel the tingling that went through him and was afraid she had gone beyond the subtle line that separates friendly affection from sexual teasing. She pulled her hand back, for fear he might turn and jump her, just to prove to her that in spite of his age . . . But he didn't move.

"Buy yourself a boat," she suggested. "Play golf. For the rest of your life, all you have to do is the things that you like to do best. Isn't that so? . . . Arnold . . ."

But Arnold didn't answer. Reassured that he wasn't getting horny, she squeezed his shoulder again.

"Arnold?" she repeated.

She pressed harder. He started to turn slowly sideways.

"No, Arnold," she said, "don't. Just sit up like a good boy."

She tried to push him back up. He fell over on her, his eyes wide open, his face set.

Arnold Hackett was dead.

She began to scream.

29

The car was no sooner into midtown, than Alan felt the shock of New York City bear down on him. The air, the heat, the haze, the stridency—heaven knows New York was familiar to him, yet he no longer recognized it.

It was the afternoon of July 30. He had only been away since the morning of the twenty-fifth. Five days had been enough for time to dilate with dizzying speed until it held a multiplicity of events and experiences that fifty years of his ordinary life would not have been able to absorb.

Those five days of love, death, and power had metamorphosed the caterpillar into a butterfly. Henceforth, it was too late for him ever to be innocent again.

"Wait for me," he told the driver of the limousine. "As soon as I finish, we'll head back out to the airport."

He looked thoughtfully at the facade of the bank.

A hundred years ago, on July 23, sweating bullets of terror, he had gone in here to cash that first $500 check. He now walked up the several steps leading to the bank's door, walked in, and headed directly for the securities window at which small shareholders were presenting their Hackett stock to be redeemed at $20 a share. He saw a bank guard shepherding the customers.

"Mr. Fischmayer is expecting me," Alan said to him. "My name is Alan Pope."

Thirty seconds later, he was shown into the luxurious office of Burger Bank's managing director. Abel Fischmayer stretched to his full height and came toward Alan with hand outstretched.

"Fischmayer," he introduced himself. "Delighted to meet you."

"Pope, same here," Alan replied. He cleared his throat and took out the deed Arnold Hackett had signed, selling his six million shares to Alan Pope.

"Mr. Fischmayer," he said, "here is a deed for six million shares of Hackett Chemical. I am turning them over to you in response to the tender which you announced."

"Fine, Mr. Pope. That is excellent."

"These shares represent a value of one hundred twenty million dollars. I owe your bank seventy million. Therefore, I would be obliged if you would pay me the difference, that is, fifty million dollars."

"Would you like a drink, Mr. Pope?" Abel asked.

"Sorry, but my plane's waiting," Alan told him. "I have to get right back."

"To France?" the man asked, his eyebrows raised.

"Could I have my check, please?" Alan ignored his query.

"Certainly," Mr. Fischmayer said with pinched lips.

He turned the combination on the lock of his middle desk drawer and took out the cashier's check.

"Here, so you may verify it," he said.

Alan calmly took the check. It was made out in his name for the unbelievable sum of "$50,000,000.00 (Fifty million dollars and no cents)." It was signed by Abel Fischmayer and two other authorized signatures that were indecipherable.

Abel looked at him, coldly and haughtily. Alan realized then that Abel, too, had found out who he was.

"Good day, sir," Alan said.

"Good day, sir," Fischmayer replied.

They did not shake hands.

Back on the chartered plane, Alan fastened his safety belt, asked the hostess to bring him a glass of champagne. He took a couple of puffs from a cigarette until the boom of the jets was heard. The idea that he was the sole passenger on this Boeing made him smile.

The plane taxied onto the runway. Alan fixed his head firmly back against the headrest, closed his eyes. There was nothing in his mind but the image of Terry.

She wasn't as classy as Mandy de Saran, but he liked her. The curves of her body, her warm smile, the two dimples in her chin, her helmet of dark hair had all gone right to Sam Bannister's heart.

"Where did you learn to speak English so well, Clarisse?" he asked.

"In London. I was an au pair girl for a couple who ran an art gallery."

"Did they have many children?" he inquired.

She laughed aloud.

"None. They were two men living together!"

"How long have you been working here at the Palm Beach?"

"A month," she told him. "I've taken the job for the season. More to have something to do than for anything else. Life at home is something of a bore. I'm married to an Englishman."

She appreciatively followed Sam's eyes as they looked her over from head to foot.

"And what do you do, Mr. Bannister?"

"I'm head of a pharmaceutical concern," he lied boldly. "In New York, of course. Could I get you something to drink?"

"Not right now, thanks. How long are you staying in Cannes?"

They hadn't declared their love yet, but considering how quickly they had gotten this far, Sam's new friend appeared to be a most promising prospect.

Sam had spotted her downstairs at the restrooms of the Palm Beach. She was sitting on a chair, reading *Vogue*, and half-heartedly listening to the tinkle of the coins that the customers emerging from the restrooms dropped in the plate as tips. The fact that she had heard steps unaccompanied by the clink of hard cash made her look up when Sam Bannister exited.

She had looked at him sharply. He had answered by nodding toward the ten-franc note he had put down on the saucer. She had smiled warmly at him and he had smiled back. Great passions often have their start in small details of this kind. Without putting up too much of a pretense, she had allowed herself to be talked into coming to his place for a drink.

"Make yourself comfortable, Clarisse," he was now telling her.

She was wearing a light cotton dress which fitted rather tightly across her chest, giving a good idea of her nipples and the seductive rings around them. Sam cleared his throat, and tried to look away. Apart from the duchess, who had taken him virtually by force, Sam had never cheated on his wife in the twenty-five years of their marriage. By a slow campaign of conjugal undermining, Crystal had finally snuffed out any inclination to stray that he might have had. Nevertheless, out of a kind of unconscious modesty, he slipped her picture into a drawer.

"Clarisse is a very pretty name," he said.

"You think so?"

They were sitting, facing one another, on two armchairs. He was desperately searching his memory to try to recapture the gestures he had found so natural long ago—the gestures that got him from the neutrality of a chair to the titillating warmth of a bed. His right hand felt like it weighed ten tons. With a constriction in his throat, he lifted it and moved it toward Clarisse's arm. When it was no more than two inches away, there was a knock on the door. The spell was broken; he'd have to start again from scratch.

Annoyed, he got up and went to the door. A girl was standing there. She had ash-blonde hair and gray eyes, and was dressed in a pair of faded jeans and a white T-shirt.

"Oh, I'm sorry, I must have made a mistake," she apologized. "I was told a friend of mine was living in Suite 751."

"What friend?" Sam asked.

"Alan Pope."

"This is his suite, all right."

"My name is Terry."

Well, so this was what Alan had fallen for!

"He's not in," Sam mumbled antagonistically.

"Do you know when he'll be back?"

"He went on a trip. I'm his friend, Sam Bannister."

"Do you expect to see him soon?" Terry asked.

"He'll be back all right, but I can't say when."

"Could you give him a letter?"

Sam took it from her, holding it cautiously between his thumb and his index finger.

"It's terribly important," Terry said.

"You can trust me," Sam told her. "I'll give it to Alan the minute I see him."

"Tell him I was called away unexpectedly," she went on. "It's all in the letter. And also, tell him that . . ."

"What? What else do you want me to tell him?"

She bit at her lips self-consciously. "Oh, nothing. It's all in the letter. Thanks again." She nodded good-bye and disappeared down the hallway.

Sam closed the door. He felt sick that Alan should have picked out such an insignificant chick when Sarah Burger was rolling out the red carpet of her fortune at his feet. Fortunately, Sam was there to watch over his friend!

He tore the letter into small pieces, went into the bathroom, and flushed them down the toilet.

After which he self-righteously and erectly went into the bedroom, where Clarisse was ready to receive him.

The Rolls-Royce turned right off the Croisette to go up the driveway of the Majestic.

From the moment he left New York, Alan had fallen asleep on the plane and not awakened again until after they were on the ground at Nice.

"Step on it, Norbert," he said, "and don't stop at the

hotel door. Drive out again and take me around to the side door."

To his consternation, Alan had just seen Sarah on a folding chair near the door, deep in conversation with Serge. Alan hunkered down out of sight on the back seat.

"Norbert," he said, "did that girl talking to Serge see me?"

Norbert squinted at the rearview mirror.

"I don't think so, sir. Miss Burger is still talking."

"Thanks. Let me off here."

He hopped out and slipped into the Majestic by the service entrance. He sneaked up to the concierge's desk.

"Seven fifty one, please."

"Your key isn't here, sir. Mr. Bannister must be up in the suite."

Alan stepped into the elevator, only to bump into Marina.

"Alan!" she gulped.

He was upset to see the traces of tears on her face.

"The most awful thing happened, Alan!" she sobbed. "He died in my arms."

"Prince Hadad?"

"No, Arnold Hackett!"

"You mean to say Mr. Hackett is dead?"

She sobbed twice as loudly.

"Dead as can be. And he died in my room. What does that make me look like?" she whimpered between sobs.

Alan took her by the shoulders and shook her gently. "Marina, come now! What did you do to him, Marina?"

Over her head, he suddenly caught sight of Sarah, who had just come into the lobby. He quickly shoved Marina back into the elevator and pressed the button for the seventh floor.

"I want to get out," said a lady in red who was carrying a black poodle in her arms. Alan had not even noticed her until now. She looked askance at them.

"I was just laying on the bed," Marina went on. "I was patting him on the head, real nice. He had just been forced to sell his business, you know, and you had to feel sorry for him. And besides, I've got to tell you something—that Hackett was your Hackett. He was your boss who fired you!"

"I know that," Alan assured her. "I know."

"Take me back to the third floor immediately," the outraged lady in red was demanding.

"As soon as we get to the seventh," Alan apologized.

The black poodle started barking threateningly.

"I just went to get him a glass of water and came back to lay down next to him—and he was dead," Marina went on.

"What did he die of?"

"Heart attack. They didn't want to drag his body through the halls, so they left him in my room. They moved my stuff to another room on the sixth floor. And they lost my straw hat on me! I don't know where any of my things are anymore!"

The door of the elevator opened as they stopped.

"Marina, we'll see each other later, and you can tell me all about it. Okay?" he said.

"You're the one who has things to tell me," she replied. "What are you doing in Cannes, anyway?"

"Will you please let me get downstairs!" the lady in red yelled at them.

Before Alan could get out, the elevator doors closed again. The lady in red tried to reach the third-floor button, but as she did so, the poodle jumped out of her arms and started barking furiously.

"I went back to your place in New York." Marina went right on talking, as if there had been no interruption. "I got sick and tired of that Harry. There wasn't any water in your apartment, so I left."

"But where did you meet Arnold Hackett?" Alan asked.

"Watch out for my dog," the lady screamed. "Jean-Paul, here! Jump, darling!" She made a hoop out of her arms for Jean-Paul to jump into. He wasn't interested.

"At Poppy's," Marina said. "You know Poppy?"

"No."

The elevator stopped again on the ground floor. The doors opened and the poodle ran out. The lady in red started to go after him, but Marina was in her way.

"Alan!" Sarah had spotted him from the lobby. She was calling shrilly. "Alan!"

Alan pushed the seventh-floor button and they were on their way up again.

"I want to get out!" The lady in red was now hysterical. "I want my Jean-Paul!"

"Hey, you in the red! Couldn't you watch where you're going?" Marina said indignantly. "You stepped on my toe!"

"I'm a personal friend of Monsieur Gohelan's," the lady protested in a huff. "I'm going to report all this. I've been coming here for twenty years. If anything happens to my Jean-Paul, I promise you—"

"Who is Poppy, Marina?" Alan asked.

"Peter's girl friend."

"What did she have to do with Arnold Hackett?"

"I don't know. I met him at her place, when I went there after I left your apartment. He asked me if I wanted to come to Cannes. All on the up and up, no hanky-panky..." Marina turned toward the lady in red as she concluded her sentence, "...you know I got no use for old people!"

The elevator came to a halt.

"Do you mean me?" the lady in red challenged.

"Yes," Marina spat at her, "and I got no use for poodles either!"

Alan slipped out the elevator door. He rang the bell at his suite.

"Who's there?" Bannister's voice came booming through.

"Me! Open up!"

"Alan?"

"Yes! You gonna open, or do I have to break it down?"

Alan could hear the lock being opened. Then he got a peek at Sam's head. Alan shoved the door, pushing Bannister back, and saw that Sam was naked.

"Again?" Alan gasped.

"I'm not alone," Sam confessed, shamefaced.

Alan looked at him with dismay. "The duchess?" he asked.

"No, the lounge attendant from the Palm Beach. Please be discreet, Alan. She's a married woman."

"Take her back where you got her! I need the living room right away," Alan told him.

"But we were just getting started..."

"Out, man! Understand?" Alan went into the bathroom. "When I come out of the shower, I'll throw you both out on your asses if you're still here," he threatened. "And you be back here in an hour. I'll have a lot of things to tell you!"

He slammed the bathroom door behind him, turned on the cold water, and burst into silent laughter.

When he got back to the foyer, showered and dried, the suite was empty. He got into his clothes, made a few notes on a pad, and dialed Hamilton Price-Lynch.

"I just got in," Alan said to him. "I'm in my suite. Will you please come over?"

Then he turned back to the figures he had written on the pad. As the doorbell rang, he shoved them into his pocket.

"Did you have a good trip, Mr. Pope?" Hamilton inquired, coming into the living room.

"Just fine, thanks."

"Everything work out as planned?"

"Exactly."

"I just had a call from Fischmayer. May I see his check, please?"

"Here it is," Alan said. "Do you have mine for me?"

"Here," Price-Lynch answered.

They exchanged checks.

Alan put his into his pocket, after making sure that it was properly made out for $100,000.

"Is that correct, Mr. Pope?"

"Right," Alan said.

"Very well, then," Hamilton said, as he handed back the check for $50,000,000 made out to Alan Pope and signed by Abel Fischmayer. "Now all you have to do is endorse this one over to the Swiss bank whose name I'm going to give you."

Alan turned his back on him, and absent-mindedly played with several bottles on the bar. Both checks were now safely in his pocket.

"Did you hear me, Mr. Pope?"

"Yes, I did."

"Then endorse it to—"

"I'm not endorsing it," Alan cut him off.

"What's that?"

"The check is made out to me. I have every intention of depositing it to my own account."

Price-Lynch started. "You must be joking."

"Not at all," Alan icily informed him. "You tried to swindle me. You used me to cover up a deceptive business practice that would have netted you $50,000,000 off the back of a customer you double-crossed."

"You think you're a big enough man to threaten me like that?" Hamilton spat at him with scorn.

"Hackett trusted you. And he died because of it."

"Everybody knows he had a bad heart!" Price-Lynch said.

"You did something unethical and immoral, Mr. Price-Lynch. And I'm surprised at you."

"What's your price?"

"I would first like to clarify matters a little, so we both know just exactly where we stand," Alan said.

"Get to the point!"

"The thing that struck me from the first moment you mentioned that tender to me was that there was no way it could possibly work. Even if you had been able to buy up all the outstanding shares, you never could have had more than forty percent. That was not enough to give you control of Hackett Chemical.

"So, in order for your dirty deal to work, you had to fulfill two conditions. First, you had to find a way to force Arnold Hackett to sell out to you. Well, since you were his banker, all you had to do was cut off his line of credit on short notice, and you had him at your mercy. Second, you needed a third party in the deal, somebody above suspicion, somebody who could buy Hackett's controlling shares from him at a bargain rate. And for that, you chose me. I was your ideal pigeon, Mr. Price-Lynch, especially after what had just happened to me."

"I'm going to give you one last chance, Pope. Keep the two hundred thousand and return my fifty million dollars, and then just disappear!" Price-Lynch said.

Alan looked at him sarcastically.

"Some words are tricky, Mr. Price-Lynch," he said. "Take the word 'disappear,' for instance. If I didn't 'disappear' before, say, after the first time I turned down your deal, it certainly was not for want of your trying to make me . . ."

Price-Lynch stiffened. "What are you trying to say?" he demanded.

"Nothing," Alan said. "Nothing at all. But we understand one another, don't we?"

"Not at all!"

Alan noted that Hamilton had lowered his eyes for a fraction of a second.

"Would you have forgotten this?" Price-Lynch said, as he took a sheet of paper out of his pocket.

Alan recognized that it was the letter he had signed four days before, agreeing to Hamilton Price-Lynch's deal. In it, he stated that he was to act as the banker's go-between.

"All I have to do is show this to the authorities to establish that you're blackmailing me," Hamilton threatened.

Alan looked him straight in the eye and did nothing to hide his amusement at the idea.

"I dare you to!" he said.

"Don't push me too far!"

"That document proves your dishonesty, Mr. Price-Lynch. No banker in the world has the right to make a tender for his own profit. That's a crime!"

"I'll raise your commission to half a million dollars," Hamilton offered.

"You're not in a position to make offers to me," Alan said. "I have another plan for myself. I intend to take control of Hackett Chemical."

Price-Lynch looked at him, unbelieving. "You are positively out of your mind!" he said.

"Mr. Hackett said that to me when I first offered to buy his shares," Alan answered. "Now, are you ready to listen to me? I'd like to make you a proposition."

"Out of your mind!" Price-Lynch was mechanically repeating.

"If you accept—and just between us, I don't see how you can turn it down—I'll offer you a commission. And it won't be five hundred thousand dollars, but five million dollars."

"What kind of nonsense is that?" Hamilton snarled.

"I'm ready to forget the past entirely. I'll return your check to you, and you give me back the six million shares of Hackett stock that I turned over to Fischmayer."

"Who'll pay for them?" Price-Lynch roared.

"You will. Of course, not out of your own pocket. You're the head man at Burger Bank. I'm asking your bank to give me a long-term loan of seventy-five million dollars, with the stock you're returning to me to serve as collateral. That'll be seventy million dollars for the purchase of the Hackett stock, and a five-million-dollar commission for you."

Alan nonchalantly glanced at his wristwatch. "I'll give

you exactly five minutes to make up your mind." He then made himself a highball and walked out onto the balcony.

For a few seconds, Price-Lynch was motionless. Then he grabbed the bottle that Alan had left on the bar, poured himself a heavy double shot, and drank it down in one gulp.

Five million dollars invested in Switzerland at twelve percent would bring him six hundred thousand dollars tax-free every year. It might not be enough to live a truly lavish life, but getting rid of Emily, and being on his own was well worth making a few sacrifices. He poured himself another shot, which he downed more pensively, and then headed out to the balcony.

Alan Pope was leaning on the railing of the balcony, staring straight in front of him. Hamilton coughed lightly.

"Mr. Pope," he said.

Alan turned slowly, as if surprised to find him there.

"I thought over your offer," Price-Lynch said.

He lit his Muratti with a shaking hand. "And I accept it."

The bed had been taken out of Marina's room. In its place, there was a board covered by a black sheet, held up by two sawhorses. On top of the board was the casket with Arnold Hackett's body in it. After the coroner's inquest had been completed, Victoria had refused to allow her husband's body to be removed to the morgue.

Their daughter Gertrude, on vacation in Europe and hastily summoned after the tragedy, had felt the same way. After presenting the usual condolences and assuring them how deeply he shared in their misfortune, Marc Gohelan had discreetly inquired of them what their plans were. A dead body in a luxury hotel presents certain problems of disposal which are quite incompatible with the establishment's usual holiday atmosphere.

Victoria and Gertrude told him that they wanted the body brought back to the United States just as soon as possible. Gohelan volunteered to carry out all the formalities necessary to charter a private plane, alert the undertakers, and clear it with the authorities. He urged the widow and the heiress to agree that it would be best to move the casket out after nightfall. But Victoria absolutely would not accept that.

"Madame," Gohelan implored her, "you must realize that we are just now at the height of the season. The hotel is swarming with people. And in broad daylight—no, please, you must understand the position I am put in."

"My husband arrived here in daylight, carrying his head high, and I don't see any reason why he should have to be sneaked out under cover of darkness!" she replied.

The only concession that she was willing to make, was that the pallbearers didn't have to wear their usual black funeral outfits.

The blinds were drawn in the bedroom. There were candles burning here and there. Through the open window, the cheerful sounds of summer vacation could be heard.

"He was an unusual man," Hamilton Price-Lynch was saying.

Sarah and Emily gave him the same look of unmitigated reproof he got every time he tried to say anything in their presence. He inwardly congratulated himself that he would not have to put up with this much longer.

"Your father happened to be walking down the hall," Victoria explained to Gertrude, "when he heard a scream. A woman had accidentally scalded herself in the shower. She suddenly opened her door, calling for help. Your father went in. It was too much for his poor heart."

This was the version that Marc Gohelan had quickly concocted to explain Hackett's presence in Marina's room.

Gertrude darted an icy look at the woman who looked like Marilyn Monroe, standing next to Lou Goldman, the movie producer, who had his arm protectively around the shoulders of his wife Julia.

"I believe you were a friend of the deceased?" Goldman whispered to Marina. "Are you returning to America for the funeral, too?"

"No, no," she said. "I just came in here to look for a straw hat. The maids lost it when they moved my things to another room."

"Did you find it?"

"No. And it's too bad, 'cause it was something I liked."

"I'm planning a huge biographical film on the life of Marilyn Monroe," he told her. "There's something about your face—"

"Yeah, I know. Everybody says so."

"Have you ever been in pictures?" he asked.

Over in another corner, head bowed, the duke was holding the hand of the Duchess de Saran. He had felt that they owed the family the courtesy of a visit before the body was shipped out. The seventh-floor waiter joined in the general mourning. He had always been unwholesomely fascinated by Hackett—the man had never come across with a tip of any kind, never even so much as a word of thanks.

"You're sure losing a wonderful boss," the waiter whispered to Richard, who was choking on his tears.

Under Gohelan's guidance, a delegation of men in white smocks had just come in.

There were no eulogies, nor any service of any kind. The men in white closed the casket, and Victoria collapsed into her daughter's arms.

Gohelan rushed out into the hall, signaled a maître d' who was standing guard some twenty yards away, then came back in and with an imperious gesture indicated to the white-smocked pallbearers to make it snappy. They lifted the casket and carried it out. Suddenly the deafening racket of a power hammer began.

In order to make sure that none of the hotel guests inadvertently came face to face with the funeral procession, Gohelan had had the idea of blocking off the hall at the level of the elevator, by having two workmen busy there, presumably making a hole in the floor. Going on the double, the pallbearers reached the dumbwaiter in no more than twenty seconds. Once the body was in there, the racket in the hall miraculously ceased. Gohelan, with a sigh of relief, returned to the room to comfort the widow and heiress.

The pallbearers went all the way down to the basement, and deposited the casket in the carpenter's shop. Everything was ready: The casket was placed on a workbench; two carpenters quickly enclosed it in a crate; once the crate was around it, there was no way of telling what was inside.

Five men in blue work clothes carried the crate out through the service entrance, then put the crate into a white van; the driver closed its doors.

Of course, word of the death of Arnold Hackett had spread through Cannes, as all rumors do. But the management of the Majestic defied anyone to say they had seen a casket being moved anywhere in the hotel during the summer vacation period.

"It can't be! She must have left a message for me!" he was saying.

Tony finished wiping the glass in his hand, while looking askance at the Rolls-Royce parked outside his restaurant.

"I'd certainly know if she had," he answered soberly.

"How about her girl friend Lucy?" Alan insisted.

"No. I think she often goes to visit friends."

"Do you know their name?"

"No, sir, I'm sorry. So many people come through the restaurant, how can we remember?"

"Let me have a straight whiskey in a glass, no ice."

Terry was gone!

No trace of her could be found anywhere. She had just vanished into thin air!

"I'd be surprised if she comes back," Tony said as he shoved the glass toward Alan. "I saw her leave with all her luggage. Not much, but it was all she had—a big sailor's duffel bag."

"How did she leave?" Alan asked.

"In a taxi."

"You remember what one?" Alan asked.

"No."

"Would you know who the driver was? Was he anyone who usually worked here in Juan-les-Pins?"

"I really didn't notice," the restaurateur answered.

"My name is Pope. Alan Pope," he told Tony. "If you should see her again, tell her I'm waiting for her. I'm at the Majestic in Cannes. She knows where . . ."

Tony looked at Alan. This was certainly not the first time he had had a lovelorn Romeo on his hands. His restaurant was a rendezvous for the cream of Juan's penniless society. He heard all about the heartaches that his customers suffered. Except that all the others had come to Chez Tony's on foot or on bikes, never before had one arrived in a Rolls-Royce.

"I wonder what could have happened to her?" Alan wondered aloud.

He had found her door locked. No note on it, no nothing. He finished what was in his glass.

"You sure you'll remember?" he asked.

"Pope, Majestic Hotel, it's engraved on my brain," Tony assured him, as he swept up the folding money Alan had put down on the counter.

Alan went back out into the street. He looked up at the building, and picked out the windows behind which he had lived moments such as he knew there would never be again.

"Where are we headed for, sir?" Norbert asked, as he held the door open for him.

"Wherever you want," Alan said wearily. "It really doesn't matter anymore."

BOOK V

30

On August 6, two days after the closing date of the tender, Alan had his car stop on Forty-second Street. New York was so hot and humid that one couldn't keep from sticking to oneself.

He went into the Rilford Building, crossed the lobby, and took the express elevator up to the thirtieth floor.

It was 10:00 A.M. In one hour, he was to appear before the board of directors of Hackett Chemical for the formality of being elected its new president. With sixty percent of the company's stock in his name, the election was, of course, a foregone conclusion. In the hallway of the company's offices, he recognized the familiar smells and sounds which he still associated with the recent abrupt end of the first phase of his life.

He saw a few former fellow workers and they greeted him in a strange, almost furtive way. He was surprised. Surely they all knew by now that he was in control of the company.

He opened the door of his old office. For four years, he

had spent his days in there—dreaming of being some-where else.

Sam Bannister saw him and quickly took his feet off the desk.

"What's got into you?" Alan asked.

"I was just studying the fluorite file," he mumbled apologetically.

Alan looked perplexed. He walked over to what had been his desk before he got fired, and pensively rubbed his fingers against its metallic rim. Then he walked to the bay window and pressed his nose against it the way Sam Bannister had seen him do so many hundreds of times during the years.

Alan had come back from Cannes two days earlier, after hiring a detective agency to try to find a trace of Terry. So far, no luck. But they said they were still trying . . .

Alan had taken rooms at the Pierre, but he hadn't gotten the kick out of it that he had had on July 24, when he spent his first night there with Ann, the travel agency girl. After the wild excitement of Cannes at the height of the season, nothing much could give him a bang anymore. Even his victory left him with a bitter taste, for the simple reason that he had no one to share it with. Except Sam.

He looked back over his shoulder. Sam had a bunch of files open in front of him and was poring over them feverishly, never raising his eyes.

"Sam," he called.

Bannister looked up.

"Yes?"

"Got problems?"

"No, I'm just busy."

"You kidding or something?"

"No, of course not," Sam mumbled, "really not, sir!"

Alan stared at him dumbfounded.

"Did I hear you call me sir?" he demanded.

"It just slipped out," Sam said, turning back to the work before him.

Alan rushed over to Sam's desk, swept away the files he was working on, grabbed him by the lapels, and jerked him up out of his chair.

"If you don't tell me right away why you're looking at me the way you are, I'll knock your silly block off your shoulders!" he roared.

"I'm not looking at you any special way. It's just that, well, I'm behind in my work..."

"Stop with the bullshit!" Alan continued in the same roar. "You barely look at me; you've hardly said a word to me since I got back; you're treating me as if I was a leper or something. If there's something bugging you, god-damn it, out with it! After all, I own the joint now. I can fix it up."

Bannister gently pulled away from him, shook his head, and stammered, "Well, that's just the point..."

"What's just the point?"

Bannister turned his eyes away. "I'm just impressed with you," he said.

"You idiot," Alan replied with a sigh of relief. "Here you had me thinking I'd done something to make you sore at me."

"Don't you realize?" Sam replied. "You're Hackett Chemical now! Nobody here in the company has been able to get over it. Even everybody down at Romano's is floored by it. They're just plain scared of you, that's all!"

"Why? What the hell has changed about me?"

"You're the boss now," Sam said.

Sam grabbed the phone, which was ringing, listened to what someone was saying, and made a face.

"Yes, sir...Certainly, sir..."

"Who is that?" Alan demanded to know.

Sam put his hand over the mouthpiece and mouthed the name Murray.

"Let me have it," Alan said. "Hello, Murray? Pope here. Come to my old office this minute!"

And he slammed the receiver down, before Bannister's admiring eyes.

"He chewed my ass out yesterday, on account of my taking off on that trip," Sam told him. "He said I had committed a gross infraction of the rules. He's going to see what he has to do about docking me..."

"You don't say!"

"Well, you know how he is," Sam lamely answered.

"He's not wrong, you know," Alan stated. "Strictly speaking, you should not have just taken off like that."

Sam's shoulders caved in under the reprimand. But Alan was pointing to the headline on a story in the morning paper, which he had brought when he came in.

PRICE-LYNCH MURDERERS
CAUGHT ON THE RIVIERA

"You know who knocked the bastard off?" Sam asked.

"The same two guys who tried to get me that time I was waterskiing. They had a contract from him to get rid of me. They were the same ones who killed Erwin Broker during the fireworks display. Cesare di Sogno was the contact man. He's been arrested, too. According to what he told the cops, Price-Lynch welched on what he owed his hit men. So he paid with his life."

Alan noticed that instead of listening to him, Sam was staring at a spot behind his head.

He turned around. Oliver Murray was standing in the doorway, about to enter.

"Mr. Pope," the personnel chief said warmly, "please accept my sincere congratulations on your promotion. No one could have deserved it more."

Alan did not take Murray's outstretched hand. He just looked icily at him, not saying a word, and then sat down behind his old desk.

"Tell me, Murray, how long have you been with the company?"

"Fifteen years, sir."

"That's quite a long time. How old are you?"

"Fifty-two, sir."

Alan was silent for a long moment. Murray, who had not been offered a seat, stood facing him.

"What's your salary?" Alan finally asked.

"Three thousand three hundred and sixty-five dollars a month, gross."

"That's a pretty fair rate of pay," Alan said with a look of concern on his brow. "If you were to be terminated, what kind of severance benefits would you have coming?"

"You intend to terminate me?" Murray gulped.

"That won't be my decision," Alan said. "I'll merely put my stamp of approval on whatever decisions are made by our new general manager, Mr. Samuel Bannister."

"Congratulations on your appointment, sir," Murray mumbled dejectedly as he bowed toward Sam.

Sam's face changed from brick red to creamy white. He was speechless.

The door opened slightly, and Patsy stuck her head in through the opening.

"Mr. Pope," she said. "Mrs. Hackett and Miss Gertrude Hackett as well as the company's sales heads, would like to see you for a few minutes before the board meeting, sir. They are in Mr. Hackett's, uh, former office. Can you meet with them there, sir?"

"I'll be right with them," Alan replied. "Murray, you can return to your office. Our new general manager will be in touch after he's had a chance to consider your case carefully."

Then, turning to Sam, he instructed, "I want you to take good care of Murray here. Don't be too tough on him, even though he is a prick. What we need in that job is a prick like him. He'll scare the shit out of the hired help. And I intend to see things hum around here!"

Suddenly energized, Sam shouted at Murray, "Well, Murray, what are you waiting for? I'd have thought your employment file would be on my desk by now!"

Alan climbed up the two flights of stairs to the executive floor. He walked up to the president's office, then paused and took a deep breath. His one final reflex surprised and amused him. He realized he had just tightened the knot of his tie and brushed off his lapels before going into the office which was now to be his own personal domain.

He knocked, waited a few seconds, and then walked in. Those who in the past had had the privilege of entering Arnold Hackett's private office used to say that he used it as a driving range. No wonder! Apart from the height of the ceiling, it seemed as long and as wide as a cathedral.

At the other end of the office, the very end of it, there was a huge steel desk facing a view of the skyscrapers rising out of New York's warm haze. And behind that desk, looking tiny in her white knit dress, was a young woman wearing large horn-rimmed glasses. It was Terry.

The blood drained from Alan's face. He fought back an impulse to run to her, to pick her up in his arms and waltz off into space. Instead, he slowly walked the hundred feet that stood between them. Finally he was in front of the desk.

"I guess you're Gertrude Hackett," he said. "How do you do?"

"And you're Alan Pope?" she answered. "I'm pleased to meet you."

"I understand you wished to see me."

"Yes. I thought we ought to meet before I turned this desk over to you. My father had named me as his executrix over my protests. But I can't say that I've executrixed very much. I'm accustomed to a different life-style."

"What kind of life-style?"

"Oh, studying and traveling. I just wanted to be free to live my own life. Can you understand that?"

"Yes, I can."

"I didn't get along very well with my father," she went on. "The only thing he respected was money; he just did not understand the values that were important to me. When I reached eighteen, I left home and struck out on my own. I'm just back from a trip to the Riviera."

"Did you have a good time?"

"Well, I did meet one sensational person."

"So did I."

"You know," she said, "I think I may not have been entirely fair to my father. I really should have shown more interest in the company that he had built. Now that I have to relinquish control of it, I'm sorry that I never really had a chance to see how it worked."

"Would you like to?" Alan asked.

"I don't really know how to do very much."

"Can you type?"

"Sort of."

"Would you be willing to give it a try?"

"Gladly," she said.

"Well, why don't you sit down at that typewriter? I'll dictate a letter to you. If you pass the test, I might be able to take you on as a secretary—on probation, of course."

Terry crossed the office and sat down at a small table with a typewriter on it. She put a sheet of paper into the typewriter, and said, "I'm ready, sir."

"Fine," Alan said in a very businesslike tone.

He began to dictate: "Dear Miss Hackett:

"In answer to yours of July 28, which I unfortunately did not receive, allow me to inform you that I love you."

He stopped a moment, then went on.

"I love you . . . I love you . . ."

"How many I-love-yous was that, sir?" Terry asked without raising her head.

"Ten—a hundred—as many as you like. Just let me go on."

"Go ahead, sir."

"Therefore and consequently, might I expect by return mail your best estimate of when our wedding day should be."

The staccato sound of the typewriter stopped. Terry slowly took her glasses off.

His legs unsteady, Alan was watching her every move. She was quite pale. And for ten endless seconds, the world stood still.

Then, in one joyous movement, they flew into each other's arms.

ABOUT THE AUTHOR AND TRANSLATOR

PIERRE REY is one of France's bestselling commercial novelists. He is known worldwide as the author of *The Greek* (over four million copies in print) and *The Widow,* which was translated into fourteen languages. *Out* was a major French novel and to date has been translated into nine languages. *Riviera*, Pierre Rey's latest book, was a bestseller in France.

HAROLD SALEMSON is a former journalist, film correspondent and film company executive. He has subtitled some two dozen foreign feature films in addition to translating over twenty books from French to English.

THE ASTONISHING #1 BESTSELLER

THE VALLEY OF HORSES
by Jean M. Auel
author of *The Clan of the Cave Bear*

Here is an unforgettable odyssey into a world of awesome mysteries, into a distant past made vividly real. In a novel that touches the very core of the human spirit, Jean Auel carries us back to the exotic, primeval world we experienced in *The Clan of the Cave Bear*—and to beautiful Ayla, the bold woman who captivates us with her fierce courage and questing heart.

( )   THE VALLEY OF HORSES (23481-1 * $4.50)
( )   THE CLAN OF THE CAVE BEAR (22775-0 * $3.95)